THE LONDON BOROUGH
www.bromley.gov.uk

Please return/renew this item
by the last date shown.
Books may also be renewed by

D1428202

30128 80259 450 0

First Published in Great Britain 2016
By Mills & Boon, an imprint of HarperCollins*Publishers*
1 London Bridge Street, London, SE1 9GF

THE MAN BEHIND THE MASK © 2016 Harlequin Books S. A.

How To Melt A Frozen Heart, *The Man Behind The Pinstripes* and *Falling For Mr Mysterious* were first published in Great Britain by Harlequin (UK) Limited.

How To Melt A Frozen Heart © 2013 Cara Colter
The Man Behind The Pinstripes © 2013 Melissa Martinez McClone
Falling For Mr Mysterious © 2012 Barbara Hannay

ISBN: 978-0-263-92074-1

05-0716

Our policy is to use papers that are natural, renewable and recyclable products and made from wood grown in sustainable forests.The logging and manufacturing processes conform to the legal environmental regulations of the country of origin.

Printed and bound in Spain
by CPI, Barcelona

HOW TO MELT A FROZEN HEART

BY
CARA COLTER

Cara Colter lives in British Columbia with her partner, Rob, and eleven horses. She has three grown children and a grandson. She is a recent recipient of an *RT Book Reviews* Career Achievement Award in the 'Love and Laughter' category. Cara loves to hear from readers, and you can contact her or learn more about her through her website: www.cara-colter.com.

To my favorite animal lover, Margo Jakobsen,
and her beloved, the true Prince of Pomerania, Phaut.

CHAPTER ONE

BRENDAN GRANT AWOKE with a start. At first he heard only the steady beat of rain on the roof, but then the phone rang again, shrill, jangling across his nerves. His eyes flicked to his bedside clock.

Three o'clock.

He felt his heart begin to beat a hard tattoo inside his chest. What good could ever come of a 3:00 a.m. phone call?

But then he remembered, and even though he remembered, he reached over and touched the place in the bed beside him. Two and a half years later and he still felt that ripple of shock at the emptiness. Becky was gone. The worst had already happened.

He groped through the darkness for the phone, picked it up.

"Yeah?" His voice was raspy with sleep.

"Charlie's dying."

And then the phone went silent in his hands.

Brendan lay there for a moment longer, holding the dead phone, not wanting to get up. He didn't really even like Charlie. They were going to start breaking ground on the lakeside living complex, Village on the Lake, tomorrow. His design had already attracted the attention of several architectural magazines, and based on the plan, the project had been nominated for the prestigious Michael Edgar Jonathon Award.

Still, as always, before they broke ground, and even after, he struggled with a feeling of it not being what he had wanted, missing the mark in some vague way he could not quite define. He recognized the stress was beginning. He was a man who needed his sleep.

But with a resigned groan, he sat up, swung his legs over the side of the bed, and sat there for a moment, his head in his hands, listening to the rain on the roof. He was so sick of rain. He certainly didn't want to go out in it at three in the morning.

Then, with a sigh, Brendan reached for his jeans.

Ten minutes later, he was on Deedee's front stoop, hammering on her door. Her house was a two-minute drive from his. Brendan turned and looked out over his neighborhood. They both enjoyed locations on "The Hill," still Hansen's most prestigious neighborhood, and even on such a ghastly night the views were spectacular.

Through wisps of mist, he could see the whole city, pastel-painted turn-of-the-century houses nestled under mature maples, clinging to the sides of steep hills. Beyond the houses and the cluster of downtown buildings, lights penetrated the gloomy gray and reflected in the black, restless waters of Kootenay Lake.

Brendan turned back as the door opened a crack. Deedee regarded him suspiciously, as if there was a possibility that by some mean coincidence at the very same time she had called him, a home invader—Hansen's first—was waiting on her front stair to prey on the elderly.

Satisfied it was Brendan Grant in the flesh, she opened the door.

"Don't you look just like the devil?" she said. "Coming out of the storm like that, all dark menace and bristling bad temper. I used to say to Becky you had to have Black Irish in you somewhere. Or pure pirate."

Brendan stepped in and regarded his grandmother-in-law with exasperated affection. Only Deedee would see a devil or a pirate in the doer of a good deed!

"I'll try to contain the bristling bad temper," he said drily. The darkness he could do nothing about. It was his coloring: dark brown eyes, dark brown hair, whiskers blacker than night. It was also his heart.

Deedee was ninety-two, under five feet tall, frighteningly thin. Still, despite the fact it was 3:15 in the morning and her cat, Charlie, was dying, she was dressed in her go-to-church best. She had on a pantsuit the color of pink grapefruit. A matching ribbon was tied in a bow in her snow-white curls.

Would Becky have looked like this someday? If she had grown old? The pain was sharp, his guilt so intense it felt as if a knife had been inserted underneath his ribs. But Brendan was accustomed to it coming like this, in unexpected moments, and he held his breath, waiting, watching himself, almost bemused.

Pain, but no emotion. A man so emotionally impoverished he had not shed a single tear for his wife.

Sometimes he felt as if his heart was a tomb that a stone had been rolled in front of, sealing it away forever.

"I'll get my coat," Deedee said. "I've already got Charlie in the cat carrier."

She turned to retrieve her coat—pink to match her outfit—from the arm of a sofa, and he saw Charlie glaring balefully at him from a homemade carrier that looked like a large and very ugly purse.

Charlie's head poked out a round hole, his ginger fur stuck up in every direction, his whiskers kinked, his eyes slit with dislike and bad temper. He made a feeble attempt to squeeze his gargantuan self out the tiny opening, but his quick resignation to defeat, and the raspy breathing caused by the effort, made Brendan aware that tonight was the end of the road for the ancient, cranky cat.

Deedee turned back to him, carefully buttoning her coat around her. Brendan picked up the cat carrier with one hand and crooked his other elbow. Deedee threaded her arm through his, and he nudged open the door with his knee, trying not to be impatient when the rain sluiced down his neck as she handed him a huge ring of keys.

"Lock the handle *and* the dead bolt," she ordered, as if they were in a high-crime area of New York City.

Both locks were sticky, and Brendan made a note to come by and give them a squirt of lubricant the next time he had a chance.

Finally they turned toward his car, inched down the steep stairs that took them from her front stoop to the road. When they reached the flat walkway, he tried to adjust his stride to Deedee's tiny steps. He was just under six feet tall, his build lithe with a runner's sleekness rather than a bodybuilder's muscle, but Deedee made him feel like a giant.

A bristling pirate of a giant.

Brendan found himself wishing she would have called one of her children to accompany her on this late-night trip to the vet's office. But for a reason he couldn't quite decipher—it certainly wasn't his graciousness—it was him she turned to when she needed anything, from a lightbulb changed to her supply of liquid meal replacements restocked.

Deedee was not a nice little old lady. She was querulous, demanding, bossy, ungrateful and totally self-centered. It had occurred to Brendan more than once that she called him because no one else would come. But Deedee was his inheritance from his late wife. Becky and Deedee had adored each other. For that reason alone he came when she called.

Finally, he had both the cat and Deedee settled, the animal on the backseat, the woman in the front. The carrier did not look waterproof and he hoped the cat would not have an accident that would bleed through to the seat. Of course, with Charlie it might not be an accident. It might be pure spite.

Regardless, the car was brand-new, all plush leather and purring power. Had Brendan bought it hoping to fill some emptiness? If so, he had failed colossally, like putting a pebble in a hole left by a cannonball. Brendan shook off the thought, annoyed. It was the lateness of the night, the strangeness of being awake at what seemed to him to be the witching hour, that made him vulnerable to uncharacteristic introspection.

He got in the driver's side and started the engine, glanced at Deedee and frowned. She looked quite thrilled to be having this middle of the night outing, not like an old woman making the painful final journey with her cat.

"Which vet are you using? Is he expecting us?"

"I'll give you directions," she snapped.

It was the tone of voice she used right before she

pronounced you an idiot, so he shrugged and put the car in drive, and pulled out into the wet, abandoned streets of Hansen.

He was determined to be patient. It was one more loss for her. Putting down her precious cat. She was entitled to be crabby tonight, and he did not want her to be alone at the vet's office as the needle went in. He did not want her to be alone when she came home without her cat.

She gave him directions, and he drove in silence, the mountains on either side of the valley making the night darker, the water hissing up under the tires. The cat's breathing was labored.

Deedee issued shrill commands for Brendan to slow down and squinted at the signs on every crossroad. Finally, she fished in her purse, took out a piece of paper and held it very close to her face.

"If you give me the address, this new car has GPS."

She contemplated that, deeply suspicious of technology, then reluctantly gave him the information.

He put it in his system. They were headed into the neighborhood that bordered Creighton Creek. A stone's throw from Hansen proper, the area was rural residential, with a collection of small, neat acreages. Because of the great location, and the land, it was a sought-after area for young professionals who had a dream of children, a golden retriever and a horse or two.

All Brendan had ever wanted, growing up the only child of a single mother, was that most elusive of things—normal. And when he'd been almost there, in a blink, everything was gone. There must have been something he could have done. Anything.

He felt the pain again, of being powerless, and again

felt himself watching, wondering if at some unexpected moment he would just break open. If he did, he was certain it would shatter him, that the pieces would be so small there would be no collecting them and putting it all together again.

But no, he was able to focus on the small, old houses of Creighton Creek, which were slowly but surely being replaced with bigger ones. Brendan's firm, Grant Architects, had designed many of the newer homes, and he allowed himself, as they drove by one of his houses— one with a particularly complicated roofline—to be diverted from the painful realization of the life he was not going to have by the reality of the one he did.

The house was beautiful. The home owners loved it. Again, he had to try and shake that feeling of having *missed* something.

"I don't recall a vet located out here," he said. "In fact, didn't I take you and Charlie to Doc Bentley recently?"

"Dr. Bentley is an idiot," Deedee muttered. "He told me to put Charlie to sleep. That there was no hope at all. 'He's old. He's got cancer. Let him go.'" She snorted. "I'm old. Are you just going to let me go? Put me to sleep, maybe?"

Brendan cast Deedee a glance. Carefully, he said, "Isn't that what we're doing? Taking Charlie to have him put to, er, sleep?"

Deedee cranked her head toward him and gave him a withering look. "I am taking him to a healer."

Brendan didn't like the sound of that, but he carefully tried to strip any judgment from his voice. "What do you mean, a healer?"

"Her name's Nora. She has that new pet rescue place. Babs Taylor told me she has a gift."

"A gift," he repeated.

"Like those old-time preachers who laid their hands on people."

"Are you kidding me?" He began to look for a place to turn around. "You need a vet. Not a nut."

"What I need is a miracle, and Dr. Bentley already told me he can't give me one." Deedee's voice was high and squeaky. "Babs's niece volunteers out there. She said somebody brought in a dog that was deader than a doornail. And Nora Anderson brought it back to life. With her *energy*."

Brendan felt his mouth tighten in a hard line of cynicism. One thing Becky and her grandmother had had in common? They loved all things "woo-woo." They actually believed in what they called psychics and mediums, had frowned at him when he had made disparaging remarks about fortune-tellers and gypsies.

An unfortunate mental picture of Nora was forming in his mind: dangling earrings, wildly colored head scarf, hideous makeup, dark blue eye shadow, a slash of blood-red on her lips.

"Can you keep a secret?" Deedee didn't wait for him to respond, but lowered her voice conspiratorially, as if dozens could hear. "Clara, over at the post office, told me she thinks from the mail that she gets that Nora is Rover. You know, from the column? *Ask Rover?*"

He didn't know.

"You can tell when you read it," Deedee elaborated, still whispering. "Nora gets right inside their heads. The animals."

"That must be helpful, so that she knows where to

send the energy to," he said, his tone deeply sarcastic. Deedee missed the sarcasm entirely, because she went on with enthusiasm.

"Exactly! I'm a great fan of *Ask Rover,* so I knew she was the one who could help Charlie. I don't drive anymore," Deedee said, as if Brendan, her favored chauffeur, didn't know that, "and I can't hear properly on the phone, so I wrote her a letter, and brought it right to the post office so I knew she'd get it the next day. She wrote me back right away saying she would send me—Charlie—some energy."

Brendan felt a kind of helpless fury claw at him. Deedee nursed the worry that Hansen's first home invader would target her. She double-locked her doors. She was suspicious of the checkout girl at the grocery counting out the wrong change! How could she fall for this?

"It worked," Deedee whispered. "Charlie got better. But then he got worse again, and she wouldn't answer my letters. I phoned, too, even though I can't hear, but I got an answering machine. I hate those. No one returned my calls. Then tonight, Charlie's breathing changed. I'm scared. I know he's dying."

Brendan hated it that she was scared, and hated it more that her fear had made her so vulnerable. "Did you send money?"

The silence was telling.

"Did you?"

"A little."

His GPS system startled them both by telling him to turn right at the next crossroad. Suddenly he wanted very much to meet the person who would use an elderly woman's fear over losing her beloved pet to bamboozle money out of her.

All the better if they rousted her from a deep sleep in the middle of the night!

He turned right; they went up a road he had never noticed before, and passed under an archway that spanned the road.

A sign hung from the archway, letters painted in fresh, primary colors. Nora's Ark.

At any other time, he might have thought it was clever little play on words. Or maybe not. He didn't like *cute*. He was an architect. He liked calculation, precision, math. He liked figuring out how large a load a beam could carry, and how to make a wall of glass that was structurally sound.

He liked the completely balanced marriage of art and science that was his work. If at the end of the project he always felt, somehow, he had missed the mark, wasn't that part of what drove him to do even better the next time? To try again for that thing, whatever it was, that was just out of his reach?

Brendan considered himself pragmatic and practical, perhaps with a good measure of cynical thrown in. He was the man least likely to give himself over to whimsy. But given that it seemed to have been raining for forty days and forty nights, he felt a strange shiver along his spine that he was arriving at an ark of any sort.

Below the sign Nora's Ark was a smaller one, announcing they were supported by the Hansen Community Betterment Committee.

His company was one of the charter members!

He shook off his annoyance, and drove over a wooden bridge that spanned a creek that was still raging with spring runoff, though it was the last day of June. Up ahead, carved out of the mountainous wilderness all around, a white house—almost a cottage—was illuminated in his headlights, surrounded by a picket fence and a yard where yellow climbing roses rioted.

Through the grim, pelting rain a light shone, warm and inviting, from inside, and the house seemed like a welcoming place, not the kind of place where a charlatan who cheated vulnerable old women would live.

Was someone awake? It was probably a good time for chanting and consulting cards. Though why do it if the mark wasn't there?

Behind the house and yard, barely visible in darkness that was slowly giving way to a soggy predawn, he could see the huge silhouette of a barn.

"Oh, we're here," Deedee breathed happily. "It looks just the way I thought it would."

That explained the appearance of the place. Homey. Welcoming. Like the old witch's cottage in *Hansel and Gretel*.

All the better to dupe people, to lure them closer.

"You wait here," Brendan said, and cut off Deedee's protest with a firm slam of the car door. He walked up a path that smelled of perfume as he crushed damp fallen rose petals under his feet.

Then, out of the corner of his eye, back toward the barn, he saw a light fly up, heard the high-pitched whinny of a horse, and, straining against the sounds of the storm, he was sure he heard the startled cry of someone in trouble. A female in trouble.

CHAPTER TWO

TURNING FROM THE house, adrenaline pumping, his instincts on red alert, Brendan Grant ran toward the barn.

At first, he thought it was a pile of old rags in the churned-up mud of the paddock adjoining the barn. The pile was faintly illuminated by the fallen flashlight beside it. Then it moved. Heedless of the mud, he put one hand on the fence, leaped it, landed, raced to the still form. It looked like a child facedown in the mud.

His sense of urgency surged as he squatted down. He knew better than to try to move whoever it was without assessing the injuries.

"Are you all right?"

Movement from the heap of rags and a squeak of distressed surprise were a relief to Brendan. Then the pile of rags flipped over.

It was his turn to be shocked. It wasn't a child, but a woman. Her hair reminded him of Charlie's—ginger, sticking up all over the place, except where a clump of mud had flattened it to her skull. But even the mud that streaked her skin could not hide the exquisite loveliness of her pale face.

Her nose was dainty, faintly dusted with copper freckles. Her lips were plump and pink; her chin had a little jut to it that hinted at a stubborn temperament. A goose egg was rising alarmingly above her right eye.

Her eyes were amazing, wide-spaced, unusually large in the smallness of her face, a color of jade that flickered with light in the grayness of the night.

If this was Nora she was an enchantress of the kind who would have no need of makeup to weave her spell.

She was obviously very woozy, because she looked at him quizzically, and then oddly, reached up and touched his cheek, a faint smile on her face, as if she did not see a dark devil arrived on the tails of the storm, but something else entirely. Something that she recognized and welcomed.

His feeling of being enchanted—however reluctantly—increased.

Then abruptly she came to her senses. She seemed to realize she was flat on her back in the middle of the night, in the mud, with a strange man who oozed menace and bristling bad temper hovering over her.

Her eyebrows knit together in consternation and she struggled to sit up.

"Hey," he said, his attempt at a soothing tone coming out of his mouth like rust, a hoarse croak. "Try not to move."

She looked as if she had no intention of following his well-meaning instruction, so he laid a hand on her shoulder. It was tiny underneath a thin jacket that appeared to be soaking up rain rather than repelling it.

He could see a little bow on what could be her pajamas at the V of her jacket.

She shook off his hand, sat up, wincing from the effort. He'd been right about her chin giving a clue to her temperament. She was stubborn.

"Who are you?" she demanded. "What are you doing out here, on my property, at this time of night?"

He was annoyed with himself that the tone of her voice increased the sense of enchantment weaving through this miserable night. Despite the lack of welcome in her words, her voice reminded him of maple syrup, rich and smooth and sweet.

She scanned his face, that initial reaction of trust, of welcome, completely gone. Now she looked wary and stubborn and maybe just a little frightened.

What she didn't have was the look of a person who would be trying to dupe an old lady out of her money.

No sense putting off the moment of truth.

"Are you Nora?"

She nodded. He let that sink in. No head scarf. No dangling earrings. Certainly no blue eye shadow, or slash of red at her mouth.

Brendan was aware that in a very short time he had started to hope the woman in a vulnerable little heap in the mud was not the same woman who had written Deedee a letter promising to heal her cat. With energy. For a fee.

He looked at her fresh face, tried to imagine dangling earrings and heavy makeup and the gypsy scarf, and found his imagination didn't quite go that far. But fresh faced or not, she'd duped Deedee. He was already disillusioned by life, so why be disturbed by the gathering of a little more evidence?

Still, for the moment she looked faintly frightened, and he felt a need to alleviate that.

"I brought a cat out," he said. "I heard a ruckus out here, saw a light and came to investigate."

She considered his explanation, but looked doubtful. He suspected he didn't look much like the kind of guy who would be attached to his cat.

"I heard you were a healer." He tried to strip judgment from his tone, but he must have looked even less like the kind of guy who would put any kind of faith in a healer than one who would be attached to a cat, because her doubtful expression intensified.

"Who did you hear that from?" she asked uneasily. Her eyes skittered toward the fence, as if she was going to try and make an escape.

"Deedee Ashton."

The name did not seem to register, but then she might be struggling to remember her own name at the moment.

"Can you tell me what happened?" he asked.

She put a hand to the goose egg above her eye.

"I don't know for sure," she said. "The horses might have knocked me over."

He scanned the corral. Three horses were squeezed against the back fence, restless and white-eyed. He didn't know much about horses, but these ones seemed in no way docile.

He told himself firmly that it was none of his business what kind of chances she took. He didn't know her. He certainly didn't care about her. Still, there was a certain kind of woman that could make a man feel he should be protective. That was the kind you really had to guard against, especially if you had already failed in the department of protecting the smaller and weaker and more vulnerable.

Brendan ordered himself not to comment. But, of course, his mouth disobeyed his mind.

"Given you're about the size of a peanut, doesn't it

seem a touch foolhardy to decide to come mingle with your wild mustangs in the middle of the night?"

She glared at him. Her look clearly said *don't tell me what to do,* which was fair.

"Unless, of course, you hoped your *energy* was going to tame them?"

Those amazing eyes narrowed. "What do you know about my energy?"

"Not as much as I plan to."

"Why does that sound like a threat?" she asked.

He shrugged.

She tossed her head at that, but he saw a veil drop smoothly over the flash of fire in those green eyes, as if *he* had hurt *her* by being a doubter. You'd think, in her business, she would have developed a thicker skin.

But he would have to deal with all that later. She had begun to shiver from being wet, but when she tried to move, a small groan escaped her lips.

He knew he shouldn't move her. But she was clearly freezing. Now was not the time to confront her about any claims she had made to Deedee. He shrugged out of his coat and wrapped it around her.

She looked as if she planned to protest his act of chivalry, but when he tucked his coat around her, he could clearly see the warmth seduced her. She snuggled inside it instead. She looked innocent, about as threatening as a wounded sparrow.

Stripping away any censure he felt about her claims of extraordinary power, he said, "Can you move your hands? How about your feet? Can you turn your head from side to side for me?"

"What are you? A doctor?" Despite the protest, she tested each of her body parts as he named it.

He touched the ugly-looking bump rising above her right eye. She winced.

"You're not lucky enough to have conjured up a doctor. You'll have to work on your conjuring a little. I'm an architect. Luckily, I have a little construction site first aid experience."

As he had hoped, at the mention of his profession—oh, those professional men were so trustworthy—her wariness of him faded, though annoyance at his conjuring remark had turned her green eyes to slits that reminded him of Charlie.

He picked the flashlight out of the mud and shone it in her eyes, looking for pupil reaction.

"Tell me about your cat," she said, swatting at the light.

"So you can send him energy?"

"Why are you here, if you're so cynical?"

He felt a shiver along his spine, similar to what he had felt when he passed under the ark sign. What if he hadn't come along when he had? Would she have lain in the mud until she had hypothermia? Would the horses have trampled her?

But he was certainly not going to let her see that for a moment he was in the sway of an idea that some power he did not understand might have drawn him here at the exact moment she needed him.

Ridiculous. If such a power existed, where had it been the night Becky had needed it?

He actually saw Nora flinch, and realized he had grimaced. It no doubt gave him the pirate look that Deedee had seen earlier.

Keeping his tone level, Brendan said, "I'm here as

the result of a comedy of errors. I thought I was on my way to a legitimate practitioner of animal medicine."

"With your cat."

He nodded.

"You don't really look like a cat kind of guy."

"No? What do cat kind of guys look like?"

She studied him, the eyes narrow again. "Not like you," she said decisively.

"So, what do I look like? A rottweiler kind of guy? Bulldog? Boxer?"

Her look was intense. If a person believed that energy crap, they would almost think she was reading his. He raised the light again, shining it in her eyes, hoping to blind her. He was not sure he liked the sensation of being *seen*.

"You're not a dog kind of guy, either."

Accurate, but not spookily so.

"In fact," she continued, "I'd be surprised if you even had a plant."

Okay. That was about enough of that.

"I never said it was *my* cat." He turned off the light and put it in his pocket. "I don't think your back is injured, so I'm going to pick you up and carry you to the house."

"You are not picking me up! I'll walk." She tried to find her feet, and glared at him as if the fact that it was his jacket swimming around her stopped her from doing so. "If you'll just give me your hand—"

But Brendan did not just give her a hand. It wasn't the jacket. The small effort of trying to get up had made her turn a ghostly white, the freckles and mud standing out in stark relief. So he ignored her protests, slid his arms under her shoulders and her knees and scooped her up easily.

She was tiny, like that wounded sparrow, and despite the barrier of his jacket, he was aware of an unusual warmth oozing out of her where he held her against his chest.

Was it because it had been so long since he had touched another human being that he felt an unwelcome shiver of pleasure?

CHAPTER THREE

UNEASILY HOLDING A beautiful stranger in his arms and feeling that unwanted shiver of something good, Brendan Grant was aware it was what he had wanted to feel when he had purchased the car. Just a moment's pleasure at something. Anything. With the car, he had not even come close.

He should have already learned *stuff* could never do it. An unwanted memory came, of standing in front of the house he now owned, with Becky at his side, thinking, *This is the beginning of my every dream come true.*

"Put me down!"

Nora's hand, smacking hard against his chest, brought him gratefully back to the here and now.

"You couldn't even stand up by yourself," he said, unmoved by her tone. "I'll put you down in a minute. When I get you to the house."

Her expression was mutinous, but she winced, suddenly in pain, and conceded with ill grace.

He strode to the house. The woman in his arms was rigid with tension for a few seconds, then relaxed noticeably. He glanced down at her to make sure she hadn't passed out.

Wide green eyes stared up at him, defiant, unblinking. If ever there were eyes that could cast a spell, it would be those ones!

Just as he got close the porch light came on, illuminating the fact that Deedee had grown tired of waiting, had exited the passenger seat of the car and was feebly trying to wrestle her cat carrier out of the back.

A boy, at that awkward stage somewhere between twelve and fifteen, who also had ginger hair like Charlie's, exploded out the front door of the cottage, and the woman in Brendan's arms squirmed to life.

His architect's mind insisted on filling in pieces of the puzzle as he looked at the boy: too old to be hers.

"Put me down," she insisted, then shook herself as if waking from a dream. "Honestly! I told you I could walk."

The boy looked as if he had been sleeping, his hair flat against his face on one side and sticking straight up on the other. But he was now wide-awake and ready to fight.

"You heard her," he said, "put her down. Who are you? What have you done to my aunt Nora?"

Not his mother. His aunt.

The boy dashed back into the house and came out wielding a coat rack. He held it over his shoulder, like a baseball bat he was prepared to swing. His level of menace was laughable. Brendan was careful not to show that he had rarely felt less threatened.

Still, he couldn't help but admire a kid prepared to do battle with a full-grown man.

Brendan closed his eyes, and was suddenly aware he didn't feel the weight of new cynicism. Instead he was acutely aware of how the sweet weight in his arms and the woman's warmth were making his skin tingle. He was aware that the air smelled of rain and rose petals, and that those smells mingled with the clean scent of her hair and her skin.

Two and a half years ago, in the night, a phone call had changed everything forever. He'd been sleepwalking through life ever since, aware that he was missing something essential that other people had. That it was locked inside the tomb, and that even if he could have rolled the rock away, he was not sure that he would.

And now, another middle of the night phone call, leading to this moment. He was standing here in a stranger's yard with a woman who either was trouble, or was in trouble, in his arms, an adolescent boy threatening him with a coat rack, Deedee oblivious to it all, struggling to get her dying cat out of the car.

Brendan was aware that the rock had rolled, that a crack of light had appeared in the darkness. He was aware of feeling wide-awake, as if he was a warrior waiting to see if it was a friend or foe outside.

For the first time in more than two years he felt the blood racing through his veins, the exquisite touch of raindrops on his skin. For the first time in so long, Brendan knew he was alive.

And it didn't make him happy.

Not one little bit.

Instead, he felt deeply resentful that the prison of numbness that had become his world was being penetrated by this vibrant, demanding capricious energy called life.

"Put me down!" Nora insisted again, hoping for a no-nonsense tone of voice that would hide the confusion she was really feeling.

She looked up into the exquisite strength of the stranger's face. Through the fabric of the expensive rain jacket he had wrapped around her, she could feel the iron hardness of his chest where she leaned into it. His arms, cradling her shoulders and her legs, were bands of pure steel.

She should have fought harder against being picked up and toted across the yard like a sleeping baby. Because it was crazy to feel so safe.

The stranger had a certain cool and dangerous aloofness about him. He had already made it clear he had heard some exaggerated claim about her energy that had allowed him to put her in the category of gypsies, tramps and thieves.

So the feeling of safety had to be attributed to the terrible knock on her head. Being in his arms made Nora achingly aware that she had been alone for a while now. Carrying the weight of her world all by herself. It was a relief to be carried for a change. A guilty pleasure, but a relief nonetheless.

Now, looking up at him, she could feel something shifting. His hands tightened marginally on her and some finely held tension played around the corners of his sinfully sensuous mouth.

The soft suede of his deep, deliciously brown eyes had not changed when he had called her a healer, his tone accusatory, but now they had hardened to icy remoteness and sparked with vague anger.

Well, he had come to her rescue and was being threatened with a coat rack. Naturally, he would react.

But now he was not the man she had awoken to, one with something so compelling in his face she had reached up and touched...

She shook that off, striving for the control she had lost when she'd accepted his arms around her, accepted being cradled against the fortress of his chest, accepted the comfort of being carried.

She could not be weak. She had to be strong. Everything was relying on *her* now. She was completely on her own since her fiancé had said, "Look, it's him or it's me."

Surely, when her sister had appointed her guardian of then fourteen-year-old Luke she had not expected that turn of events! Karen had thought she was entrusting her son to a home, to a stable, financially secure environment that would have two parents, one her sister, Nora, affectionately known within the family as "the flake," the other a highly respected stable person, a vet with his own practice.

But the highly predictable world Karen had envisioned for Luke didn't happen. When everything had fallen apart between her and Vance, Nora had risked it all on a new start.

She *had* to be strong.

"Look," Nora said, "you really have to put me down."

The man ignored her, looking flintily past her to Luke.

To get his attention off her nephew, and to show she meant business, she smacked the stranger hard, against the solid wall of his chest. It felt ineffectual, as if she was being annoying, like a bug, not powerful like a lioness.

Still, when his arm slid out from under her knees, and she found herself standing, albeit a bit wobbly, on her own two feet, instead of feeling relieved she felt the oddest sense of loss.

He had carried her across her yard with incredible ease, his stride long, powerful and purposeful, his breath remaining steady and even. It was the kind of strength a person might want to rely on.

If that person hadn't made a pact to rely totally on herself!

Get a grip, Nora ordered silently, moving away from the man. She was genuinely relieved that Luke dropped the coat rack and came to her side.

Casting a look loaded with suspicion and warning at the man who had carried her, Luke got his shoulder under her arm and helped her toward the house.

"What happened? Did he hurt you?"

"No. No. It wasn't him. I couldn't sleep and I went to check the animals. One of the new horses must have spooked and knocked me over."

"Why would you go out in the corral by yourself?" Luke asked.

"My question precisely." The man's voice was deep and calm, steady.

"Those horses were wild when they were brought in," Luke said accusingly. "That one took a kick at the guy unloading him."

She didn't like it one little bit that it felt as if the two were forming an alliance against her!

Why had she gone into the corral when the horses were so restless? Probably she hadn't even thought about it, overly confident in her ability to calm animals.

Since she was a little girl she had found refuge from her mother and father's constant bickering by bringing home broken things to fix. Tiny wounded birds, abandoned cats, dogs near death.

Inside, Nora was still the girl who had been seen

by family and school chums as an eccentric, a kook, and she was more comfortable hiding her gifts than revealing them.

Which made her very uncomfortable with whatever this stranger thought he knew about her.

Would Karen have ever made her guardian of Luke if she knew Vance would not be in the picture? Probably not. She would have known her sister could not be trusted to control impulses like jumping into a corral full of flighty horses in the middle of the night!

Nora was solely responsible for Luke. What if he'd found her out there in the mud? Hadn't he been traumatized enough? She was supposed to be protecting him!

Still, it was unsettling to her that what she remembered, in far more detail than her lapse of judgment before entering the corral, or the moments before being knocked over and knocked out, was the moment after.

Coming to, Nora had opened her eyes to find this man bent over her. His expression was intense, and he was breathtakingly handsome. Dark, thick hair was curling wetly around perfect features—a straight nose; whisker-roughened cheeks; a faintly cleft chin; firm, sensuous lips.

A raindrop had slid with exquisite slowness down his temple, over the high ridge of his cheekbone, onto his lip.

And then, in slow motion, it had fallen from his lip to hers.

Perhaps it was the knock on the head that had made the moment feel suspended, made the raindrop feel as if it sizzled in the chill of the night. Made her reach out with the tip of her tongue and taste that tiny pearl of water.

Perhaps it was the knock on the head that made her feel like a princess coming awake to find the prince leaning over her.

Through it all, Nora had been caught hard by eyes that mesmerized: velvet brown suede flecked with gold, a light in them that was mostly solid strength, with just the faintest shadow of something else.

Something she of all people should know.

Woozily, she had reached out and let the palm of her hand caress his bristly cheek, to touch that common ground she recognized between them.

He had gone very still under her touch, but he did not move away from it. She had felt a lovely sense of safety, that this was someone she could rely on.

But then the wooziness was gone, just like that, and she'd remembered she was in her paddock. And that she was alone out there with a man who had no business being on her property at this time of the night.

Nora's instincts when it came to animals were beyond good. Some people, including her ex-fiancé, Dr. Vance Height, whom she had met while working as an assistant in his veterinary practice, were spooked by what she could accomplish with sheer intuition.

But Vance was a reminder that Nora's good instincts did not extend to men. Or much else about life. With tonight being an unsettling exception, her perception was fabulous when it came to dealing with hurt, frightened animals.

Or writing her quirky, off-beat column *Ask Rover*, a column she had never admitted she was behind, because she had come across Vance reading it in her early days at his office, and he had been terribly scornful of it.

The intuition was not so good at helping her stretch her modest income from the column to support both the animal shelter and Luke. Thankfully, as the shelter became more established it was starting to receive financial support from the community of Hansen.

Her intuition was also not proving the least helpful at dealing with a now fifteen-year-old nephew who seemed intent on visiting his hurt and anger over the death of his mother on the whole world.

Feeling foolish now for that vulnerable moment when she had reached up and let her hand scrape the seductive whiskery roughness of the stranger's cheek, and more foolish for allowing herself to be carried across her yard by a perfect stranger, Nora shook off Luke's arm. She was supposed to be protecting him, not the other way around.

She turned and faced the man, folding her arms over her chest.

She had been, she was certain, mistaken that they shared anything in common. Looking at him from this angle, she found he looked hard and cold, and she had, as was her unfortunate habit, given her trust too soon.

"Where did he come from?" Luke asked in a suspicious undertone.

For all she knew he could be an ax murderer! Anyone could say they were an architect! She ran an animal rescue center. Anyone could say they had brought a cat.

She knew he wasn't a cat person, one likely to be ruled by the kind of sentiment that would drive him out on a night like this for the well-being of a cat.

But behind the man, she suddenly became aware of an old woman in a ghastly pink outfit. As Nora watched, the woman gave a grunt of exertion and freed a large container from the backseat of a car that was as gray as the night and sleek with sporty expense. The man turned to her, stepped back and took a large carpet bag from her.

Nora registered two things at once: how protective he seemed of that tiny, frail woman, and that there was indeed a cat! Its head was sticking out of a kind of window in the side of the carrier. One didn't have to have any psychic ability at all to know the cat did not have now, and probably never had had, a pleasing personality.

"I'm Brendan Grant," he said.

The name seemed Scottish to Nora, and with the rain plastering his hair to his head, running unchecked down the formidable, handsome lines of his face, it was just a little too easy to picture him as a Scottish warrior. Strong. Imperious to the weather.

Determined to get his own way.

What was his own way?

"And this is my grandmother, Deedee, and her cat, Charlie." The faint hiss of angry energy seemed to intensify around him. His mouth had become a hard line. He was watching Nora closely for her reaction.

"I'm sorry?" she said. What on earth was he doing here at this time of the night with his grandmother and her cat?

Still, whatever it was, it did dilute some of the threat she felt. Though not an expert, she was still fairly certain architect ax murderers did not travel with an entourage that included grandmothers and cats.

His voice calm and ice-edged, he said, "Deedee has been made certain promises concerning Charlie. And she has paid in advance."

Nora didn't have a clue what he meant. But she did realize the threat she felt was not of the ax-murderer variety.

It was of the raindrop-falling-from-lips variety. She was aware her head hurt, but was not at all sure this feeling of being caught off balance was caused by the knock to her head.

"I don't know what you're talking about," she said firmly.

She became aware that something rippled through Luke. She felt more than saw his discomfort. She cast her nephew a glance out of the corner of her eye.

Uh-oh.

"Look," the man said quietly, the commanding tone of his voice drawing her attention firmly back to him. "You may be able to pull the wool over the eyes of an old woman, but I'm here to look after her interests. And you should know that if you've swindled her, you can kiss the support of the Hansen Community Betterment Committee good-bye."

Kiss the support of the Hansen Community Betterment Committee good-bye? Nora couldn't let her panic show.

"Swindled your grandmother?" she asked instead. Below the panic, she could feel the insult of it! His caustic remarks about her energy and her being a healer were beginning to make an awful kind of sense.

"I wouldn't be surprised if the police became involved," Brendan said, the quiet in his voice making it all the more threatening.

CHAPTER FOUR

THE POLICE? NORA felt a sense of panic, as if her world were tilting.

Still, she could not cave before him. She was about to insist that he was the one trespassing on private property, except that at the mention of the police, she realized she wasn't the only one panicking.

Nora saw Luke go rigid.

There'd been an unfortunate incident at school involving the police way too recently.

Luke claimed to have *borrowed* a bicycle. Apparently without the full understanding of the bicycle's owner, which was why the police had become involved. Luke had talked to the other boy, and the whole thing, thankfully, had blown over.

Now her nephew met her eyes, pleading, and then ducked his head, drawing a pattern in the wet ground with his bare toe.

Nora glanced back at Brendan Grant and saw he had not missed a thing. He was watching Luke narrowly, and her sense of him being a warrior intensified. His look did not bode well for her nephew.

What had Luke done now? She was acutely aware of having failed in her responsibility to her nephew by going into the corral by herself tonight. Now every protective instinct rose in her.

"Nobody swindled me," Deedee said plaintively. "She sent me energy for Charlie."

"For a price," Brendan added softly.

Nora knew she had not sent anyone any energy. And certainly not for a price! But Luke was squirming so uncomfortably she wanted to hit him with her elbow to make him stop drawing attention to himself.

Because no matter what he had done, Luke was no match for Brendan Grant. Not in any way. Not physically, nor could her poor orphaned nephew bear up under the anger that sparked in the man's eyes.

Taking a deep breath, she said brightly. "Oh, I remember now. Charlie."

Luke cast her a glance loaded with gratitude and relief, and she might have allowed herself to relish that, especially coupled with the fact he had taken up a coat rack in her defense. Moments when her nephew actually seemed to like her were rare, after all.

But Brendan Grant looked hard and skeptical, and she needed to stay focused on the immediate threat of that.

She put together the few clues she had. One of her gifts was an acute ability to focus on detail. Brendan and Deedee had arrived in the middle of the night. From what she could see of the cat, he was ill, the lateness of the hour suggested desperately so.

"Charlie's been sick, right?" she said.

"That's right!" Deedee said eagerly.

Brendan's expression just became more grim.

"You said you'd send him energy," Deedee reminded her. "You said to send money. I sent fifty dollars."

"Fifty dollars?" Brendan snapped. "Deedee! You said you sent a *little* money."

"In terms of what my cat is worth to me, that is a small amount." The woman gave him a look that was equal parts sulk and steel.

"So there you have it," Brendan said to Nora, exasperated. "If you play your cards right, she'll sign over her house to you. You won't need the support of the Hansen Community Betterment Committee. Is that how this operation of yours works?"

"Of course not!" Nora said, feeling the heat rising in her cheeks. "I'm sure it was just a mistake. I must have thought the money was a donation."

She tried to keep her voice steady, but was not sure she succeeded.

"Uh-huh." He sounded cynical, and rightfully so.

Nora wanted to whirl on Luke and shake him. She had never even raised her voice to him, but their whole future was at stake here. And worse, if he had sent that letter, and taken that money—and who else could it possibly be?—he had stolen from a vulnerable old woman. How could he? Who was he becoming? And why couldn't she stop it?

Again she felt the weight of responsibility for her choices. Karen would have never entrusted her to raise her nephew alone. She would have been able to predict this catastrophe coming.

With great care, Nora kept herself from looking askance at her nephew.

"Let's get in out of the rain," she suggested, trying to keep her voice steady. Because he had given her his jacket, the rain had soaked through Brendan's shirt, which was now practically transparent.

She was aware she didn't really want Brendan Grant, with his bristling masculine energy and wet, clinging shirt, invading her house. She'd been here only a little while, but it had quickly become a sanctuary to her. On the other hand, she desperately needed to buy some time, to take Luke aside and figure out what he had done.

And fix it.

Yet again.

But a glance at the unyielding features of the man who had made her feel momentarily so safe told her this might not be so easy to fix.

The house was not what Brendan expected of a charlatan's house. There were no crystals dangling in the door wells and no clusters of herbs hanging upside down from their stems. There was no cloying scent of incense.

"Lovely," Deedee breathed with approval, standing in the doorway, taking it in.

"Disappointing," Brendan said.

In fact, he found the house was cozy and clean. An uneasiness crawled along his neck as they passed through a living room where a pair of love seats the color of melted butter faced each other across a coffee table where some of those yellow roses from the yard floated in a clear glass bowl.

"Disappointing?" Nora asked.

"No black cat. No cauldron on the hearth."

Nora shot him a look. She really was the cutest little thing. Again he had that feeling of coming awake. He didn't want to notice her, but how could he not? Her hair was a mess, standing straight up, strawberry-blonde dandelion fluff. Her eyes were huge in a dainty mud-streaked face. She looked more frightened now than when he had first found her.

The scam revealed. But her shock seemed genuine, and so did her distress.

"Look," Nora said in a defensive undertone, "I take in sick and abandoned animals. I don't claim to be a healer."

Her nephew snorted at that, and she shot him a glare that he was completely oblivious to.

Deedee, deaf anyway, hadn't even heard.

"As for black cats and cauldrons, I certainly don't do witchcraft!"

Her muddy, soaked clothes, and his jacket, swam around her, and he guessed she would be determined not to remove her coat and reveal the pajamas underneath.

He wasn't sure why. The pajama bottoms, which he could see, were filthy, but underneath the mud they were plaid. Utilitarian rather than sexy.

They came to the kitchen, and Nora turned on a light to reveal old cabinets painted that same cheerful shade of yellow as her sofas and roses. The floor was old hardwood planking that gleamed with patina. He smelled fresh bread.

There was a jar full of cookies on the counter, and notes and pictures were held by magnets to the front of a vintage fridge. There was a wood-burning stove in one corner, and an old, scarred oak table covered with schoolbooks.

The uneasiness returned. He thought of those wonders of granite and steel that people wanted for their kitchens these days, that he designed, and suddenly he knew what the uneasiness was. They somehow had all missed the mark.

For all the awards that decorated the walls of his office, he had never achieved *this*. A feeling.

He shook it off, looked back at Nora. The caption under her high school yearbook picture had probably read "Least likely to bamboozle an old woman out of her money."

But somebody had. The nephew? The kid practically had a neon sign over his head that flashed Guilty, but on the other hand, didn't all kids that age look like that? Slinky and defensive and as if they had just finished committing a crime?

What surprised Brendan was that he was interested at all in who did it. And if it was her nephew, to what lengths she would go to protect him.

But that's what happened when you came alive. Life, the interactions of people, their relationships and motivations interested you.

It was a wound waiting to happen, he warned himself.

"Put the cat there." Nora pointed to a kitchen island, a marble top fastened to solid wooden legs, and he set the cat carrier down, surreptitiously checking the bottom for any dampness that might have transferred to the seat of his new car.

He knew it said something about the kind of person he was that he was relieved to find none.

"He's been very sick," Deedee said. "Just like I told you in the letter."

"Maybe you could remind me what you wrote in your letter."

In the light of the kitchen, Brendan could see a knob

growing alarmingly on Nora's forehead. She was wet and covered in mud.

And Brendan Grant was surprised there was a part of him that still knew the right thing to do. And was prepared to do it.

"The cat will have to wait," he heard himself say firmly, in the tone of voice he used on the construction site when a carpenter was insisting something couldn't be done the way he wanted it done.

And the people in the room reacted about the same way. Deedee swung her head and glared at him. Nora looked none too happy, either.

"I want to take a look at you," he insisted. "If you don't need a trip to the emergency ward, you certainly need a shower and a change of clothes before you check out the cat."

"I can have a look at the cat first."

So she wanted what he wanted. For this to be quick. Look at the cat. Tell them what they all already knew about Charlie's prospects for a future. Of course, what they wanted parted ways at finding out who was guilty of taking money from Deedee, and what the consequences were going to be.

Still, handled properly, the whole drama could unfold and conclude in about two minutes, in and out.

Heavy on the out part. He wanted to head home and go back to bed.

His old life—that cave that was comforting in its lack of intensity, in its palette of grays—beckoned to him. But it seemed to him that nothing was going to go quite as he wanted.

Which he hated in and of itself. Because one thing

Brendan Grant wanted, in a world that had already scorned his need for it, was control.

"You first, then the cat," he told Nora.

Deedee, in typical fashion, appeared annoyed that her agenda was being moved to the back of the line. But Nora looked annoyed, too. It told him a lot about her when she folded her arms over his coat.

Independent. Possibly newly so. No one was going to tell her what to do. Brendan wondered again what the pajamas she was so determined to hide looked like.

"You already told me you aren't a doctor," Nora said.

"Doctor or not, a head injury is nothing to take lightly. They can be sneaky and deadly. It will just take me a minute to look at you."

"I'm fine."

"Deadly?" The boy got a panicky pinched look around his eyes. "Let him look at you!"

Nora, seeing his distress, surrendered, sinking onto a kitchen chair with ill grace.

"That was quite a hit to your head. Do you think you were knocked out?" Brendan moved close, brushed her hair away from the rapidly growing bump.

Every part of her seemed to be either wet or covered with mud. How was it her hair felt like silk?

"I'm fine."

"That's not what I asked," he said mildly.

"I don't think I was knocked out." She offered this grumpily.

"But you can't say for sure?"

She didn't want to admit it, but Brendan could tell she didn't remember, which was probably not a good sign.

Nora knew what date it was, her full name and her

birthday. He noted that she was twenty-six, though she looked younger. He also noted, annoyed, that he was interested in her age.

And apparently her marital status. There was no ring on her finger, no signs—large shoes, men's magazines, messes—that would indicate there was any male besides the boy in residence.

Brendan hated that he was awake enough to notice those things, to wonder at her history, what had brought her and her nephew to this remote corner of British Columbia.

Doing his best to detach, he asked more questions. She remembered what had happened right before she was knocked down and right after, though she did not remember precisely what had knocked her down. She could follow the movement of his finger with her eyes.

"You seem fine," he finally decided, but he felt uneasy. A concussion really was nothing to fool around with.

"She is fine," Deedee snapped. "Meanwhile, Charlie could be expiring."

"I'll just have a quick look at the cat," Nora said.

"He's lasted this long. I'm sure he can wait another five minutes. You need to go have a shower and put on something dry."

"Are you always this bossy?"

He ignored her. "If you feel dizzy or if you vomit, or feel like you're going to be sick, you need to tell me right away. Or Luke after I leave. You may have to get to the hospital yet tonight."

She looked as if she was going to protest. And then she glanced down at herself, and surprised him by giving in without a fight.

"All right. Luke, come with me for a minute. You can see if you can find a shirt that will fit Mr. Grant. He's soaked."

That explained her easy acquiescence. She was going to go talk it over with the kid. They were going to get their stories straight and figure out who had done what.

Brendan already knew precisely what she was going to do. She had already started to set it up when she'd said the money had been taken by accident, mistaken for a donation. She was going to take the blame.

Personally, Brendan was strongly leaning toward the conclusion her nephew had done it. How could she possibly think that not letting him accept responsibility was going to do the boy any good?

"Brendan?"

He turned to Deedee, impatient. Was she really going to insist that cat come first again? She did love to have her own way, largely oblivious to the larger picture.

"I'm not feeling well," she said.

He scanned her face. She loved to be the center of attention. But the fear he saw was real.

"My heart's beating too fast," she whispered.

He crossed the room and lifted her frail wrist. Her pulse was going crazy. She searched his face, ready to panic, and he forced himself to smile.

"Let's make it a double header," he said. "We'll take you to the hospital and they can check out Nora at the same time."

He cast Nora a look.

Her protest died on her lips as she read his face and then glanced at Deedee.

"You're right," she said. "I think I need to go to the hospital."

CHAPTER FIVE

AT HIS AUNT's declaration, panic twisted the boy's features, but only for a second. He took in the situation in the room, his gaze lingering on Deedee. Brendan saw calm come to him, almost as if he had breathed in the truth.

"What about Charlie?" Deedee half whispered, half sobbed. "I can't leave him! Not when he's—"

The steadiness remained in the boy's eyes as he looked to Brendan and then his aunt. "I got the cat," he said, and Deedee relaxed noticeably, slumped against Brendan.

Ninety-two. Deedee could die right now. She could go before the cat. Life liked to put ironic little twists in the story line.

Becky, young and healthy, gone at twenty-six. To this day, it seemed impossible.

A week before she had died, she had said to him, out of the blue, "If I die first, I'll come back and let you know I'm all right."

"You won't be all right," he'd said, uncomfortable with the conversation, pragmatic to a fault. "You'll be dead."

So far, she hadn't been back to let him know anything, even how to keep on living. So he'd been right. Dead was dead.

And he'd been prepared to deal with it tonight with Charlie. Not Deedee. Not on his watch. With a sense of urgency he was trying to disguise, and feeling somewhat like the ringmaster at a three-ring circus, Brendan pulled his cell phone from his pocket and herded all his charges back out the door into the rain.

"Can you get in the back with her?" he asked in an undertone. "Kick my seat if anything changes. You know how to monitor her pulse?"

Nora nodded and climbed in the backseat of the car with Deedee. Luke and the cat got in the front with Brendan. The car smelled of new leather and luxury. It screamed a man who had arrived.

The type of man who would never see anything in the slightly eccentric owner of a struggling animal shelter.

Not that she cared who found her attractive and who didn't! Good grief! The lady beside her could be having a heart attack. This was not the time or place!

Starting the car, Brendan never lost focus. He tucked the phone under his ear. "Hansen Emergency? It's Brendan Grant here. I'm on my way in. I have a ninety-two-year-old woman who has a very fast pulse. No history of heart problems. No chest pain. I also have a young woman who has had a head injury. Who's the doctor on call tonight? I know you're not supposed to tell me, but I want to know."

Nora took it all in. How his name had been recognized, how the name of the on-call doctor had been surrendered to him with a token protest only.

She took in his confidence as he dialed another number. "Greg? Sorry to wake you. Becky's grandmother is not well."

Becky? She'd thought it was *his* grandmother!

"Who's Becky?" she asked Deedee.

"My granddaughter. Brendan's her husband."

Married. Why would that feel the way it did? Like some kind of loss? Why didn't he wear a ring? Nora hated married men who didn't wear rings. They were sneaky, they were looking for—

"She died," Deedee said tiredly.

"I'm so sorry," Nora said, and thought of what she was sure she had seen in his eyes when he'd first leaned over her. The common ground. Now she understood it. Sorrow.

"In a car accident," Deedee went on. She was talking too loudly, the way people who are hard of hearing did. "Brendan doesn't talk about her. I need someone to cry with sometimes. But he never will. He didn't even cry at the funeral."

It was said like an accusation, and so loudly the man in the front seat could not miss it. Nora watched his face in the light coming from the dash. He didn't even flinch. It was as if he was cast in stone.

But she had seen the pain spilling into his eyes in that first unguarded moment when he had stood over her in the paddock.

"People all grieve in their own way," Nora said, and saw him cast her a quick glance in the rearview mirror before he reached for his phone again. "And it seems to me maybe he's there for you in other ways that are just as important."

Not everyone would be chauffeuring an elderly

woman and her sick cat around the country in the middle of the night!

"Of course, you're right," Deedee murmured, and leaned her head on Nora's shoulder. Nora had her hand on the woman's wrist and noticed, gratefully, the pulse was slowing to normal.

She listened to the deep gravel of Brendan's voice as he spoke on the phone.

"And I have a head injury, too. I think mild concussion, but a confirmation would be good. See you there. We're five minutes out."

He clicked the phone shut and stepped on the gas. The night was wet and the roads had to be slippery, but he oozed calm confidence as he navigated the twisty, mist-shrouded road into Hansen. The powerful car responded as if it were a living thing.

The way a man handled a powerful car told you a lot about him. The way a man handled an emergency told you a lot as well. Not that they were tests, but had they been, Brendan Grant would have passed with flying colors.

His calm never flagged. Not on the wet roads, not as they pulled into Emergency, not as he helped his grandmother out of the back of the car. There were obviously benefits to being emotionally shut down.

"What about Charlie?" Deedee wailed again.

"I'll stay with him," Luke said. "Out here. I'm not going in there."

Nora doubted that he was ever going to get over the thing he had about hospitals. He'd spent too much time in one while his mother was sick. He hated them now.

Brendan didn't question why, just flipped a set of keys at Luke. "Her house is three blocks that way. The address is on the chain. I presume you have your cell phone with you and that your aunt has the number?"

"Why can't I stay here?"

"Because if that cat pees in my car," he said in a low tone that Deedee didn't hear, "it really isn't going to survive the night."

Nora was appalled, but it was a guy thing, because Luke chuckled. Then he sobered. "You're trusting me to go into her house?"

Brendan's eyes locked on his. "Is there any reason I shouldn't?"

Luke ducked his head and didn't say anything.

"I don't know how long we'll be here. Get some rest. Let the cat out of that purse, near his litter box if you can locate it. If your aunt is released, you're going to have to look after her for the rest of the night."

Luke glanced at the address on the key chain. "I hope none of my friends see me with this dorky thing," he muttered, but Nora did not miss the fact that he looked pleased—if somewhat guilty—about Brendan's trust.

"I could drive him," she said tentatively, "and come back. I really don't need—"

Brendan gave her a look that was so don't-mess-with-me it made her stomach feel as if it was doing a free fall from ten thousand feet. She just didn't have the energy to take him on.

In the hospital, she had that same sense that you could tell a lot about a man by the way he handled an emergency. Again he passed. He handled the nurse with confidence that was palatable, not the least intimidated by her officiousness. In fact, the exact opposite might have been true. He was obviously well-known in the community, and respected. The nurse treated Brendan as if he was part of that inner circle of the emergency ward.

Interestingly, Vance had been terrible at emergencies. He became so flustered if a badly injured animal was brought in that he could not inspire confidence in anyone. You would have thought with practice he would have gotten better, but he never did. He liked catering to the pudgy poodle set, doing routine checkups and giving shots, neutering, and cleaning teeth.

In fact, he'd opted for regular hours only and hired a young vet to handle the nighttime emergencies, and finally any emergency at all.

A few weeks ago, Nora had heard he was engaged to that young vet. Up until then she had nursed a secret fantasy that he was going to show up on her doorstep, confess the error of his ways and beg her to take him back.

She shook it off. For whatever the reason—she suspected because Brendan Grant made things happen— she found herself ushered into an examination room in record time.

In short order, a young doctor was in, a nurse at his side.

"How's Mrs. Ashton?" Nora asked.

"Old," he said with a resigned smile. "We're going to keep her for observation. So, Brendan says a bump on the head? Maybe knocked out?"

"Maybe," Nora admitted.

"How do you know Brendan?" he asked.

"It's a long story."

The doctor laughed. "That's what he said. He designed our house and supervised the build. He's an amazing architect."

Great! In her weakened state, Nora just had to know Brendan Grant was an all-around phenomenal guy.

The doctor repeated some of the questions Brendan had asked her earlier, shone a light in her eye, got her to follow the movement of his finger.

"I should keep you for observation, too."

"I can't!" she said. "I have animals that will need feeding in—" her eyes flew to a nearby clock "—two hours."

The doctor sighed. "He said you'd say that. I'm going to send you home, but with strict instructions what to watch for. And what to do for the next few hours. Any dizziness, any nausea, any loss of consciousness, you come right back in. I'll give you a handout with symptoms you need to watch for over the next few days. Sometimes even weeks later symptoms can come up."

After having the nurse go over the sheet with her, they let her go. Brendan was in the waiting room.

"You didn't have to wait."

"Uh-huh. How were you going to get home? And collect your nephew?"

"Taxi, I guess."

"And would the taxi driver be watching you for signs of concussion?" Brendan held up duplicates of the instructions the doctor had given her.

The truth was she was glad she did not have to worry about a taxi right now, or how to find Luke. She was glad this man was in charge. And she might have a concussion, so it was okay to be weak. Just this once. Just for tonight.

The animals needed to be fed in a few hours.

She felt like weeping.

Brendan was watching her closely.

"Are you okay?"

"Yes," she said firmly.

But just as if he hadn't heard her, he slipped his arm around her waist, and just as if she hadn't claimed she was okay, she leaned heavily into him.

They collected Luke and, since no one had any idea when Deedee would be home, recaptured Charlie. Nora tried to stay awake and couldn't. She awoke to find herself in Brendan Grant's arms for the second time that night.

There was absolutely no fight left in her.

None.

Because Luke was bringing Charlie into the house instead of out to the barn. She didn't allow any of the animals in the house. How could she? If she did, soon they would be overrun!

But she just didn't have the energy to make a fuss about it right now. Instead, she snuggled deep into Brendan's reassuring strength and let him carry her into her house and up the stairs to her room.

"Is she okay?" Luke asked, pointing Brendan to a room on the right of a narrow hallway. He disappeared with Charlie and the cat carrier into a doorway farther up the hall.

"She's just done in," Brendan assured him. He nudged open the door and hesitated on the threshold of Nora's room.

It was confirmed she was completely, one hundred percent single. No man could be trusted with so much white: white walls, white curtains, white pillows, white bedspread. Her room reminded him of innocence. There was something alarmingly bridal about it.

And that was the last thing Brendan wanted to be thinking of as he carried Nora Anderson across the threshold!

He looked down at her and felt a wave of relief. Still wrapped in his too large jacket, mud from head to toe, she was the world's least likely bride. In fact, her bridal vision of a room was about to be damaged by her muddy little self.

Brendan took a deep breath, stepped in, and quickly made his way to the bed, where he set her on the edge.

Luke appeared in the doorway. "Anything I can do?"

"Oh, Luke," Nora said. "Where did he come from? You know the rules. We can't have animals in the house."

Brendan turned, expecting to see Luke had Charlie. Instead, he had a black-and-white kitten riding in the palm of his hand.

"This one's different," Luke said. "I'm calling him Ranger."

"We don't name them!"

Luke looked mutinous. "I'm keeping him. For my own."

Nora chewed her lip. "We need to talk about that," she said.

"But not tonight," Brendan said firmly. "Luke, can you get rid of the kitten for now, and find me a flashlight?"

He disappeared and came back, with no kitten, but a flashlight.

"Shine it right in your aunt's eyes. Do you see what it does to her pupils? That's called dilation. It's very important that both her pupils are dilating in the same way. I need you to try it."

The boy grasped the flashlight without any hesitation. Brendan was going to take it as a good sign that Luke was not nearly as rebellious as his aunt was.

"Yes, her eyes are doing the same thing. The black part is getting smaller when I hold the light up."

"Don't talk about me like I'm not here!"

"Good. That's exactly what you are looking for. You need to wake her up every hour after I leave and check her eyes. If you see a change you need to call 9-1-1."

"There's no need to frighten him!" Nora protested.

"I'm not frightening him. I'm asking him to step up to the plate. I'm treating him like a man."

Luke puffed up a bit at that.

"Well, he's not a man."

And then deflated.

"He's not a child, either."

The boy puffed up again.

"Either he checks you or I stay for the night."

She blanched at that, then folded her arms over her chest with ill grace and glared at him. That settled, Brendan conducted some very simple tests on his unwilling patient while Luke watched.

"The doctor already did this."

"Luke needs to see what to do."

Finally, Brendan was satisfied. "Do you need anything? A drink of warm milk, maybe?"

"Oh."

There was something kind of sweet and kind of sad about her surprise that anyone would look after her.

"That would be nice," she said shyly.

"Luke, can you go warm some milk?"

Luke left and Brendan leaned over and pulled off her shoes. Gently, he tugged the jacket off her.

"I can do it!"

"It's not as if you're in a see-through negligee."

She scowled at him, but let him free each of her limbs from the jacket.

He pretended not to notice her pajama top at all, but it was adorable. How was it a pink pajama top with kittens on it that said Purrfectly Purrfect Me could be more sexy than a negligee?

"Stand up for a minute," he ordered. She did, and he deftly pulled back the white quilt. Surprise, surprise, pure white sheets.

He guided her under the covers. She sank into her bed, then struggled to sit up. "Set the alarm. I have to be up. I have to feed the animals in two hours."

The clock was holding down some papers on a bed-side table. He could tell now wouldn't be the best time to relate what the doctor had told him. She had to rest. Completely. For at least twenty-four hours. She wasn't even supposed to look at a computer screen or read. So he pretended to set the clock.

He looked back at the bed, and her eyes were already closed, her breath coming out in soft puffs.

So much for the warm milk.

He went and looked at her. He felt the oddest desire to kiss her, not passionately, but a good-night kiss, like a father might give a child. Protective. Happy she was safe.

Happy he had managed to keep at least one person safe from the perils of life.

Brendan went down the steps. The kitchen was empty; no milk was out or on the stove. Luke was stretched out on the living room couch.

The empty carrier was beside him, and Charlie, a cat

who hated both animal and man equally, was stretched out over the boy's chest. The black-and-white kitten, Ranger, was curled into Charlie's belly. They were all fast asleep.

Brendan moved closer. Charlie didn't even look like the same cat. He certainly didn't sound like it. The death rattle Brendan had heard earlier was gone.

Maybe he had died. Brendan reached out uneasily and touched him. The cat's fur was warm beneath his fingertips and the animal sighed.

He yanked his hand back. There was no such thing as a healer, he told himself, annoyed. Nora had barely glanced at the cat, anyway.

The boy's cell phone was on the coffee table, and Brendan picked it up and checked. Sure enough, Luke had set the alarm to go off every hour on the hour. But the boy couldn't be trusted to cook milk. Besides, he looked exhausted, with dark circles under his eyes, his face pale and taut, even in sleep.

Brendan suddenly knew he couldn't leave them alone with this.

He could feel it. Around the boy. And around her. They'd both been carrying it for too long.

Brendan flicked through the settings on the phone, turned off the alarm and slowly climbed back up the stairs to Nora's room.

CHAPTER SIX

OUTSIDE THE DOOR of that terrifyingly bridal bedroom, Brendan flicked open his own cell phone.

Logically, he knew he could not take this on right now. He had a deadline coming up. Village on the Lake was an amazing opportunity, and he knew the condo project would be the most prestigious of his career to date.

But once before he had chosen work when there was another choice to be made. He had been driven by his need to succeed, driven to outrun the ghosts of his own childhood, driven to be worthy of a wife who came from far different circumstances than he had.

He had needed to be something, or prove something, to have something he didn't have, and he had made a choice that had left him with nothing at all.

That choice had left his heart trapped behind a wall, in a yawning cavern of emptiness.

Could you come to the same fork in the road again? And make a different choice? Not one that would change what had been, nor could alter what had already transpired, but one that changed who you could be?

He shook off the thoughts, finished dialing. His secretary's voice came over the answering machine.

"You've reached Grant Architects. We can't take your call right now, but we'll get back to you as soon as we can."

"Linda, I won't be in today." Added to all the work that Nora and her nephew undoubtedly did themselves, Deedee was in the hospital. She would need company. And word-search books and updates on Charlie. Brendan had no doubt she would be the world's most impatient patient.

"There is a possibility—" horrible as it was, he recognized it was a real possibility "—that I might not be in this week. Send—" he named a junior architect "—to supervise the Village."

And then he closed his cell phone and contemplated the magnitude of what he had just done. He didn't miss work. Not ever.

And then, anticipating it would start ringing right at seven—with fires to be put out, clients, construction site foremen, Linda protesting time off was impossible—he shut it completely off.

He knew there were going to be a lot of questions about his absence. Saying it was uncharacteristic was an understatement.

There were going to be a lot of questions.

And he was not at all sure he had any answers. Because niggling at the back of his mind was the thought that he didn't want to be there when they broke ground on Village on the Lake. He didn't want to be there as his plan took on life. He already knew that his feeling of dissatisfaction would grow in proportion to the buildings taking shape, becoming more and more real.

He slid through the door of the bedroom. There was a chair—white, of course—beside her bed and he took it, a bit guiltily, because his clothes were a little the worse for wear also. He was tempted to put his cell phone back on to use the alarm, just as Luke had intended to do.

And then Brendan was annoyed with himself that he had lasted less than a minute without wanting to rely on his cell phone, so stubbornly didn't turn it back on.

It was part of that relentless busyness that had helped him survive. Just like putting even more ungodly hours in at work than he had before the accident.

Something in him *wanted* to stop. That astounded him. Something in him wanted to rest, and be introspective.

Was part of him ready to heal, to crawl back into the light, shielding his eyes from the brilliance? And maybe, just maybe, was this a place where things like that happened? Where something that was dead in a man could be resurrected?

Maybe it was. Look at that cat down there.

Honestly, Brendan could not believe he was entertaining such thoughts—totally unfounded in any kind of science, totally whimsical, the magical thinking of a little boy.

Mommy, I'm going to buy you a castle someday. I promise.

The memory of those words shook him, and he shivered as though someone had walked across his grave. Hadn't he known from the minute he had driven under that sign that things were about to go sideways?

Annoyed with himself, he sought refuge in the way he always had, but on a point of pride would not turn on his phone to check the weather or the stock report. He prowled restlessly. Starting with the virginal whiteness, the room told him things about her that she might have preferred he didn't know.

There was a picture of her and Luke on her dresser. But none of a man. There was a stack of bills there, too. Why would she have those in her room, unless she wanted to worry over them in private, protect the boy from anxiety?

There was a laundry basket on the floor, full of neatly folded items. She would have been devastated that her underwear was on top. It reminded him of her pajamas, utilitarian, not sexy. There was no jewelry on the dresser, no nod to that feminine longing for the pretty and the frivolous.

If he was a man who felt things, he might have felt a little sad for her and what the room told him about her. Snowed under with responsibility, alone, and sworn off the small pleasure of celebrating her own prettiness.

And then his eyes went to the papers stuck under the alarm clock. They looked like letters, and he shifted over and cut his eyes to them. He wasn't going to read personal mail.

Only they didn't look personal. In fact, the letter on top began "Dear Rover."

Intrigued, remembering Deedee had said something about Nora being *Ask Rover,* he picked up the letter.

"Dear Rover," he read, "I have a new boyfriend. He is everything I ever dreamed of. Handsome. Funny. He has a good job. There is only one problem. I have a thirteen-year-old malamute cross named Sigh. They hate each other. What should I do?" It was signed "Confused."

The handwriting changed. Though still feminine, it was Rover's—make that Nora's—response, Brendan realized. Further intrigued, he saw she had answered and then crossed it all out. He took the chair next to the bed and squinted to read through the scribbles.

Dear Confused,
Though dogs are capable of such emotions as jealousy, quite often they are better judges of character than human beings. What effort has your prince made to win over your dog? Has your new love been sensitive to the fact your dog is aging, and you might have to soon say good-bye? Has he done one single thing to make that moment easier for you? I'm afraid, from a dog's point of view, he sounds like a jerk. I think you would be better off without him. I am not sure I could be trusted not to bite him, possibly in a place that would make it difficult for him to reproduce. Thank you for your question, though really questions where the answers are of such a life-altering nature might be better answered by your best friend, your mother or your priest. Best barks, Rover.

This was crossed out, but it seemed to him with a certain reluctance.

Brendan felt his lips twitching. He flipped to the next page.

Dear Confused,
Thirteen is very old for a malamute. Do you want to make such a weighty decision based on a dog who will not be with you much longer?

This, too, had been crossed out.

He flipped the page, looking for her answer, but instead found a different letter.

Dear Rover,
My dog, an English bulldog named Petunia, won't come in the basement laundry room. She sits outside the door and howls and shakes. Do you think I have a ghost? —Haunted

Again, there were two replies. The first, with a big X through it, said:

Dear Haunted,
English bulldogs are known for many lovely traits, intelligence not being among those. Your laundry room is unlikely to be haunted so much as presenting a myriad of smells and sounds beyond poor Petunia's ability to comprehend them. This situation is unlikely to ever get better, so you could save yourself a great deal of frustration by leaving Petunia upstairs while you go to the basement to do laundry. If you give her a chew bone before you go, there is a good chance she won't notice you are gone until you get back.

The second response was measured, and made no comments about the intelligence of bulldogs. It explained that laundry rooms had strange sounds and smells, that Petunia needed to be introduced to the elements separately and slowly, and that dog treats would help.

Still smiling, Brendan set the papers back on the table.

It penetrated his exhaustion that something was different than when he'd arrived.

For a moment he couldn't figure out what it was.

And then he did: it was absolutely quiet. He got up and went to the window. It wasn't just that night was melting into daybreak. The rain had stopped. And on the horizon was something he hadn't seen for forty days and forty nights.

He blinked like a man emerging from a cave.

Or maybe he hadn't seen it since the night his wife and his unborn child had died.

On the horizon, the sun was coming up.

"Hey, sweetheart, what's your name?"

Nora shook herself groggily. She stared up at the man looking at her, felt his hand on her shoulder.

"Not sweetheart," she said, certain it was a dream and closed her eyes.

That hand on her shoulder, a light in her eyes, "what day were you born?" and then wonderful sleep claiming her again.

"Just for a second, follow my finger with your eyes."

Nora awoke with a start. Sunshine splashed across her bed. Sunshine! The warmth of it was a delight.

All night she had had strange dreams that Brendan Grant was in her room, but now she glanced at the chair where she was sure he had sat, and could clearly see it had been but a dream. The chair was empty.

Sunshine! She looked at the clock. It was noon!

"Oh goodness! The animals!" She sat up too quickly and it made her feel dizzy. She was aware her head hurt, and other parts of her felt bruised.

How was it possible to feel so good, filled with wonderful dreams, and so bad at the same time? Physically aching, sick that she had slept through looking after her animals.

She lay back down, just for a moment.

"Hey."

Brendan Grant was standing in her doorway. Despite the fact he was in the same shirt as last night, and it had been wet, and dried wrinkled, and his hair was rumpled and his face becoming shadowed with whiskers, he looked amazing. Handsome, oozing confidence, one of those superannoying guys who took charge.

Superannoying unless you happened to be in need of someone to take charge!

"Don't sit up. Doctor's orders. You have to rest. All day."

She couldn't let on for a single second that, in her weakened state, she found that take-charge attitude ever so slightly attractive.

"I can't rest all day! I have to look after the animals."

"I've got it covered."

She scowled at him so he would never guess how much those words meant to her.

"You sat with me all night," she said. She knew she should be appreciative. It came out sounding like an accusation.

"I did."

"That's an unexpected kindness to the stranger you think swindled your grandmother."

"I was hoping you'd talk in your sleep."

"Did I?" she asked, aghast.

"What are you afraid of? A confession? Don't you remember? I asked you questions every time I woke you up."

"Yeah, like what my name was. And my birthday."

He slapped himself on the forehead. "Shoot. I didn't take advantage."

For some reason she blushed, as if he meant taking advantage in a different way. He lifted an eyebrow.

"I didn't take advantage like that, either," he said softly.

"I wasn't suggesting you had," she said primly. Feeling terribly vulnerable, she pulled her quilt up around her chin. "If you'll excuse me, I need to get dressed. I need to look after my animals."

"They're all looked after."

"But how?"

"Luke helped."

"Oh," she said uneasily. She didn't really like the thought of Brendan being alone with Luke, interrogating him.

"Don't worry, he didn't tell me a thing."

She didn't like that she was transparent, either!

"Even though I shamelessly tried to pry information out of him."

"About?" she asked, attempting a careless tone.

"I started small, building up to the big question. I asked where you were from, and he said from a nice place, not a dump like this. I asked how long you had been here, and he said too long, and I asked how old he was and he said nineteen."

"We're from Victoria, we've been here six months and he just turned fifteen."

"Then I asked him who took the money from Deedee."

She held her breath.

"He said lots of people open the mail. The place is

practically overrun with volunteers. He said he thought some of those old ladies were pretty shifty looking." Brendan was watching her way too closely. "Are they?"

She felt backed into a corner. Of course her volunteers were not shifty looking! But she wasn't calling Luke a liar, either. She fidgeted with the quilt and didn't answer.

"I thought I'd better find out for myself who looked shifty. So I had Luke call some of them to come help with morning chores. Funny, I can't really see any of the ones who showed up stealing from my grandmother, but I interrogated them, anyway."

"You did not," she said skeptically.

"I did. They all admitted to opening mail. None of them looked guilty, though. None of them remembered a letter from my grandmother. Of course, I'm not sure any of them would have remembered what they had for breakfast this morning. Don't you have a system for dealing with mail? It doesn't seem very efficient that anyone who feels like it, or wanders by the mailbox, opens the letters."

"Systems are not my strong suit."

"Neither is volunteer selection. If the ones who showed up today are any indication, it's kind of like having my grandmother for a volunteer. The old biddy brigade."

Now he sounded like Luke!

"They are invaluable to me!" The truth was Nora needed some young, strong people to volunteer, but they just weren't who showed up when she put an ad in the paper. She hated it that the weaknesses in her organization were so blatantly apparent to him after an hour or two.

"But you can't let any of your current volunteers near a large animal. They can't do any heavy work. One's afraid of dogs and one is allergic to cats. They all hate the parrot. Who bites."

"That's Lafayette. Did he bite you?"

"Of course he bit me. Luke says he bites everyone. Before saying things that would make a sailor blush. In three languages."

"Did you put antiseptic on it?"

"Who's looking after who?"

He was gazing at her keenly. She had sounded way too much like she cared. He was a tyrant, obviously. He'd waltzed in here and completely taken over. She couldn't just let him!

"I don't want to get sued. After infection sets in and your finger falls off. Then you sue me, and at your recommendation, I've lose the funding from the Hansen Community Betterment Committee."

"I haven't decided about a recommendation to the HCBC. Yet."

"And please don't alienate all my volunteers."

"I couldn't alienate your volunteers if I tried, and believe me, I did. But oh, no, they came around the barn after me, promising me cookies, brownies and roast beef dinner. And talking about what a nice girl you are. And available. 'What a shame. No boyfriend. And so pretty, too.'"

"I don't have a boyfriend because I don't want one," Nora told him, and felt a crimson blush go up her cheeks.

"Some jerk broke your heart," Brendan said, and his tone was light, but his eyes were not. They darkened with a menace that made her gasp.

He was seeing way too much, and it had to stop!

"Get out of my room. I need to shower and get dressed."

He sighed theatrically. "It's as hard to pry information out of you as it is out of your nephew. Do you need help?"

Her mouth fell open. She gasped like a fish on a bank.

He laughed, backed into the hall, his hands in cowboy surrender, and shut the door. But he had to get in the last word.

"If you're dizzy or feel like you're going to vomit, call me. Even if you're naked."

CHAPTER SEVEN

NORA WAS GLAD Brendan Grant was on the other side of that door and couldn't see her face. *Even if she was naked?*

He was trying to shock her, and she was not going to give him the satisfaction of responding.

"Especially if you're naked," he called through the door.

So much for not giving him satisfaction. Nora picked up her shoe from where he had pulled it off her foot last night. She hurled it at the door and heard his hoot of pleasure that he had gotten to her.

She looked around her bedroom. Her world felt like a big mess, with chaos everywhere! Even her beautiful Egyptian cotton sheets, one of the things she had treated herself to before she became guardian to a very expensive fifteen-year-old, were dirty. Her sense of messiness increased when she went into the en suite bathroom and saw herself in the mirror.

Her hair, face and clothes were smudged with mud. She looked like a terrible cross between a cast member of *Oliver* and, with the lump rising over her eye, Quasimodo. Luckily, she told herself, she was not in the market for a man, and especially not a man like the one who had totally invaded her world.

Still, it did not feel lucky at all that *that* man was intent on invading her world when she looked like this! Somehow around a guy like that, a woman—any woman, even one newly sworn to fierce independence—wanted to look her best.

She desperately needed these moments to collect herself. The water of the shower was an absolute balm. She told herself it wasn't weakness that made her apply the subtlest hint of makeup. It was an effort to regain some confidence. And hide her bruises. And erase first impressions!

After showering and applying makeup, with far more care than she would have wanted to admit, Nora chose a flattering shirt, short-sleeved and summery as a nod to the sun finally making an appearance, and designer jeans, remnants of her old life when she'd bought designer things for herself and never worried about money.

She convinced herself the makeover worked. She convinced herself she felt like a new woman.

She felt ready to battle for her independence! Ready to fight any inclination to lean on another!

Brendan was alone in her kitchen. She paused in the darkness of the hallway before he knew she was there.

Despite her vow to be unaffected by him, it was hard not to take advantage of that moment to study him.

There was no doubt about it. Brendan Grant was a devastatingly attractive man with that dark hair and matching eyes, the slashing brows and straight nose and strong chin. He radiated a subtle masculine strength, a confidence in himself that was not in any way changed by the fact he was in a wrinkled shirt or his hair was roughed or the planed hollows of his cheeks were darkening with whiskers.

The annoying fact was her kitchen was improved by a man standing at the counter, supremely comfortable in his own skin, eating cookies.

"Sorry," he said, when he saw her. "I helped myself."

"No, that's good. I should have told you to make yourself at home."

But she was stunned by the longing that statement awakened in her. A man like this making himself at home? The image somehow deepened her definition of home, made it richer and more complex, and filled her with yearning.

She recouped quickly. "Speaking of which, you need to go home. You must be exhausted. And want a shower. And a change of clothes. And don't you need to check on your grandmother?"

"But who is going to make sure you don't do anything you're not supposed to do?"

"Luke will. Where is Luke?"

Brendan nodded toward the living room, and she went and peeked. Luke was sitting on the sofa, feet on the coffee table, head nodding against his chest. Charlie was sprawled out across his belly, kneading, the way contented cats do. The kitten was perched on his shoulder, batting at a strand of his hair, and Luke swatted it as if a fly was bothering him in his sleep.

"If only such cuteness could last," she said ruefully.

Brendan came and stood beside her. She could feel his presence, even though he didn't touch her, energy tingling off him.

"Ditto for Charlie," he said. "It's not as if he's a nice

cat. He's waited under Deedee's sofa and attacked my ankles. You think that doesn't make you nervous?"

Brendan chuckled. And so did Nora. It was a small thing. A shared moment of amusement. It made her need to get rid of him even more urgent.

As if he sensed the danger of the moment as acutely as she had, he frowned. "Charlie seems way better than he was last night. Are you, er, doing something?"

"No. There's nothing to do, I'm afraid. How old is he?"

"Seventeen, I think."

"That's pretty old for a cat," she said carefully.

"I think so, too. Unfortunately, Deedee has a friend whose cat made it to twenty-three."

"I wouldn't tell her Charlie is feeling better," Nora suggested.

She knew it was an opportunity for him to make a crack about her missing an opportunity to get some more money out of Deedee, but he didn't take it.

"Okay, I won't tell her. Though it is obvious, even to me, a tried-and-true cynic, that he is feeling better." He added, "I'm going. Do not do a single thing today. Do you hear me?"

"Are you always so masterful?" she said, raising an eyebrow, unimpressed.

"Why?" he asked softly. "Do you like masterful?"

"No!" She'd better be careful. She didn't have a shoe handy to throw. Instead, she quickly changed tack. "I'll catch up on some of my inside things."

She was giving in just a little, to make him go.

"You're not even supposed to read. Except your symptom sheet, which tells you not to read. And don't use the computer. No answering *Ask Rover*."

She stiffened. "What do you know about *Ask Rover?*"

"There were some letters beside your bed."

"You read my mail!"

"It was lying out. I had to think of a way to stay awake. Sorry." He didn't sound contrite.

She *hated* that he knew.

And then she didn't.

Because he said, "I liked the first response better. The dog knew the guy was a jerk." And Brendan smiled at her, as if he actually *liked* it that she was *Ask Rover*. "Is that the one you'll use? About biting him where it counts?"

Nora could feel her face getting very red. That had not been meant for anyone to see.

"No," she said, "it won't be."

"That's a shame."

And it sounded as if he meant it!

"I'll be back," he said.

"No!"

That sounded way too vehement.

"You've done enough," she amended hastily. "I'm very appreciative. Really. But I can take it from here."

"Uh-huh," he said, without an ounce of conviction. He gave her one long look, and then patted her shoulder and was gone.

And suddenly she was alone, in a house that was changed in some subtle and irrevocable way because he had spent the night in her bedroom and eaten cookies at her kitchen counter.

And just as she had a secret side that answered letters to *Ask Rover* exactly the way she wanted to, she had a secret side that listened to his car start up and said,

Usually when a man spends the night something a little more exciting happens! Maybe next time.

"There isn't going to be a next time," she informed her secret side.

But, of course, there was. Because he had said he was coming back, and he did. One of the volunteers must have told him when they did evening chores and feeding, because he was there promptly at seven. Nora peered out the living room window at him getting out of his car.

He was dressed more appropriately, in a plaid jacket, and jeans tucked into rubber boots. Really, the ready-to-grub-out-pens outfit should have made Brendan less attractive. And didn't. At all.

Nora breathed a sigh of relief when he made no move toward the house. Luke, bless his heart, was already at the barns. She was glad to be rid of him, too. He had absolutely hovered all day, Charlie in his arms and Ranger on his heels.

She knew, somehow, she should have insisted he take the cats with him when he went to do chores, and leave them in the barn, but she hadn't.

Charlie didn't like her, and had retreated under the sofa as soon as Luke left, then slunk off up the stairs, probably to Luke's room. It didn't matter. She didn't have to lay her hands on him to know his life force was leeching out of him. The antics of the kitten entertained her, but didn't occupy her enough for her to outrun her own thoughts.

Which let her know her relief that Brendan had headed for the barns instead of the house was pretended relief. Part of her wanted him to come up here. Which probably explained why she was still in the designer jeans and top, and not her pj's despite a full day of doing nothing.

Unless you counted catching up on movies. She scowled at the TV. Since he'd arrived—since she knew he was out there—she had no idea what was going on in the movie.

Then she heard them coming. She felt like a high school girl waiting for her prom date. She checked her buttons. Ran a hand through her hair. Tried to pull her bangs over the bump on her forehead. She tried to decide how to sit so that it looked as if she was completely surprised and a little bored by the fact Brendan was coming to her house.

Luke let him in, so he didn't knock.

And then he was standing there, filling her space, gazing at her, and her silly heart was beating way too hard.

"How are you feeling?" he asked.

If she told him the truth about her racing pulse, she'd probably be whisked off to the hospital, just as Deedee had been. "Bored."

He looked past her to the TV. "What movie?"

Why hadn't she thought of that when she was preparing to see him again?

She snapped it off. "Something silly. I just turned it on to keep from going crazy."

"Uh-huh."

"It's that pirate one," Luke said, coming back with Charlie. "It's for babies, but she's seen it three times. Because of Johnny Jose." He rolled his eyes disparagingly.

Brendan's lips were twitching as if her crush on

Johnny Jose was amusing. "So you're feeling all right? No signs of dizziness? Not feeling sick?"

"I'm fine." If he said uh-huh she was going to scream. Instead he stuck his hands in his pockets and rocked back on his heels and studied her. She tilted her chin defiantly.

"This is cool, Auntie Nora. Brendan gave the old lady a tablet so she can see some video of Charlie while she's in the hospital."

How, exactly, could you steel yourself against something like that?

Or what followed. Luke put down Charlie, got out a piece of string and tied a lump of hay to it. "This is a mouse," he narrated. Then he pulled it across the floor.

The black-and-white kitten exploded across the room after the hay. Luke shouted with laughter. It was the most animated she had seen her nephew in a long, long time. And then he went and dangled the string in front of the couch, where Charlie had retreated.

A ginger paw came out and swatted. Then swatted again. Then both paws shot out, and Charlie grabbed the "mouse" with such strength he pulled it from Luke's hand, yanking it under the couch with him.

Brendan lowered the phone that he had been recording the scene with, and stared at the place where Charlie had disappeared. "That is like the old Charlie," he said uneasily, "the one who likes to attack ankles."

"Did you get it?" Luke asked, then sighed. "Not that Mrs. Ashton will be able to figure out how to open it. Auntie Nora wouldn't be able to."

Why don't you just tell him all my secrets? Crush on Johnny Jose. Computer illiterate. Ask Rover. He's going to know me better than I know myself if this keeps up.

Brendan still looked faintly dazed. "I'll go see Deedee and make sure she got it. I can show her on my phone if she didn't figure it out. I'll be back first thing tomorrow for chores."

Nora opened her mouth to protest. First, she didn't think it was a good idea for him to show that footage to Deedee. Second, she didn't think he should come back here.

But she saw Luke's quick look of pleasure before he masked it by snaring the mouse from under the couch and getting Ranger going again.

He liked Brendan. He wanted to believe the cat was getting better. Couldn't she just let life ride, for once?

"Good job with the horses," Brendan said to Luke. "Remember not to let your aunt anywhere near them. And be sure and check her one more night. Can you do that?"

"You had me at the deadly part," Luke said, glancing up from the kitten, and he and Brendan exchanged a grin.

Three days later, Brendan was still showing up to do chores. Nora had started to do a pretty good job of hiding out, which was necessary because chores always finished with Brendan and Luke coming to the house to produce a new video of Charlie. Not only was the aging cat alive and well, but he seemed to be improving.

Deedee was home from the hospital, but confined to bed. She was so impressed with the changes in Charlie she hoped to leave him at Nora's Ark a bit longer.

But enough was enough! Nora was completely recovered. Really, there had been nothing to recover from.

A whole lot of fuss about nothing.

And she'd had enough of hiding out in her own

home. It was time to tell Brendan Grant, nicely, that he had to exit her life. Goodbye. Nice meeting you. Get lost. Could he take Deedee's cat home to her at the same time?

Charlie was in the house. Luke was getting way too attached to him—he seemed to like him even more than the kitten—and Nora seemed to be the only one determined to remember that there was going to be no happy ending for the old cat.

It was way too obvious to her that there were no happy endings, period, and it was a crazy thing to hope for.

She wasn't hiding out today. She was waiting in the living room, her plan firmly in place. She was getting rid of them—the cat and Brendan Grant. And at the same time, she was getting rid of this part of her that wanted so desperately to attach itself to the possibility of happy endings.

She rehearsed from the moment she heard his car. *Thanks so much. Quite capable. Very independent. Lots of volunteers. No room for the cat. Vamoose, both of you.*

And then the door opened, and Luke and Brendan didn't come into her space so much as they spilled into it, like sunshine piercing the dark. Brendan's head was cocked to Luke. She heard his low laugh at something her nephew said.

Her plan faltered.

Brendan Grant was here to help. She wasn't sure if he had intended to help her nephew, but it was certainly a possibility. Look how good he was with his grandmother. Still, whether it had been his intention or not, she saw subtle changes in Luke with this positive daily male influence.

When, she wondered, had she become this woman? So interested in protecting herself that she thought she didn't have to show one speck of gratitude to someone who was helping her. And helping that tiny two-person unit that was her family.

She was Luke's main role model. She had a responsibility. Was that what she wanted to teach him about life? Protect yourself at all costs?

So what if she found Brendan attractive? Surely she could control herself! It would be akin to meeting Johnny. You wouldn't be helpless. You wouldn't throw yourself at him. You wouldn't embarrass yourself or him.

You would act as though your heart was not beating a mile a minute. As though you were a mature woman capable of great grace and confidence.

You would step up to him and look him in the eye. And smile.

"Hi, Brendan," she heard herself say, calm and mature, a woman she could be proud of. "Thanks so much for all your help around here. I really appreciate it."

That would have been good enough. More than good enough.

So why did she have to add, "I made lasagna tonight. There's extra. Do you want some?"

"Aunt Nora makes the best lasagna. Lots of cheese," Luke said, and his hope that Brendan would stay was somehow heartbreaking.

Too late, Nora wondered what she was letting them in for.

Particularly when Brendan said, "It would take a better man than me to turn down homemade lasagna. Especially the kind with lots of cheese."

CHAPTER EIGHT

WHAT THE HELL was he doing? Brendan asked himself as he sat at Nora's table for the second night in a row. Lasagna last night. Meat loaf tonight.

"You wanna stay and play Scrabble?" Luke asked, oh so casually, as if he didn't care what Brendan's answer was.

And out of the corner of his eye he watched Nora, as he always watched Nora, and saw her tensing, caught just as he was between wanting him to go and wanting him to stay.

"Scrabble?" he said. "I'm not staying to play Scrabble."

Luke tried to hide how crestfallen he was. Nora got a pinched look about her mouth and eyes.

It should have confirmed he could not stay here to play Scrabble. Instead he heard himself saying, "Don't you know how to play poker?"

And when they both shook their heads, he said, "I guess it's about time you learned."

An hour later Luke was rolling on the floor laughing. Brendan's own stomach hurt from laughing so hard. The rock had been rolled away and light was penetrating into every corner of that cave.

He needed to stop. He needed to ponder hard questions. He needed to slow down, roll the rock back in place, regroup, retreat, rethink.

Why was he doing this? The truth? Something in him was watching that damned cat getting better and better. Something in him was surrendering, resisting his efforts to be logical, telling him that if that cat could be healed, maybe he could, too.

Healed from what? he asked himself. Until he had passed under that Nora's Ark sign, hadn't he been blissfully unaware of his afflictions?

No, that wasn't true. There hadn't been one blissful thing about his life. It had been cold and dark and dank and gray. Certainly there had been no moments of laughter like this.

He had managed to avoid his demons—guilt, dark despair, crippling loneliness—by filling the confines of the space he had chosen with ceaseless work, by never stopping.

He had thought if he stopped he would find his afflictions had run along with him, silent, waiting.

He thought if he ever stopped, those tears that had never been cried would begin to flow, and would flow and flow and flow until he was drowning in them and in his own weakness.

His hardened heart behind its wall, a life that yawned with emotional emptiness, that had protected him.

And now Nora's laughter was lapping against it, like water against a refuge built of mud, lapping away, steadily eroding the defenses.

How could you defend against moments like these?

"You are," he told her, "without a doubt the worst

card player I have ever seen. Give that deck to Luke before you mark it so badly I'll own your house."

"What do you mean, mark it?"

Luke took the cards from her. "See this bend you made here? Now everyone knows that's the ace of spades."

"Oh," she said, the only one who didn't know.

And she simply didn't have the face for poker! She frowned at bad hands. She chewed her lip if they were really bad. Her eyes did a glow-in-the-dark thing if it was a good hand.

"Your aunt is a wash-out at this game. You have some promise, though. You have to have some ability to lie to be a good poker player."

Luke flinched as if he'd been struck. He ducked his head. He dealt them each a hand and glared at his. And then he set them down, face up. He cleared his throat and looked Brendan right in the eye.

"I did it," he blurted out. "I opened the mail. I sent Deedee the letter. I took the money."

Honestly, Brendan did not want to like this kid.

But coupled with the defense of his aunt with the coat rack, and how hard he worked out there in the barn every day, how good he was with that cat and all the animals, the confession meant there was some hope for the boy.

If Nora didn't manage to kill him with kindness first.

Because his aunt put down her cards—a royal flush, not that she would recognize it—and glared at Luke, ready to fight for him, ready to believe in him. "Luke! No, you didn't!"

"Let him do the right thing," Brendan said quietly.

The words made Nora want to weep. It confirmed

what she already guiltily believed. She was making the wrong choices for Luke over and over again.

Nora hated that Brendan was right. And she hated that he had come into her house and her life and had taken control as naturally as he breathed.

But most of all, she hated the sense of relief she felt that she didn't have to figure out how to fix it. She hated what it said about her that she had been prepared to lie to protect her nephew. And she hated, too, that she felt the same way she had felt in Brendan's arms. Not so alone. Carried.

"Why don't you tell us what happened?" Brendan suggested.

Nora appreciated his tone. Mild but stern. Not about to take any nonsense.

Luke glanced at her, and she nodded, not missing the look of relief on his face. He'd been carrying the guilt for too long.

"I was opening the mail for Nora's Ark and found Deedee's letter. She didn't say Charlie was dying. She just said he wasn't feeling well. I decided to play along. So I wrote her and said sure I'd send some energy. But that she should make, er, a donation."

"You told her to send money," Brendan said flatly, not willing to allow Luke to sugarcoat it.

"Okay. I did."

"But why? You have money," Nora asked plaintively.

"I didn't have enough."

She felt herself pale. Enough for what? Why did a fifteen-year-old boy need fifty dollars that he couldn't ask her for?

Cigarettes? Alcohol? Drugs?

Karen, I have failed. Colossally. Why did you leave me with this?

Given the road she was going down, at first she thought Luke's answer was a relief.

"The police were hassling me about the bike. The guy I borrowed it from, Gerald Jack-in-the-Box—"

"Jackinox," she corrected automatically, thinking, *It's about the bike. Not drugs.*

"Whatever. He said he'd make it go away if I gave him fifty bucks."

Her sense of relief evaporated. "That's blackmail! Tell me you didn't ask Mrs. Ashton for fifty dollars to give to him! Oh, Luke, why didn't you come to me?"

He at least had the grace to look a little shamefaced. "I asked her for fifty bucks. Cash. In the mail. When the money actually came, I was shocked. And I felt guilty. So I sat down and thought I'd send her stupid cat—I didn't know him then—some energy."

"What do you mean by that?" Brendan asked, his voice stern.

"Well, just the way my aunt does it."

"And what way is that? That your aunt does it?"

"That's not important!" Nora said. Her way with animals had always made her a bit of a novelty—and not always in a good way—to those who knew about it. Brendan Grant already knew way too much about her. He'd guessed she'd been betrayed. He knew she had a secret crush on Johnny Jose. He'd read *Ask Rover* and knew she wrote it. Enough was enough!

But annoyingly, Brendan trumped her with Luke. By a country mile.

"She puts her hands on the animal and then closes her eyes and goes all quiet. So that's what I did. Only

I had to pretend the cat was there. I sort of imagined
light going around him. It was dumb, because I didn't
have a clue what the cat looked like. I didn't picture
him being so ugly. I mean, not that he's ugly once you
get to know him."

"That's the same with all things, and people, too,
Luke," Nora said, not wanting to miss an opportunity
to help him see things in a way that would make him
a better person.

Luke and Brendan both rolled their eyes.

"Right," Luke muttered. "Anyway, it freaked me out
because I got all warm, like the sun came out, and it was
pouring rain that day. It freaked me out even more when
Mrs. Ashton wrote that it worked, so I just threw out
her letter. And erased her messages. Geez, she called
about a dozen times a day. I was a wreck trying to get
to the answering machine before my aunt."

Nora cast Brendan a glance. He didn't look at all
sympathetic to Luke feeling like a wreck trying to keep
his treachery hidden.

"Why," Brendan asked carefully, "did it freak you
out when you thought it worked? You could have been
into some real cash."

"I didn't like the way it felt."

Nora's sweet sensation of relief was tempered somewhat when Luke shrugged and sent her a look. "Who
wants to be like her?"

Even though she was used to his barbs, it hurt. And
even though it was the story of her life. She was careful not to let how badly it hurt show.

Over the years, some people saw what she did as a
gift, but most saw it as just plain weird. She was cautious about showing people that side of herself. Even

in the column, she didn't reveal she wrote it, didn't always say exactly what she wanted to say, tempering it with what people wanted to hear.

Nora glanced at Brendan. He was watching her. She had the uneasy feeling he saw everything, even the things she least wanted to reveal.

Again she had that aggravating feeling. Instead of feeling exposed, she felt in some way not alone.

She tore her eyes away from him, forced herself to focus on her nephew. "Luke, do you understand how terrible this is? You gave false hope to a poor little old lady—"

"No one would resent being called old more than Deedee," Brendan said mildly, "and we won't even go into the poor part."

"The point is she was afraid to lose her cat, and Luke played on her fear and took her money."

"I needed the fifty bucks!"

"You allowed that boy to blackmail you! I have to call his parents."

"That's why I didn't tell you! Dammit, Auntie, I didn't really have permission to borrow his bike. Do you have to be so gullible?"

Brendan's tone remained mild enough, but there was steel running through it. "You don't use language like that in front of women. And your aunt is not the guilty party here. You are. What really happened with the bike?"

Nora was aware she should have said that, not him. She felt it again, though. The tempting weakness of liking the fact she was not handling this alone.

"I took it," Luke said, jutting out his chin defiantly. "I stole Gerald's bike because he was mean to me. He made fun of my hair in front of the whole class. You think it's not hard enough being new? And everybody knowing your aunt does voodoo?"

"Voodoo," Brendan said, with just a trace of approval.

"What do you mean, everybody knows I do voodoo?" Nora asked, horrified. "I don't! I run a shelter for abused and abandoned animals. That's all!"

"No, it isn't," Luke said wearily.

And suddenly she wondered if it had been about Luke's hair at all. Or if it had been about her.

"Anyway," Luke continued, "Gerald said he'd back my story that I borrowed the bike if I gave him fifty dollars."

"You've made everything worse," Nora said, but not too strongly. It was bad enough Luke was being teased about his hair. He was being teased about her, too! She was an adult and she could barely handle the mockery. That was why she wrote her column in secret.

"I think the question now is how are you going to fix all this?" Brendan asked.

"Naturally, we'll give your grandmother back her money," Nora said, hearing the resignation in her voice.

"No. *You* won't," Brendan said.

"Excuse me?"

"Luke did it. He needs to figure out how to make amends to her."

"What's amends?" Luke asked suspiciously.

"Just what it sounds like. You broke something, you mend it."

He pondered that. "I don't know how."

"I'll give you a chance to figure it out."

Luke seemed to be back to his old self, arms folded

over his narrow chest, bristling with barely contained hostility.

Take charge, Nora ordered herself, so she added, "Figure it out. With no computer. And no cell phone."

"That sucks," the boy said, and got up from the table and marched away.

"You're bossy," Nora said to Brendan, feeling somehow she had to hide the fact that she was so grateful someone was helping her through this.

"You've already said that."

"Sorry to bore you by repeating myself." She needed time to gather herself. Needed to show leadership, and wasn't. She was letting Brendan take charge.

Only because it had been a strange week. She'd been injured. She'd let down her guard around Brendan. Invited him into her life.

Still, it was a new blow that Luke was being teased at school because of her.

"Tell me what you've heard about me," she said to Brendan.

"Deedee heard you were a healer. She was making biblical references, about the laying on of hands. She's expecting a miracle."

Nora groaned softly. "I'm sorry. Do you think that's what Luke's classmates are hearing about me, too?"

"I assume some version of that. You bring a dead dog to life, and you're the talk of the town."

"I didn't bring a dead dog to life!"

"You're not used to small towns, are you?"

"No."

"It's like that game you played in junior high school. The teacher whispers, 'The green tree on Main Street is dying,' to the first kid in the line, and they whisper it to the next. But twenty kids later it has become 'Mrs. Green killed her husband on Main Street with a tree branch.'"

"We never played a game like that in school."

"A shame. The power of distortion would not be such a surprise to you. What really happened with the dog?"

"He'd been hit by a car. He was knocked out. Not dead."

"Technicalities. So, you have no gift with animals?"

"I didn't say that. I've always liked animals, sometimes a whole lot more than people. There is an energy element to animals that is very strong, and I seem to be able to connect with that. But I'm not a vet, and I don't try to take the place of one."

"Ah."

She had said enough. But despite her vow to herself to keep the barriers up between her and Brendan, it felt strangely and nicely intimate to be sharing her kitchen with him, telling him things she didn't always feel free to say.

"What I have no gift with, I'm afraid, is adolescent boys," she added, since she seemed bent on confessing private things about herself.

"I see cookies in a jar and good food on the table every night. There are drawings on the fridge and homework being done. Where are his folks?"

She could not quite keep the shaking from her voice. "My sister died."

"And his dad?"

"He went before Karen. Luke's never said anything to you? You guys have been doing chores together for days."

"Yeah, well, you know guys."

But she didn't. She didn't know guys at all. That was probably part of the problem with Luke.

Brendan sighed. "We don't talk about *deep* things. Discussion runs to who is the best hockey player in the world. Last night's baseball scores. Who can clean a cat cage the fastest and with the least gagging."

Nora really didn't want to confide one more thing to this man. But she heard herself saying, "I'm not sure that Karen would have trusted me by myself with this. She saw my fiancé, Vance, as the stable one, a vet with a well-established practice. I'm afraid I've always been seen as the family black sheep."

"It seems to me your sister would think you were doing well at making a home for your nephew."

"So, now you know! I'm an orphan," Luke exclaimed from the doorway. "Doesn't that just suck? Who even knew there was such a thing anymore?"

Nora hadn't seen him reappear, but there he was, bristling defensively.

"And you think that isn't bad enough?" Luke continued, jerking his head toward her. "She was going to get married. And then Vance wouldn't marry her. Because of me."

CHAPTER NINE

NORA'S MOUTH FELL open. Her eyes clouded with tears. She'd had no idea Luke knew about that awful conversation between her and Vance.

"Just because I glued his stupid golf clubs to his golf bag."

"Why'd you do that?" Brendan asked mildly.

"He didn't want Auntie Nora to get me a skateboard, because I'd been suspended from school. So she didn't. So I glued his golf clubs to his bag. Super Duper Gobby Glue works just the way it says in the commercial."

"I'll remember that," Brendan promised.

"'It's him or it's me,'" Luke quoted. His mimicry of Vance might have been hilariously accurate, if it wasn't for the context. "She picked me. Dumb, huh?"

And then Brendan said, his voice steady as a rock, "I don't think it's so dumb."

Despite the fact Nora could have done without her whole life story being exposed, she could have kissed Brendan, she felt so grateful.

Unfortunately, that made her look at his lips.

The thought of kissing Brendan Grant made her dizzier than the bump on her head.

"You don't think it was dumb that she picked me?"

Luke said, and the hopeful look in his eyes tugged at her heartstrings. He quickly covered it. "Sure. I just took money from your grandmother."

"You know everybody makes mistakes. Your aunt Nora when she got engaged to a jerk."

Her heart filled with the most unreasonable gratitude that someone saw Vance's defection as a statement about him, not about her.

"He was a jerk," Luke said. "A sanctimonious, know-it-all, stuck-up jerk."

Nora's mouth fell open. First of all, she'd had no idea Luke's dislike of Vance had run so deep. Second, she had no idea that he could use a word like *sanctimonious* correctly.

"She should have asked Rover," Brendan dead-panned, and then he and Luke cracked up. Brendan must have caught her disapproving expression, because he sobered.

"So, everybody makes mistakes," he said. "When you took that money from Deedee, it was a mistake. What matters is whether you choose to grow from them or not."

"What kind of mistakes have you ever made?" Luke challenged, not laughing anymore. Nora could tell he wanted to believe there was hope that a mistake could turn out okay, and was afraid to believe at the very same time.

Which she understood perfectly, of course.

Brendan hesitated. He tossed his cards down on the table. For a moment, it looked as if he wasn't going to say anything at all.

Then, his voice so soft she felt herself straining to

hear it, he said, "My wife died because of a terrible mistake I made. She was carrying our baby."

Nora laid her hand on his, almost unbearably grateful that Brendan had seen how great Luke's need was. And possibly hers. That he had overcome so tremendous an inner obstacle and given something of himself to both of them confirmed that her instincts had been right, after all.

There was a common place between them.

But it seemed to her that common place was the most frightening thing of all. It asked her to put aside her past injuries and her petty fears. It asked her to think less about protecting herself and more about reaching out to another human being.

Reaching out to animals was easy. Human beings were far more complicated.

She wasn't ready. She ordered herself to withdraw her hand.

And yet her hand, as if separate from her mind and linked to her soul, stayed right where it was.

Brendan could not believe he had said that to Nora and Luke. What if these were the words that broke open that dam of emotion within him?

But no, the dam was safe. He had not cried then, and he would not cry now. Still, there was nothing he hated more than sympathy. He waited for her to say something that would make him regret confiding in them even more than he already did.

But Nora said nothing at all. Instead, with a tenderness so exquisite if felt as if the dam of emotion was newly threatened, she laid her hand on top of his.

For a moment he felt only the connection, her small

hand covering part of his larger one, the softness of her palm against his toughened skin.

But then he was stunned by the warmth that began to pour from her hand, some energy vibrating up his wrist into his arm. It felt as if his whole body was beginning to tingle.

And suddenly, the world's greatest cynic believed what he had only suspected until now.

She could heal things.

The light shining in her eyes almost made him believe she could heal the most impossible thing of all: a heart smashed to pieces.

For a stunned second, he felt his throat close. But then he fought it.

Because who would want that fixed? For what reason? So that it could be smashed again? So that a man could face his impotency over the caprice of life all over again?

He jerked his hand out of hers, and she stiffened, guessing it, correctly, as rejection. Then she had the good sense to look relieved. She actually glared at her hand for a minute, as if it had mutinied and acted on its own accord.

She turned rapidly from him, ran a hand over her eyes, winced when she touched the bump on her head.

"I should get some footage of Charlie for Deedee and then go," he said.

Luke, looking pensive and solemn, went and got the cat.

Nora was completely composed when she turned back to Brendan.

"Thank you for telling us. I know it was hard for you.

And yet he needed to hear it. He's known you only a short time, but he looks up to you."

Brendan shrugged, withdrawing, uncomfortable.

Luke came back with Charlie and set him on the counter.

The cat gave a yowl of indignation and made for the edge, as if he fully planned to leap to the floor.

Brendan stared. This was a cat that had barely been able to lift his head a few days ago. "What are you feeding him?"

Luke made a quick grab and caught Charlie by the back of the neck. The cat hunkered down, resigned but unhappy.

"There's no cure for old age," Nora told Brendan gently. "There's nothing that stops life from unfolding in its natural order."

As Luke lifted his other hand so that both of them rested on the cat, Brendan was aware again of that vibration, of an energy he didn't understand. It was almost as if the light in the room changed.

The cat stopped struggling. It was as if Charlie had been tranquilized. He closed his eyes and a deep purr came from him.

Luke jerked his hands away. He took the cat off the counter, set him on the floor, watched him scoot off. Uncaring that there would be no pictures tonight, he shoved both hands in his pockets. His face was white and his voice was brimming with anger.

"Life's natural order?" he spat out. "My mom was thirty-four. What's natural about that? Oh, and Aunt Nora is a healer, all right. Ask anyone. My mom always talked about my auntie Kookie, how her room was filled with mice and birds and cats and dogs, and she could heal them all."

"Luke, that's an exaggeration. I liked animals. I couldn't—"

But he cut her off. "I was here when they brought that dog in. It was dead."

"It wasn't," Nora said. "Obviously it wasn't."

"And then she puts her hands on it, and *poof,* he's alive and wagging his tail. And in three days he's running around the yard, bringing me sticks to throw.

"But when it really counts? When it's cancer? Forget it! Who would want a gift like that, anyway? That's why I don't want to be like her! You can't change anything that matters."

And then he spun on his heel and followed the cat, and Nora and Brendan stood in frozen silence as he thumped up the stairs.

"How did he know Charlie has cancer?" Brendan asked.

"He doesn't," Nora said too quickly, her troubled eyes on the empty doorway her nephew had gone through. "His mom—my sister—died of cancer. I'm sorry, I don't think there's anything more I can do for Charlie. You should take him home to Deedee. She can spend his last days with him."

Brendan could feel weariness like a dull ache in his bones.

Not just because it was late, either.

It was the weariness of it all.

A boy who had lost everything and who already knew you could not change anything that really mattered. A woman who was trying desperately to help him through it, even though she had lost, too.

Brendan realized he had actually been thinking that cat was getting better. Had been bringing Deedee pictures, instead of preparing her to face yet another loss.

This was the truth he had been doing his best to outrun for two and a half years. It was just as Luke had said. When it really counted?

A man was powerless.

And there was no feeling in the world quite as bad as that one.

Luke came back down the stairs. He looked as if he had been crying, and Brendan almost envied him those tears, the release they brought from the inner storm.

The boy's face was white and strained with the manful effort of trying not to let everything he was feeling show. He had Charlie tucked under his arm, an unwilling football.

"I'm going to fix him! And I'm going to pay you back your money, too!" Luke stomped back up the stairs.

Nora bit her lip, sent Brendan an imploring look.

He shrugged. He wanted to be a dyed-in-the-wool cynic, but the past few days had challenged that. The aunt had something. He had felt it when she'd touched his arm.

And Luke had something, too. That cat was acting better, even if he wasn't actually getting better.

Though that something that Nora and Luke had— that gift with things wounded—was not necessarily what they needed.

Despite the shrug, he knew his indifference was pretended. Caring had crept up on him.

Brendan recognized their lives were a web he could get tangled in.

Was already tangled in, whether he wanted to be or not. And he didn't want it. He'd spent a long time locked in his lonely place, avoiding entanglement.

He walked out the door, refusing to look back at Nora. Free of the enchantment of her house, walking through the warmth of the early summer evening to his car, Brendan Grant vowed to himself he wasn't coming back here. Not until it was time to pick up Charlie.

Dead or alive.

Nora loved the barn. It had taken a dozen volunteers and a hundred man-hours to make the falling-down old structure into an animal shelter, but now it was perfect. She was in the small-animal section, two rows of roomy cages facing a sparkling clean center aisle.

After a night like last night, she needed the peace she felt working alone here. She had a rock-and-roll station blasting, music from the fifties. It was partly to keep her moving through the exhaustion after twenty-four hours of being woken every hour on the hour. It was partly a nice distraction from her whirling thoughts.

But the animals loved music. Humming along, she reached inside the rabbit cage, picked up a droopy-eared bunny she had named Valentine, and tucked him into her bosom.

He wriggled against her, snuggling deeper.

"You want to dance, sweetheart?"

"Sure."

She whirled. Brendan was standing there, watching her. The rabbit must have taken the sudden hard beating of her heart as a warning of imminent danger, because he scrambled out of her arms, over her shoulder and down her back. He hit the floor running.

Brendan reached behind him and closed the door to prevent bunny escape, then turned back to her.

How unfair that he looked even better in the pure afternoon sunshine streaming through the windows high up the walls than he had looked last night.

He must have come from work. He had on a white shirt and gray pants. A tie was loosely knotted at his throat. He looked handsome and sure of himself, a model for *GQ,* only more real.

And she still had a lump the size of a baseball on her forehead, and was wearing a charming blue smock of the one-size-fits-all variety that swam around her.

"I—I haven't seen you for a few days," she stammered. She hoped there was nothing in her voice that revealed how she had waited. And watched.

And hated herself for both.

"Busy at work," he said.

"What are you doing here now?"

"Deedee insisted. Luke's been sending her pictures, but she had to come see for herself."

Nora had no idea Luke had been sending on pictures of the cat. She probably would have asked him to stop, if she knew. What did they all think was going to happen?

"Yesterday he sent a video of that old cat playing with a ball."

She looked closely at Brendan. "Please tell me you don't believe that animal is going to get better?"

He shrugged. "I don't know what to believe, Nora. The thing is, *I'm* getting better. And I never believed that would happen."

"What do you mean, better?" she whispered.

He rolled his shoulders. "I've been in total darkness. I can feel the light trying to get through. There are cracks in the wall and light is seeping in, and every time I patch one crack, another one appears."

It felt as if she couldn't breathe. As if she was going to cry. It felt as if she could run to him and put her arms around him and whisper him home.

To her.

"But the walls have become who I am, so when they crumble, will I crumble, too?"

"No," she whispered. "You won't."

"Uh-huh."

The feelings were too strong. To hide how totally vulnerable she felt, Nora got down on her hands and knees and looked under a set of cages. Valentine stared back at her.

And then Brendan was on the floor beside her. His scent, clean and masculine, overrode every other smell in the building. It was not lightening the mood, having him so near, though he, too, seemed to want to back off from the intensity of the previous moment.

"I think he stuck his tongue out at me," he said.

"Like life," she said. "When you most want control, it will stick its tongue out at you."

"Oh boy," Brendan muttered, "I can see it coming now. *Ask Valentine.*"

She laughed and he smiled.

"There he is." He reached under the row of cages; his shoulder brushed hers; Valentine hopped away.

Nora shot back before she did something really dumb, something she would regret forever, and crawled along the floor. "Valentine," she crooned, "come here."

"I dropped Deedee off at the house. Luke said you were down here."

Did that mean Brendan *wanted* to see her? She

glanced sideways at him, just as he shoved himself under the bank of cages.

"You're ruining your clothes," she said.

He ignored her. "I'm being outsmarted by a rabbit."

Valentine hopped from underneath and took off down the row.

Brendan crawled out, dusted himself off, stood up. "Can't you call him back with your energy?"

She glanced at him, annoyed at the barb, and then saw the little smile playing across his face. He was teasing her. Something dangerous rippled down her spine.

The awareness of him shivered more intensely around her. It was nice to be teased by him.

For a moment, she was going to fight it. The intensity, the subtle invitation to bring him into the light.

And then she found she couldn't. By his own admission he had been in darkness. By his own admission he had come here to her.

With an inner sigh of surrender, Nora decided to play. To be the one thing she never was. Totally herself. She had been so serious for so long. She could not resist the temptations of this moment.

CHAPTER TEN

NORA PLACED HER fingers on her temples, squinched her eyes shut tightly and hummed. "Uzzy, wuzzy, fuzzy bunny, let this poem call you home."

She opened one eye when she heard Brendan snicker. "Is it working?"

"That is the worst spell I've ever heard."

"Oh," she said, widening her eyes innocently. "Have you heard many?"

"Thankfully, no."

"Why don't you try?"

He seemed to debate for a moment. Why did her heart begin to beat faster when he gave in to it, too? To the invitation of life not being so serious. A smile tugged at the corners of that sinful mouth.

"How about a carrot instead of an incantation?" he suggested.

"If he was starving, we might have a hope. As you know, since you've been doing it, he's quite well fed. Still…" she went to the fridge at the end of the aisle, removed a bag and handed Brendan a carrot "…we can try. If it doesn't work today, it might work by midweek."

They went back down the aisle, her on one side, him on the other, peering under cages.

"Now that Deedee's feeling better, is she going to make a decision? Is she going to take Charlie home? Or to the vet?" Nora asked.

"She has her own ideas, as always, none of which involve relieving you of Charlie. She seems to have come for a visit. Luke and she were in deep conversation when I left."

"Luke and Deedee? Seriously?"

"Seriously. Hey! Here he is! Here bunny, bunny, bunny." Brendan was down on his knees again, peering under a sink. As she watched, reluctantly enchanted by a man willing to wreck a thousand-dollar suit for a rabbit, he held out the carrot in the palm of his hand. Valentine edged toward him, he made a move to grab him and the bunny leaped sideways and hopped away.

"He's waving his tail at me. Like a middle finger. Wow. Even I can read his energy."

Nora giggled. Brendan turned and glared at her, but a smile lurked in his eyes. "Let's see if he'll fall for the bait again."

Really, she knew if they left the rabbit alone, he'd eventually get hungry and come out. But it was too fun trying to catch him with Brendan.

Together they chased that bunny all over the barn, acting silly, making faces, doing voices, crawling under cages, and in and out and over obstacles. They called suggestions to each other, and whispered plans, as if he could overhear them, and they laughed at Valentine's impudence.

Finally, they had him.

"Companies pay money for this," Brendan said. "It's called team building."

It occurred to her they had been a team. And it had

felt good. Why was it every time she was with him something happened that made her feel the delicious if guilty pleasure of not being alone?

Now she focused on him and the bunny. She could tell a lot about a person from how he handled an animal.

For a moment Brendan looked as if he intended to hand Valentine to her.

But then his expression softened, and he held the bunny firmly in the palm of his hand, his fingers tapered over the rib cage. He pulled him in close to his chest, stroking Valentine's snubby little nose with one gentle fingertip.

There was something about watching a strong man with a fuzzy bunny that could melt a person's heart. Nora felt some terrible weakness unfurl in her at his tenderness with Valentine, in his decision to come into the light. She was annoyed with herself for feeling as if she had unintentionally given Brendan a test, and she was just as annoyed that he had passed.

"Okay, I think I remember where the little monster lives." He put Valentine back in the cage, closed the door and turned to her.

"Deedee's not going to take him home. I figured it out. She can't bear the thought of being with Charlie when he dies. Though I guess we're all wondering if he's going to die at all. He keeps improving."

"It's temporary."

"You sound certain of that."

"I am. I wish Luke wouldn't have taken it on. He's setting himself up for heartbreak."

"And he's had enough," Brendan guessed softly. "And so have you."

The look in his eyes was the one she had seen that

rainy night when she had come to in the horse pen, when she had reached up and touched his cheek in welcome.

A person could drown in a look like that, throw herself willingly into those deep pools of understanding.

Instead, she congratulated herself for trying to back off.

"When you work with animals that are unwell, you expect a certain amount of grief. I've developed strategies for not getting attached. I don't name any of the animals."

"You named Lafayette."

She could say he had come named, but he hadn't. "Who would get attached to *him?*" she said, a bit defensively.

"How about Valentine?"

"Okay, so the odd one slips by my guard. But now that I have this beautiful facility, I don't ever let animals in the house. To prevent attachment, and also, where would you draw the line?"

"But Luke has Charlie in the house. And Ranger."

She bit her lip. "I know I should be stricter."

"But you took it as a good sign that he cared about something," Brendan guessed, and then reached forward and brushed her hair away from the bump on her head. "He cares about you. He told me he woke you up every hour on the hour."

"He did."

"And how are you feeling?"

"Exhausted."

"Funny, you didn't look exhausted when I came in."

She blushed, remembering that he had caught her dancing.

"In fact," he said, cocking his head, listening to the music blaring, "don't we have some unfinished business? Didn't you ask me to dance?"

Her mouth fell open. Of course she had not asked him to dance! He knew she had been talking to the bunny! What was he doing?

What was *she* doing? Because she found herself playing along, again. Boldly, almost daring him, she held out her hand.

Come, then, into the light.

And felt as if the bottom was falling out of her world when he took it. Because it was only then that she recognized what darkness she had been in.

Grieving her sister. And Vance's abandonment when she'd needed him most. Weighed down by extra responsibility. Wanting desperately to be everything Luke needed, and knowing in her heart she had been falling short.

She took Brendan's hand and smiled at him, and it felt as if for the first time in a long, long time that smile was coming straight from her heart.

What was he doing? Brendan asked himself.

Ever since that first smile had tickled her lips, a desire had been growing in him, and it felt as if his fate was sealed when she'd giggled today. When she'd laughed, chasing that bunny through the barn.

Brendan was not sure he could ever find his way to the light, or if the light could ever penetrate the darkness around him. He was not even certain he wanted it to, because it could mean the loss of the grip he had on the pool of pain inside of him.

Still, watching the cat change, watching Charlie

playing, seemed nothing short of a miracle. What had he started to believe?

However nebulous he was about what he wanted for himself, Brendan was aware of what he wanted for Nora. He wanted to make that light go on in her. He wanted something in her life to be fun and carefree.

It hit him like a ton of bricks what she needed, and why he felt so compelled by her need.

She was in the same situation his mother had once been in, a single parent struggling to be both parents, struggling to do everything right.

His mother's struggles had shaped Brendan, made him driven, made him want things for his own family that he and his mother had not had, and could not have even dared to hope for.

Now, looking at Nora, he could see the strain in her face, the stress in the droop of her shoulders.

It looked as if it had been a long, long time since she had laughed, or had anything approaching fun in her life.

The weight of the whole world seemed to be on those slender shoulders

It was not his job to lift it, Brendan Grant told himself. He'd managed to not get tangled in the web of life for a long time. Yet the last few days...

But that begged the question about the kind of man he had become. Hadn't he said to the boy last night that a mistake could be turned into an opportunity? To become something better?

Brendan had made a terrible mistake that night two and a half years ago.

He'd let Becky drive alone on a bad night. He should

have been with her. She had begged him to go. She'd been so excited.

A pressing project at work. No, no, I'll meet you there. I'll come up later tonight. You'll wake up to my handsome mug in the morning. I promise.

He hated these thoughts. He hated that he was questioning himself. That he could see light, and was being drawn toward it. He hated it that he was coming back to life.

There was no reason he had to be here anymore. Nora didn't need him.

Except that she did.

Life was asking more of him. And there was that ironic twist again. It was asking him to show someone else how to lighten up, how to have fun. But in doing so, he was coming closer to finding his own light. What if this time it broke down the walls all around him and pierced his heart like a lightning bolt?

It would be so easy to walk away from a challenge like that! But if he let the legacy of his love for his wife be bitterness, somehow he had failed.

If he could ignore the need of these two people, in a situation so like the one his mother and he had once been in, it wouldn't matter how many beautiful houses he designed and built.

What if the child Becky had carried had already been born? What if he'd had to figure out how to make a life for both of them *and* deal with his grief?

That's the situation Nora was in. She was grieving her sister and trying to make a life for her nephew.

If he didn't do a single thing to lighten that burden when her need was so obvious to him, Brendan was not sure he would ever get the bitterness of failure off his tongue.

"So," he said, making a decision, cocking his head to the music. "Do you know how to jive?"

Ridiculous to feel as if it was the bravest and most risky thing he had ever done.

"No!" she stated, then asked skeptically, "Do you?"

"Of course not. Well, maybe a little. From high school dance class."

"Interesting school you went to! Word games *and* dance class," Nora said.

"Let's teach each other," he said. And then he pulled her in close to him. She put her hands up, pushing away from him, keeping a small barrier between her and his chest. She was tense and unsure.

Well, she should be. Maybe she was asking the question he needed to ask.

So he lightened her burden. And made her smile. Then what? What happened next?

But this moment stole his questions about the future. Her huge green eyes locked on his face, her pulse beating harder than that rabbit's in the delicate hollow of her throat.

"Relax," he heard himself say softly. He was still holding her hand, and rested his other hand on the soft curve between her rib cage and her hip.

She did relax, looking at him with fearful expectation.

"Okay," he said, "just like dance class. One, two, three, one, two, three."

They shuffled along the aisle between the cages. She looked down at her feet, her tongue caught between her teeth.

"I'm surprised you asked me to dance," he said. "You aren't very good at it."

"I thought I was pretty good when it was Valentine I was dancing with!"

"Uh-huh."

"I was. Not so inhibited."

"There's no cause to be inhibited," he said.

"Yes, there is! I'm going to step on your toes—"

"I can handle it. Steel toes." The truth was he'd had to force himself to go to work today. He had wanted to be here instead. He had missed it here as he had not missed getting to Village on the Lake every day.

She glared down at his feet. "They are not!"

"Specifically made for construction sites. They are."

"I'm going to look foolish."

"There's no one here to worry about."

"What about you?"

"I'd love to see this—" he pressed a finger into the little worry line in her forehead "—disappear. Just give yourself to it. Just for a minute."

She hesitated, then he felt the exact moment she surrendered shiver up the length of her entire body.

"Now," he said softly, "you should try moving your hips."

"You first!"

"Just us and the bunnies. And a few cats."

"And a parrot who swears."

"Ah, Lafayette, the finger eater. Hard to find a home for him, I assume?" The distraction of talking about the parrot worked. Brendan was moving and she was going with him.

"Hard to find a home for him? Impossible. Except for young men of a certain age who would take him to use as a novelty item at their frat parties. I couldn't allow that."

"That sounds just a bit like, um, attachment."

"Well, it isn't. That horrible parrot is probably going to teach Luke new words."

"There are no words that are new to a fifteen-year-old boy."

While she contemplated that, Brendan decided to up the difficulty level.

"I'm going to pull away from you, but keep holding your hand. Up in the air like this. Walk beside me."

"This isn't a jive," she said. "I think it's a minuet."

"Nope. No hips in minuets."

"Did you learn that in dance class?"

She was becoming quite breathless. He pulled her back to him, put his hand on her waist, leaned his forehead to hers. "Get ready to spin under my arm."

She did.

"Now spin back. We're good," he declared.

"We're not. We're terrible."

"Ask Valentine if you don't believe me. Get ready for the dip."

"Dip? No! Brendan! We'll fall."

CHAPTER ELEVEN

"FALL? ON MY watch? I don't think so. Relax. Trust me."

Nora giggled. Then relaxed, and then trusted him.

And at that exact second of giving her trust completely, his arm went behind the small of her back and she was literally swept off her feet.

Just like that she found her back arched, totally supported by his strength. Just like that they were in balance. In harmony. He held her suspended there. She gazed into his eyes. And then he pulled her in hard to his chest.

She leaned against him, feeling the steady, solid beat of his heart. They were both breathing hard, and she started to laugh. She laughed until the tears flowed.

"OhmyGod," she said. "I haven't laughed like that for so long!"

He was watching her intently, a little satisfied smile playing on his lips.

As if he had planned this. Give the poor beleaguered aunt a break from the monotony of her life.

It had been a nice thing to do.

But while she'd been losing control, he'd been gaining it.

And that was enough of that.

"Brendan, that was so much fun. I hardly know how to thank you."

Except that she did. She knew only one way to bring him totally into this place of light with her.

And before she could stop herself or think of the consequences, letting the momentum of the dance carry her, she was on her tiptoes, taking his lips with hers. And that's when the bottom really fell out of her world.

Brendan Grant's lips were like silk warmed through with honey.

Nora considered herself something of an expert on energy, but nothing could have prepared her for this exchange.

His energy was pure and powerful.

It swept through her, until it felt as if every cell in her whole body was vibrating with welcome for what he was.

A life force. Compelling. All-encompassing.

And that was before his kiss deepened. Taking her. Capturing her. Promising her. Making her believe…

…in the breadth and depth and pure power of love.

She broke away and stood staring at him, her chest heaving, her mind whirling, her soul on fire.

She didn't want to believe! Belief had left her shattered. Her belief in such things had left her weak and vulnerable and blind.

And she was doing it again.

Love! How could the word *love* have entered the picture? She hadn't given it permission! She hadn't invited it into her life! If anything, she was actively avoiding such a complicated twist to her already overwhelming life.

Realistically, she knew next to nothing about this man.

Except that he had known sorrow.

And that he was good to his deceased wife's grand-mother.

And had given her nephew a chance.

And could hold a bunny with tenderness.

And could turn an ordinary moment into a dance.

And had made her laugh.

And was afraid of crumbling along with the walls that came down.

The truth was that Nora felt she knew more about Brendan Grant in less than twenty-four hours than she had known about Dr. Vance Height in more than two years.

"I don't know wh-what got into me," she stammered, and could feel the heat moving up her cheeks. She had kissed a stranger. It didn't matter that she felt she *knew* him. That was crazy. That was the illusion!

"I need to go. I need to go check on Luke. And Charlie. And your grandmother. And—"

"Hey!" He stepped in close to her, touched her cheek, looked deep into her eyes. "Don't make it more than it was. A spontaneous moment between a healthy man and a beautiful woman."

She stared at him.

It was nothing to him. Well, of course! No matter what she read into it, they did not know each other. While she was falling in love, he was building his walls higher.

"I—I'm not beautiful," she stammered. Of all the things she could have said, why that?

"Yes," he said, his voice husky, his thumb moving down her cheek and scraping delicately over her lip. "Yes, you are."

Because she had *needed* to hear that. Had needed someone to see the woman in her.

And for a moment she thought he was going to kiss her again. And she knew, despite her attempt at re-solve, she would not do a single thing—not one single thing—to stop him.

But then he stepped back from her, shoved his hands into his pockets.

"How about if I start on the chores? While I wait for Deedee?"

Pride and a need for self-protection made Nora want to refuse. But if she said no, he would know that some-thing he had dismissed as nothing had shaken her right to her core.

And practicality took over. As he had pointed out, her volunteers were largely little old ladies. Here was someone who could do the heavy work. She couldn't turn it down.

"Do you think I could get you to move some hay bales?"

"Sure, just show me what you need done."

Trying to shake off that awareness of him—a need that he had unleashed within her and that she intended to fight with her whole heart—Nora led him through the small-animal section.

She was going to pretend nothing had happened.

But it was harder, as she watched him walk through her world with easy familiarity, pausing to scratch a cat's ear, to stick his finger through mesh to tickle a kitten. Even the hamsters seemed to recognize him, and scurried to the wire to say hello.

They stopped in front of the colorful parrot, which at once swore loudly at Nora, using a term so derogatory to females it made her flush. Then the parrot switched to French.

Brendan's lips twitched. His voice stern, he said, *"Lafayette, fermez la bouche."*

"Ooh," she teased, unable to resist, even though she knew the dangers of teasing, "you speak French. What did you say?"

"Romantic gibberish," he said, wagging a fiendish eyebrow at her. "It means shut your mouth."

And the tension that had been building between them since their lips met exploded into laughter once again.

"What do you do with animals like Lafayette?" he asked when the laughter stopped. "The ones that won't be adopted for whatever reason?"

"I'm pretty new at this. I've only had the shelter open for six months. Demand for adoptable pets has outstripped animals coming in. I even found a home for a white rat! So far, that's a decision I haven't had to make."

"Maybe you should have a plan," he suggested.

She decided it would make her feel way too vulnerable to let him know how she dreaded the day she would have to make that decision, let alone plan for it.

They continued through the barn, and the dogs went crazy when they saw Brendan. With easy confidence, he moved into each pen and opened the door out to the run.

There were three dogs in residence, a black Lab with only three legs, which had been found out wandering. The cocker spaniel, Millie, had been brought in because her owner couldn't afford the diabetes medication. The puppy was of an unknown breed. A week ago he'd been a matted and flea-infested mess, wary of people. Now he gamboled after Brendan.

"I don't suppose you want to take one home?" Nora asked ruefully. "The dog with three legs?"

"You had me pegged right as a guy who wouldn't even have a plant."

It was a warning to her, whether he knew it or not.

Not a man to pin any kind of romantic dream on.

But she already knew that. She was so done with romantic dreams. Though there was something about being dipped over a man's arm that could breathe them back to life in anyone, even a more hardened soul than her.

And there was something about seeing him with animals that told the truth about who and what he was, even if he didn't know that himself.

"You'll have no trouble finding a home for this little guy," he said of the enthusiastic puppy. "I'm not so sure about Long John Silver over there. Really, you should have a plan."

"I don't want a plan!" she said. "What? After six months get rid of him? How could I walk by that cage every day if time was counting down?"

"That sounds a bit like attachment to me."

"Well, it isn't!"

It felt so much more powerful to be annoyed with him than it had felt being in his arms.

Finally, they arrived at a large stack of hay, and without being told, Brendan got a wheelbarrow and began to pull bales down. Nora went back to cleaning cages, putting in food and changing water.

Her annoyance, unfortunately, could not be sustained in light of how hard he was working for her.

The awareness was roaring in her ears, sizzling through her veins. She could not help sneaking peeks at him. There was a certain poetry to a male body hard at work, and she was sworn off romance, not dead! Still, these kind of temptations—dancing, laughing, watching him pull eighty-pound bales down and shift them effortlessly to the wheelbarrow—were going to chip away at her resolve.

Thankfully, her cell phone buzzed, and when she took the call there was a rescue she needed to go to. That was going to do double duty by rescuing her from the tingles on her skin and on her lips.

"Gotta go," she said, her tone deliberately breezy. "Iguana found on the loose in Hansen Lakeside Park." She ordered herself to thank him, and then to tell him not to come back. Diplomatically, of course. *Nothing here that Luke and I can't handle, especially now that school is out for the summer.*

But, weakling that she was, she found herself looking at Brendan's lips. She decided she needed to think about it before doing something rash and irrevocable.

Which probably described her decision to kiss Brendan Grant! Rash and irrevocable. Everything she did around him, from here on out, had to be measured and thought out carefully.

Everything she did around him now? From here on out? Hmm, not exactly the thoughts of a woman who was going to look at a man and tell him never to come back!

Three days later, Nora was scowling at her computer screen. Iguanas *did* eat dark, leafy greens. Except not the one she had. He was probably ill, and his owner had not been able to afford the vet bills. She made a note to pack up the iguana to take to her appointment with Dr. Bentley this afternoon. The vet was good enough to donate a few minutes to the animal shelter one day every week, and could also be counted on for emergencies.

She was aware that even as she did these routine tasks, her mind was not on them.

It was on Brendan Grant. He had brought his grandmother out every day for a few minutes, quite early in the morning, before he had to be at the office.

Nora couldn't very well tell him to stay away when Deedee wanted to see Charlie, refused to take him home, and couldn't drive herself.

Without being asked, without checking in, Brendan headed for the barn, and every morning after he left, Nora went out to see all the bales moved, the horse pen cleaned, the large bags of dog food organized, the aisle swept.

He didn't come to the house.

And she didn't go out. In fact, knowing now what time he came, she would sometimes scurry for cover just as he was pulling into the driveway.

Though it felt as if she was fighting her inner demons. That spontaneous dance haunted her. As did the laughter. And his lips on hers. He was out there right now. She could just go down…

She heard the front door open, flicked her curtain back. She saw Deedee making her slow way back to the car, Luke holding her arm and helping her in. Brendan was nowhere in sight, but if she waited just a minute, Nora knew that he would be.

Then Luke came back in the house, and she heard

him taking the stairs two at a time. She quickly flicked the curtain down and stared at her computer screen.

He stopped off in his room, and when he came up behind her a minute later, Charlie was drooping over Luke's crossed arms as if doing an impression of a leopard in a tree.

"Do the animals ever talk to you?" her nephew asked in a troubled voice, scratching Charlie's ears. "I mean, not in words, but you get, like, a feeling from them and know exactly what they're thinking?"

"Give me an example."

He took a deep breath. "Charlie is ready to go. He's tired. And he hurts. And he's a cat. Cats are clean. He doesn't want to be losing control of himself, if you know what I mean. You know why he's staying?"

She shook her head.

"Because he loves her. Deedee. And she's not ready to let him go."

In the past few days it was becoming apparent to Nora that Luke shared her gift, only his was a more intense version. Were animals really talking to him? Or was it just one more example of how her crazy decisions were affecting him?

Karen would not have approved of Luke being certain he knew what animals were thinking! She had certainly never approved of Nora's abilities.

"Remember Mr. Grant said I had to make a mend?"

Nora nodded, not correcting him that it was "amends."

"That's how I'm going to do it. By getting her ready."

"How are you going to do that?"

"I don't know. But she thinks it's by mowing her lawn. I'm going to bring Ranger with me."

Nora gazed at her nephew, and he had a look of resolve on his face. Not like a boy, but a man.

For the first time in a long, long time, Nora didn't feel worried, even though to someone looking in it might seem as if she should.

Luke was communicating with animals! Or thought he was. That probably needed a psychiatrist, not what she was feeling.

He was taking on the gargantuan task of getting Deedee ready to lose her pet. It was a failure getting ready to happen.

Protect him.

But this was probably why her sister had wanted her and Vance as Luke's guardians. Because Nora felt proud of him for taking on the impossible. And as if there was a slim hope, after all, that her nephew was going to leave the world better than he found it.

Somehow the changes in Luke and her own feeling of optimism seemed linked, not to the wonderful summer weather they were suddenly enjoying, but to this man who was in her life while not being in it.

It was all beginning to feel like the scariest thing that had ever happened to her. In that nice scary way like anticipating someone jumping out from behind a bush at you on Halloween, or riding the biggest roller coaster at the amusement park.

Luke went to the window. "Brendan's coming up from the barn now. I'll catch a ride with him into town and mow Deedee's grass."

Nora wanted to scream no, the very same way she wanted to scream no as the roller coaster was inching up that final climb. But just like then, it felt as if it was already too late. She could see all their lives getting more and more tangled together.

Besides, when she looked at the simple bravery revealed in her nephew's face, Nora knew she had to be as brave as he was.

She joined him at the window and saw Brendan striding across her yard.

"He must change for work later," she said out loud, admiring the way faded jeans clung to his legs, to the leanness of his hips. A plaid shirt was tucked into his belt, but open at the throat. Her eyes skittered to the firm line of Brendan's lips.

She had to be brave. Whether she wanted to be or not.

"It's Saturday," Luke chided her.

"Oh. Now that you're on summer holidays, I forget sometimes."

"That's my flaky aunt. Who doesn't know what day it is?" But he said it with gruff affection, then added, "Gotta go. I'll call you later."

Luke put his hand on her shoulder, dropped a casual kiss on her cheek. He squinted at the computer screen.

"It's not because we're giving him the wrong diet. Iggy ate something," he said.

"Iggy? Luke, we try not to name the animals."

"It's not really a name, just short for iguana. Dr. Bentley's going to have to x-ray him. How could an iguana swallow a house?"

And on that note, her nephew was gone, Ranger peeking out his hoodie pocket. He went back outside, and moments later, she heard him calling, "Brendan? I'll come with you. I'm going to mow Deedee's lawn. That's if Deedee can look after my kitten."

Nora twitched back the curtain just in time to see Luke hand Ranger to Deedee.

The old woman stared at the kitten. For a moment, she looked mad, as if she might give it back. But then her face softened, and she tucked Ranger into her breast and got into the car.

Brendan looked up at her, as if he'd known she was watching all along. He gave her a small smile and a thumbs-up. As if they were raising this boy together. She let the curtain fall back into place.

CHAPTER TWELVE

MIDAFTERNOON, NORA WAS thinking of Luke's words while she stood in Dr. Bentley's office looking at the X-ray of Iggy's digestive tract, and not his words about mowing the lawn, either. About how an iguana could swallow a house. The X-ray clearly showed a little toy house lodged in the reptile's digestive system.

"An iguana will eat anything," Dr. Bentley said.

The vet donated many of his services to the animal shelter, but was not volunteering an operation on an iguana, and she couldn't ask. Now what? They had a reserve fund, but to use it for an expensive procedure for an animal she had no hope of finding a home for?

She remembered being thankful, just days ago, that she had never had to face this situation.

Maybe you should have a plan. She hated it that Brendan Grant had been right. He had that look of a man who was always right. Who was logical and thought things through and never did anything impulsive or irrevocable.

We would be a well-balanced team, she thought, before she could stop herself.

"I need a minute to think," she said.

"Take your time."

She wrestled Iggy back into his cage and lugged him out to the waiting room. She had three choices. She could bring him home to die. She could have the vet speed up the process, which would be more humane. Or she could find the money for the procedure.

Her cell phone rang and she looked at the number coming in.

"Hey, Luke," she said, trying to strip the conflict she was feeling from her voice.

"It's not Luke. I borrowed his phone."

"Why?" It was him, the one who was always right. Maybe she'd call him that. Mr. Right. Then again, maybe not. She did not want to be thinking of Brendan Grant as Mr. Right in any context.

There was no Mr. Right! It was a fairy tale to keep females from empowering themselves! Ditto for thinking she was falling in love with him. Just another fairy tale.

"Because we're standing out in Deedee's yard and he handed it to me." A pause, and his voice lowered. "And because I wasn't sure if you would answer if you saw it was me."

"What would make you say that?" she said cautiously.

"I thought you were avoiding me."

Was she that obvious? It was embarrassing, really.

"Why would I be avoiding you?" she asked.

Silence. She thought of the boldness of taking his lips with her own, and shivered. She thought of the word *love* coming unbidden to her after she had kissed him.

He moved on without answering the question. They both knew exactly why she was avoiding him.

"I told Luke I'd take him for a milkshake. He did Deedee's lawn and then started on her shrub beds. They're pretty overgrown. He's worked really hard. I can't believe you've lived here six months and not been to the Moo Factory. His exact words were '*we never do anything fun.*'"

"We do fun things," she protested.

"Oh, yeah? Like what?"

We played a few hands of poker, once.

She knew it said something simply awful about her life with her nephew that, aside from that, nothing came to mind.

"We rented *Star Wars* last week."

"Really? That sounds like fun redefined."

"Are you being sarcastic?"

"It comes naturally to me, like breathing."

"We play Scrabble," she said triumphantly. "When I can get him away from the computer." Too late, she remembered they had invited Brendan to play Scrabble. He'd been unimpressed.

"Fun intensified."

She remembered his face that evening Luke had suggested Scrabble. But she was on a mission now to prove they had fun.

"And Luke showed me how to play virtual bowling!"

"Wow!"

It let her know how wise her avoidance strategy was. He was sarcastic. It was hard to hold that fault in the forefront, though, in light of his good deed. He was taking her nephew for ice cream.

"I bet you threw the bowling ball backward."

"How could you know that?"

"Psychic. That should help me fit right in on the farm."

"Oh!"

"I warned you. Sarcastic."

"How did you really know? About the bowling ball?"

"I've played that game."

"Oh, so *you* threw the ball backward?"

"No." Suddenly he seemed impatient with the conversation. "Anyway, I thought I should ask your permission before I took Luke for ice cream."

It was so respectful it could make a woman forgive sarcasm. Or at least one who did not have her guard way up.

"That wasn't necessary. Of course you can take him." Ridiculous to somehow feel deflated that she wasn't being invited.

Then Brendan said, "Luke would like you to come with us."

Not *him*. Luke.

She looked at the sick iguana. And suddenly was overcome by weakness, not wanting to have to make this decision herself.

"I'm at the vet's office with Iggy, an iguana who has eaten something."

"Iggy," Brendan repeated slowly. "I thought you told me you didn't name them?"

"Who would get attached to an iguana?" she said, but the truth was maybe she already was. She didn't want to bring him home to die. Or put him to sleep.

She told Brendan what was going on. It was his chance to say *I told you so,* but he didn't, and she felt it was another test he'd passed.

Another one that she hadn't meant to give him.

"You have a contingency fund?" he asked.

"Yes, but Brendan, that money would be so much better used educating people not to buy iguanas as pets. And the contingency fund isn't huge. What if I spend it on him, and then have an emergency next week?"

"On something with a little more of a cute factor than an iguana?"

She didn't mean to, but she started to cry. And she wasn't sure if it was because of the damned iguana that she'd been foolish enough to accept a name for, or because Brendan had gone virtual bowling with someone else who had thrown the ball the wrong way.

Or because it wasn't his idea to ask her out for ice cream.

It was Becky he'd played that silly game with. At a Christmas function? Everyone having hysterics at her lack of coordination.

He realized, holding the phone, that this was the first time he'd had a memory of Becky that made him *feel* anything. It was as if, after she died, he had started focusing on his failure to protect her, and that had erased all the good things from his mind.

But somewhere, had he also thought that thinking of the good would be *that* thing? That thing that would break him wide-open?

His contemplation of his treacherous inner landscape was cut blessedly short when Brendan heard a soft snuffling noise on the other end of the phone line. He tried to dismiss it as static, but the hair on the back of his neck prickled.

Maybe he *was* psychic. "Are you crying?"

The truth was his inner landscape seemed less treacherous than that.

The truth was he knew Nora Anderson had been avoiding him. And the truth was, he knew it had been a good thing. For them to avoid each other. Look at how quickly his intention to be a Good Samaritan by making her laugh had become complicated. By her hips under his hands. And then by her lips. On his.

"N-n-no."

But she was. Crying. Was it over an iguana? He was pretty sure she had said she was used to dealing with tragedy with animals. She had strategies for not getting attached.

Not that she seemed to stick to any of them!

An awful possibility occurred to him. Maybe it was because he had just thought of his wife that he was suddenly aware how quickly things could go sideways.

"Have you been having outbursts since you hit your head?" he asked.

"I am not having an outburst!" Now Nora was insulted.

Brendan was astounded that he felt guilty. When he'd been dancing her down the aisle of the animal shelter, he really should have been asking her concussion-related questions. And instead of doing the easy thing, and avoiding her and all the complications that her lips had caused in his uncomplicated life over the last few days, he should have been evaluating her medical condition.

"Have you been to see a doctor?" he asked.

"I don't need a doctor!"

"Look, outbursts can be a sign of concussion—"

"I am not having an outburst!" Each word was enunciated with extreme control, and then the phone went dead in his hands. Nora Anderson had hung up on him!

It seemed to Brendan that hanging up on someone could be evidence of an outburst.

Luke, flushed from heat, his hair flattened by sweat, came out of the flower bed, a tangle of bramble in his gloved hand. "Is Aunt Nora coming with us? For ice cream."

"I'm not sure what your aunt is doing." Except he was sure she was crying over an iguana. "Has she, er, been having outbursts?"

"What does that mean?"

"Crying. Snapping."

"Oh. You mean PMS."

Brendan wasn't sure if he should reprimand Luke or not, but a look of such deep masculine sympathy passed between them that he just couldn't.

Luke seemed to contemplate the fact his aunt might be a little off today. "Maybe just bring me back a milk-shake," he muttered, and disappeared into the garden again.

Then he peeked back out. "Can you get something for Deedee, too? And just a little dish of vanilla for Ranger. I'll pay for it." He glanced toward the house. "She's trying not to. But she likes him. Ranger."

There seemed to be a bit of that going around. People trying not to like each other, and liking each other anyway.

Luke was a prime example. It was damn hard not to like this kid.

And that went ditto for his aggravating aunt.

Knowing she wasn't going to appreciate it one little bit, Brendan made his way to the vet's office.

Nora was sitting in the waiting room, doing her best to look like a woman who would not cry over an iguana. The iguana was in a cage at her feet. It had a ribbon around its neck. Who tied a ribbon around the neck of an iguana they planned not to get attached to?

When she saw him, she folded hands over her chest.

"I. Can. Handle. It. Myself."

"Uh-huh." It was the first time he'd seen her in a dress. Or in clothes that fit, for that matter. It was a denim jumper. She had amazing legs. It was kind of like Ranger, hard not to like something so adorable.

He ignored her glare and took the seat next to her. "Have you decided what to do then?"

He slid her a look. She gnawed her lip. He knew darn well that meant she hadn't. He remembered how her lip tasted.

What was he doing here?

Trying to do the right thing, he reminded himself sternly. Brendan took one more quick look at her, and then got up and sauntered past the receptionist and into the back to talk to Herb Bentley.

"Okay," Brendan said, coming back into the waiting room. Nora was fishing through her handbag, looking for tissues. "Let's go for milkshakes."

While she was sipping her shake, he could grill her about concussion symptoms. He would look up a complete list of them on his iPad while waiting in line. There was always a line at the Moo Factory on Saturday.

She looked stubborn. "In case you've forgotten, I have to make a decision about the iguana."

"I've already made it," he said. He picked up the cage and put it on the receptionist's desk.

Nora bristled, balled up a tissue in her fist. "You made the decision? But you can't!"

It wasn't exactly an outburst, but it certainly seemed as if she might be on the edge of one.

Patiently, Brendan told her, "I told Doc I'd pay for the operation. Let's go have ice cream."

"I didn't tell you about Iggy because I needed you to fix it!" she said.

"Whatever."

"No! It's not whatever! I told you because I needed a little tiny bit of feedback. I needed to not feel so alone. I trusted you. I didn't tell you because I needed the decision made for me."

She looked as if she wanted to stick her fist in her mouth after she admitted that. About not wanting to make the decision by herself. She had let it slip how alone she felt in the world.

He looked at her lips.

Well, that shouldn't last long. Her being alone. At the moment, she was the best kept secret in Hansen. When word got out, every unattached guy for a hundred miles would be beating a path to her doorstep. Brendan didn't even want to question the hollow feeling that realization caused in the pit of his stomach.

But only, he told himself, because he knew she'd made a bad choice once. Only because he knew it would destroy that kid up there slaving away in his grandmother's garden if Nora did it again.

Why was he worried about her? She claimed not to like attachments. On the other hand, she was already attached to the iguana, and God knew there were lots of lizards around.

"My paying for the procedure is no big deal," he explained patiently. "You could be having cognitive difficulties, postconcussion, that were making it hard for you to make a decision."

"I don't like iguanas. But that doesn't mean I want to have the decision whether he lives or dies in my hands."

"Well, now it's not. There. Solved."

"Oh!"

"Irritability," he said sagely. He knew it would be wiser to keep that observation to himself, but he was surprised to find a part of him was actually enjoying this little interchange.

"I am not having cognitive difficulties! And I'm not irritable."

He raised an eyebrow.

"It's justified irritability, not knocked-over-the-head irritability!"

"It just seems a teensy bit out of proportion. I mean, I thought you'd be—" he considered saying grateful, and then said "—happy. I just don't see that it's a big deal."

"You paying is a big deal. I'll pay you back," she said stubbornly.

"Consider it a donation."

"No."

"You really need a board of directors to answer to."

"And it's you making the decision that's a big deal."

"Wouldn't it be forgivable if I made the decision based on the presumption you might be having cognitive difficulties? Even if you weren't?"

He blinked at her. He happened to know he had eyelashes women found irresistible. He wasn't opposed to using them as a weapon when backed into a corner.

She stared at him. Blinked herself. Looked away.

"Talk about cognitive difficulties," she muttered. He was pleased that she suddenly lost her desire to argue with him. Still, she couldn't just give in! Let him have the last word!

"I will pay you back."

"Fine. I'll take it out in milkshakes. A lifetime supply. I like licorice."

"A lifetime supply? How much *is* the procedure going to cost?"

Seeing the worry creasing her brow, he cut the amount in half and was rewarded for his little lie when she looked relieved.

"There is no such thing as a licorice milkshake," she said.

"That just shows you've never been to the Moo Factory."

"Besides, if you think other people making decisions for you is no big deal, *I'll* pick the flavor of your lifetime supply."

It was all turning lighter. He could tell it was against her will. Maybe she *was* experiencing cognitive impairment!

"Have at it," he said drily. "I've never met a flavor of ice cream I didn't like."

"Apparently," she muttered. "Licorice? Yuck!"

He held open the clinic door for her and she went outside to the parking lot, eyed his vehicle suspiciously. "Where's Luke?"

"At the last minute, he said he didn't want to come. He asked us to bring something back for him so he could keep working. And he asked me to bring something back for Deedee, too. And Ranger. He said he'd pay for theirs."

"My nephew, Luke Caviletti, said he'd pay?"

"Yeah."

"You're sure? He's the kind of gangly kid with red hair."

But her attempt at humor was meant to cover something else and it failed. Her face crinkled up. She did a funny thing with her nose and squinched her eyes hard.

The facial contortions didn't help her gain control. He could tell she was making a valiant, valiant effort not to cry again. The tears squeezed out anyway.

He wanted to just shove his hands in his pockets and wait it out. But he was helpless against what he did next.

"Maybe…I…am…having…just…a…little…bit… of…cognitive…impairment." She was scrubbing at her eyes with that balled up tissue.

He went to her and pulled her against him, wrapped his arms around the small of her back and held on tight.

He could feel the wetness soaking into his shirt.

And the warmth oozing out of her body.

And her heart beating below his.

Now, for his own protection and for hers, would be a great time to confirm that emotional changeability was definitely a sign of concussion.

But somehow those words about the proven correlation between concussion and emotions got trapped in his throat and never made it to his mouth.

Somehow his one hand left the small of her back, went to her hair and smoothed it soothingly.

That feeling was back.

Of being alive.

Only standing there in the vet's office parking lot, with sunshine that felt warmer after the months of rain, with her body pressed into his, Brendan was aware he didn't feel resentful of waking up, of being alive. Not this time.

Not at all.

CHAPTER THIRTEEN

"OKAY," BRENDAN GRANT said, consulting his iPad. "Are you getting headaches?"

"You are spoiling the best milkshake I have ever had."

"Just answer the question, ma'am," he said, in a voice that reminded her of a policeman.

Nora leveled him a look that she hoped would get him to stop. He *was* wrecking a perfect moment. They were sitting at a picnic table across from the Moo Factory, in Hansen Lakeside Park. Iggy had been granted a stay of execution. Luke had actually offered to spend his own money buying another human being—and a kitten—ice cream.

The sun had brought everyone to the park. Children were screaming on nearby playground equipment, some boys were throwing a Frisbee, a young couple was pushing a baby carriage. Nora watched the small family and identified the emotion she was feeling as envy.

"They look like they would provide the perfect home for a three-legged dog," she said to Brendan when she saw that he had noticed her watching them.

"Now who is spoiling the moment? Can you stop worrying about your animals for one minute and focus on the question? Lack of focus! It's on this list of symptoms!"

"I seem to be getting a headache right now." Nora was trying so hard to steel herself against him, but honestly, when he turned on the charm? It was nearly hopeless. That thing he had done with his eyelashes? The big, innocent blink?

Criminal, really.

"I'm being serious!" he insisted, glancing at his iPad and then scowling back at her. As long as he didn't blink!

"So am I!"

"You have a headache?"

"Yes."

He scrutinized her, and looked as if he was going to scoop her up and rush her off to the hospital. Really, she didn't quite know what to do with all this chauvinistic caring.

What if she just surrendered to it? She'd had a bump on the head. She could be forgiven a weak moment.

"Could be brain freeze. From the milkshake," she told him.

"Ah." He looked genuinely relieved, but she wasn't letting him off the hook yet.

"Of course, it could be from being nagged by an exceedingly annoying man!"

His lips twitched a little, with amusement, not annoyance. He didn't look the least contrite. In fact, he consulted his tablet again. "I'm not being exceedingly annoying. I'm being mildly annoying. For your own good."

She rolled her eyes and took a long sip of her milkshake. Huckleberry Heaven really was heaven. But to be sitting across the table from a man like this on such a gorgeous summer day, and be asked about your cognitive function?

"Are you having any foggy feelings? Like you can't concentrate?"

Only when you blink at me.

"Would that be the same as lack of focus?"

He considered this thoughtfully.

"Can I taste your milkshake?" she asked him.

"I'm going to put yes for that one. What does tasting my milkshake have to do with feeling foggy?"

"I've never tasted a licorice milkshake before. I've decided to live dangerously, since a blood vessel in my head may be perilously weakened, getting ready to explode as we speak."

He glared at her.

She put a hand to her forehead, swayed. He furrowed his brow, baffled.

"My best impression of pre-aneurism," she told him.

She wasn't sure what it was, but he brought out something zany in her, a kind of lack of inhibition that she had not experienced often.

She liked it, especially when he shoved his milkshake across the table to make her stop. Before he gave in and laughed.

She put his straw in her mouth. She was way too aware of the fact that her lips were where his had been. She thought maybe he liked it, too. He suddenly didn't seem nearly so interested in his silly questions. Instead, he watched her suck on his straw, and there was something so intense in his eyes it made her shiver.

"Whoo, that's cold," she said, to explain the shiver. She suspected he was not fooled. She pushed the shake back across the table at him. "Not to mention surprisingly good."

Deliberately, his eyes still locked on her, he took the straw. He was caressing the damn thing with his lips.

It was the closest she'd ever been to being kissed without actually being kissed. What he was doing with that straw was darn near X-rated. She shoved her milkshake across to him.

"Want to try mine?" she asked softly. She was encouraging him!

Apparently he did want to try hers. Intensity sizzled in the air between them as he grasped her shake, lifted it to his mouth, took the straw between his teeth and nipped before closing his lips over it.

"What else do you want to do?" he asked softly. "To live dangerously. Before the blood vessel in your head lets go."

The thing was, he was kidding. But the other thing was it was no joke. Life was not predictable. Her sister the health nut, dead in her early thirties. His wife in a car accident.

Suddenly, it seemed to Nora that she had not taken nearly enough chances. That she had not lived as fully as she should have.

If it was all going to be over, what had she missed?

It was easy to see the answer right now, with him sitting across from her, doing seductive things to her straw. The sun was gleaming in his dark hair; the faintest shadow of whiskers were appearing on the hardhoned planes of his cheeks.

She had missed the glory of being with a man like this.

And just letting go.

Enjoying wherever life took them, even if it was dangerous. Especially if it was dangerous!

"I want to rent one of those things down there." Nora pointed to a colorful booth and a dock. Parked beside the pier were flat-bottomed boats that had pedals in them.

She realized she wasn't kidding. She wanted to forget Iggy and a three-legged dog she could not find a home for. She wanted to forget an old lady whose cat, despite a reprieve, was going to die. She even wanted to forget poor Luke and the weight of her responsibility to him. She wanted to forget she had *Ask Rover* columns due, and bills to pay that relied on that column to pay them.

She just wanted to go out on the water and play.

"I think," she said slowly, "I want to live as if I'm dying."

"That's a song," he said.

She looked at him. She screwed up all her courage. "So, do you want to sing it with me?"

"Sure," he said, and it didn't even reduce her pleasure when he added, "So I can watch for more symptoms."

While he went down to the dock and arranged to rent the boat, Nora called Luke to tell him his milkshake was going to be late.

He said it was okay. He and Deedee had gotten tired of waiting and were eating pie, anyway.

"Don't ever eat pie cooked by someone really ancient," he warned Nora in an undertone. "I don't think she remembered to put sugar in it. It might be really old, too, like it's been in her fridge for three weeks."

"Don't eat it!" Nora declared.

"I can't hurt her feelings," Luke whispered, and then said good-bye and hung up.

She was still contemplating that when Brendan returned. Luke didn't want to hurt someone's feelings. It really was shaping up to be a perfect day.

"Okay, sailor," Brendan said, coming up to her and passing her a life jacket, "let's go."

Nora wondered if it was because they had been trapped inside so long because of the rain that they gave themselves so completely to an afternoon of playing on the water in the sunshine.

The boat, if it could be called that, was an awkward contraption. It was propelled forward, ever so slowly, by two people side by side, pedaling with all their might. Steering took some getting used to. There was no steering wheel. In order to turn the boat, one person stopped pedaling and the other kept going. The boat would start doing a painfully slow arc.

With much shouting and laughter she and Brendan headed out of the bay into the lake. They had not counted on the wind coming up and creating a tiny bit of chop. They had rented the boat for an hour, but by the time they got it back to the dock they had been wrestling with it, trying to get it back to shore against a headwind and a small swell for over two hours.

"Oh, boy," he said, "if that was your idea of living dangerously, I'd hate to see dull."

"It wasn't dull! It was fun!"

"Uh-huh."

"So, you pick something dangerous then, if you're so great."

"All right. I'll come for you tomorrow at ten."

"We're going to do something dangerous together? Tomorrow at ten?"

"Unless you're too chicken."

But she wasn't. She felt as brave as she ever had. That feeling lasted until the next morning, when precisely at ten, Brendan roared into her yard.

He was on a motorcycle.

It was dangerous all right, Brendan thought. They had taken the ferry across the lake and he was navigating the road that twisted along the north shore. It wasn't dangerous because the road had more dips and hollows and rises and falls than a roller coaster. It wasn't dangerous because of the tourists pulling trailers or boats backed up the traffic, and the locals took incredible chances getting by them.

No, it was dangerous because Nora Anderson was curled against his back, holding him hard and tight, so close that he doubted a piece of tissue paper could be inserted between them. It was dangerous because instead of being the least frightened, she was shouting with laughter and egging him on to new feats of daring.

They stopped for lunch at a pub midway down the lake, and when she pulled her helmet off and freed her flattened hair, her nose was sunburned and her cheeks were rosy from the wind and she was shining with happiness.

She looked carefree and young, and he found himself wishing that she would look like that all the time.

Over steak sandwiches, on a deck that stretched over the blue waters of the lake, they talked of Iggy's recovery and laughed about Luke eating Deedee's pie. Brendan told Nora about something funny that had happened at work, but was aware of not saying a single thing about Village on the Lake, which was supposed to be a pinnacle point in his career. She shared some of her ambitions for Nora's Ark with him.

It wasn't so much what they said as how he felt. Relaxed. At ease. As if he had known her forever, and she was the easiest person in the world to spend time with.

She sipped a beer; he stuck with water. Navigating the road, and his growing feeling for Nora, was going to take him having complete control of his senses! No impairment of any kind.

"You know what I did last night?" he asked.

"Cleaned licorice splotches off your shirt?"

"After that."

"Worked?"

He realized he was surprised that the answer to that was not yes. He always worked. But he hadn't last night.

"I looked up back columns of *Ask Rover* on the internet."

She blushed scarlet and took a swig of her beer. "Why would you do that?"

"Curious."

The blush deepened. "So, now you know. Nut job."

He frowned. "Are you kidding?"

"No. I never let anyone know I write that."

"But why?"

"All I ever wanted was to be normal. Not be laughed at. Not seen as eccentric or weird. I wanted to be popular and surrounded with friends. Instead, I had this thing, a strange ability to offer comfort to injured animals. My family used to tease me that I would have been burned at the stake if I'd lived in a different age.

"I can connect better with animals than people. It's

kind of like mind reading, only without words. I pick up on the animal's energy. My family thought I was strange. The kids I grew up with thought I was a woo-woo. I learned to keep all that stuff that is outside the norm pretty secret."

"So, when you write *Ask Rover,* are you picking up that energy thing, even from a distance?"

She scanned his face, saw he wasn't mocking her at all, but genuinely interested. "I'm not sure how much of it is picking up something from a distance, and how much of it is reading those letters really carefully."

"There are a lot of letters," he pointed out slowly, "from satisfied readers who are amazed by how applicable your advice is to their situation. How could you know that dog that had been shaking for a week had a broken tooth? How could you know that missing cat had gone in the appliance repairman's van?"

"They're just educated guesses…and a feeling. My weird little gift to the world. I hope you won't tell anyone it's me." She saw something in his face that looked stubborn. "It's for Luke's sake, too. So he can have a normal life here."

"What do you want for him?"

She sighed. "The things I couldn't achieve for myself. Popularity. A house full of friends. I don't want the fact that I do something different to make people laugh at him or judge him."

"You know, Nora, people make judgments. For instance, you know that dark period of history your family talked about, where they burned witches at the stake? They associated cats with witches, so they killed them, too.

"And when they killed the cats, the rat population

exploded. And rats carried bubonic plague. Before that was over, twenty-five million people were dead."

"I'm not sure I get what you're saying."

"People make judgments. Lots of those judgments they make are just plain wrong. Somehow, we all have to find our own truth."

He hesitated. "I liked *Ask Rover,* but I *loved* the crossed out rough drafts that I read beside your bed that night. Does any of that stuff ever make it past the final cut?"

"No. Never."

"I wish it did."

She laughed, self-deprecating. "I don't think the world is ready for *Ask Nora.*"

"That's where I think you are wrong. The world could use a little more Nora at her brilliant, funny, insightful best. The world could use a little more of the real thing."

"If I cry are you going to ask if I'm h-having an outburst?" she stammered.

"No," he said. "I'm going to do this."

And he did the most dangerous thing of all. He kissed her. He kissed her long and hard and deep. He kissed who she really was, not the tiny piece of herself that she chose to show the world.

"I shouldn't have done that," he said, pulling away from her.

"But why?" she asked, her eyes round with wonder and wanting.

He shrugged. "We should go."

"No. I feel as if, when you read the columns beside my bed, you uncovered part of my heart, whether

I wanted you to or not. That's not fair. Not unless you show me something of yours."

Brendan looked at Nora, and struggled with it. To show her who he really was. To crawl out from under the crushing weight of his guilt.

Her hand was suddenly on his. He could feel that energy of hers. Promising to lead him out of darkness toward the light, to roll the stone away from the entrance to the cave once and for all.

He still might have resisted.

If she had not proved one more time her intuition was uncanny. Nora said, "Tell me something about you. That's secret. Not just any secret. Your deepest secret."

He was torn completely, between not wanting to trust and for once letting his guard down. He had told her the world needed what was real about her. Could the same be said for him?

Nora knew things. She knew how to heal things. Look at Charlie. Just from being around her, under the same roof as her, the cat was pulling further away from dying every day.

So why had she asked this question? About secrets? The light in her eyes beckoned him in the direction he would not have chosen to go. The light in her eyes made him brave when he wanted to turn tail and run.

The long season of rain was over, and the sun had come out. Could his life be the same?

He took a deep breath. He told her something no one knew about him.

"I feel like a failure as an architect," he said.

"But you're very successful."

"I've never, ever, not even once stood in front of a

house I've completed, and felt pride. I've always felt like I missed something. So there you have it, my secret."

She studied him for a moment. And then she said, "That's not really the secret. It's just the first layer of it."

"What?"

"I'd be willing to bet my newly repaired iguana that that sense of not being good enough has a root somewhere."

"It's not like I feel *I'm* not good enough!" he protested, but her gaze called him out.

He realized he hadn't even told Becky all of it, but been vague about his beginnings. Wasn't that part of how he had failed her?

"My mom was never with my dad," he said, and had to clear his throat to go on. "She got pregnant, he didn't care. She never said it, but I suspect it was a case of unrequited love that culminated in a one-night stand. Who knows? Maybe she even used the pregnancy to try and trap him. But if she did, it backfired badly and left her young, uneducated and totally on her own. She was tired and bitter toward every man in the world except one, and that was me."

He shrugged, tried to laugh it off. "So there you have it, a genuine bastard."

There was something fierce in the way Nora was looking at him, as if she was seeing more, much more than he had intended for her to see.

"No," she said softly, "That's still just a layer of it. There's more. Tell me the rest."

This was her gift, then, unveiled. Her intuition calling to the broken place inside of him, coaxing it toward her light.

"We were poor," he heard himself saying. "There

seems to be this little trend where its popular to say you were poor, poor meaning you didn't go out to restaurants to eat, or you didn't get forty gifts under the Christmas tree, or you didn't have the cool designer label clothes like everyone else.

"People who were really poor? They don't brag about it."

There. That was enough. He'd told her he felt dissatisfaction with his work. That he was illegitimate, and that he'd grown up poor. Those were his secrets.

But not all of them. And she knew. He could feel her energy pulling the words from him. Or maybe they had just wanted out for so long, they could not be stopped now that they had started.

Like the tears, if he ever let them fall.

"We were the desperate kind of poor. My mom worked as a maid at a motel, and in private houses, in the mornings, and a waitress in the evenings. Every penny counted. Sometimes we didn't have food. Sometimes we got evicted because we couldn't pay the rent.

"I grew up knowing it would be up to me to make my mother's every sacrifice worthwhile. She managed somehow—I have no idea how, and probably would have rather she put food on the table—to squirrel away a little money for me to go to university. I worked three different jobs. I got scholarships. She lived long enough to see me graduate.

"Once she died, I moved across the country to Hansen. There was a small architectural firm here. I told myself it was for a job opportunity, but I think it was to leave all that behind.

"And then I met Becky. To tell you the truth, I couldn't believe a girl like her would look at a guy like me. She had grown up extremely well-to-do, the daughter of one of Hansen's old rich families. She was the swimming pool in the backyard, vacation home at Vale, finishing school in Switzerland kind of rich.

"I slammed the door on who I used to be," he said. "I was ashamed of it. I didn't tell anybody what I'd come from, let alone this rich girl who was crazy in love with me. I thought if she knew it all, she'd never say yes when I asked her to marry me."

"But didn't she ask?"

"Of course she asked. I think, at first, she thought it was part of my mystique that I didn't say much about my past."

He stopped himself. He was revealing way too much. No one cared about this stuff! But he looked at Nora, and he could see she cared. And he could see that the light in her eyes was not going to let him go, that he would not feel released until he told all of it.

"I felt I had to be worthy of Becky's faith in me. It wasn't enough to pay the bills every month. No. I had to succeed. I had to have all the trappings of success.

"When my boss decided to retire, we worked on my being able to buy the firm from him. And then, at the very same time, Becky's family home came up for sale. It was exactly the kind of house my mom had cleaned when I was a kid. She called them castles."

It was really time to stop. But it seemed as if that little boy who had promised his mother to buy her a castle was talking, and wasn't going to be quiet until he'd said it all!

"Sometimes if school was out for the day, or I was home sick, I got to go with her to those fancy houses.

"For a kid who was living in a two-room shack on

the wrong side of the tracks, that kind of house was a castle. A special room for dining? Four bathrooms? Hardwood floors and Turkish rugs and good art, and amazing chandeliers. The kids had bedrooms decorated in themes. In one house, the boy had a pirate room and the girl a princess room. I grew up on the phrase 'when my ship comes in.'"

It seemed to him he could stop right there. That he should stop right there. But it was as if a dam had broken inside him, as if something toxic was flowing out and with each word he spoke he felt cleaner and freer.

It was a free fall. He was free-falling into the light in her eyes, trusting that he could survive the landing. He took a deep breath. He was going to tell it all.

CHAPTER FOURTEEN

"Becky, quite sincerely, didn't care if we bought that house. But I cared. I felt responsible for keeping her in the style she was accustomed to.

"I was stretched way too thin. I didn't want her to go to work. I felt that would make me a failure, mean I couldn't provide for her. I started working all the time, trying to make it all happen.

"She was becoming increasingly frustrated, trying to get through to me. She was beginning to see what she had mistaken for mystique was my inability to connect with her. She told me I wasn't fun anymore. That nothing was fun anymore."

And here it was, finally, the worst of it. The part where he'd killed a good woman who had done nothing wrong but love him.

"I didn't want to have a baby," he said, his voice hoarse from talking too damn much. "I thought it would just be one more stress. I didn't know she was beyond caring what I wanted. She was trying to save *us,* and I didn't even know we were in trouble.

"She'd booked us a ski weekend. Was I happy about it? No. Annoyed. Why was she spending money on frivolous things?

"But she wanted us to do something fun. She wanted us to be romantic. She had some big news to tell me. News worth celebrating. News worth spending money on.

"The day we were supposed to go, something came up at work. It seemed urgent at the time. Now I wonder if I made it urgent so that she would know I was still annoyed about spending money and taking the weekend off from work. I told her to drive up to the ski hill without me, that I'd meet her there later that night.

"She was upset with me when she left. It started snowing hard while she was on the road. She lost control of the car, skidded off the road and hit a tree. She was killed instantly. I found out her big news, the reason for our celebration, from the coroner. That she was pregnant. The baby died, too. She had stopped taking the pills. I know because I found them in our medicine cabinet after. When I was wondering if there was anything strong enough in there to end my misery, to end the endless question I asked myself.

"*Was* the fact that she was upset with me a contributing factor in the accident? Probably. And if work was everything before that, it was even more after. Aside from pills in the cabinet, it was the only way I could stop the guilt. The only way.

"You know, a week before she died, she said to me, 'If I die first, I'll come back and let you know I'm all right.'

"And I didn't hear the love in that. I just said, 'You won't be all right. You'll be dead.'

"She never has," he heard himself whisper. "She never has let me know she's all right. Because she isn't. And it's my fault that she isn't.'"

He waited to feel sorry that he had told Nora, sorry that he had exposed so much of himself to her, sorry that just as he now had a better idea of who she was from reading her column, she had a better idea of who he was.

He waited for her to say the wrong thing.

That he should absolve himself, or that Becky *was* all right, or that it wasn't his fault at all.

But she said nothing.

Nora didn't even look at him; she was looking out over the mirrorlike, serene waters of the lake. Her eyes were pools of deep calm.

He had to let her know who he really was. He had to. It was a compulsion he couldn't stop.

"I've never cried for her," he said. "Not the night they told me. Not at her funeral. Not once."

He thought that would make Nora yank her hand from his. But instead, her grip tightened. She left her hand where it was, and her touch had energy in it. Acceptance. Strength. Healing.

Suddenly Brendan felt an enormous sensation of freedom. He was still free-falling. It was the same as flying.

He had expected telling her would bring him to his knees, unleash that bottled-up torrent of grief.

Instead, it had given him wings.

From that moment of trust, an unexpected bond grew between them, and together they flew into the sun of summer.

They simply could not get enough of each other. Luke was part of the magic, somehow. Over Nora's sputtering protests, Brendan taught him how to ride the motorcycle in her driveway. And then he taught her. Just as with poker, Luke had potential, she had none.

The three of them sneaked away in the heat of the day to go to the beach and swim and play in refreshing, icy waters. They rented kayaks, which were more fun than the cumbersome pedal boats. They took the three-legged dog for long hikes in the cool of the forest.

With Iggy recovering under the kitchen table, and Charlie on Luke's lap, they played poker in the evening. Brendan even let himself be talked into Scrabble.

Increasingly, Brendan and Nora found ways to be by themselves. He took her to enchanted places, like the waterfall that cascaded out of the rocks on the Hidden Valley Trail. They ate picnics, and lay out on the grass, sometimes staying late enough to watch the stars pop out in inky skies.

Village on the Lake seemed the least important thing Brendan had ever done.

Important was reading over Nora's latest draft for her column. Important was taking Luke and Charlie to visit Deedee.

It was on one of those occasions that Brendan decided it was time to address the Charlie issue.

"Maybe it's time for Charlie to come back here to Deedee's. He's getting better." Brendan and Luke were doing dishes. Nora and Deedee were outside on her porch in the rocking chairs, Charlie on the elderly woman's lap.

"No," Luke said, and cast a troubled look through the screen door. "No. He's not getting better. He's holding."

But given what Charlie had looked like just a short time ago, wasn't "holding" a miracle?

Brendan smiled to himself. He had gone from being the world's biggest cynic to believing in miracles.

That was a miracle in and of itself.

And wasn't that what love did? Create miracles? Turn the ordinary into the extraordinary?

Love.

Brendan contemplated that word, shocked by it.

But what else could make everything ordinary feel as though it was infused with light?

Even the hunger he felt for physical connection with Nora—holding her hand, brushing her hair away from her face, touching her lips—was a miracle of feeling alive, of feeling eager about life.

He took pleasure in showering her with little gifts: a gold necklace with two hearts entwined, a set of tiny silver hoop earrings. Girlie gifts that she was so uncomfortable accepting and then wore with such feminine pleasure.

He took her to public places, like Shakespeare on the Lake, in the natural amphitheatre at Lakeside Park. He had a barbecue at his house and introduced her to his friends and business associates. She still wouldn't let him tell anyone she was *Ask Rover,* though.

And it hit him right then, as she was standing at his kitchen sink, after all the guests had gone.

He went and put his arms around her, and breathed in deeply of her hair. She turned and caught him hard and they clung to each other.

And then she stretched up and he stretched down.

And their lips met right in the middle.

And he knew.

In the depth and passion and soul of that kiss, Brendan Grant knew the truth. He loved her. And he put her slightly away from him and he saw the truth shining in her. She loved him, too.

"I want to stay the night," she whispered.

But he knew that would never work for him. And it would never really work for her, either.

What he was feeling for Nora wasn't a one-night-stand kind of thing.

There would be people who said it was too soon, and that he couldn't possibly know, and that he was rushing things.

But it wasn't too soon. When he counted back the days, he realized he had known her for six weeks. Somehow they had become the best six weeks of his life. He did know, and in this life, where things could turn around so quickly, was there ever a moment to waste?

He had never in his whole life so badly wanted to do something right. He put her away from him. "You need to go home."

She looked wounded, and he touched her swollen bottom lip with his thumb, nearly caved in with yearning. Gave in to the desire to kiss her one more time.

This time when they pulled away they were both panting. His shirt was tugged out of his slacks where her hands had crept under it, splayed themselves across his flesh with an urgent wanting.

He broke away from her. "Go home."

Tomorrow he would go out to Nora's Ark with his motorcycle and pick her up. He would have the most gorgeous ring he could find in Hansen in his pocket. He would have champagne and strawberries, and he'd carry them to a viewpoint in the mountains where he could show her the whole world.

And then he'd ask her to marry him.

But for now? She had to go home before he did something that disrespected her and the enormous love he felt for her.

"Go home," he said gruffly.

He lay awake for a long time that night, thinking that soon his bed would not be empty. That soon his life would not be empty. He lay awake thinking of how he would propose. The exact words he would say.

He lay awake picturing the light that would come on in her when he went down on bended knee in front of her....

When he finally slept, he dreamed.

Becky had finally come to him. She was in a meadow filled with brown-eyed, wild sunflowers. She was in long skirt, and she was dancing, just like Nora had been dancing that day with the bunny. There was a blanket spread out in the grass, and a baby was sitting on it, his pudgy fist full of wildflowers.

And Becky was holding something, too, just like Nora had been holding Valentine.

Her face shining with joy, Becky whispered, "We're all right. Can't you see that we're all right? All of us."

And he moved closer to her, wanting to see her, wanting desperately to tell her how sorry he was for not knowing what he had when he had it. He moved toward her, needing to see the baby on the blanket and the baby she was holding.

But then he stopped short.

Because it wasn't a baby she was holding so tenderly to her bosom.

It was Charlie.

Brendan woke covered in sweat, to the sound of the

ringing phone. He knew before he picked it up exactly what had happened. He actually considered not answering.

All this time he had been free-falling. Now he considered the possibility he was not going to survive the landing.

He picked up the phone. As he had known, it was Luke.

"Charlie's gone," he said.

Brendan almost said, "I know," but he didn't.

"You don't have to come," Luke said.

But he did. He had to go and be with them.

"I'll be there in a few minutes."

When he arrived, Luke was holding Charlie, with Nora sitting beside him, holding his hand.

She gave Brendan a beseeching look that said, *Take this pain away,* and he felt all the angry impotence of not being able to.

"I'll go out and dig a hole," he offered.

"No, I'm taking him to Deedee's." Luke said. "I made a box for him." He got up, carrying the lifeless cat, cuddling him against his narrow chest.

He brought back a box clumsily made of wood, the corners painstakingly sanded. It had a picture of Charlie lacquered onto the lid. Beneath the picture Luke had carved Charlie's name.

It was not a box that had been whipped up in the less than an hour since Charlie had died.

Nora lost control when she saw it.

But Luke didn't. He opened it up and laid the cat on the soft white towel inside. He put on the lid, and turned to Brendan, who felt as if his control was an elastic band being stretched thinner and thinner.

All this time, while he'd been having fun and romancing Nora and convincing himself love could fix everything and that the cat was going to get better, Luke had been getting ready for a different ending. A realistic one.

"We need to take him to Deedee's," Luke said. "I'll call her and let her know we're coming."

Considering how Deedee had had issues around being there when the cat died, Brendan wasn't so sure that was a good idea.

"We'll bury him there," Luke stated, as if it was all decided. Brendan might have suggested they bury the cat here, but he was terrified if he opened his mouth all that would come out would be a wail of fury and impotence.

Silently, with Nora beside him crying helplessly, Luke in the back, quiet and pale, with the cat in the box on his lap, Brendan drove them to Deedee's.

She was waiting, dressed in black. Luke gave her the box, and she stared at it, ran her fingers over the carving of the cat's name, bent and kissed the picture. And then they all followed her out to the yard.

Brendan saw that while he'd been laughing, and packing picnics and buying trinkets, and watching stars come out, Luke had not just been bringing back a neglected flower bed. He'd been preparing a resting place.

The bed that had been such a mess was now fully weeded. Underneath a rosebush, Luke had dug a square hole. It had been there for a while; white rose petals had fallen inside.

Luke took the box from a quietly weeping Deedee and gently laid it in. A shovel was set unobtrusively against the fence, and he went and got it and began to fill the hole.

Deedee wailed.

It reminded Brendan of how she had sounded when they had buried Becky, that day he had stood there and not shed a tear.

Nora put her arm around those thin, caved-in shoulders of Becky's grandmother.

"Let's go in," she said. "I'll make you a cup of tea." They moved toward the house. Brendan stayed outside with Luke.

"I'll do it," Brendan offered, moving to take the shovel from him.

Luke's grip on it tightened. "No," he said, his voice fierce and strong and determined. "I have to finish it. I'm making a mend."

Brendan shoved his hands into his pockets and rocked back on his heels. He was so aware of his own stupidity. Over the last while, his guard had come down. He had let himself hope that everything could be all right.

In a world where it never was.

He listened to the steady thump of dirt hitting the top of that painstakingly crafted wooden box. He thought of Charlie inside, still and silent. Had he actually thought the cat was going to live?

Dead was dead.

He thought of how powerless he had been to stop anything.

Even falling in love, when that was what he knew he could not do. He knew he could not do it, because the light had broken through the cracks in his cave, undermined the strength of the walls.

Everything felt as if it was shattering around him.

Luke glanced up. "Are you okay?"

The youth was watching him way too closely, with that look so much like his aunt's. You could hide nothing from these two; they *saw* you, right to your soul.

Brendan pinched the bridge of his nose. He swallowed hard. He tried to breathe, and when none of that worked, he spun on his heel and walked away.

"Go home," Brendan had said to her. His face had been ablaze with love and with promise for a future.

But that had been before Charlie died.

She tried to think if he had said a single word at that solemn, sad little ceremony in Deedee's backyard.

Nora didn't think he had. And then he had left without saying goodbye.

There was no way she could have known that those last words to her had stopped short of the future. What he must have meant was go home, go away, it's over.

Those magical days ended as quickly as they had begun. Just like that, the phone stopped ringing, the motorcycle stopped appearing in the yard.

What had changed? Charlie had died. That meant they needed him more, not less. At first, Nora felt furious with Brendan for letting them down.

This was when Luke needed to know he could count on someone else.

She needed to know that.

She had phoned and left Brendan a message. Had practically begged him to be there for her nephew. Had hoped he would hear her own unspoken need.

But he had not come.

Like a lovesick teenager, she had waited by her

phone for him to call and offer some explanation, but no call came because there was no explanation.

Trying to protect Luke, she went through the motions. She even managed to rise above her own pain to think of Deedee.

She was bringing Deedee a casserole as Brendan was leaving. He saw her and searched for a way to escape. There was none.

He looked awful, as if he wasn't eating or sleeping. There were dark circles under his eyes and it made her want to go to him, wrap her arms around him and hold him.

But he was glaring at her, and then he crossed his arms over his chest, waiting, his face a mask. Holding him would be like trying to hold a porcupine.

She had to fight such weak impulses in herself, anyway. He had broken her heart. He had broken Luke's heart. And she wanted to comfort him?

He needed to be brought to task, and she was just the woman to do it!

She didn't bother with the niceties. She didn't say hello, or ask where he'd been or why he hadn't called.

She said to him, her voice low with fury at his betrayal of her and her nephew, "What are you hiding from?"

He smiled a tight, horrible, icy smile. "I don't know what you mean."

"You made a mistake," she said. "But not the one you think."

"Excuse me?"

"You think the mistake was letting Becky drive that night. But you had started to make the mistake long before that."

CHAPTER FIFTEEN

"WHAT ARE YOU talking about?" Brendan said.

She could hear the coolness in his voice, but he wasn't shutting her down or shutting her up. He was the one who, over the summer, had given her a voice, and now he would just have to live with the consequences of that.

"She wanted to love you. While you were busy trying to impress her with someone you weren't, she wanted to love you. That's why she got pregnant. She sensed you pulling further and further away. She wanted you back."

"You can't know that."

"I can."

"Stop it. You don't know anything about me."

"I know you're hiding. From pain. From life. From love."

For one full minute she held her breath. He was hearing her. He was leaning toward her. He wanted it all: that place of refuge, the home, the love.

He wanted it all, and she could tell the exact moment he remembered the price. His face closed.

"That's rich," he said coldly. "This from the woman who never tells anyone who she really is?"

And then he turned and walked away.

The fury dissipated a bit that night as she contemplated that. She had taken a chance through these long days of summer. She had shown him who she really was. She had been zany and carefree, and she had let her intuition out.

Though maybe never quite so much as she had on Deedee's front steps this afternoon.

And she thought he had liked who she really was. Maybe even loved it.

But then, softly, it came to her. The point wasn't really what he liked or didn't like. The point was that *she* had liked it! She had loved it. She had loved living in that place of freedom, without masks.

As long as she was hiding any part of who she really was, she recognized she would never have power.

She recognized something Brendan Grant might not have known.

You could protect yourself by being alone. But that required nothing of you. Life required something. And that was that you become who you really were, under any circumstance.

Life went on. Nora had a boy to raise. School was starting again soon. He needed school supplies and clothes. She needed to get on with the business of living.

She had even stopped writing *Ask Rover,* and now was very aware she needed to start again.

So on that first day of school, after Luke had gotten on the bus, Nora went through the piles of letters she'd received, and she didn't pick a single easy one. She didn't pick one that said, "Sambo will not stop pooping on the floor," or "Buffy attacks the mailman."

She picked one that said, "My dog is sick. Do I spend the money to make him well, or do I give up?" She picked one that said, "My kids want a dog so badly, but I'm a single mom and I feel overwhelmed already." She picked one that said, "I work long hours and am never home. Is this fair to my dog?"

She picked them, and with Iggy, the most lovable iguana ever born, snoozing on top of her feet, she answered them, from the place deep in her heart that had always whispered to her.

That place that other people didn't always understand, because it was so pure and uncorrupted.

It was a place of untainted instinct and uncontaminated intuition, and it was who she had always been and who she wasn't going to be afraid to be anymore.

And when she was done answering them, she changed her byline. It said *"Ask Rover, by Nora Anderson."*

When she was finished, she went out and visited with her volunteers, telling them there would be a meeting soon, and to please bring ideas about better organizing the jobs and having systems in place for dealing with difficult situations like Iggy.

When Luke came in, she was busy making cookies for him.

"How was your first day at school?"

"It was okay."

But she could tell it wasn't. "What happened?"

"Gerry wanted another fifty bucks."

"I'm calling his parents! This is outrageous. I should have called them—"

Luke put his hand on her shoulder. She realized she was looking up at him, and that he had grown a lot over the summer.

"I went to the police station at lunch hour. I told them the truth. I told them I stole the bike."

Her mouth fell open. He had grown a lot in every way.

"Did you tell them that boy is extorting money from you?" she sputtered.

"No," he said. "I just took away the reason he could extort money from me."

"I'm going to call his parents."

"No," he said, "you're not. I'm not giving it one more ounce of energy. It's finished."

"Are you going to be charged? For stealing the bicycle?" She could feel that old, desperate worry clawing at her. That she was doing it all wrong.

That she had let Brendan into their lives, trusted him, and now Luke was dealing with the loss of a male he had looked up to. And he was trying to navigate difficult situations on his own. Why had he gone to the police? He should have talked it over with her! What if he was charged?

"The sergeant I talked to said it was unlikely I would be charged."

Something was different about Luke since Charlie had died. Instead of tearing him down, it was as if the death of the cat had helped him come into his own, and in such a genuine way that not seeing Brendan did not seem to be bothering him.

Luke had used the word *energy* so easily a moment ago, and suddenly, just like that, she could see his, and feel it.

Just like that, she knew who her nephew was, and who he would always be. She knew she had not done things wrong, after all.

Except maybe for one thing.

She realized he could handle an adult discussion. "I'm sorry about Brendan," she said. "I'm sorry that I let you become attached to him, and that he doesn't come around anymore."

When Luke looked at her, she realized he did so with eyes that were wise, the eyes of an old soul.

She knew in that second it was never going to be what she had hoped for him.

He was never going to be the popular kid, the one who laughed lots and was at the heart of all the fun.

It was never going to be like that.

It was going to be better.

He was introspective. Somber. Strong. Intuitive.

"Brendan not coming here is not about me," Luke said slowly. "It's not about you, either."

"What's it about?" she whispered.

"It's about hope. He hoped he didn't have to hurt anymore. When Charlie died, it reminded him he did. He was crying when he left Deedee's that day we buried Charlie."

Nora felt herself go very still. "Brendan was crying?"

"He didn't want me to see, but I did."

The words hit her like hammer blows. She'd been making it all about her. While she'd been breaking free, Brendan had been building up the walls of his prison.

And she had let him. She had accepted his strength. Accepted the fact that he wanted to be responsible for her and for the whole world. She had leaned on that, and come to depend on it.

She'd let him believe he was in charge of the whole world. She had relished that sense of being looked after!

And then Charlie had died, reminding him that protecting everyone and everything was a hopeless job. One he could not do. He withdrew, nursing the sense of failure and powerlessness that he'd had to face for the first time when his wife died.

"How'd you get to be so smart?" Nora asked Luke softly.

He snorted and was just a fifteen-year-old boy again, not a wise sage who had been born again and again and again.

"If you think I'm so smart," he said, snatching a still warm cookie from the sheet, "tell my math teacher."

Brendan stared down at the plan. It was after ten and he was still in the office. One of the fluorescent lights had started flickering a few hours ago, and now it felt as if his headache was flickering in unison with it.

He heard a door open somewhere in the building and ignored it. Janitorial staff.

He scowled at the plan, dissatisfied.

"You look happy."

He stiffened at the sound of her voice, straightened and glanced at the door. She was there. Her ginger hair caught the light and looked like a flame around her head. Her eyes were deep and soulful, and filled him with a sense of regret for the choice he had made.

To walk away. It was as if he had walked away from a pool of water beckoning a man who had crossed the desert.

But of course, he had walked away because he understood the nature of a mirage.

Even though he turned from her swiftly, masked that reaction of pleasure at seeing her, she did not go away.

She came and stood beside him, so close he could smell that cinnamon-and-citrus smell that was hers and hers alone.

He inhaled it as if it were that pool of water and he was that man dying of thirst.

"That's a pretty house," she said, looking down at the plan.

He ordered himself not to be drawn into discussion. To fold up his plan, fold his arms over his chest and drive her away.

But a man, any man, was only so strong.

And loneliness had made Brendan weak. He would just drink in her scent and her presence for a while longer. A few minutes.

"The house is okay," he said.

"Really? What don't you like about it?"

It's not what he didn't like about it. It was what he didn't like about *him*. He used to focus only on the house, and the function of it. He had never wondered about the lives that would be lived inside.

"It's a pretty house, for a lovely young couple."

"And?" she prodded.

"They've never known a moment's agony over anything."

"And?"

"And I hope they never do."

"But?"

"But I doubt it, because life doesn't go that way."

"That's right, it doesn't," she said, ever so gently, just as if he hadn't let her down. As if he hadn't let Luke down.

"That little baby they loved so much, that they were

cooing over and bouncing up and down on their knee while they sat across from me in my office?"

"What about the baby?"

"It will probably take them through the fires of hell one day. It could get sick, or experiment with drugs, or get bullied at school."

"That's what love does," she said, as if she was agreeing with him. "It leaves you wide-open to all kinds of pain."

"And this pretty little house wouldn't help any of that. It won't help it and it won't stop it."

"No," she agreed, "it won't. Because you don't have that kind of power."

"We're not talking about me."

"Yes, Brendan, we are—the one who builds houses, the one who chose to build houses because he always longed for a home. The one who wanted so badly for that home to protect all who enter there."

"Why are you here?"

"I've come to take you home. Not to a house. I've come to take you home to my heart."

"See?" he said with a snort of pure derision, doing what needed to be done, trying to wound her, trying to drive her away. "They were all right about you. You are a pure flake."

"Yes," she said sweetly. "Yes, I am. But I'm your flake."

"You're not my flake. I don't need a flake."

"You do. Desperately."

"What could you possibly know about my need?"

"Everything."

He scowled.

"I'm intuitive, remember? A healer. I know what you need."

Don't even ask her, he ordered himself. "What do I need?" he asked, masking his desperation with a sneer.

"You took a chance," she said. "You loved. And you felt as if it made you weak instead of strong."

Accurate, but not spookily so. He kept his arms folded over his chest, his expression cynical.

"You need a place," she said softly, "where you can put away your armor."

His mouth fell open. He clamped it shut.

"You need a place where you don't always have to be the strong one. Where it's okay to fall when the parachute doesn't open."

Now it was getting spooky.

"Where someone is going to be there to catch you."

"It sounds like a good way to get squashed like a bug on a windshield," he said.

"That's exactly how I'd want to go."

"Like a bug on a windshield?" he said cynically.

"In the service of love," she said simply. "You'll need a strong woman, Brendan. A relationship not based in her need and you providing, but based in true equality.

"Based in the recognition that, on some days, you'll hold her up, and other days, made strong by your love when she needed it most, she will hold you up.

"I'm that woman."

She sounded absolutely certain.

"I love you," Nora said with quiet composure. "And I'm never stopping. Not if it hurts me. Not if you won't let me. I'm still going to love you. I'm going to be wide open, and if it brings pain, I'm ready to accept that as part of the price of living fully, not tucked away in a cave somewhere."

He knew he had never said a single word about a cave to her. Never.

"So," she finished, her courage shining from her eyes, enough courage for both of them, "you might as well come along for the ride."

"You're crazy."

"I know," she said. "Ask Rover."

He fought the impulse to smile, but he had to fight hard.

And then she did the one thing he could not fight. The one thing that stole what remained of his strength.

She moved in close to him. She slipped her hand behind his neck and pulled his face to hers. She searched his eyes and found what she wanted there, because she smiled.

He recognized it instantly, identical to that very first smile he had seen from her when he had turned over a pile of rags in a paddock on a rainy night. It was a smile that knew exactly who he was and welcomed him.

And then she kissed him.

And he, weakened, kissed her back.

Only, the strangest thing happened. As her lips laid claim on him, his surrender became not weakness, but strength.

It felt as if she had somehow captured every one of those tears he had cried after that damn cat had died. She had captured them, and now she poured them back into his emptiness.

The energy washed off of her, and into him. Brendan could feel the life flowing back into his body, like water over parched earth.

He could feel himself opening instead of closing.

He could feel himself becoming everything he was ever meant to be, and then more. More than he had ever hoped he could be.

He lifted her slight body to him, and cradled her against his chest.

This was his home. This was what he had struggled to capture with his building designs his whole life, and this was why he had always had a sense of failure.

Because the most essential thing had been missing. Home was not a building. It was the spirit that filled it.

EPILOGUE

BRENDAN SAT BESIDE Nora in the crowded Hansen High School auditorium. They had endured the speeches, and with each one being duller and longer than the last, he wished Nora, Hansen's most celebrated citizen, had accepted the invitation to speak.

Once she had changed her column to *Ask Nora,* amazing things had begun to happen. The internet blog had been a sensation. A book of her columns and blogs had followed, and it had been on the bestseller list for eight straight months. And then she'd been approached to do a radio show.

So, as Hansen's most celebrated citizen, Nora had been asked to give the commencement address at the high school graduation.

But she had said no—it was Luke's day, not hers. Which had been a relief to Brendan, because what if the baby decided to come midspeech, and they had to leave fast?

They had long since sold Brendan's house on "the Hill."

When the acreage next to Nora's became available, they had purchased it. They had worked on the plan for the new house together. It wasn't the biggest house he'd ever built, and it certainly wasn't the grandest.

And yet it was filled with the secret that made a house something beyond a collection of sticks and stones. It was filled to the rafters with laughter and companionship and healing. Somehow Lafayette had made it in there, and so had Iggy. And the dog with three legs, who came when they called "Long" or "John" or "Silver." There was a descendant of Valentine named Cupid, and Ranger, and a small pasture that contained two sheep, Bo and Peep, and a burro named Burrito.

Nora's property had been sold at cost to Nora's Ark, now registered as a charity, with a board of directors and an army of volunteers running it. Though she still crossed the fence when a sick animal arrived in the middle of the night, even if she had not been called. She always knew a new animal had arrived, always knew when her special gifts were needed.

And more often than not, Luke was right beside her.

As each name was read out, a graduate walked across the stage.

It occurred to Brendan you could tell a lot about these kids from the way they crossed that stage. You could tell if they were shy. Or outgoing. Or plain old trouble. You could tell by the way they walked if they were going to be ambitious or complacent, if they were going to take the world by storm or just ride a lazy current through it.

"Ohh," Nora sighed quietly beside him.

He turned and looked at her, ready if need be to disrupt the ceremony, to pick up his wife, just the way he had picked her up all those years ago, and race for the door.

But she gave him a reassuring smile and placed his hand on the swell of her stomach. The baby kicked at his palm, as if impatient to make its entrance into the world. One day he or she would be crossing this stage. What would the way he or she walked say about all of them who had helped raise this child?

Brendan had deliberately chosen aisle seats. Now he glanced back toward the door, making sure the way was clear, judging how long it would take him to reach it with Nora in his arms.

But Nora and Luke had both assured him today was not the day, and for a reason Brendan still could not decipher, they knew these things. But still, he needed to be prepared. They had their way, he had his.

"Luke Caviletti."

Brendan turned his attention fully to the stage.

He had offered Luke his name a year ago, but Luke had said no. He didn't need the name to feel he was a valued part of the family. He had wanted to carry his father's name into the future.

As he came across the stage, that was what Luke looked like, a beam of pure light heading for the future. Brendan hadn't expected to feel anything at this graduation except too warm and bored, so his sudden emotion took him by surprise. He didn't try to pinch his nose, or swallow, or breathe it away. He just let it come, grateful to feel, to be alive, to have this moment of glorious pride and emotion.

He had helped raise this young man, and through the tears that blurred his vision, he could see every single thing about him.

Out of the corner of his eye, he saw the tears of joy and pride sliding down Nora's face, also. Brendan moved his palm from her stomach, took her hand in his and squeezed ever so gently.

Luke had never become what Nora had dreamed of—the popular kid who filled up their house with his friends and noise and activity.

What he had become was so much better.

He had become himself: strong, quiet, calm, certain in the gift he had to give the world. Neither Nora nor Brendan had been surprised when this young man, once terrified of hospitals, told them he would use the money Deedee had left him to become a doctor.

Luke had that same incredible quality that Nora had, the one that made people call her a healer. Only in him, it was more intense, more defined, something tangible in the air around him.

When Brendan had first met Nora, she had just lost her sister. And her fiancé. And yet despite that, she had never hesitated to be of service. She had been there for her nephew. She had provided a place of refuge for the lost and wounded of God's creatures.

Luke had that same ability to rise above what had hurt him, and use his life experience in service. He would make an unbelievable doctor.

And Brendan was learning from both of them. Village on the Lake was completed. People had moved in. They loved it there. It had won a Most Livable Community award. But now he understood exactly why all those early plans had always left him dissatisfied.

He had tried to use his work to shore up a wounded ego in service to nothing more than himself.

There was no satisfaction in that, no matter how many awards you won.

But today a different plan took center stage. He was designing a housing complex for single parents of limited income. It wasn't utilitarian or bare bones. It was beautiful.

Nora had been right. He had embraced the science of architecture with his mind, but his heart had always known it would lead him where he was meant to be. For what he really wanted was to create *home*.

Not just for him and Nora, for the baby and Luke.

No, for those afraid to dream. For those who had nothing to hope for. For those who had been abandoned, who had been crushed and were afraid.

The housing complex Mary Grant Court bore the name of his mother. Brendan loved it. He woke up every day filled with energy, excited to go to work, happy in a way he had not even known it was possible for a man to be happy.

Energy was really not the mystery he had once thought it was. You could see its power in a thunderstorm. It was energy harnessed when you turned on a light. Energy ran through each amazing thing on the planet Earth, all those invisible particles of matter moving so fast they gave the illusion of being solid.

But there was a place where energy transformed. And that place was the great mystery. It didn't remove pain; it married it. It didn't alter life experience; it merged with it. It fused with all things and became something larger than itself.

And that was when it became more than energy.

Then it became a force that could turn a pile of lumber and a load of concrete into that most blessed of places, a home.

Then it became the force that could heal the broken.

Then it became the force that could raise the dead.

Many people called it many things.

Brendan called it love.

And knew that he was the most blessed of men that he had been allowed to know it.

* * * * *

THE MAN BEHIND
THE PINSTRIPES

BY
MELISSA McCLONE

With a degree in mechanical engineering from Stanford University, the last thing **Melissa McClone** ever thought she would be doing was writing romance novels. But analysing engines for a major US airline just couldn't compete with her 'happily-ever-afters'. When she isn't writing, caring for her three young children or doing laundry, Melissa loves to curl up on the couch with a cup of tea, her cats and a good book. She enjoys watching home decorating shows to get ideas for her house—a 1939 cottage that is *slowly* being renovated. Melissa lives in Lake Oswego, Oregon, with her own real-life hero husband, two daughters, a son, two lovable but oh-so-spoiled indoor cats and a no-longer-stray outdoor kitty that has decided to call the garage home.

Melissa loves to hear from her readers. You can write to her at PO Box 63, Lake Oswego, OR 97034, USA, or contact her via her website: www.melissamcclone.com.

To Jan Herinckx for introducing us to
Chaos and the world of dog-showing!

Special thanks to: Terri Reed, Jennifer Shirk,
Jennifer Short. And the Immersion Crew: Margie
Lawson, Elizabeth Cockle and Lori Freeland.

CHAPTER ONE

THE INCESSANT BARKING from the backyard of his family's palatial estate confirmed Caleb Fairchild's fear. His grandmother had gone to the dogs.

Cursing under his breath, he pressed the doorbell.

A symphony of chimes filled the air, drowning out the irritating barks. Forget Mozart. Forget Bach. Only a commissioned piece from a respected New York composer would do for Gertrude Fairchild, his grandmother who had founded a billion-dollar skin care company with his late grandfather in Boise, Idaho.

Caleb was here to put an end to her frivolous infatuation with man's best friend. It was the only way to keep Fair Face, the family company, successful and profitable.

The front door opened, greeting him with a blast of cold air and a whiff of his grandmother's floral scent perfume.

Grams.

Short white curls bounced every which way. She looked fifty-seven not seventy-seven, thanks to decades of using her own skin care products.

"Caleb! I saw your car on the security camera so told Mrs. Harrison I would answer the door." The words rushed from Grams's mouth faster than lobster tails disappeared from the buffet table at the country club. "What are you doing here? Your assistant said you didn't have any free time this week. That's why I mailed you the dog care prototypes."

He hadn't expected Grams to be so excited by his visit. He kissed her cheek. "I'm never too busy for you."

Her cornflower blue eyes danced with laughter. "This is such a lovely surprise."

Sweat trickled down his back. Too bad he couldn't blame the perspiration on the warm June day.

He adjusted his yellow tie then smoothed his suit jacket. But no matter how professional he looked, she wasn't going to like what he had to say. "I'm not here as your grandson. I need to speak with you as Fair Face's CEO."

"Oh, sweetheart." The warmth in her voice added to his discomfort. "I raised you. You'll always be my grandson first."

Her words hit him like a sucker-punch. He owed Grams... everything.

She opened the door wider. "Come in."

"Nice sari," he said.

Grams struck a pose. "Just something I had in my closet."

He entered the foyer. "Better add Bollywood to your bucket list."

"Already have." She closed the door. "Let's go out on the patio and chat."

Chat, not speak or discuss or talk. Not good.

Caleb glanced around. Something was...off.

Museum-worthy works of art hung in the same places. The squeaky dog toys and ravaged stuffed animals on the shiny hardwood floor were new. But the one display he expected to see, what he wanted to see, what he longed to see was missing from its usual spot.

His throat tightened. "Where are the—"

"In the living room."

Caleb walked around the corner and saw the three-foot U.S. Navy aircraft carrier replicas showcased on a brand-new wooden display case. He touched the deck of the USS *Ronald Reagan*.

Familiar. Soothing. Home.

"I've been making some changes around here," Grams said

from behind him. "I thought they deserved a nicer place than the foyer."

He faced her. "Gramps would like this."

"That's what I thought, too. Have you eaten lunch?"

"I grabbed something on my way over."

"Then you need dessert. I have cake. Made it myself." She touched Caleb's arm with her thin, vein-covered hand. "Carrot, not chocolate, but still tasty."

Grams always felt the urge to feed him. He knew she wouldn't give up until he agreed to have a bite to eat. "I'll have something before I leave."

A satisfied smile graced her glossed lips.

At least one of them was happy.

Back in the foyer, he kicked a tennis ball with his foot. "It's a miracle you don't break a hip with all these dog toys laying around."

"I might be old, but I'm still spry." His grandmother's gaze softened. She placed her hand over her heart. "Heavens. Every time I see you, you remind me more and more of your father. God rest his soul."

Caleb's stomach churned as if he'd eaten one too many spicy Buffalo wings. He strived hard to be nothing like his feckless father. A man who'd wanted nothing to do with Fair Face. A man who'd blown through money like a hedge fund manager's mistress. A man who'd died in a fiery speedboat crash off the Cote d'Azur with his girlfriend du jour.

Grams' gaze ran the length of Caleb. She clucked her tongue. "But you've got to stop dressing like a high-class mortician."

"Not this again." Caleb raised his chin, undaunted, and followed her out of the foyer. "You'd have me dress like a rugged, action-adventure movie star. A shirtless one, given the pictures you share on Facebook."

They walked by the dining room where two elaborate chandeliers hung above a hand-carved mahogany table that sat twenty.

"You're a handsome man," Grams said. "Show off your assets."

"I'm the CEO. I have a professional image to maintain."

"There's no corporate policy that says your hair can't touch your collar."

"The cut suits my position."

"Your *suits* are a whole other matter." She pointed at his chest. "Your tie is too understated. Red screams power. We'll go shopping. Girls these days are looking for the whole package. That includes having stylish hair and being a snazzy dresser."

And not taking your grandmother's fashion advice.

They walked into the kitchen. A basket of fruit and a covered cake stand sat on the marble counter. Something simmered on the stove. The scent of basil filled the air. Normal, everyday things, but this visit home felt anything but normal.

"Women only care about the balance in my bank account," he said.

"Some. Not all." She stopped, squeezed his hand, the way she'd done for as long as Caleb remembered. Her tender touch and her warm hugs had seen him through death, heartbreak and everyday life. "You'll find a woman who cares only about you."

Difficult to do when he wasn't looking, but he wasn't telling Grams that today. One piece of bad news a day met her quota. "I like being single."

"You must have one-night stands or friends with benefits."

He flinched. "You're spending too much time on Facebook."

A disturbing realization formed in his mind. Discussing sex might be easier than talking to Grams about her dog skin care products.

She placed her hands on her hips. "I would like great grandchildren one of these years while I can still get on the floor and play with them. Why do you think I created that line of organic baby products?"

"Everyone at the company knows you want great grandchildren."

"What's a woman to do?" She put her palms up. Gold bracelets clinked against each other. "You and your sister are in no rush to give me grandbabies while I'm still breathing."

"Can you imagine Courtney as a mom?"

"She has some growing up to do," Grams admitted, but without any accusation or disappointment. She walked into the family room with its leather couches, huge television and enough books on the floor-to-ceiling bookshelves to start a library. "Though I give you credit for at least proposing to that money-grubbing floozy, Cash-andra."

Unwelcome memories flooded him. His heart cried foul. Cheat. Sucker. "Cassandra."

The woman had introduced herself to him at a benefit dinner. Smart and sexy as hell, Cassandra knew what buttons to push to become the center of his universe. She'd made him feel more like a warrior than a businessman. Marriage hadn't been on his radar screen, but when she gave him an ultimatum, he'd played right into her hand with a romantic proposal and a stunning three-carat engagement ring only to find out everything about her and their relationship had been a scam, a ruse, a lie.

"Cash-andra fits." Grams held up three fingers. "Refusing to sign the agreed-upon prenup. Two-timing you. Hiring a divorce attorney before saying I do. No wonder you're afraid to date."

He squared his shoulders. "I'm not afraid."

Not afraid of Cassandra.

Not afraid of any woman.

But he was…cautious.

After Cassandra wouldn't sign the prenup, he'd called off the wedding and broken up with her. She'd begged him for a second chance, and he'd been tempted to reconcile, until a private investigator proved the woman was a gold digger in the same league as his own mother.

Grams waved a hand in the air, as if she could brush aside bad things in the world. Light reflected off her three diamond rings, anniversary presents from his grandfather. "I shouldn't have mentioned the Jezebel."

At least Caleb had gotten away relatively unscathed except for a bruised ego and broken heart. Unlike his father who'd wound up with two kids he'd never wanted.

She exited the house through the family room's French doors.

Caleb followed her outside to see new furniture—a large gleaming, teak table surrounded matching wood chairs, a hammock and padded loungers.

The sun beat down. He pulled out a chair for his grandmother, who sat. "It's hot. Let me put up the umbrella."

Grams picked up a black rectangular remote from the table. "I've got it."

She pressed a button.

A cantilevered umbrella opened, covering them in shade.

He joined her at the table.

"What do you think about the dog products?" Gertie asked.

No birds chirped. Even the crickets seemed to be napping. The only thing he heard was an occasional bark and his grandfather's voice.

Do what must be done. For Fair Face. For your grandmother.

Caleb would rather be back in his office dealing with end-of-quarter results. Who was he kidding? He'd rather be anywhere else right now.

"Interesting prototypes," he said. "Appealing fragrance and texture."

Gertie whistled. "Wait until you see them in action."

Dogs ran full speed from around the corner. A blur of gray, brown and black. The three animals stopped at Grams's feet, mouths panting and tails wagging.

"Feel how soft they are." Pride filled her voice as if the dogs were as much a part of her gene pool as Caleb was.

He rested his hands on the table, not about to touch one of her animals. "Most fur is soft if a dog is clean."

"Not Dozer's." She scooped up the little brown dog, whose right eye had been sewn shut. Not one of her expensive show dogs. A rescue or foster. "His hair was bristly and dry with flakes."

"Doggy dandruff?"

"Allergies. Animals have sensitivities like humans. That's why companies need to use natural and organic ingredients. No nasty chemicals or additives. Look at Dozer now." She stared at the dog with the same love and acceptance she'd always given Courtney and him. Even before their father had dumped them here after their mother ran off with her personal trainer. "That's why I developed Fair Face's new line of animal products."

Ignoring the gray dog brushing against his leg, Caleb held up his hands to stop her. "Fair Face doesn't manufacture animal products."

Grams's grin didn't falter. "Not yet, but you will. I've tested the formulas on my consultant and myself. We've used them on my dogs."

"I didn't know you hired a consultant."

"Her name is Becca. You'll love her."

Caleb doubted that. Most consultants were only looking for a big payday. He'd have to check this Becca's qualifications. "You realize Fair Face is a skin care company. Human skin."

"Skin or fur. Two legs or four. Change…expansion is important if a company wants to remain relevant."

"Not in this case." He needed to be careful not to hurt Grams's feelings. "Our resources are tied up with the launch of the organic baby care line. This isn't the time to expose ourselves to more risk."

Lines tightened around her mouth. "Your grandfather built Fair Face by taking risks. Sometimes you have to put yourself out on a limb."

"Limbs break. I have one thousand one hundred thirty-three employees who count on me to make sure they receive paychecks."

"What I'm asking you to do is not risky. The formulas are

ready to go into production. Put together a pilot sales program and we're all set."

"It's not that simple, Grams. Fair Face is a multinational company. We have extra product testing and research to ensure ourselves against liability issues." The words came out slowly, full of intent and purpose and zero emotion. His grandmother was the smartest woman he knew, used to getting her way. If he wasn't careful, he would find himself not only manufacturing her products, but also taking one of her damn dogs home. Likely the one-eyed mutt with soft fur. "I won't expose Fair Face to the additional expense of trying to break into an unknown market."

Grams sighed, a long drawn out sigh he hadn't heard since Courtney lost her passport in Prague when she was supposed to be in Milan.

"Sometimes I wish you had a little more of your father in you instead of being so buttoned-down and by-the-book."

The aggravation in her voice matched the tension cording in Caleb's neck. The tightness seeped to his shoulders, spilled down his spine. "This isn't personal. I can't afford to make a mistake, and you should be enjoying your retirement, not working in your lab."

"I'm a chemist. That's what I do. You didn't have this problem with the organic baby line." Frustration tinged each of her words, matching the I-wish-you'd-drop-it look in her eyes. "I see what's going on. You don't like the dog care products."

"I never said that."

"But it's the truth." She studied him as if she were trying to prove a hypothesis. "You've got that look. The one you got when you said it didn't matter if your father came home for Christmas."

"I never needed him here. I had you and Gramps." Caleb would try a new tactic. He scooted his chair closer. "Remember Gramps's marketing tagline."

"*The fairest face of all…*"

"His words still define the company today. Fifty years later."

Caleb leaned toward her, as if his nearness would soften the blow. "I'm sorry to say it, but dog products, no matter how natural or organic or aromatherapeutic, have no place at Fair Face."

"It's still my company." She enunciated each word with a firm voice punctuated by her ramrod posture.

Disappointing his grandmother was something his father did, not Caleb. He felt like a jerk. One with a silk noose around his neck choking him.

"I know that, but it's not just my decision." A plane flew overhead. A dog barked. The silence at the table deepened. He prepared himself to say what he'd come here to say. "I met with the department heads before coming over here. Showed them your prototypes. Ran the numbers. Calculated margins."

"And..."

"Everyone has high expectations for your baby skin care line," he said. "But they agree—moving into animal products will affect Fair Face's reputation, not enhance our brand and lead to loss of revenue, anywhere from 2.3 to 5.7 percent."

Caleb expected to see a reaction, hear a retort. But Grams remained silent, her face still, nuzzling the dog against her neck. "Everyone thinks this?"

He nodded once.

Disbelief flickered across her face. She'd looked the same way when she learned his grandfather had been diagnosed with Alzheimer's. But then something sparked. A spark of resignation. No, a spark of resolve.

"Well, that settles it. I trust you know what's best for Fair Face." She sounded doting and grandmotherly, not disappointed and hurt. "Becca and I will figure out another way."

"Another way for what?"

Grams's eyes darkened to a steely blue. "To manufacture the products. You and those suits at Fair Face are wrong. There's a market for my dog skin care line. A big one."

The sun's rays warmed Becca Taylor's cheeks. The sweet scent of roses floated on the air. She walked across the manicured lawn in Gertie's backyard with two dogs—Maurice, a Norwegian elkhound, and Snowy, a bichon frise.

The two show dogs sniffed the ground, looking for any dropped treats or a place to do their business.

She tucked her cellphone into her shorts pocket. "Don't get sidetracked, boys. Gertie is waiting for us on the patio."

Becca had no idea what her boss wanted. She didn't care.

Gertie had rescued Becca the same way she'd rescued the foster dogs living at the estate. This was only a temporary place, but being here gave them hope of finding a forever home.

Maurice's ears perked.

"Do you hear Gertie?"

The two dogs ran in the direction of the patio.

Becca quickened her pace. She rounded a corner.

Gertie and a man sat at the teak table underneath the shade of the umbrella. Five dogs vied for attention, paws pounding on the pavement. Gertie waved.

The man next to her turned around.

Whoa. Hello, Mr. Gorgeous.

Tingles skittered from Becca's stomach to her fingertips.

None of the dogs growled or barked at the guy. Points in his favor. Dogs were the best judges of character, much better than hers.

She walked onto the patio.

The man stood.

Another wave of tingles made the rounds.

Most guys she knew didn't stand. Didn't open doors. Didn't leave the toilet seat down. This man had been raised right.

He was handsome with classical features—high cheekbones, straight nose, strong jawline. The kind of handsome women showed off to girlfriends.

The man stepped away from the table, angling his body toward her. His navy pinstriped suit was tailored, accentuating wide shoulders and tapering nicely at the hips. He moved with the grace of an athlete, making her wonder if he had sexy abdominal muscles underneath.

Very nice packaging.

Well, except for his hair.

His short, cookie-cutter, corporate hairstyle could be seen walking out of every high rise in downtown Boise. With such a gorgeous face, the man's light brown hair should be longer, a little mussed, sexy and carefree, instead of something so… businesslike.

Not that his hair mattered to Becca. Or anything about him.

His top-of-the-line suit shouted one thing—Best in Show.

She might be a dog handler, but she didn't handle his type.

They didn't belong in the same ring. He was a champion with an endless pedigree. She was a mutt without a collar.

She'd tried playing with the top dogs, the wealthy dogs, once before and landed in the doghouse, aka jail.

Never again.

But looking never hurt anybody.

Gertie looked up from the dogs at her feet. "Becca. There's someone I want you to meet."

He was tall, over six feet. The top of her head came to the tip of his nose.

Becca took two steps closer. "Hello."

His green eyes reminded her of jade, a bit cool for her taste, but hey, no one was perfect. His eyelashes more than made up for whatever reserve she saw reflected in his gaze. If she had thick, dark lashes like his she would never need to buy mascara again.

She wiped her hand on her shorts then extended her arm. "I'm Becca Taylor."

His grip was strong, his skin warm.

A burst of heat shot up her arm and pulsed through her veins.

"Caleb Fairchild." His rich voice reminded her of melted dark chocolate, rich and smooth and tasty.

Wait a minute. Fairchild. That meant he was…

"My grandson," Gertie said.

The man who could make Becca's dream of working as a full-time dog handler come true. If the dog products sold as well as Gertie expected, Becca would have the means to travel the dog show circuit without needing to work extra part-time jobs to cover living expenses.

Caleb Fairchild. She couldn't believe he was here. That had to mean good news about the dog products.

Uh-oh. Ogling him was the last thing she should be doing. He was the CEO of Fair Face and wealthy. Wealthy, as in she could win the lottery twice and not come close to his net worth.

"Nice to meet you." Becca realized she was still holding his hand. She released it. "I've heard lots about you."

Caleb's gaze slid over her as if he'd reviewed the evidence, passed judgment and sentenced her to the not-worth-his-time crowd. "I haven't heard about you until today."

His formal demeanor made Jane Austen's Mr. Darcy seem downright provincial. No doubt Mr. Fairchild thought he was too good for her.

Maybe he was.

But she wouldn't let it bother her.

Her career was not only at stake, but also in his hands.

"Tell me about yourself," he said.

His stiff tone irritated her like a flea infestation in the middle of winter. But she couldn't let her annoyance show.

She met his gaze straight on, making sure she didn't blink or show any signs of weakness. "I'm a dog person."

"I thought you were a consultant."

A what? Becca struggled for something to say, struggled and came up empty. Still she had to try. "I...I—"

"Becca is a dog consultant," Gertie said. "She's a true dog whisperer. Her veterinary knowledge has been invaluable with product development. I don't know what I'd do without her."

If Becca wasn't already indebted to Gertie Fairchild, she was now.

Gertie shot a pointed look at Caleb. "Perhaps if you dropped by more often you'd know what's going on."

Caleb directed a smile at his grandmother that redefined the word *charming.*

Not that Becca was about to be charmed. The dogs might like him, but she was…reserving judgment.

"I see you every Sunday for brunch at the club." Caleb's affection for his grandmother wrapped around Becca like a thick, warm comforter, weighing the scales in his favor. "But you never talk about yourself."

Gertie shrugged, but hurt flashed in her eyes so fast Becca doubted if Caleb noticed. "Oh, it just seems like we end up talking about you and Courtney."

"Well, I'm here now," he said.

Gertie placed her hand over her heart and closed her eyes. "To dash all my hopes and dreams."

Becca's gaze bounced between the two. "What do you mean?"

Caleb touched Gertie's arm. "My grandmother is being melodramatic."

Opening her eyes, Gertie pursed her lips. "I'm entitled to be a drama queen. You don't want our pet products."

No. No. No. If that was true, it would ruin…everything. Gertie wouldn't go forward with the dog products without her company backing them. Becca forced herself to breathe. "I don't understand."

Gertie shook her head. "My grandson, the CEO, and his closed-minded cronies at *my* company believe our dog skin care line will devalue their brand."

"That's stupid and shortsighted," Becca said.

Caleb eyed her as if she were the bounty, a half-eaten mouse or bird, left on the porch by an outdoor cat. "That's quite an opinion for a…consultant."

"Not for a dog consultant." The words came out more harshly than Becca intended, but if she couldn't change his mind she would be back to living in a singlewide behind Otto. Otto, her parents' longtime trailer park manager, wore stiletto heels with his camouflage, and skinned squirrels for fun. "Do you know how much money is spent annually on pets?"

"Billions."

"Over fifty billion dollars. Food and vet costs are the largest portion, but analysts project over four billion dollars are spent on pet services. That includes grooming. Gertie's products are amazing. Better than anything on the market."

Gertie nodded. "If only my dear husband were still around. He'd jump on this opportunity."

"Gramps would agree with me." Caleb frowned, not a sad one, more of a do-we-have-to-go-through-this-again frown. "Fair Face is not being shortsighted. We have a strategic plan."

Becca forced herself not to slump. "So change your plan."

"Where'd you get your MBA?" he asked.

Try AA degree. "I didn't study business. I'm a certified veterinary technician, but my most valuable education came from The School of Hard Knocks."

Aka the Idaho Women's Correctional Center.

"As I explained to my grandmother, the decision about manufacturing the dog skin care line is out of my hands."

Caleb's polite tone surprised Becca, but provided no comfort. Not after she'd poured her heart and soul into the dog products. "If the decision was all yours?"

His hard, cold gaze locked on hers. "I still wouldn't manufacture them."

The words slammed into Becca like a fist to her jaw. She took a step back. But she couldn't retreat. "How could you do this to your grandmother?"

Caleb opened his mouth to speak.

Gertie placed her hand on his shoulder. "I'll help Becca understand."

He muttered a thank-you.

"This decision is in the best interest of Fair Face." Gertie sounded surprisingly calm. "It's okay."

But it wasn't.

Becca had thought that things would be different this time.

That she could be a part of something, something big and successful and special. That maybe, just maybe, dreams could come true.

She should have known better.

Things never worked out for girls—women—like Becca. And never would.

CHAPTER TWO

A FEW MINUTES LATER, Becca stood where the grass met the patio, her heart in her throat and her back to Gertie and Caleb. Dogs panted with eagerness, waiting for the ball to be thrown again.

And again. And again.

Playing fetch kept Becca's shoulders from sagging. She would much rather curl up in the kennel with the dogs than be here. Dogs gave her so much. Loyalty, companionship and most importantly love. Dogs loved unconditionally. They cared, no matter what. They accepted her for who she was without any explanations.

Unlike…people.

"Come sit with us," Gertie said.

Us.

A sheen of sweat covered Becca's skin from the warm temperature, but she shivered.

Caleb had multi-millions. Gertie had hundreds of millions. Becca had $8,428.

She didn't want much—a roof over her head, a dog to call her own and the chance to prove herself as a professional handler. Not a lot to ask.

But those dreams had imploded thanks to Caleb Fairchild. Becca didn't want to spend another minute with the man. She glanced back at her boss.

"Please, Becca." Gertie's words were drawn out with an

undertone of a plea. Gertie might be more upset about Fair Face not wanting to take on her new products than she acted.

Becca whipped around. Forced a smile. Took a step onto the patio. "Sure, I'll sit for a few minutes."

Caleb was still standing, a tall, dream-crushing force she did not want to reckon with ever again.

Walking to the table, she didn't acknowledge his presence. He didn't deserve a second look or an "excuse me" as she passed.

Gertie had to be reeling, the same as Becca, after what he'd said.

I still wouldn't manufacture them.

Becca's blood boiled. But she couldn't lose it.

She touched Gertie's thin shoulder, not knowing how else to comfort her employer, her friend. The luxurious feel of silk beneath Becca's palm would soon be a thing of the past. But it wasn't the trappings of wealth she would miss. It was this amazing woman, the one who had almost made Becca believe anything was possible. *Almost*...

"I'm so sorry." A lump burned in her throat. Her eyes stung. She blinked. "You've worked so hard and wasted so much time for nothing."

Gertie waved her hand as if her arm were an enchanted wand that could make everything better. Diamonds sparkled beneath the sun. Prisms of lights danced. If only magic did exist....

"None of this has been a waste, dear." Gertie smiled up at Becca. Not the trying-hard-to-smile-and-not-cry of someone disappointed and reeling, but a smile full of light and hope. "The products are top-notch. You said so yourself. Nothing has changed, in spite of what Caleb thinks."

He gave a barely perceptible shake of his head.

Obviously he didn't agree with his grandmother. But Gertie didn't seem deterred.

That didn't make sense to Becca. Caleb was the CEO and

had final say. She sat next to Gertie. "But if Fair Face doesn't want the products…"

"You and I are starting our own company." Gertie spoke with a singsong voice. "We'll manufacture the products without Fair Face."

Our own company. It wasn't over.

Becca's breath hitched. Her vision blurred. She touched her fingers to her lips.

The dream wasn't dead. She could make this work. She wasn't sure how…

Gertie had always spoken as if working with Fair Face on the products was a done deal, but if going into business was their only option that would have to do. "O-kay."

"Your consultant doesn't sound very confident," Caleb said to Gertie. "Face it, you're a chemist, not a businesswoman." He looked at Becca. "Maybe you can talk some sense into my grandmother about this crazy idea of hers."

Becca clenched her hands. She might not know anything about business, but she didn't like Caleb's condescending attitude. The guy had some nerve discounting his grandmother.

Forget jade. The color of his eyes reminded her of cucumbers or fava beans. Not only cool, but uninspiring.

Change and *taking a risk* weren't part of his vocabulary. But they were hers. "Makes perfect sense to me. I'm in."

"Wonderful." Gertie clapped her hands together. "We'll need an advisor. Caleb?"

A horrified look distorted his face, as if he'd been asked to face the Zombie Apocalypse alone and empty-handed. He took a step back and bumped into a lounge chair. "Not me. I don't have time."

His words—dare Becca say excuse?—didn't surprise her. The guy kept glancing at his watch. She'd bet five bucks he had his life scheduled down to the minute with alarms on his smartphone set to ring, buzz or whistle reminders.

"You wouldn't leave us on our own to figure things out." Gertie fluttered her eyelashes as if she were some helpless female—about as helpless as a charging rhino. "You'll have to make the time."

His chin jutted forward. Walking across burning coals on his hands looked more appealing than helping them. "Sorry, Grams. I can't."

Good. Becca didn't want his help any more than he wanted to give it. "We'll find someone else to advise us."

Gertie grinned, the kind of grin that scientists got when they made a discovery and were about to shout "Eureka!" "Or…"

"Or what?" Becca said at the same time as Caleb.

"We can see if another company is interested in partnering with us." Gertie listed what Becca assumed to be Fair Face's main competitors.

Caleb's lips tightened. His face reddened. His nostrils flared.

Well played, Gertie.

Becca bit back a smile. Not a scientific breakthrough, but a way to break Caleb. Gertie was not only intelligent, but also knew how to get her way. That was how Becca had ended up living at the estate. She wondered if Caleb knew he didn't stand a chance against his grandmother.

"You wouldn't," he said.

"They are my formulas. Developed with my money in my lab here at my house," Gertie said. "I can do whatever I want with them."

True. But Gertie owned the privately held Fair Face.

Becca didn't need an MBA from a hallowed ivy-covered institute to know Gertie's actions might have repercussions.

Caleb rested his hands on the back of the chair. One by one, his fingers tightened around the wood until his knuckles turned white.

Say no.

Becca didn't want him to advise them. She and Gertie needed help starting a new business. But Becca would rather not see Caleb again. She couldn't deny a physical attraction to him. Strange. She preferred going out with a rough-around-the-edges and not-so-full-of-themselves type of guy. Working-class guys like her.

Being attracted to a man who had money and power was stupid and dangerous. Men like that could ruin her plans. Her life. One had.

Of course, Caleb hadn't shown the slightest interest in her. He wouldn't. He would never lower his standards. Except maybe for one night.

No, thanks.

Becca wanted nothing to do with Caleb Fairchild.

Caleb was trapped, by the patio furniture and by his grand-mother. This was not the way he'd expected the meeting to go. He was outnumbered and had no reinforcements. Time to rein in his grams before all hell broke loose.

He gave her a look, the look that said he knew exactly what she was doing. Too bad she was more interested in the tail-wag-ging, paw-prancing dogs at her feet. No matter, he knew how to handle Grams. Her so-called consultant was another matter.

Becca seemed pleased by his predicament. She sat with her shoulders squared and her lips pursed, as if she were looking for a fight. Not exactly the type of behavior he would have ex-pected from a consultant, even a dog one.

He would bet Becca was the one who talked Grams into making the dog products. Nothing else would explain why his grandmother had strayed from developing products that had made her and Fair Face a fortune.

It had to be Becca behind all this nonsense.

The woman was likely a con artist looking to turn this consulting gig into a big pay off. She could be stealing when Grams wasn't paying attention. Maybe a heist of artwork and jewelry and silver was in the works. His wealthy family had always been a target of people wanting to take advantage of them. People like Cassandra. Grams could be in real danger.

Sure, Becca looked more like a college student than a scam-mer. Especially wearing a "No outfit is complete without dog hair" T-shirt and jean shorts that showed off long, smooth, thoroughbred legs.

She had great legs. He'd give her that.

But looks could be deceiving. He'd fallen for Cassandra and her glamorous façade.

Not that Becca was glamorous.

With her short, pixie-cut brown hair and no makeup she was pretty in a girl-next-door kind of way. If he'd ever had a next-door neighbor whose house wasn't separated by acres of land, high fences and security cameras.

But Becca wasn't all rainbows and apple pie.

Her blue eyes, tired and hardened and wary, contradicted her youthful appearance. She wasn't innocent or naïve. Definitely not one of the princess types he'd known at school or the social climbers he knew around town. There was an edge to her he couldn't quite define, and that…intrigued him.

Worried him, too.

He didn't want anyone taking advantage of Grams.

Speaking of which, he faced his grandmother. "It's not going to work."

Grams glanced up from the dogs. The five animals worshipped at her feet as if she were a demigod or a large slice of bacon dressed in pink. "What's not going to work, dear?"

A smile tugged on the corners of Becca's mouth, as if she were amused by the situation.

Caleb pressed his lips together. He didn't like her.

Any consultant with an ounce of integrity would have taken his side on this. But what did he expect from a woman who wore sports sandals with neon-orange-and-green toenail polish to work? He bet she was covered with tattoos and piercings beneath her clothing.

Sexy images of her filled his mind.

Focus.

He rocked back on his heels. "If you partner with one of Fair Face's competitors, the media will turn this into a firestorm. Imagine how the employees will react. You're the creative influence behind our products. How will you reconcile what you do for one company with the other?"

"Animal products for them. Human products for Fair Face." A sheepish grin formed on Grams's lips. "It was only a thought."

A dog tried to get his attention, first rubbing against Caleb's leg then staring up at him. Seemed as if everyone was giving him the soulful-puppy-look today. "A ploy."

Grams tsked. "I can't believe you think I'd resort to such a tactic."

Yeah, right. Caleb remembered looking at what colleges to attend and Grams's reaction. Naval Academy, too dangerous. Harvard, too far. Cal Berkeley, too hippy. She'd steered him right where she'd wanted him—Stanford, her alma mater. "I'm sure you'd resort to worse to get your way."

That earned him a grin from Becca.

Glad someone found this entertaining. Though she had a nice smile, one that made him think of springtime and fresh flowers. An odd thought given he had little time to enjoy the outdoors these days. Maybe it was because they were outside.

"I shouldn't have to resort to anything," Grams said. "You promised your grandfather you'd take care of us."

Something Caleb would never forget.

That promise was directing the course of his life. For better or worse given his grandmother, his sister, Fair Face and the employees were now his responsibility. He grimaced. "I'm taking care of you the best way I know how."

Grams rubbed a gray dog named Blue, but she didn't say a word.

He knew this trick, using silence to make him give in, the way his grandfather had capitulated in the past. But Caleb couldn't surrender. "Grams—"

"Gertie, didn't you mention the other day how busy Fair Face keeps your grandson?" Becca interrupted. "It might be better to find someone else to help us, since Caleb is so busy."

Whoa. Becca wanted to be his ally?

That sent Caleb's hinky-meter shooting into the red zone. No one was that nice to a total stranger. She must want him out of the way so she could run her scam in peace.

"Good idea," he said, playing along. Maybe he could catch Becca in a lie or trip her up somehow. "I'm not sure I'd have a few minutes to spare until the baby product line launches, if then. You know how it is."

"Yes, I do." Grams tapped her fingers against her chin. "But I like keeping things in the family."

So much for taking her formulas to a competitor. "You wouldn't want me to ignore the company, would you?"

His grandmother's gaze narrowed as if zooming in on a target—him. "Who's trying to guilt who now?"

He raised his hands in surrender. "Fair enough."

"Maybe Caleb knows someone who can help us," Becca said.

He would rather his grandmother drop this whole thing, but once Grams saw what starting her own business entailed, she would decide retirement was a better alternative. He would get someone he trusted to advise them, someone to keep an eye on Becca, someone to steer his grandmother properly. Caleb would still be in control, by proxy. "I'm happy to give you a few names. I know one person who would be a good fit."

"I suppose it's worth a try," Gertie said.

"Definitely worth a try." Enthusiasm filled Becca's voice. "We can do this."

We? Us? Caleb straightened. Becca acted more like a partner. He needed to talk to his grandmother about what sort of contract she had with her "consultant." Something about Becca bothered him. She had to be up to no good. "I'll text you the names and numbers, Grams."

"Send Becca the list. As you said, I'm a chemist not a businesswoman."

"Will do." Caleb glanced at his watch, bent and kissed his grandmother's cheek. "Now, if you ladies will excuse me, I need to get back to the office."

Grams grabbed hold of his hand. Her thin fingers dug into his skin. "You can't leave. You haven't had any cake."

The carrot cake. Caleb had forgotten, but he couldn't forget the pile of work waiting for him on his desk. He checked his watch again.

"Gertie baked the carrot cake herself. You need to try a piece." Becca's voice sounded lighthearted, but her pointed look contained a clear warning. Caleb had better stay if he knew what was good for him.

Interesting. The consultant was being protective of his grandmother. Usually that was *his* job. Becca's concern could be genuine or a ruse—most likely the latter—but she was correct about one thing. Eating a slice of cake wouldn't take *that* long. No reason to keep disappointing Grams. He could also use the opportunity to ask his grandmother for more information about her dog consultant.

Caleb placed his arm around his grandmother. "I'd love a piece of your cake and a glass of iced tea."

Dogs raced around Becca, jumping and barking and chasing balls. She stood in the center of the lawn while Gertie went into the house to have Mrs. Harrison prepare the refreshments.

Playing with the dogs was more fun than sitting with Caleb on the patio. Becca saw no reason to make idle chitchat with a man eager to eat his cake and get out of there. At least, she couldn't think of one.

She much preferred four-footed, fur-covered company to dismissive CEOs. Dogs were her best friends, even when they were a little naughty.

"You're a mess, Blue." Becca picked strands of grass and twigs from the Kerry blue terrier's gray hair. "Let's clean you up before Gertie returns."

Dogs—no matter a purebred like Blue or a mutt like Dozer—loved to get dirty. Gertie didn't mind, but Becca tried to keep the dogs looking half decent even when playing.

Blue licked her hand.

Bending over, she kissed his head. "Such a good boy."

"You like dogs."

Becca jumped. She didn't have to turn around to know Caleb was right behind her, but she glanced over her shoulder anyway. "I love dogs. They're my life."

His cool gaze examined her as if she were a stock he was deciding to buy or sell, making her feel exposed. Naked.

Her nose itched. Her lungs didn't want to fill with air.

He stepped forward to stand next to her. "Your life as a dog consultant?"

"Gertie came up with that title," Becca said. "But I am a dog handler, groomer and certified vet tech."

"A jill of all trades."

That was one way to look at it. Desperate to make a living working with animals and to become a full-time professional dog handler was another. "When it comes to animals, particularly dogs."

Snowy and Maurice chased each other, barking. Dozer played tug-of-war with Hunter, a thirteen-inch beagle, growling. Blue sat at Becca's feet, waiting. "I need to put the dogs in the kennel."

Confusion clouded Caleb's gaze. He might as well have spoken the question on his mind aloud.

"Yes, Gertie has a kennel."

"How did you know what I was thinking?"

"Your face." Becca almost laughed. "I'm guessing you don't play a lot of poker. Unless you prefer losing money."

Caleb looked amused, not angry. That surprised her.

"Hey," he said. "I used to be quite good."

"If the other players were blind."

"Ha-ha."

"Well, you don't have much of a poker face."

At least not with his grandmother. Or with Becca.

He puffed out his chest. "We're not playing cards. But you're looking at a real card shark."

She liked his willingness to poke fun at himself. "I believe you."

"No, you don't."

Heat rushed up her neck. "Okay, I don't."

"Honest."

"I try to be." He wasn't talking about poker any longer. She picked up one of the balls. "It's important to play fair."

Caleb's eyebrow twitched. "Do you have a good poker face?"

"You realized I didn't believe you, so probably not."

"No aces up your sleeve?"

"Not my style."

"What is your style?"

"Strategy over deceit." Becca couldn't tell if he believed her, but she hoped he did. Because he was Gertie's grandson, she rationalized. "That's why I'd never sit at a poker table with you. You're too easy to read. It would be like stealing a bone from a puppy."

"A puppy, huh?"

"A manly pup. Not girly."

He grinned wryly. "Wouldn't want to be girly dog."

His gaze held hers. Becca stared mesmerized.

Something passed between them. A look. A connection.

Her pulse quickened.

He looked away.

What was going on? She didn't date guys like him. Even if she did, he was too much of a Boy Scout. And it was clear he didn't like her. "I have to go."

"I want to see the kennel."

"Uh, sure." But she felt uncertain, unsettled being near him. She pointed to the left. "It's down by the guest cottage."

Caleb fell into step next to Becca, shortening his stride to match hers. "How did you meet my grandmother?"

She called the five dogs. They followed. "At The Rose City Classic."

He gave her a blank stare.

Funny he didn't know what that was, given Gertie's interest in dog showing. "It's in Portland. One of the biggest dog shows on the West Coast. Your grandmother hired me to take Snowy into the breed ring. Ended up with a Group third. A very good day."

Blue darted off, as if he were looking for something—a toy, a ball, maybe a squirrel.

Becca whistled for him.

He trotted back with a sad expression in his brown eyes.

Caleb rubbed his chin. "I have no idea what you just said."

"Dog show speak," Becca said. "Snowy won third place in the Group ring. In his case, the Non-Sporting group."

"Third place is good?"

"Gertie was pleased with the result. She offered me a job taking care of her dogs, including the fosters and rescues, here at the estate."

"And the dog skin care line?"

"She sprang that on me after I arrived."

A look of surprise filled his eyes, but disappeared quickly. "Sounds like you're a big help to her."

"I try to be," Becca said. "Your grandmother's wonderful."

"She is." He looked at her. "I'd hate to see anyone take advantage of her kindness."

Not anyone. Becca.

The accusation in his voice made her feel like a death row inmate. Each muscle tightened in preparation for a fight. The balls of her sandals pressed harder against the grass. She fought the urge to mount a defense. If this were a test, she didn't want to fail. "I'd hate that to happen, too."

The silence stretched between them.

His assessing gaze never wavered from hers.

Disconcerted, she fiddled with a thread from the hem of her shorts.

Caleb put his hand out to Dozer, who walked next to them. Funny, considering he'd ignored the dogs before.

Dozer sniffed Caleb's fingers then nudged his hand.

With a tender smile, he patted the dog's head.

Becca's heart bumped. Nothing was more attractive than a man being sweet to animals. A good thing Caleb's physical appearance was pretty easy to overlook given his personality and suspicions.

"You helped me with my grandmother," he said. "Trying to get me out of the way?"

At least he was direct. She wet her lips, not liking the way he raised her hackles and temperature at the same time. "It's obvious you don't want to work with us."

"I don't have time," he clarified.

"There's never enough time."

Dozer ran off, chasing a butterfly.

"It's a valuable commodity," Caleb said.

"Easy to waste when you don't spend it in the right ways."

"Experience talking?"

"Mostly an observation."

Maurice, the Norwegian elkhound, approached Caleb. The dog could never get enough attention and would go up to anyone with a free hand to pet him.

He bent over.

And then Becca remembered. "Wait!"

Caleb touched the dog. He jerked back. A cereal-bowl-sized glob of dark and light hair clung to his hand. "What the…"

Maurice brushed against Caleb's pant leg, covering the dark fabric in hair also.

Oh, no. She bit the inside of her cheek.

"This overweight husky is shedding all his fur." The frown on Caleb's face matched the frustration in his voice. "Enough to stuff a pillow."

"Maurice is a Norwegian elkhound. He's blowing his coat." The guilty expression on the dog's face reminded her of the time he'd stolen food out of the garbage can. She motioned him over and patted his head. This wasn't the dog's fault. Unlike Caleb, she was used to the shedding, a small price to pay for his love. "They do that a couple times a year. It's a mess to clean up."

"Now you tell me."

His tone bristled, as if she were the one to blame. Becca was about to tell him if he spent any time here with his grandmother he would know about Maurice, but decided against it. If she lightened the mood, Caleb might stop acting so…upset. "Look at the bright side."

His mouth slanted. "There's a bright side?"

"You could be wearing black instead of navy."

He didn't say anything, then a smile cracked open on his face, taking her breath away. "I guess I am lucky. Though it's only dog hair, not the end of the world."

If he kept grinning it might be the end of hers.

Caleb brushed the hair away, but ended up spreading it up his sleeve and onto the front of his suit.

"Be careful." She remembered he had to return to the office. "Or you'll make it…"

"Worse." He glanced down. Half laughed. "Too late."

It was her turn to smile. "I have a lint roller. I can clean up your suit in a jiffy."

Amusement filled his eyes. "I thought you liked dog hair."

"Huh?"

"Your T-shirt."

She read the saying. "Oh, yes. Dog hair is an occupational hazard."

"Yet you keep a lint brush."

"You never know when it'll come in handy."

"Do you make a habit of cleaning men's clothing?"

His tone sounded playful, almost flirty. That made no sense. Caleb wouldn't flirt with her. She rubbed her lips together. "Not, um, usually."

Something—interest or maybe it was mischief—flared in his eyes. "I'm honored."

Nerves overwhelmed her. A guy like Caleb was nothing but trouble. He could be trying to cause trouble for her now.

She took a deep breath. "Do you have other clothes with you? Getting the dog hair off your pants will be easier if you aren't wearing them."

"Easier, but not impossible."

Becca pictured herself kneeling and rolling the lint brush over his pants. Her temperature shot up ten degrees. She crossed her arms over her chest. "You can use the roller brush yourself."

He grinned wryly. "My gym bag is in the car."

An image of him in a pair of shorts and a T-shirt stretched across his muscular chest and arms rooted itself in her mind.

Wait a minute. Did he say gym bag? That meant he had time to work out, but no time to spend with Gertie.

Becca's blood pressure rose, but she knew better than to allow it to spiral out of control. Judging him wasn't right. People did that with her and usually got it wrong. Maybe his priorities had gotten mixed up. She'd give him the benefit of the doubt. For now.

"Go change," she said. "I'll put the dogs in the kennel and grab the lint brush out of guest cottage."

"Using the guest cottage as your office?"

"I live there."

His mouth dropped open. He closed it. "You live here at the estate?"

"Yes."

"Why?"

The one word dripped with so much snobbery Becca felt as if someone had dumped a bucket of ice-cold water on her head.

He waited for her to answer.

A hundred and two different answers raced through her mind. She settled on one. "Because Gertie thought it would be for the best."

"Best for you."

"Yes." But there was more to it than that. "Best for Gertie, too."

Confusion filled his gaze. "My grandmother doesn't lack anything."

He sounded so certain, not the least bit defensive. A good sign, but still…

Becca shouldn't have brought this up, but her affection for Gertie meant Becca couldn't back down now. She wanted Caleb to stop blowing off his grandmother. "Gertie thought living here would make it easier for me to do my job without having to drive back and forth all the time. But I also think she wants me here because she's lonely."

"My grandmother lonely?"

The disbelief in his words irritated Becca. She'd realized this as soon as she got to know Gertie, yet her own grandson couldn't see it. "Yes."

"That's impossible," he said without hesitation. "Gertie Fairchild has more friends than anyone I know. She's a social butterfly who turns down invitations—otherwise she'd never be home. She has the means to go out whenever she wants. She has an entire staff to take care of the house and the grounds. No way is she lonely."

What Caleb said might have been true once, but no longer. "Gertie does have a staff, but we're employees. She has lunch twice a week with friends. But she hasn't attended any parties since I moved in. She prefers to spend time in her lab."

"The lab is keeping her from her friends."

"I believe your grandmother would rather spend time with her family, not friends."

"You believe?" He grimaced. "My sister and I—"

"See her every Sunday for brunch at the club, I know. But since I arrived neither you nor your sister have stopped by. Not until you today."

"As I said—"

"You've been busy," Becca finished for him.

Caleb shot a sideways glance at the house. "All Grams has to do is call. I'll do whatever she asks."

"Gertie asked for your help with the dog care products."

"That's…"

"Different?"

A vein at his neck throbbed. "You've got a cush job living here at the estate. I'm sure my grandmother's paying you a bundle to take care of a few dogs and prance them around the ring. What's it to you anyway?"

He sounded defensive. She would, too. Realizing you'd screwed up was never easy. Boy, did she know that. "Gertie's helped me a lot. I want her to be happy."

"Trust me, she's happy. But you have some nerve sponging off my grandmother, helping her with her wild dog-product scheme and then telling me how I should act with my family."

Not defensive. Overconfident. Cocky. Clueless.

Caleb Fairchild was no different than the other people who saw her as dirt to be wiped off the bottom of their expensive designer shoes.

At least she'd tried. For Gertie's sake.

Becca reached out her hand. "Give me your jacket."

"You're going to help me after trying to make me feel like a jerk?" he asked.

Mission accomplished. If he felt like a jerk he had only himself to blame. "I said I'd help. I only told you the truth."

He didn't look as if he believed her. They were even. She didn't trust him.

"As you see it," he said.

She met his gaze straight on. "I could say the same about your truth."

They stood there locked in a stare down.

Stalemate.

"At least we know where we stand," he said.

Becca wasn't so certain, but she knew one thing. Being with Caleb was like riding a gravity-defying roller coaster. He left her feeling breathless, scared to death, and never wanting to get on again. She didn't like it. Him.

She held up his jacket. "And just so you know, I'm not doing this for you. I'm doing it for Gertie."

CHAPTER THREE

BY THE TIME Caleb changed into a pair of shorts and a T-shirt and then returned to the patio, the table had been transformed with china, crystal glasses and a glass-blown vase filled with yellow and pink roses from the garden. Very feminine. Very Grams. "You've gone all out."

"I enjoy having company." Beaming, Grams patted the seat next to her. "Sit and eat."

Caleb sat next to her. He stared across the table at Becca. What was she doing here?

He wanted to speak to Grams alone, to talk about Becca and his concerns about the so-called dog consultant and if she was exploiting his grandmother's generosity.

Sneaky scam artist or sweet dog lover? Becca seemed to be a contradiction, one that confused him.

On their way to the kennel, he'd sensed a connection. Something he hadn't felt in over a year. Maybe two. Not since... Cassandra. But he knew better than to trust those kinds of emotions with a total stranger.

Becca wasn't his usual type—Caleb casually dated high-powered professional women—but he'd found himself flirting and having fun with her until she'd had to ruin the moment with her ridiculous grandmother-is-lonely spiel.

Becca was wrong. He couldn't wait to prove how wrong.

He sliced through his cake with his fork. The silver tines pinged against the porcelain plate.

As if he wanted or needed anything from Becca Taylor other than her lint roller.

"You must be hungry," Grams said.

Nodding, he took a bite.

Becca drank from her glass of ice water.

"Do the dogs usually stay in the kennel all day?" he asked.

A rivulet of condensation rolled down her glass. She placed it on the corner of the yellow floral placemat. "No, they are out most of the time, but if they were here they'd be going crazy over the cake."

"Dogs eat cake?" he asked.

Becca refilled her water from a glass pitcher with lemons floating on the top.

A guilty expression crossed Grams's face. "I never give them a lot. Never any chocolate. But when they stare up at me as if they're starving, it's too hard not to give them a taste."

"Those dogs know exactly how to get what they want." Laughter filled Becca's eyes. "They're spoiled rotten."

"Nothing wrong with being spoiled and pampered," Grams agreed.

"Not at all." Becca sounded wistful. "I'd love to be one of your dogs."

Her words surprised Caleb. She didn't seem like the primping and pampering type. But what did he really know about her? He sipped his iced tea.

She picked up her fork and sliced off a bite of cake. Her lips parted.

Fair Face made a lipstick that plumped lips, making them fuller and, according to the marketing department, more desirable. Becca's lips were perfect the way they were.

She raised the fork.

Like a moth to a blowtorch, Caleb watched her, unable to look away. He placed his glass on the table.

She brought the fork closer to her mouth until her lips closed around the end.

The sweat at the back on his neck had caused the collar on his T-shirt to shrink two sizes in the past ten seconds.

She pulled out the empty fork. A dab of enticing frosting was stuck on the corner of her mouth.

A very lickable position.

What the hell was he thinking? Caleb wasn't into licking. At least not his grandmother's employee, one who claimed to know more about Grams's than he did.

The woman was dangerous. Caleb forced himself to look away.

If making him feel worse had been Becca's goal, she'd succeeded. Not only worse, but also aggravated. Annoyed. Attracted.

No, not attracted. Distracted. By the frosting.

His gaze strayed back to the creamy dab on Becca's face.

Yes, that was it. The icing. He placed his fork on the plate. Not the lick…

"Please don't tell me you're finished?" Grams asked, sounding distressed he hadn't eaten the whole slice.

The last thing Caleb wanted was more cake. He needed to figure out what was going on with Becca, then get out of here. "Letting the food settle before I eat more."

He sneaked a peek at Becca.

The tip of her pink tongue darted out, licking her top lip to remove the bit of frosting before disappearing back into her mouth.

Caleb stuck two fingers inside his collar and tugged. Hard. The afternoon heat was making him sweat. Maybe he should head to the gym instead of back to work. Doing today's workout at the gym might clear his head and help him focus on the right things.

He wiped his mouth with a yellow napkin. Becca should have used hers instead of her tongue to remove the icing.

Maybe Becca was trying to be provocative and flirty. Maybe Becca saw dollar signs when she looked at him as Cassandra had. Maybe Becca didn't want him to object to her involvement with Gertie. His grandmother had to be the mark here, not him.

"The cake is delicious. Moist," he said. "The frosting has the right amount of sweetness."

Eyes bright, Grams leaned forward over the table. "I'm so happy you like it. I've been working hard on the recipe."

With a sweet grin that made him think of cotton candy, Becca motioned to her plate. Only half the slice remained. "I think you've perfected it."

Grams chuckled. "Took me enough attempts."

"I've enjoyed each and every slice." Becca patted her trim waistline. "As you can tell."

"Nonsense," Grams said. "You have a lovely figure. Besides, a few slices of cake never hurt anybody. Men like curves, isn't that right, Caleb?"

He choked on the cake in his mouth. Becca's curves were the last thing he should be looking at right now. Not that he hadn't checked them out before. "Mmmm-hmmm."

"See," Grams said lightheartedly.

Warm affection filled Becca's eyes. "I'm sold."

Caleb's gaze darted between the two women. Grams treated Becca more like a friend than an employee. That was typical of his grandmother's interactions with her staff, including the dowdy Mrs. Harrison, a fortysomething widow who preferred to go by her last name.

Still, Grams and Becca's familiarity added to his suspicions given the differences in their social status, personalities and ages. His grandmother always took in strays and treated them well. Becca seemed to be playing along with her role in that scenario, but adding a twist by making sure she was becoming indispensable and irreplaceable.

Something was definitely off here. "Grams is an excellent baker."

"You should have been here on Monday," Becca said. "Gertie knocked it out of the park with her Black Forest cake. Seriously to-die-for."

"Black Forest cake?" he asked.

Grams nodded with a knowing gleam in her eyes. "Your favorite."

That had been only three days ago. Caleb stared at his plate.

Carrot cake was Courtney's favorite. Grams had made his favorite earlier in the week. Puzzle pieces fell into place like colored blocks on a Rubick's Cube. A seven-layer lead weight settled in the pit of Caleb's stomach. "How many cakes do you bake a week?"

"It depends on how long it takes us to eat one," she answered.

The question ricocheted through him, as if he were swinging wildly and hitting only air. "Us?"

"Becca. The estate staff. My lab assistants. Whoever else happens to be working here," Grams explained. "Sometimes Becca takes the leftovers to the vet clinic when she covers shifts there."

Wait a minute. He assumed his grandmother paid Becca well and allowed her to live in the guest cottage rent-free. Why would Becca work at a vet clinic, too? Especially if she was running a con?

"Sounds like a lot of cake." Caleb tried to reconcile what he was learning about Becca as well as Grams's cake. "I didn't realize you enjoyed baking so much."

Grams raised a shoulder, but there was nothing casual or indifferent in the movement. "Can't have one of my grandchildren stop by and not have any cake to eat."

But I also think she wants me here because she's lonely.

Damn. His chest tightened. Becca was right. Grams was lonely. Regret slithered through him.

Thinking about the number of cakes being baked with anticipation and love and a big dose of hope made it hard to breathe. He figured Grams would be out and about doing whatever women of her age did to pass the time. Lunches, museums, fundraisers. He'd never thought she would go to so much trouble or imagined she would be sitting at home and waiting for her grandchildren to stop by.

His promise and his efforts blew up like a fifty-megaton bomb.

So much for taking care of Grams. He'd failed. He hadn't taken care of her. He'd let her down.

Just like his...dad.

Guilt churned in Caleb's gut. He opened his mouth to speak, but wasn't sure what to say. "I'm sorry" wasn't enough. He pressed his lips together.

"Did you have something you wanted to say?" Grams asked.

Caleb looked up. His grandmother was speaking to Becca.

Of course *that* woman would have something to say, a smug remark or a smart-aleck comment to expose his failure aloud. Anything so she could rub a ten-pound bag of salt into the gaping hole over his heart.

"No," Becca said, but that didn't soothe him, because she had an I-told-you-so smile plastered on her face. She looked pleased, almost giddy that she'd been proven correct.

How deeply had she ingrained herself in Grams's life? He was concerned how well Becca could read his family. He needed to find his grandmother a new consultant, one with a better education, wardrobe and manners. One he trusted.

Becca's silly, sheep-eating grin made the Cheshire cat look as if he were frowning. She raised a forkful of cake to her mouth. Each movement seemed exaggerated, almost slow motion as if she knew he was waiting for her to make the next move and she wanted to make him suffer.

Good luck with that.

Caleb couldn't feel any worse than he was feeling. He had to do something to make this up to Grams.

"You can have another slice after you finish yours," Grams said.

"One is enough for today," he said. "But let me know when you bake another Black Forest cake, and I'll stop by."

A dazzling smile on his grandmother's face, the kind that

could power a city for a day, reaffirmed how lonely she must be in spite of her money and friends. That loneliness made her vulnerable to people who wanted to take advantage of her, people like Becca.

"I'll do that," Grams said.

He ground the toe of his running shoe against the tile.

In spite of his thinking he'd been a doting grandson, his phone calls, text messages and brunch on Sunday hadn't been enough. Grams wanted to spend face-to-face time with her grandchildren, to chat with them and to feed them.

Caleb's overbooked calendar flashed in his mind. His arm and shoulder muscles bunched, as if he'd done one too many Burpees at the gym.

He was so screwed.

No, that wasn't right.

This was his grandmother, not some stranger.

He'd made a promise, one he intended to honor if it killed him. And it might do that unless Caleb could figure something out. A way to spend more time with Grams. Make more time for her. Find time...

Becca's fork scraped against the plate.

Food.

That gave him an idea.

He had to eat. So did Grams.

Mealtimes would allow him to eat and appease his grandmother's need to see her grandson at the same time. The question was how often. Brunch was a standing date. Dinner once a week would be a good start.

"Let's have dinner next week on Wednesday. Invite Courtney to come," he suggested. "I'm sure your cook can whip up something tasty for us. You can make dessert."

Grams shimmied her narrow shoulders, as if she were a teenager bursting with excitement, not an elderly woman.

Maybe once a week wouldn't be enough. His chest tightened.

"That sounds wonderful," Grams said. "Do you think Courtney can make it?"

The anticipation in Grams's voice made one thing certain. His sister would be at the dinner if he had to buy her a pretty, expensive bauble or a new pair of designer shoes. Grams was worth it. "Yes. She'll be here."

Grams looked as if she might float away like a helium balloon. "Excellent, because I can't wait for Courtney to meet Becca."

Caleb rolled his shoulders, trying to loosen the knots. He didn't want Becca at dinner. The woman had overstayed her welcome as far as he was concerned. This meal was for his family, not employees.

He flashed her a practiced smile, so practiced people never saw through it. But the way Becca studied him made Caleb wonder if she was the exception to the rule. He tilted his head. "Join us for a glass of wine on Wednesday."

Becca brushed her knuckles across her lips. "I don't want to intrude on your evening."

"You aren't intruding," Grams said before Caleb could reply. "You're having dinner with us."

"No," he said at the same time as Becca.

His gaze locked on hers for an uncomfortable second before he looked away. Only ice remained in his glass, but he picked it up and sipped.

The woman was…unpredictable. One more thing not to like about her. He was more of a "load the dice ahead of time so he knew what he was going to roll" kind of guy. He didn't like surprises. He'd bet Becca thrived upon them.

Grams's lip curled. "Caleb."

Becca studied her cake as if a magic treasure were hidden inside. "It's okay, Gertie."

No, it wasn't. Caleb deserved his grandmother's sharp tone. "What I meant is Courtney is a lot to take in if you're not used to being around her. I have no doubt they'll name a Category 5 hurricane after her one of these days."

"Your sister can be…challenging at times," Grams said.

Understatement of the year. Courtney was the definition

of drama princess. The rest of the earth's population was here to make his sister look good or help her out. Nothing he tried stopped her from being so selfish. Not even making her work at Fair Face in order to gain access to her trust fund. "We don't want Courtney to overwhelm Becca and make her want to hightail it out of here."

On second thought getting Becca out of the picture was exactly what he wanted to happen. No way would Grams start a business venture on her own. Caleb might have to rethink this.

"Becca won't be overwhelmed. She's made of stronger stuff than that," Gertie said.

"Thanks, but you need this time alone with your grandchildren." Becca's eyelids blinked rapidly, like the shutter on a sport photographer's camera. "I can't make it anyway. I'm covering a shift for a vet tech at the twenty-four hour animal hospital on Wednesday."

"That's too bad," he said.

She toyed with her napkin, her fingers speeding up as if someone had pressed the accelerator. A good thing the napkin was cloth or it would be shredded to bits.

"It is," Becca said. "But I'm sure you'll have a wonderful time together."

Her saccharine sweet voice sounded relieved not to be a part of the dinner. Maybe she had seen through him. That would be a first. "You'll be missed."

As much as a case of poison oak.

A dismayed expression crossed Grams's face, washing over her like a rogue wave. Her shoulders hunched. "You're working that night, Becca?"

The tremble in her voice sent Caleb's pulse accelerating like a rocket's booster engine. Unease spiraled inside him. He reached for his grandmother's hand, covering hers with his. Her skin felt surprisingly warm. Her pulse wasn't racing. Good signs, he hoped. "Grams? You okay?"

She stared at her hands. "I forgot about Becca working on

Wednesday. I do have an assistant who reminds me of things, but…"

Grams shook her head slowly, as if she were moving through syrup not air.

Caleb understood her worry. His grandfather had suffered from Alzheimer's, a horrible disease for the patient as well as the family. Being forgotten by the man who'd held their lives together for so long hadn't been easy. But even at the worst of times, Grams had dealt with the stress of the disease with raw strength and never-ending grace and by making jokes. He'd never seen his grandmother act like this. Not even when she'd been stuck in bed with an upper respiratory infection over a year ago. "No worries. You've had a lot on your mind."

"That's right," Becca agreed.

Caleb wondered if she knew something about Grams's health, but hadn't told anyone. Except Becca looked genuinely concerned.

Grams gave his hand a feeble squeeze. "I should be able to remember a detail like Becca's work schedule."

"I never told you about next week's schedule." Becca's voice was soft and nurturing and oh-so-appealing. "I received the call this morning about what shifts I'll be covering. You haven't forgotten anything."

"I haven't?" Grams asked.

Hearing the unfamiliar uncertainty in her voice worried Caleb.

"Nope," Becca confirmed.

Whether his grandmother had forgotten or not, she seemed so much older and fragile. Time to call her doctor. He patted her hand.

"I'm going to stick around this afternoon." This would cause havoc with his schedule, but he needed to be here for Grams. He could use the time to figure out what was going on with Becca. "I can finish up my work here, then we'll have dinner."

Grams straightened. All signs of weakness disappeared like a wilted flower that had found new life. Her smile took twenty years from her face. Her eyes twinkled. She pulled her hand from beneath his and rubbed her palms together. "That will be perfectly splendid."

Huh? Her transformation stunned him.

"Maura, the new cook, is making lasagna tonight. She's using my recipe for the sauce," Grams said to him. "Becca loves my sauce, don't you?"

Amusement gleamed in Becca's eyes. "I do."

Caleb didn't know what she found so funny. His grandmother's health was nothing to laugh about. "Sounds great, but let's phone your doctor first."

"Nothing is wrong with me." Grams waved off his concern, as if he'd asked if she wanted a slice of lemon in her iced tea. "I had a complete physical two months ago. Dr. Latham said I'm healthy, with a memory an elephant would envy."

That didn't explain what had happened with her only moments ago. "A call won't take long."

Grams's lips formed a perfect O. She leaned toward him. "You're worried about me."

No sense denying the obvious. He nodded.

She touched the side of his face, her touch soft and loving. "You have always been the sweetest boy."

He blew out a frustrated puff of air. "I haven't been a boy for a while."

"Very true, but I remember when you ran around the house naked." She looked at Becca while heat rose in his cheeks. "He never wanted to wear clothes unless it was a superhero costume or camouflage."

Forget the doctor. Might as well call the coroner. For him. Cause of death—embarrassment. "I was what? Three?"

"Three, four and five. It seems like yesterday," Grams said with a touch of nostalgia. She stood. "Please don't worry about me. I'm fine."

Caleb wasn't sure about that. He rose.

She motioned him to sit. "Eat the rest of your cake. I'm going to tell Mrs. Harrison you're staying for dinner."

"I'll go with you," he said.

Becca gave him the thumbs-down sign.

Caleb would have to be blind to misinterpret that signal. He sat. "Or I can finish my cake."

"Do that. Then use the study to work." The words were barely out of Grams's mouth before she bounced her way toward the house.

The French doors slammed shut.

Caleb leaned over the table toward Becca. He might not like her. He sure as hell didn't trust her, but she was the only one he could ask. "What is going on with my grandmother?"

Becca understood Caleb's concern. She'd been worried, too, until she realized Gertie was faking her memory loss. Becca glanced at the house, biting back a smile. "I imagine your grandmother's in a mad rush to get to the pantry for the ingredients for a Black Forest cake."

Caleb's eyes darkened to an emerald-green. Make that the color of steamed broccoli. His mouth pinched at the corners. "What?"

"You know how you talked about your grandmother using ploys to get her way?"

His gaze narrowed. "Yes."

"Gertie played both of us by pretending to be a forgetful granny."

"She wouldn't."

"She did." It was all Becca could do not to bust out in a belly laugh. "You'd better work on your poker face or prepare for more of her antics, since it worked so well."

"Huh?"

"You not only stayed for cake, but you're having dinner here."

He rubbed the back of his neck. "Grams played me like a well-tuned Stradivarius, didn't she?"

"Perhaps not that well-tuned."

"Touché."

"Your grandmother is the smartest woman I know."

"You seem pretty sharp yourself."

Warmth emanated from Becca's stomach. She hoped the heat didn't spread all the way to her face. No one except Gertie had ever called Becca sharp. "Thanks, but what she was doing wasn't hard to figure out."

"What tipped you off?" he asked.

He leaned back in his chair, looking more relaxed and comfortable. Different. More approachable. The workout clothes looked mouthwateringly good on him.

"Becca?"

Oops. She'd been staring. Her cheeks warmed. A pale pink, she hoped. "I hadn't told Gertie about my work schedule. But when she looked at your hand on hers and didn't look away, I knew something was up."

"I thought it was strange, but Grams knows how to push my buttons when she wants. She had me worried about her health."

"Desperation can drive a person to do things they normally wouldn't."

He tossed Becca one of those you've-got-to-be-kidding looks. "My grandmother is not desperate."

"I'd be desperate if someone I loved kept blowing me off."

"You don't have to keep rubbing it in. I'm going to spend more time with her."

"Glad to hear it." Becca had expected Caleb to be angry, not repentant. This softer side of him surprised her, given his obvious suspicions about her. Appealed to her, too. "You have no idea how lucky you are. Gertie is amazing. Don't take her for granted."

"You really seem to care about Grams."

Becca nodded. "I wish she was my grandmother."

"Do you have family close by?" he asked.

"Southern Idaho. I don't see them much." Becca didn't like the conversation turning toward her. She stood. "I have to go."

Caleb scooted back in his chair. "Where are you going?"

"To get your suit."

"Before you go." He stood. "One question."

"What?"

"Are Grams's dog products that good?"

"Will you believe what I say?"

"I asked your opinion."

He hadn't answered her question. Maybe he had a better poker face than she thought. "The products are so excellent, they'll sell themselves."

"You sound certain. Confident."

"I am," she said. "The line is going to make a fortune, but it's better that Fair Face isn't manufacturing the products."

His jaw tensed. "I thought that's what you and Grams wanted."

"It was, but not now."

"Trying to get rid of me?"

"Sort of."

His eyes darkened. "Why is that?"

"If Fair Face doesn't believe in the products, they won't be willing to put all their resources behind them," she said. "Fair Face will do enough, just enough, to appease Gertie. The line might not fail, but it won't succeed as well as it could with the right backing and support."

"For a dog consultant, you know a lot about business."

Becca hated that his words meant as much as they did. They shouldn't. "Not really. It's common sense."

"Not having Fair Face involved means more money for you."

She hadn't thought about that. "More money would be great."

"I'm sure it would be."

As if Caleb could understand what money would mean to her. He'd never gone hungry because there wasn't enough money for groceries. He'd never worn thrift-shop clothes and duct-taped shoes. He'd never left prison with nothing except a backpack and an appointment with a probation officer.

"Thinking about how you're going to spend all that money?" he asked.

"Thinking about our next step," she said. "I'll give you my number. Text me the names and numbers of possible advisors."

"No need."

Her heart dropped. "What do you mean?"

"I know the perfect person to help you and Grams."

She fisted her hands in anticipation. "Who?"

"Me."

No. No. No. Every nerve ending shrieked. "You said you didn't have time."

"That was before you made me realize I've been neglecting my grandmother and should spend more time her."

Oh, no. Becca had brought this upon herself. "You should be doing something fun with Gertie, not working with her."

"You said she liked to work."

"She does. But…" Becca swallowed. "You don't want to ignore Fair Face."

"I'll work it out. This way I'll be able to help you, too." He sounded so confident, as if nothing could stop him. "I can answer any questions you have, make sure things stay on track, maybe provide angel funding. That should make you happy."

The lopsided smile on Caleb's face told Becca he expected her to be anything but happy about this. Goal achieved, because she was very unhappy at the moment. "I—"

"Trust me."

She would never trust a man with so much money and power. She chewed the inside of her cheek. "I hate to put you out like this. It really isn't necessary."

"No worries. Honest." The charming smile spreading across his face made her breath hitch. "Besides, I'm not doing this for you. I'm doing it for my grandmother."

CHAPTER FOUR

THE NEXT AFTERNOON, Caleb left his office and rode in a limousine to his grandmother's estate. He hoped the element of surprise would work in his favor today. Unlike yesterday when he'd been caught off-guard by most everything.

Spending time with Grams and being her advisor were the perfect ruses for Caleb dropping by unannounced. He could keep on eye on Becca until he figured out what she was up to.

The estate's housekeeper, Mrs. Harrison, answered the door. She told him that Grams was in the lab, which he expected, and Becca was in the study, which he hadn't.

Every nerve ending went on alert.

She shouldn't be allowed to have free rein on the estate. She shouldn't be allowed to sit in the same study where his grandfather put together Fair Face. She shouldn't be here at all.

He stood in the doorway of the study, watching Becca.

With a laptop at her left, she hunched over the desk, pencil in hand, scribbling notes on paper. She wore a green T-shirt. He assumed she had on shorts, but he saw only crossed long legs and a bare foot swinging beneath the desk.

"Working hard?" Though he imagined her brainstorming ways to con Grams out of money rather than actual work.

Becca's gaze jerked up. Her eyes widened. She set her pencil on the desk. "Caleb. I didn't know you were stopping by."

"I thought I'd see if you have any questions about the business plan we talked about last night."

"That's what I'm working on."

Convenient. Unless she was lying. He took a step toward her. "Let me see what you've done."

She frowned. "I only started this morning."

"I'm your advisor," he said in an even voice. No reason to make her aware of his suspicions. "It's my job to keep you headed in the right direction."

And make sure she didn't hurt what mattered most to him.

Becca eyed him warily. "I didn't realize CEOs micromanage their employees."

"You don't work for me." If Becca did, he would have fired her yesterday when she gave away her true intention.

Trying to get rid of me?

Sort of.

Not sort of. He had no doubt she'd wanted him gone so she could scam Grams out of as much money as possible. That was why he'd agreed to advise them, why he'd participated in a conference call on the way over here, why he'd be checking in with them daily.

To protect Grams. To protect Fair Face.

"But I'm advising you." For now. He'd hired a private investigator to do a background check, but until the man reported back Caleb was sticking close to her, even if it messed up his schedule. "I take that role seriously."

She straightened the papers and handed the stack to him. "Here."

He ran his thumb over the edges. Too many to count quickly. "A lot of pages for starting this morning."

Her mouth tightened. "I didn't plagiarize, if that's what you're suggesting."

Her defensive behavior suggested she knew Caleb was onto her. No reason to be all that subtle about his suspicions. Maybe she'd get scared and take off on her own. That would make things simpler, especially with Grams.

Tension, thick and unsettling, hung in the air.

Underneath the desk, her foot swung like a pendulum

gone crazy. Back and forth, speeding up each time the blur of fluorescent-painted toenails came toward him.

"I wasn't suggesting anything." Caleb didn't trust Becca. But he couldn't deny she…intrigued him. He held the papers in the air. "Only making an observation."

"I found a business plan template online," she said to his surprise. "The website explains what to write where and gives you text boxes to fill in. You download the plan into word processing software."

"Handy."

"Yes."

Caleb read through her rough draft, making mental notes as he went. He set the plan on the desk.

"So?" she asked, her voice full of curiosity.

"Not bad." He waited for a reaction, but didn't get one. She either didn't care or had tight control of her emotions. He would go with apathy. "Hold off on working on the executive summary until the business plan is complete. That way you'll have a better idea of who and what the company is all about."

She rested her elbows on the desk and leaned forward. Her V-neck T-shirt gaped, giving him an enticing peek of ivory skin, beige satin and cleavage.

He enjoyed the view for a moment, felt his temperature rise and then looked away. This wasn't the time to be distracted by a nice, round pair of breasts.

"What else?" she asked.

Becca sounded interested, not apathetic, as if she wanted to know what was wrong and how to fix it. That was unexpected.

Caleb picked up the business plan and scanned the pages again. He'd read through enough business plans over the years with his personal venture capital/angel fund to offer some quick fixes. "This is a good start, but you need specific goals and a more concrete direction. The product descriptions are excellent, but you're missing pricing information or market comparisons. You'll need hard facts, start-up costs, projected balance sheets. 'The products will sell themselves' isn't a sales and marketing strategy."

Her shoulders slumped. "There's so much more to this than I realized."

"That's what I was trying to tell you and my grandmother yesterday." The more discouraged they got, especially Becca, the better. "There are easier ways to make money than starting your own business."

She stared at her hands. "Making money has never come easy for me or people I know."

"My grandfather told me hard work always pays off."

"I've heard your grandfather was a wonderful man, but sometimes hard work doesn't put groceries in the cupboard." Without a glance Caleb's way, she made notes on another piece of paper. "Anything else I should add?"

"Make these fixes first, then I'll review it again." He handed back her pages. "Writing something like this is an iterative process."

"That sucks, since Gertie wants the plan finished tonight."

Grams could be impatient. When she'd presented the baby products, she'd wanted them on the market in less than three months. It had taken almost a year. "I'm surprised she didn't want it done yesterday."

"Two dogs needed baths last night. Otherwise, she would have told me to get it done. In a nice way, of course."

Grams could be firm, but "in a nice way" described her perfectly. "When did you move in?"

"February."

Four months ago. Had it been that long since he'd been to the estate? He couldn't remember. "You've had plenty of time to figure out how my grandmother operates."

"She's the best boss. Ever."

So adamant. Loyal. The woman deserved an Oscar nomination for her acting abilities. "Grams likes getting her way."

Becca stared down her nose at him. "Most people do."

"You?"

"If it ever happened, I'd probably like getting my way."

If. Probably. Her words raised more questions.

"But I never get my way," she added. "Let me tell you. It sucks."

Caleb had never met a woman like Becca Taylor. She might be a scammer, but the way she spoke her mind was…entertaining. She added color and expectation into predictable life. He would miss that when she was gone. But he would survive.

The next day, Becca finished her morning run with Maurice. She walked to the kennel with the dog at her side.

Sweat covered her face and dripped from her hair. Her legs trembled from the exertion. "Let's get you put away so I can see what Gertie needs."

"My grandmother wants you up at the house."

The sound of Caleb's voice sent goosebumps prickling Becca's skin. A strange sensation, given how sticky and hot she felt at the moment.

But strange and Caleb seemed to go together. Three visits in three days. For someone claiming to be busy, he had a lot of time to check up on—make that "advise"—her. Though today was Saturday, and based on his casual attire, a pair of cargo shorts and a T-shirt, he wasn't going into the office today.

"You run," he said.

"The dogs run." She opened the kennel door. The blast of cool air refreshed her, kept her temper in check. "I hold the leashes and get dragged along."

"You're not a runner."

"Do I look like a runner?" She glanced back at him. "Don't answer that."

Caleb smiled, but whether his smile was genuine or not remained to be seen. He followed her into the kennel, the door closing behind him. "Why do you run if you don't like it?"

She not only didn't like running, she didn't like Caleb being underfoot. His wide shoulders and height made the spacious kennel feel cramped and stuffy.

"Some of the dogs prefer it to walking." Becca opened the door to Maurice's space complete with pillow bed and a doggy door that led to his own grassy dog run. She unhooked his leash and let him loose inside. The dog went straight for his stainless steel water bowl. "So we run."

"You really are a dog person."

"Muscle tone is important. Dog judges don't like to see flabby or fat dogs in the ring."

"You run the little ones, too?"

"I walk them." She checked each of the dog bowls to make sure they had enough water to get them through the next couple of hours. "How briskly depends on their legs."

"When do you walk them?" he asked.

"I already did." She wished he'd go bother someone else. Maybe he was trying turn on the charm and play nice. But he looked good today. He exuded confidence, and a part of her wanted to reach out and grab some for herself. That was bad. Becca didn't want to notice anything about Caleb Fairchild. She was thinking about him too much as it were. Maybe she was lonely. An animal control officer she'd met at the animal hospital had mentioned meeting for coffee. Going on a date with him might take her mind off Caleb. "They'll get another walk later if it's not too hot."

"Sounds like they are lucky dogs."

"Anyone who is fortunate to have Gertie on their side is a lucky dog."

"Including you?"

"I'm the luckiest." She motioned to the door. "I need to see what Gertie wants."

"I'll go with you."

Figures. "I'm sure you want to spend as much time with your grandmother as possible."

"That's right."

Liar. Becca bit her tongue to keep from saying the word aloud. Caleb spent twice as much time with her than Gertie.

Okay, his insights on the business plan had been useful.

Becca would give him that much credit. But the way Caleb watched her, as if trying to catch her doing something wrong made her so self-conscious she was having trouble sleeping. Something she hadn't had since leaving prison. She didn't like it. Didn't like him.

Maybe if she kept working hard and proved herself writing the business plan, Caleb would continue visiting his grandmother, but leave Becca alone. She hoped so because whenever he came close physical awareness shot through her like an electric shock.

She found Gertie, dressed in a lab coat and black pants, sitting on a bar stool at the kitchen's island. Mrs. Harrison washed vegetables. A young woman named Maura, who helped cook and clean, stood at the stove, stirring whatever was inside a saucepan.

"You wanted to see me," Becca said.

"Yes." Gertie clapped her hands together. "I have some news. A sort of good news/bad news kind of thing."

Becca had never known Gertie to have any bad news until today. "Start with the bad so we end on a high note."

"I can't go with you to the dog show in Oregon next weekend," Gertie announced.

Becca's chest tightened. She took a step forward. "Is anything wrong?"

"Oh, no, dear. I'm fine, but I found out an old friend is being thrown a surprise party. It's not something I can miss."

That wasn't really bad news. Not compared to some of the bad news she'd dealt with in the past. She would miss Gertie's company, but her employer needed to get out of the lab more. "Go have fun. I'm used to doing shows on my own."

"You won't be alone." Gertie bounced from jeweled slipper to jeweled slipper and back again. "That's my good news. Caleb is going with you so he can see the products in action."

No. No. No.

Becca staggered back until she bumped into something solid and around six feet tall.

Caleb.

She jumped forward. "Sorry."

"No worries."

Maybe not for him, but this wasn't good news at all. A weekend with Caleb watching her every move, waiting and hoping she screwed up. Not to mention the strange way he made her insides quiver. She couldn't let this happen. "Have you ever been to a dog show before?"

"No, but I need to know how the products work in order to help you."

Caleb would hate wasting time at a dog show. She had work to do, but he would be standing or sitting around, bored out of his mind. She wouldn't have time to entertain him or be subjected to another of his inquisitions.

There had to be a way to convince him not to go.

On Monday, the clip of Caleb's Italian leather wingtips against the estate's hardwood floor echoed the beat of his heart. Working with Becca on the business plan, he'd learned two things about her: she was from a small town outside Twin Falls, Idaho, and her father's first name was Rob. Information his private investigator had used to perform a background check.

The jig was up. Caleb had known his instincts were right about her.

His hand tightened around the manila folder containing irrefutable proof Becca Taylor was trying to scam his grandmother. He strode into the estate's solarium with one goal in mind—get Becca away from his grandmother. "Hello, Grams."

"Caleb." She lounged on a chaise holding a glass of pink lemonade complete with a pink paper umbrella. "Thanks for letting yourself in. I was standing most of the day, and my feet hurt."

He kissed her cheek. "You shouldn't spend so much time in the lab."

"It's what I do."

Not for long. The crazy dog care line would soon be nothing but a footnote in Grams's life, a distant memory along with Becca. He crinkled the edge of the folder. "Where's your consultant?"

"At the animal hospital." Grams placed her drink on a mosaic end table she'd purchased in Turkey. "You're stuck with me."

"I came to visit you."

Grams placed her hand on her chest. "I'm touched. What did you want to talk about?

He sat in a damask covered chair next the chaise. "Becca."

Grams's eyes softened with affection. "Becca has been spending so much time writing and revising the business plan. You'll be impressed."

Caleb doubted that, but he reminded himself to be conscious of his grandmother's feelings. "I learned disturbing news today. Becca Taylor isn't who you think she is."

"I know exactly who Becca is." Grams sounded one hundred percent confident. "She's a sweet, hardworking woman and my friend."

One who takes, takes, takes before hightailing it out of there.

"Your friend Becca, aka Rebecca Taylor, is a convicted criminal. She spent three years at the Idaho Women's Correctional Center." Caleb expected to see a reaction, but didn't. Maybe Grams was trying to take it all in. "We're not talking shoplifting, Grams. Theft, trespassing and vandalism."

Grams tapped her finger against her cheek. "How did you find out?"

"A private investigator." He raised the folder in the air, careful to keep his excitement out of his voice. "I know you consider Becca a friend and she's been helping you, but she's taking advantage of you. Fire her. Get her out of the guesthouse. Out of your life. Before she hurts you and robs you blind."

"Just because a person makes a mistake in the past doesn't mean they'll repeat it in the future."

"She is a crook." He didn't understand why his grandmother

was being so understanding. She should be upset, furious. Maybe she was in shock. "I'll bet Becca learned more ways to break the law while she was in jail."

Grams picked up her pink lemonade and stared into the glass. "Becca told me all about her time in prison."

"You knew about this?"

"She told me everything before she accepted my job offer."

Outrage choked him. "Yet you hired her anyway? Let her move in?"

"She made a youthful mistake."

He scoffed. "That mistake landed her in jail."

"She paid the price for her actions. Learned her lesson."

"We're not talking about an overdue library book." He stared at his grandmother in disbelief. "You can't have a criminal working for you. It's not safe."

"Becca would never hurt me."

"She is a convicted—"

"I respect her honesty and integrity," Grams interrupted. "I'm not going to hold the past against her. Neither should you."

"Don't make me out to be the bad guy here. I didn't rob anybody," he countered. "I'm trying to look out for you, Grams. That's what Gramps wanted me to do. You have a big heart. People have taken advantage of you in the past."

"People need the opportunity to make a fresh start."

Caleb's jaw tensed. "You gave my father plenty of fresh starts. He blew every single one."

"Becca is nothing like him."

"That's true," Caleb agreed. "My father was never in jail."

"Your father had his own issues," Grams said. "But even if he'd gone to jail, it wouldn't have changed the way I felt about him. People deserve another chance."

Everyone meaning Becca. And…his father.

A weight pressed down on Caleb's chest, squeezing the air out of his lungs and the blood out of his heart. "How many fresh starts did you give my father?"

"If your father were alive today, I'd be giving him another

chance the way I'm doing with Becca. That's what you do when you love someone."

"Rebecca Taylor is a complete stranger."

"To you. Not to me. I care what happens to her," Grams said. "And I'm much more interested in the woman she is today than the girl she was at eighteen."

Caleb pressed his lips together. This wasn't how he'd imagined the conversation going. "You don't know if she's told you the truth. Read the report, then you can decide—"

"I've made my decision about Becca. Nothing is going to change my mind, but you should talk to her about this and appease your concerns."

"You're that sure about her."

"Yes," Grams said. "I want you to be sure about Becca, too. Talk to her about your concerns. Let her explain what happened."

That would be a complete waste of time.

Nothing Becca had to say would change his mind.

Absolutely nothing.

Grams's eyes implored him. "Please, Caleb. Speak with Becca. For me."

Screw Caleb Fairchild for delving into her business.

Becca balled her hands. The tenth floor of Fair Face's corporate headquarters was the last place she wanted to be tonight.

"Mr. Fairchild will see you now," a middle-aged uniformed security guard said. "Follow me."

Becca walked down an empty hallway. The fifth draft of the business plan inside her gray-and-black messenger bag bumped against her hip.

She adjusted the bag's strap. She wasn't even sure why she'd brought the plan along. Maybe to show Caleb she'd been working, not plotting a crime against his grandmother.

As if he would believe her.

She glanced at the guard. "It's quiet."

"Most folks have gone home," he said.

The carpet muted their footsteps, unlike the correction facility where sound echoed. Instead of passing walled cells with solid metal doors and slits for windows, she passed offices with mahogany wood doors and brass nameplates. No one whispered her name or called her something nasty. No one shot dagger-filled stares or tried to beat her up when the guards weren't looking.

But the memories hit her hard. The sounds. The smells. The bone-chilling cold she could never seem to shake even during the long, hot summers.

Becca crossed her arms over her chest.

She wanted to forget about all that. Not relieve the worst three years of her life to appease Caleb Fairchild's curiosity. But she would talk to him…for Gertie's sake.

At the end of the hallway, the guard pointed to an office with its door open. A light was on inside. "That's Mr. Fairchild's office."

She wondered if Mr. Fairchild had asked the guard to stick around outside his office while they spoke. After all, she was a hardened criminal. She forced a tight smile. "Thanks."

She entered the office.

Big. She hadn't expected the office to be this large, complete with a round table surrounded by six chairs, a couch and coffee table, a large desk, chairs, bookcases along her right side and floor to ceiling windows on the two far corner walls.

Then again, Caleb Fairchild was the CEO.

He sat at his desk, a portrait in concentration as he stared at his computer monitor.

Caleb looked every bit the handsome business executive—if you liked that type. Even though it was past quitting time, every strand of his hair was in place, his tie knotted tightly around his neck and his sleeves unrolled. The only thing missing was his suit jacket.

He looked clean cut, respectable and proper. But as with Whit who'd gotten her in so much trouble, Becca knew looks could be deceiving. Caleb was a shark waiting to attack and take her out. Exactly the sort she tried to avoid. But tonight she was venturing into his water without a harpoon or any way to defend herself except her word against his suspicions.

It wasn't going to be pretty.

Though he still hadn't noticed her, so maybe she had a chance of surviving. She cleared her throat.

Caleb's cool, assessing gaze met hers.

A chill shivered down her spine.

He stood. "Good evening, Becca."

She saw nothing good about it. He had some nerve hiring a P.I. As if she would have lied about her past to his grandmother. She'd dealt with enough liars and fakes growing up and while she was in jail to ever want to be one.

Becca bit the inside of her cheek.

"Close the door so we have some privacy," he said.

She hadn't seen another person in the building except the security guard. Guess he would be hanging around out in the hallway. Figured. She closed the door.

"Thanks." He motioned to one of the two black leather chairs in front of the large desk. "Have a seat."

Standing wouldn't give her that much of an advantage over sitting seeing as she was out of her element and on his home turf. She crossed his office, removed her messenger bag then sat, sinking into a chair. She ran her fingertips along the buttery soft leather. This furniture was much nicer than anything in her parents' house. "Gertie said you had questions for me."

His gaze didn't waver from Becca's. "You don't waste any time."

Her temperature increased. No doubt stress from his hawk-like gaze. He saw her as a vulture circling over his grandmother. "You've made it clear you're a busy man."

He walked around the front of the desk and sat on the edge.

Needing something to do with her hands, Becca picked dog hair off her skirt.

She'd spent an hour trying to figure out what to wear, finally deciding on one of her dog-show suits—teal skirt, matching three-quarter-sleeve jacket and a lace-trimmed camisole underneath. She wasn't sure what the proper attire was for explaining one's prison record, but this was better than a pair of Daisy Duke shorts and a camisole.

"Tell me how you ended up in prison," he said matter-of-factly.

Becca took a deep breath. She glanced around the room, not really seeing anything. She took another breath, then met his gaze directly. "I was an idiot."

He drew back with confusion in his eyes. "Excuse me?"

"I did something really stupid." Becca rubbed her face. "I fell for a guy. I thought he liked me, so I trusted him. Big mistake."

One corner of Caleb's mouth rose, but she wouldn't call it a smile. Not a half-one, either. "You're not the first to be led astray by their heart."

He sounded as if he'd been there, done that, got the T-shirt. But being led astray and wearing prison garb for three years were totally different things.

Becca had been so naive to think a rich boy like Whitley would want her—a girl from the trailer park. Yet he'd made her feel so…different. Special. Glamorous. Trying to be cool had enticed her to be reckless. She raised her chin. "I should have known better. Whitley was the brother of a girl I'd gotten to know through dog showing. They were wealthy. I wasn't. But Whit didn't seem to care."

"Whit is the man."

"Boy," she clarified. "I couldn't believe when he asked me out for a smoothie. I wanted him to like me, so I tried to be the type of girl he'd want to date, even if that wasn't who I was. I fell…hard."

So hard she'd found herself thumbing through a bridal magazine at the grocery store and imagining what color dresses the bridesmaids should wear. "I'd recently graduated high school. It was summertime. We went out almost every night and then…"

Memories hit strong and fast. The flashing of red and blue

lights. The accusations. The tears. The handcuffs scraping her wrists. Being read her Miranda rights.

Someone touched her shoulder.

She jumped.

Caleb held up his hands as if surrendering. His eyes were dark. Concerned. "Sorry. You looked miles away for a second."

Not miles, years. She stood, backing away from him. "Just…remembering."

"This is hard for you."

Becca nodded, not trusting her voice. A compassionate person would tell her to stop.

Not Caleb.

He didn't say a word, but remained perched on his desk as if he might attack at any minute. Not so much a shark now—more like a dangerous hawk ready to swoop down on his prey.

On her.

A thrill fissured through her. So not the reaction she should have around him.

Becca shouldn't react to him at all. Or notice all these little details about him.

She hated that she did.

CHAPTER FIVE

BECCA WALKED TO one of the bookcases, the one closest to the office's door and farthest away from Caleb. Oh, he was handsome and could turn on the charm faster than she could blink. Tonight she saw an edge to him she hadn't see before, an edge that appealed to her.

But she knew his type all too well.

Whatever she said tonight would fall on deaf ears. He'd been suspicious of her since the day they met. Nothing was going to change his mind about her.

He'd likely agreed to attend the dog show, not to see the new products in action, but to watch her because of her criminal past.

"I'm not a bad person," she said.

"I never said you were."

But he hadn't said she wasn't, either.

No one cared about the truth. "Guilty" was all that mattered to people. What happened hadn't been forgotten. And wouldn't be. It followed her everywhere.

Or had until she'd met Gertie.

Caleb wouldn't be as understanding. That was why this was so hard for Becca.

She noticed a black-framed photo of him and another man. Both men were attractive. The other guy wasn't as handsome as Caleb, but as fit with a muscular V-shaped physique. A triangle folded American flag with military ribbons sat on the shelf above the picture.

Becca realized she was procrastinating. Might as well get this over with. She looked over at Caleb.

His dark gaze met hers. "Take your time."

"I don't want to drag this out any longer." Telling him what had happened was the only thing that would loosen the tension in her neck. "Whit asked if I wanted to hang out with him and some of his friends. I said yes, thinking things must be getting serious if he wanted to introduce me to his friends."

"A reasonable assumption."

"Reasonable, but wrong," she admitted. "He was interested in me, but not as a girlfriend. I was being set up to be the patsy. The scapegoat. The one they could blame if their plans to break in to the bank president's house to steal cash to buy drugs went south."

"They don't sound like the Honor Society kids."

"Some were. Others were jocks. But they were no better than a gang of hoodlums. They just wore designer clothes and drove nice cars."

"You were part of it."

"No. I had no idea what they were planning." She forced herself not to make a face at him and read the titles of the business books on the shelf instead. A few military strategy type books were mixed in with the marketing and finance titles. "Whit said we were going to hop the fence and go hot-tubbing while the guy was on vacation. I was wearing my bikini underneath my clothing and had a towel crammed in my bag."

But not even those things, including the panties and bra she'd brought to change into, had mattered to the police.

"It wasn't until we were inside the house and not in the backyard that I realized what they were planning. But I thought Whit liked me, so I..."

Becca bit her lip. She couldn't bring herself to say the words.

"You went along," Caleb finished for her.

She nodded. Embarrassed, regretful and ashamed. "I was

trying to fit into Whit's world. I was afraid to speak up, so I just followed his lead."

"I take it things didn't turn out as planned."

"No one knew about the high-tech security system in the house. The police caught us inside, and then…"

Her chest tightened with Whit's betrayal. Becca took a breath and another. It didn't help. "Everyone turned on me. Pointed their fingers at me. Blamed me. They said it had been all my idea. I had picked the lock. Stolen the money."

"But the police should have—"

"The police believed them. Why wouldn't they? My dad had spent time in the county jail for getting into a fight. I was the resident trailer trash. No one was surprised to find me involved in something like this. Not to mention my fingerprints were all over the evidence."

Caleb's eyes widened. "How did that happen?"

She understood the disbelief in his tone. Her parents and lawyer had sounded the same way. "Whit had me wrapped around his little finger. *Open the door, gorgeous. Hold this tool, beautiful. Have you ever seen this much money before? Want to hold it?*"

She hadn't, and she did.

"But the other kids were accessories to the crime," he said. "Whit, too."

"True, but they had high-priced attorneys who managed to get the charges reduced or dropped."

"That doesn't seem fair."

"It wasn't. But life has never been fair to people like me." Caleb's privileged upbringing would affect one's perspective as much as growing up in a trailer park had hers. "Luck wasn't on my side, either. I'd turned eighteen two days before, so was legally considered an adult. My parents couldn't afford a lawyer so I was assigned a public defender. Due to the evidence and witnesses…"

"Whit and his friends cut a deal."

Becca nodded. "My lawyer recommended a plea bargain."

"You took it."

"I wanted to fight the charges, but my parents thought three years in prison was better than the alternative, so I did what my lawyer wanted."

Caleb didn't say anything.

That didn't surprise her. She stared at a photograph of Caleb surrounded by bikini-clad supermodels. There was another picture of the Fairchild family—Caleb, a young woman who must be Courtney, Gertie and her late husband. All four people looked so happy and carefree with bright smiles on their faces.

Becca wondered what it would be like to feel so happy and content. Just once she would like to know.

"You must have been scared," Caleb said.

"Terrified." She still was some days, but he didn't need to know that. "I understand if you don't believe me. But it's what happened."

"A hard lesson to learn."

She walked back to the chair, but remained standing. "I wouldn't wish the three years I spent locked up on anybody. Not even the kids who set me up me that night."

"Regrets?"

"I know people say you shouldn't have regrets, but if I could go back to change that one night I would. Being in jail…it sucked. But I learned my lesson. I'm not going to try to be someone I'm not ever again."

She waited for him to ask the inevitable questions about whether she was part of a gang or if she had a girlfriend or something else he might have seen on television.

"I'm sorry," he said finally.

Her gaze jerked up. "Excuse me."

"I'm sorry you had to go through that."

She didn't say anything. She wasn't sure what to think of his words or the sentiment behind them.

"So what happened after you got out of jail?" he asked.

"I tried to start where I left off. But it wasn't as easy as I thought that it would be."

"Why not?"

"I kept filling out applications and being turned down for job interviews. Even though I'd done my time, people still saw me as a criminal."

He shifted positions on the desk. "What did you do?"

"I'd been planning to go to college to become a vet tech before all this happened, so applied to a few programs and eventually got accepted to one. I used the scholarships I'd won through dog showing and worked every odd job I could find to cover tuition. But after I had my degree, I ran into the same problems as before. I couldn't find a veterinary clinic back home that would hire me."

"Your past."

"My past is very much my present. I fear it always will be. As our conversation tonight proves once again."

He stared at the carpet.

Feeling guilty? Becca hoped so, and she wasn't going to back down. "They say you can't be tried twice for the same crime, but that's only in a court of law. People don't forget, and they hold a grudge. I moved to Boise because I thought I'd have more opportunities here."

"Have you?"

"A few," she said. "I found a job at an animal hospital. A professional dog handler I'd known through 4-H as a kid and as a junior handler in AKC took pity on me and asked if I wanted to be her apprentice. That's how I met Gertie."

"My grandmother doesn't care about your past."

"Gertie is one in a million." Thinking about Gertie made Becca want to smile for the first tine since she'd left the estate earlier. "I wish more people were like her. But they're not."

They were more like Caleb.

That was one reason she preferred the company of dogs to people. Dogs were more loyal, understanding, loving.

"Any other questions?" she asked. "I'm happy to give you the name of my former probation officer. Though he can't guarantee I'm not trying to scam your grandmother."

A blush colored Caleb's cheeks. "She told you."

"She warned me."

"This isn't personal." He sounded defensive. "I'm only try-ing to protect her."

"As you should," she agreed. "If I weren't your target, I'd say your chivalry is sweet even if it's…misguided. But this isn't the first time it's happened to me. I know it won't be the last."

"You're resigned to that."

"Annoyed by it, too. But what am I going to do?"

Nothing she'd done so far had changed people's opinion of her. But that hadn't stopped her from trying. From work-ing the worst shifts at the animal hospital to busting her butt doing whatever Gertie asked, Becca had wanted to earn peo-ple's respect, to be…accepted for who she was now. Not who she'd been before.

"You could move out of Idaho," he said.

"I'm far enough away from my parents as it is."

"Family is important to you."

"It's all I've got."

"Me, too," he said.

A warm look passed between them. Becca found herself getting lost in Caleb's eyes. What was going on? She never ex-pected to have anything in common with Caleb. Well, except for liking chocolate cake and Gertie. But he was more com-plicated and different from what Becca expected.

"Grams told me you've been working on a revised business plan. Did you bring it with you?" he asked.

"Business plan?" She blinked at the sudden change of topic. "I have it. But I didn't think you were still going to advise us."

"Why not?"

"You only agreed because you had doubts about me."

"That's true."

Her heart fell. Spilling her guts hadn't changed anything. She shouldn't feel as disappointed as she did. "You still have doubts."

"I told my grandmother I would help her," he said. "I'm not going back on my word."

She respected Caleb for being a man of his word, especially when his agreeing had meant so much to Gertie. But he hadn't denied still having doubts about Becca.

That had happened before.

It would happen again.

But she was surprised how much it hurt now.

Caleb was wrong about Becca.

Wrong about her motives. Wrong about her past.

He loosened his tie.

Caleb had misjudged her. Completely.

What she'd said about struggling after getting out of prison jibed with the private investigator's report. She'd admitted her father had spent time in jail, too.

Her education and experience wouldn't give her the knowledge to pull off a big financial scam. Though he couldn't deny the possibility of a theft on a smaller scale.

He glanced up from Becca's business plan.

In her teal suit, standing by one of his bookcases, she looked like a consultant. Professional. Knowledgable. A world apart from the woman he'd met in his grandmother's backyard.

But whether dressed to the nines or in bright orange prison garb, she was the same woman. A woman eager to rebuild her life. A woman he found himself wanting to learn more and more about.

Her story about Whit sounded all too plausible to Caleb. He knew guys like that, his father was like that, his experience with Cassandra had been like that.

Becca was most likely exactly what she seemed to be—a hopeful dog whisperer who was caught up in one of his grandmother's schemes through no fault of her own.

Moving a foot away from him, Becca pulled out a book, read the inside flap, then placed it back on the shelf. She did the same with another.

Con artists, like his Cassandra, were good at sob stories, but Becca seemed too genuine, her behavior too natural and awkward and uncomplicated. She didn't appear to be a threat, but he'd deal with her if that changed.

For now, Caleb would go along with his grandmother's gamble. A part of him admired Becca. That was rare.

But he still had to be careful for all their sakes.

"You're welcome to borrow any of the books," he said.

"Is there one you'd recommend?"

"Strategic Marketing and Branding."

Becca touched each of the book spines with her fingertip, searching for the title. She pulled one out. "Here it is."

"You know the market and the industry, but having a thought out branding strategy can make all the difference," he explained. "The book will be a good introduction to the buzzwords and approaches being used."

She studied the front cover. "Thanks."

"You're welcome."

He thought she would walk back toward his desk. She didn't. Instead she kept looking at the items on the shelves.

"The USS *Essex.*" Becca studied one of the small replicas of aircraft carriers. "Gertie has a larger version of this in her collection."

"Gramps was assigned to the USS *Essex* during the Korean War. He fell in love with aircraft carriers. Grams used to give him the models on special occasions."

"What a wonderful gift." Becca bent to take a closer look at the shelf containing the models. Her skirt rose in the back, showing off her firm thighs. "The USS *Vinson.*"

His groin tightened. He tried not to stare. "Yes."

"I've seen that one, too." She straightened. "Your grandfather had large replicas at home and small models here at the office?"

"The smaller ones are mine."

She glanced his way. "Yours?"

He nodded, a part of him wishing she could be his tonight.

Whoa. Where had that come from?

He'd been working too hard if his mind was going…there.

Grams hadn't mentioned if Becca had a boyfriend, but Caleb imagined she did. A man who thought nothing of carrying lint rollers, doggy treats and poop bags wherever he went.

Someone totally opposite to Caleb.

He couldn't keep a plant alive, let alone be responsible for a pet. It wouldn't be fair to a dog or cat or fish.

Not that he wanted a girlfriend. He dated when he had time, but kept things…light. It was easier that way, given his schedule.

He secured her pages with a binder clip. "Excellent work on the business plan."

A smile tugged at her lips. He waited for one to explode and light up her face. The right corner lifted another quarter of inch before shooting back into place as if she'd realized she was going five miles per hour over the speed limit and needed to slow down before getting pulled over.

She smiled for Grams, but not him.

That bothered Caleb. He wanted a smile.

Becca bit her lip, gnawing at it like a piece of jerky, a stale piece. "I don't think it's ever going to be ready."

"Iterative process, remember?"

She shrugged.

Ah-ha. A perfectionist. Caleb had a couple on his staff—hard workers—but their never-satisfied, not-good-enough tendencies made end-of-the-quarter more stressful. "What you've done so far is pretty impressive."

Something—pride, maybe?—flashed in her eyes. But the same wariness from before quickly took over. "You think?"

He nodded. "It's obvious you've been working hard revising the drafts."

"That's what Gertie pays me to do."

"You're doing it very well." He would have known that if he'd listened to his grandmother instead of telling her to fire her consultant. He was sure Grams wouldn't let him forget that, either.

Becca straightened, as if he'd finally gotten her attention. Or she liked what he'd said.

"There are a few areas where you'll need to do more research," he added.

"Manufacturing, for sure. And the product containers are giving me a real headache." She was one step ahead of him. "Everything is priced based on quantity. Making that initial order seems to be based on magic."

"A Magic 8 Ball, actually."

"You're…" Her gaze narrowed. "Kidding."

"Had you going for a minute," he teased.

Amusement gleamed in her eyes. "Twenty seconds tops."

"Forty at least."

Her smile burst across her face like the sun at dawn.

He couldn't breathe.

"Thirty," she said playfully. "Not a nanosecond longer."

With her eyes bright and her face glowing, she looked… gorgeous. It was his turn to speak, but Caleb didn't know what to say. All he could do was stare.

She studied him. "Have you ever consulted a Magic 8 Ball?"

"No, but my sister Courtney had one. Swore it worked."

"And you kidded her about that."

"I'm her older brother. Of course I did."

"I'm not surprised," Becca said. "You're not the kind of person who leaves things up to chance, let alone a fortune-telling game."

Interesting observation and dead-on. "Why do you say that?"

She motioned to the books on the shelf. "The business books mixed in with military ones. Strategy. War. That suggests you like to be prepared. Know what you're up against. Have a solid plan and an exit strategy. You take a tactical approach. At least you did with me."

"I may have had some bad intel."

"It happens."

She didn't sound upset. That was a relief. "You're observant."

Becca lifted one shoulder. "I keep my eyes open so I know what's going on."

A lesson learned. No doubt because of what had happened to her when she was younger. Caleb was the same way thanks to Cassandra. Interesting that he and Becca had been used in similar ways. Though hers had been much worse. "It's not good being caught off-guard."

"Nope." She motioned to the other shelf with his memorabilia. "Was the flag your grandfather's?"

"Yes. From his funeral."

She pointed to one of the photographs. "Who's this?"

Caleb crossed the office, picked up a framed photo of him with Ty Dooley. "My best friend since third grade. He's in the navy."

"The two of you look like you could be brothers."

"Ty's like a brother." He was living the dream for both of them. Right now Ty was downrange somewhere classified. Caleb couldn't wait to see him again. "We planned on being in the navy together."

A grin spread across her face. "You wanted to follow in your grandfather's footsteps."

Caleb's muscles tensed. He'd never told anyone that except Ty. Becca guessing that made Caleb feel stripped bare and vulnerable. He didn't like it. He nodded once.

She studied him, her gaze sharp and assessing. "Military service is honorable, but you're following in your grandfather's footsteps by being Fair Face's CEO."

True, but Caleb felt no satisfaction. He'd wanted to be the kind of man his grandfather had been and nothing like his father.

Becca pointed to another photograph of Caleb with itty-bitty-bikini-clad supermodels clinging to him. "Most men would kill to be in your position."

He wasn't "most men."

The decision to run Fair Face had never been his to make. His worthless father hadn't wanted anything to do with the family company. To say that everything had fallen to Caleb was an understatement. He'd had to grow up fast. "What's the saying…? The grass is always greener."

"I wouldn't have expected that kind of longing from you."

Of course she wouldn't. But this—he glanced around the office—was never who he'd expected to be growing up. He'd dreamed about being a navy SEAL for as long as he could remember. Not the CEO of a skin-care company. "I'm sure there's something you wanted to be when you were growing up."

Becca nodded. "A vet. But I was a kid then. Very naive about how the world worked."

"Me, too," he said. "But that's what being a kid is all about. Dreaming of doing what sounds cool without understanding our places in the world."

"Too bad you couldn't trade jobs with your friend Ty for a week. Bet he'd enjoy hanging with supermodels while you swabbed decks on a ship or sub."

Caleb nearly laughed. An M4 rifle was more likely to be found in his best friend's hands, not a mop. Ty was one of the elite special ops guys, a navy SEAL, stationed in Virginia Beach on a Tier One team. Caleb would love a taste of Ty's life. "Fun idea, but I doubt I'd like swabbing decks."

"So you're more into adventure," she said. "Bet you'd like Special Forces kind of stuff. Best-of-the-best kind of thing."

Caleb didn't understand how she kept nailing him. He moved away from her. "What guy wouldn't?"

"Some might not, given the danger and risk involved, but I can see why it would appeal to you."

"Why is that?"

She tilted her chin. "The leadership skills you've honed as CEO would be useful even if the arena was different. Teamwork, too. No more profit margins, but life-or-death stakes. Kick-ass missions that would be more stressful than anything you've dealt with, but exciting due to the physical and mental challenges. You'd be surrounded by smart people. I'd assume someone who wasn't intelligent wouldn't last long, but in corporate America brainpower doesn't appear to be a prerequisite for rising to the top. At least here at Fair Face."

She might lack business experience, but she had what Grams would call gumption. "Not liking my grandmother's dog products doesn't mean employees here are stupid."

"Liking the products would prove they were smart." Becca stared at the photo of him and Ty again. "I think the real draw to your friend's lifestyle is loyalty. To the country, the service, your teammates. Heaven knows, you're loyal to your family."

Caleb couldn't move. Breathe. Blink.

How did she know this about him? A woman he'd known less than a week. One he'd underestimated.

"I suppose being in the navy would be more interesting work than sitting in meetings all day wondering what SPF of sunscreen would sell best," she added.

He found himself nodding.

"My only question is if joining the navy was so important to you, why didn't you enlist?" she asked.

"My family. Fair Face," he admitted. "They needed me."

"You wouldn't have been in the navy forever."

"No, but I was needed here. What I wanted to do…" He glanced at the photograph of Ty and him. "It was secondary."

Her eyes softened. "You love your family."

"Everyone loves their family."

"Not everyone would sacrifice their dreams."

Caleb shrugged, but the last thing he felt was indifference. He rubbed the back of his neck. He didn't want to have this conversation. He glanced at his watch, more out of habit than anything else. "It's getting late. I'll walk you to your car."

"Thanks, but that's not necessary," she said, a hint of a tremor in her voice. "My car is at the Park & Ride lot. I rode the bus into downtown."

"You took the bus?"

"Gas is expensive."

His grandmother had to be paying her a bundle, plus providing a free place for her to stay. Not to mention her job at the animal hospital. "You can't have money trouble."

She glared at him.

Forget daggers—Becca was firing mortar in his direction. He turned his hands palms up. "What?"

"I never said I couldn't afford it." Becca shot him a get-a-clue look. "Why should I want to waste my hard-earned cash to drive into town so you could try to get me fired?"

Stubborn. She also looked cute when she was angry. "Saving money is always good, especially when there's a motive or desire behind it. My grandfather taught me to save for a rainy day."

"Rain, thunderstorm, monsoon." Her fingers tightened around the strap of her messenger bag. "You never know what the future holds."

Caleb's life proved that was true.

"It's best to be prepared for anything." Well, almost anything. He hadn't been prepared for Becca. He should drive her home and see how deep her stubbornness ran. He shoved his laptop into his bag. "Come on, I'll walk you out."

CHAPTER SIX

WALKING ACROSS THE lobby of Fair Face's corporate headquarters, footsteps echoing on the tiled floor and questions swirling through her brain, Becca eyed the man next to her.

Caleb Fairchild looked like the perfect CEO in his gray suit—acted like one, too—but underneath the pinstripes was another man. A man who dreamed of adventure. A man who longed to serve his country. A man who sacrificed those dreams for his family.

Becca wondered if he ever let that side of himself show to anyone except his best friend. She would like to see it.

She'd been immune to pretty faces, charming smiles, killer eyes since the judge dropped the gavel in the courthouse in Twin Falls, Idaho. She went on occasional dates with working-class guys and cowboy types to have a little fun, but she always kept things casual. She was afraid of being burned again. She hadn't met anyone she'd wanted to get closer to. Getting closer to a guy made her vulnerable, a way she didn't like feeling.

Not that she wanted to get close to Caleb. But she had to admit the guy interested her. In a way she hadn't been interested in…well, forever. That was…a problem.

Her parents had a great marriage in spite of their financial struggles. But Becca knew finding a man who could accept her and her past wasn't going to be easy. Maybe that was why she hadn't been looking too hard to find "the one."

They passed another employee who was staying late that

evening. Caleb greeted him by name, the third in the past five minutes. "I hope you know how impressed we all were with those new label designs, Anthony. Great work."

The employee, an older man with gray hair and wire-rimmed glasses, walked away with a proud grin on his face and standing two inches taller.

"Do you know every single person who works here?" she asked.

"No, but everyone wears a badge," Caleb said. "That helps with the names."

Considerate of him, even though he'd accused her of trying to steal from Gertie. "The employees seem to appreciate your effort."

"They work hard." Caleb opened one of the double glass doors for her. "It's the least I can do."

"Thanks." His manners had impressed Becca the first time they'd met. She was impressed now in spite of his accusations. But she wouldn't allow herself to be taken in by him. Caleb Fairchild was no different from any other rich guy. She walked outside into bright daylight and stifling heat even though it was after seven at night. "The temperature hasn't dropped at all."

Two construction workers wearing paint splattered coveralls and carrying hard hats, walked toward them with tired smiles.

Caleb removed his suit jacket and draped it over his left arm. "Welcome to summer in Boise."

A fluorescent green food truck idled curbside with a line of customers waiting. The scent of garlic and rosemary filled the air. Becca's mouth watered. She stared at the plate of noodles and pork being dished up through the window.

"Hungry?" Caleb asked.

"A little." She hadn't eaten lunch. "Whatever they're cooking smells good."

"It does."

A siren wailed.

Goosebumps covered her skin in spite of the heat. She hated

sirens. The sound brought back too many memories, memories she wanted to forget.

Hearing the handcuffs lock around her wrists. Being shoved into a police car. Feeling the heartbreak of betrayal.

Becca crossed her arms in front of her chest and forced herself to keep walking.

She wished she could forget. She wished others could forget, too. She wished people would trust her.

Not just people. A person. Caleb.

The realization disturbed her as much as the siren.

Caleb's opinion didn't matter. And if she kept telling herself that she might finally believe it.

Stop thinking about him!

The sound faded into the distance.

With a deep breath, she lowered her arms then pointed to a white sign about ten feet in front of them. "This is where I catch the bus."

Caleb looked around at the few people waiting. "Let me drive you to the Park & Ride lot. I can follow you back to Grams's place and we can have dinner."

Becca's breath caught in her throat. She opened her mouth to speak. No words came out. She tried again. "Thanks, but there's no need for you to go to so much trouble."

"I need to eat, too." He whipped out his cellphone. "I'll see if Grams has eaten or not."

Dinner with Gertie, not a date with Caleb.

Becca should be relieved, not disappointed. The guy had serious doubts about her. He was everything she didn't want in a man. He was likely asking her to make amends for making her come here tonight. Of course, she'd never said yes to either the ride or dinner.

Caleb flashed his phone, showing her a text exchange. "Mrs. Harrison was going to warm something up for Grams, but she would rather have pizza. Does salad and a pepperoni pizza with mushrooms sound good?"

"Sounds great." The words escaped before Becca could

stop them. Darn, she knew better. On the bright side, Gertie would be thrilled to have her grandson there again and Becca wouldn't have to worry about making dinner tonight.

He typed on his phone. Messages pinged back and forth. "We're all set. Grams will have the pizza delivered."

Becca glanced at the bus stop, then looked at Caleb. "Back to Fair Face."

"My car is in the parking lot of the building next door," Caleb said.

"Gertie said there was parking available beneath Fair Face."

"There is."

This wasn't making sense. "Why aren't you parked there?"

"I prefer to let the employees and visitors use the closer spots."

Becca didn't want to be more impressed. She didn't want to like him, either. But she was. And she did in spite of a growing list of reasons she shouldn't. The guy took his responsibilities seriously.

She sneaked a peek at his profile. So handsome and strong and determined.

Maybe he took things too seriously.

A few minutes later, Caleb opened the door leading to a bank of elevators, blasting her with cool, refreshing air.

She stepped inside and waited for him to join her. "Please don't think you have to add me to your list."

"What list?"

"The list of people and things you have to take care of."

His eyes widened. His lips parted. Shock turned to confusion followed by a blank expression. "What do you mean?"

Maybe he was better at poker than she thought. If Becca hadn't been paying attention, she would have missed the play of emotion across his face. "Seems like you're the one responsible for taking care of your grandmother, your sister, Fair Face and your employees. I wouldn't want you to think I need taking care of, too."

"I didn't think that," he said. "You seem capable of caring for yourself."

She nodded. "But it makes me wonder."

"What?"

"Who takes care of you?"

His eyes clouded. His posture stiffened. "I take care of myself. I also know Ty has my six."

"Your friend in the navy."

"Best friend," Caleb said.

"I wish I had a best friend like that."

"You don't?"

"I haven't had a best friend since I was in seventh grade." Cecily Parker had lived in the trailer park for six months. The best six months of Becca's childhood. She and Cecily did everything together—rode the school bus, ate lunch in the cafeteria, had sleepovers. "Her mom met some guy online and moved to Cincinnati. Never heard from my friend again."

"What stopped you from getting a new best friend?"

"No one wanted to be friends with the kid who lived in the trailer park."

"You don't live in a trailer now."

"No, but making friends is different when you're older."

"That's true."

But some things hadn't changed.

Becca hadn't spent the last few years trying to get her life back together to make the same mistake again with Caleb. He wasn't Whit, but Caleb was rich, handsome and powerful, the kind of man who could get away with anything. The kind of man who wouldn't think twice about breaking her heart.

She needed to be smart about this, about him.

She'd agreed to a ride and dinner, but that was all. He could advise them. Help them. But keeping her distance from him would be her smartest move. Even if that was the last thing she wanted to do.

After dinner, Caleb walked out onto his grandmother's patio. Becca Taylor intrigued him. He didn't need a PhD to realize she didn't want to spend one more minute in his company.

Her not saying a word on the drive to the Park & Ride lot had been his first clue. The way she'd sat at the opposite end of the table, as far away from him as possible, had been his second clue. The way she'd scarfed down her pizza and salad, as if a bomb was about to explode if she didn't eat fast enough, and excused herself without wanting dessert had been his third and fourth clues.

No other woman had been so blatant in their dislike of him.

A door opened behind him.

"I thought you were heading home," Grams said.

Him, too. But something had stopped him from leaving. Not something. Someone. "I thought I might check on Becca first."

"She seemed preoccupied over dinner," Grams said.

He felt responsible. "Telling me what happened wasn't easy for her."

"But she did."

"Becca was very open about it." More so than he would have been if he'd been the one asked to explain.

"Do you still think she's trying to fleece me?"

You still have doubts.

Earlier this evening, the hurt in Becca's voice had sliced through him, raw and jagged and deep. But she was correct. He still had doubts. Becca was a stranger, an unknown quantity.

"People have ulterior motives and hidden agendas." Both his ex-fiancée and his mother, the definition of a gold digger, had had them. "That's human nature."

"Becca wouldn't hurt me or anybody."

Caleb wished he had Grams's confidence. But that was a lesson he should have learned from his father's mistakes. Instead, it had taken Cassandra to teach him that trust was something to be earned, not given freely to a stranger. "Maybe I'll feel that way after I get to know Becca better."

Though she knew him well enough. She understood him better than his family. Better than Cassandra. Better than everybody else in his life with the exception of Ty.

That bothered Caleb. If the wrong people knew too much, they could use that to their advantage. They could hurt you.

"I'm sure you will." Grams touched his arm. "It's getting late. Check on Becca, then head home."

"Will do." He hugged his grandmother. "And before I forget, thanks for the pizza and the cake."

Grams beamed. "This is your home. You're welcome anytime."

Being here brought back good memories and feelings of contentment. "Thanks."

Caleb followed the lighted path away from the patio. Stars filled the dark sky. Satellites circled above. The moon hung low.

A beautiful night. One he would have been spending alone in his loft working if not for Becca. Sure, he could have seen the sky from the twenty-foot windows, but he much preferred being here.

A cry filled the air. Not a human. A dog. In pain.

Adrenaline surged. Caleb broke into a run.

Becca.

The moans continued. Barking from other dogs, too.

Caleb knew it was a dog hurting, but his heart pounded against his ribs.

What if he was wrong? What if she was hurt?

He quickened his pace, his breath coming hard and fast.

Only the porch light was on at the guest cottage. He continued to the kennel.

The door was open, the lights on.

He ran inside.

Dogs stood at the front of their kennels barking and agitated.

He glanced around.

Becca sat on the floor, her legs extended. A stethoscope hung around her neck. She wore an ivory-colored lace-trimmed camisole that stretched across her chest. Her suit jacket covered the dog lying across her lap. The animal was the one who'd shed all over Caleb.

What was the dog's name? Morris?

No, Maurice. The Norwegian elkhound.

Caleb kneeled at Becca's side. Touched her bare shoulder. Ignored her soft skin and warmth beneath his hand. "What's going on?"

"Maurice." She rubbed the dog. "His stomach is distended. He's gassy and in pain."

The dog looked miserable. The other dogs wouldn't stop barking. Maurice wouldn't move.

"Is it serious?" Caleb asked.

"I don't know. I'm not sure what's wrong," she said. "The staff only uses products Gertie's made or approved, so I'm not worried about chemical poisoning. But if Maurice ate too much, there's the risk of bloat. His stomach could flip. Elkhounds aren't as prone as other breeds, but his pulse is high. Heart rate, too. I gave Gertie a call, but she didn't answer."

"She was on the patio with me."

"I'm going to take Maurice to the animal hospital where I work. I'd rather not take any chances."

Becca spoke calmly and in control, but worry filmed her eyes. He wanted to kiss it away. Hell, he wanted to make the poor dog feel better, too. "I'll let my grandmother know."

About to reach for his cellphone, Caleb realized he was still touching Becca's shoulder. He hadn't noticed. The gesture felt so natural, so right. Maybe because she was so different from other women he'd known, especially Cassandra. Maybe that was why Becca felt…safe. He lowered his arm then pulled out his phone.

"Tell Gertie not to worry," Becca said. "The door to the food cabinet door was ajar. Maurice might have gotten into there and gorged himself on whatever he found."

The dog released a groan that sounded as if someone was rolling his innards through a pasta machine.

The other dogs barked. Two howled.

Becca made soothing sounds and kept rubbing Maurice. "I bet you got into the food. Is that what happened, boy?"

The dog's gaze didn't leave hers.

Caleb thought that was one smart dog. Well, except for overeating.

"It's okay," Becca said. "You're not in trouble. Not at all."

Her soft voice was like a caress against Caleb's face, even though the words were for the dog's sake, he wished they were for him.

"You're going to have to go to the vet." She kissed Maurice's head. "You won't like that, but I'll be with you."

Caleb touched the dog. "I'll drive you."

"Thanks, but I've got a crate in the backseat. I need to move my car closer to make things easier on Maurice."

"I'll stay here with him while you do that."

"He'll shed on you."

"It's only dog hair," Caleb said. "And you have a lint roller."

The corners of her mouth curved in an appreciative smile. She stood. "Thanks. Be right back."

He took her place. The dog didn't seem to mind.

"It's okay, boy." He rubbed Maurice's head. "You're in good hands. Becca's going to take care of you."

Two brown, sad eyes met Caleb's. The look of total trust and affection sent the air rushing from his lungs. It was as if the dog understood.

Maybe Maurice did.

Caleb took a breath then leaned over so he could whisper in the dog's ear. "You're one lucky dog. I wish Becca liked me half as much as she cares for you."

But she didn't and wouldn't.

For the best, he told himself.

Too bad a part of him wasn't so sure.

Becca parked outside the kennel, left the engine idling then opened the car's back door.

Maurice was going to be fine. Just fine.

Repeating the words over and over again, she ran to the kennel.

If anything, she was wasting her time, gas and Gertie's money. Becca would be happy to waste all three as long as Maurice was okay.

She entered the kennel. Froze.

Caleb sat on the floor, in his designer suit, with Maurice's head resting on his lap. He rubbed the dog, talking in a soft voice.

Her mouth went dry.

The tenderness in Caleb's eyes as he stared at the dog sent Becca's heart thudding.

Her pulse rate kicked up a notch, maybe two.

Wait a minute. This was the same man who didn't trust her, who didn't like her, who wanted her fired.

But she couldn't help herself. He'd cranked up the charm without even realizing the affect this would have on her. Best to dial that down ASAP.

She cleared her throat. "How's he doing?"

"Not feeling too well, are you, boy?"

The sweet way Caleb spoke to the dog tugged at her heart-strings. Ignore it. Him. "Thank you for sitting with him. I can put him in his crate now."

Before Becca blinked, Caleb was on his feet. He picked up the dog easily, helping out both her and Maurice. "I'll carry him."

At the car, they loaded Maurice into the crate. She double-checked the latch to make sure it was secure. All set.

Caleb opened the driver's door.

"I appreciate your help." She hadn't known what to expect from Caleb, but his assistance with Maurice hadn't been it. "Tell Gertie I'll call as soon as I know anything."

"I'll check on the other dogs, then wait with Grams until you call. She wants to go with you."

"It could be a long night."

"That's what I figured," he said. "She opened the food cupboard to get dog treats earlier. She feels awful for not double checking the door was shut."

"Tell her not to worry. We'll get Maurice fixed right up."

"If not…"

"Let's not go there."

Their gazes met. Held. The same connection she'd felt the first day they'd met. But this wasn't the time to analyze things. Not with Maurice in pain.

Caleb kissed her cheek.

More of a peck, if she wanted to be technical, a brush of his lips over her skin. But her heart pounded. Warmth rushed through her.

"For luck," he said.

Becca resisted the impulse to kiss him back, only hard on the lips. She couldn't afford the distraction. Maurice needed her. She forced herself into the driver's seat then buckled her seat belt.

This wasn't the time or the place for more kisses. Most importantly this wasn't the man she should be kissing.

Not tonight. Not tomorrow night. Not ever.

Four hours later, Becca pulled into the guest cottage's driveway. Every muscle ached from tiredness. Her eyelids wanted to close. But she wasn't going to sleep much tonight.

Not when she needed to watch Maurice.

She glanced in the rearview mirror. "We're home, handsome."

The dog didn't make a sound. He must be exhausted after all the tests and X-rays. Not to mention his stomachache.

Becca grabbed her purse, exited the car and locked the door.

"Want a hand?"

Caleb.

He walked toward her, silhouetted by the porch light. He'd removed his jacket and tie, undone two buttons at the top of his shirt and rolled up his sleeves.

Her heart stumbled. "You're still here."

"I didn't want to leave Grams alone."

Becca wished she'd been the reason. Pathetic. But she was

pleased Caleb realized the difference between live-in staff and her grandson. "I hope she's not awake."

"She went to bed after you called."

"You should have gone home."

"It's fine." He spoke as if staying up half the night was no big deal. Maybe not for him, but she appreciated it. "Too bad the dog gorged himself on so many treats."

She nodded. "You should have seen the X-rays. Half his tummy was full."

"Last time he'll do that."

"Oh, no. He'll do it again if given the chance." Becca opened the crate's door. "Elkhounds will eat until they make themselves sick. They are food fiends. I knew something was wrong when he wouldn't eat his dinner."

Maurice lumbered out of the car as if each step hurt.

"Poor boy." Caleb picked up the dog. "Where do you want him?"

"On my bed," she said. "He's sleeping with me tonight."

"You really are a lucky dog."

Becca's cheeks heated. She was relieved for the darkness so Caleb couldn't see she'd blushed. "Not that lucky, considering the diet he'll be going on to get ready for the show this weekend."

Caleb was supposed to go, but he hadn't mentioned anything. Maybe he'd changed his mind.

She hoped not.

Wait a minute. That wasn't right. She didn't want him to go.

The cottage door was unlocked. She followed Caleb through the living room and into the bedroom. A sheet covered the comforter. Dogs spent so much time in here that cut down on her having to do laundry.

He gently set the dog on the bed. "Here you go, lucky dog."

"Thanks." She straightened the sheet then rubbed Maurice. "You should go. It's late."

Caleb's gaze narrowed on her. "You're exhausted."

"Long day. I'll sleep in a little while." She glanced at the dog who had curled up on her side of the bed. "I want to make sure he doesn't take a turn for the worse."

"Take a nap. I'll watch him."

A nap would be great, but she couldn't impose on Caleb. "That's nice of you to offer, but it's too late. You have to be at work in the morning."

"I'm the CEO," he said. "Grams won't complain if I show up late."

"This is *my* job."

Caleb tucked a strand of hair behind her ear.

A tremble ran through Becca. She didn't want to react to him, but couldn't help herself. He had a strange effect on her.

"It's mine tonight," he said.

A part of her wanted to let him take over, to not have to do everything herself tonight. She'd been on her own for so long with only herself to depend upon. But she couldn't…

Not when Caleb took care of so many others.

She raised her chin. "I'm not your responsibility."

"No, but how about we say you and Maurice are for the next couple of hours?"

The beat of her heart matched the quickening of her pulse. "You're making it hard for me not to like you."

His eyebrows wagged. "There's a lot to like."

His lighthearted tone made her smile. Something she hadn't thought possible at this late—make that early—hour. "Maybe, but it's hard to tell with dog hair all over you."

His mouth quirked. "You're covered in dog hair, too."

Becca didn't have to look to know it was true. "I'm always covered in dog hair."

"Grab some clothes." He kicked off his leather shoes. "Get comfortable on the couch."

"This is my bedroom."

"Not tonight." He crawled into bed with Maurice. The dog moved closer to him. "The boys have taken over."

"Are you always this bossy?" she asked.

"Yes," he said. "Get some sleep. Us boys will be fine. Won't we, Maurice?"

As if on cue, the dog licked Caleb's hand.

"See," he said.

Becca stared at him with a tingly feeling in her stomach. Funny—or maybe not so funny—but she could get used to "the boys" being here.

CHAPTER SEVEN

THLURP.

What was that? Caleb opened his eyes. Daylight filled the room. A mass of black and grey fur stood over him.

Thlurp.

A tongue licked his cheek.

He bolted upright.

Maurice's moist nose and his warm, smelly mouth were right in Caleb's face.

"Morning breath is one thing." Caleb turned away. "But yours is toxic."

The dog panted, looking pleased.

"At least you're up and about," Caleb said. "You must feel better."

Maurice stood on top of him. His paws pressed into Caleb's thighs.

"You're too big to be a lap dog."

The dog didn't listen. He plopped down, making himself at home on top of Caleb's legs.

"Okay," he relented. "You can sit here for a minute. But no longer."

"Are the boys having trouble this morning?" Becca asked.

The sound of her voice brightened his day like the first rays of sunshine through the window.

Caleb peered around the dog to see Becca standing at the foot of the bed.

She wore a pair of striped fleece pants and a tie-dyed ribbed tank top. Her hair was messy, as if she'd crawled out of bed or in her case, off the couch. Totally hot.

Waking up to Becca licking his face would have been much better. Too bad she couldn't join Caleb in bed now. He wasn't in the market for a relationship, but a fling would be fine. Fun.

Becca yawned, stretching her hands overhead.

His gaze shot to her chest, rising with her arm movement.

"You didn't wake me," she said.

He was staring. Gawking at her breasts. Not good. He looked at her face. "You were tired."

"So were you."

He'd checked on her in the middle of the night. She'd looked so peaceful with a slight smile on her face. He'd thought how appealing inviting her into bed with him would be. He'd imagined carrying her to bed. But that had bad idea written all over it. So he'd covered her with the blanket she'd kicked off and returned to bed with Maurice. "I wasn't."

"You stayed up all night."

"Not all night." Caleb's gaze kept straying to her tank top. "Once Maurice settled down, I dozed."

Becca moved closer.

The scent of her filled Caleb's nostrils. Wanting more, he breathed in deeper this time.

She touched the dog, leaning into him. Her hand brushed Caleb's thigh, sending shivery sparks up his leg.

"He looks better this morning," she said. "I'll take him outside."

"I took him outside around three."

Her lips parted, full and soft and kissable. If not for the dead weight on his lap, he would have tried to kiss her.

"I didn't hear you," she said.

"We were quiet." He glanced at the digital clock on the nightstand. "It's only five-thirty. Go back to bed."

"You're in my bed."

A sensual awareness buzzed between them.

A comfortable queen-size bed. A beautiful woman. A couple hours to kill until he was due at the office. This was looking pretty good.

"I'll scoot over. Maurice won't mind." Caleb moved closer to the far edge. It would be better if Maurice gave up his turn on the bed and went to the couch, but the dog didn't seem like the selfless type. Becca had that role locked up.

She watched him.

"The dog's on my side." Caleb kept his tone light, half-joking so he wouldn't scare her off. He patted the empty spot on the mattress. "Plenty of room for you now."

Her gaze shifted from him to the bed. "Better be careful, who you invite into bed, Mr. Fairchild."

"It's your bed."

"Then you should be even more careful. You wouldn't want to give away any corporate secrets over pillow talk."

He grinned. "Who said anything about talking?"

"You're full of surprises this morning."

He would be happy to surprise her more. All he needed was the opportunity and an invitation. "You're seeing only what you want to see."

"I'm seeing a pot and a kettle. Which one are you?" Amusement twinkled in her eyes. "I'd say the pot. But I suppose it doesn't matter, since they're both black."

Damn. Caleb shouldn't be so attracted to her. This went deeper than her looks. She challenged him, kept him on his toes. He liked that.

His ex-fiancée had always tried to suck up and sweet-talk him. Most women went along with him, rarely disagreed, as if he wanted a yes-woman instead of someone who spoke her mind and pushed his buttons.

Not that he wanted a woman. But he'd take this one for the morning. Hell, he'd stretch it to lunchtime if she were game. "That makes you the kettle."

"Works for me," she said. "I love kettle corn."

What was it about Becca Taylor that could get him turned on talking about cookware and popcorn?

Keeping his distance was the smart course of action if he wanted to avoid a complicated and messy situation. But leaving Becca's bed, especially if there was any chance of her climbing in it, didn't appeal to him in the slightest.

A fling would be fun. Easy. Safe.

And then Caleb remembered where he was....

The guest cottage at his grandmother's estate. With Grams's employee. His advisee.

A woman who made it hard to think straight when he was around her. A woman who knew too much about him. A woman who was the definition of dangerous.

Alarm bells sounded in his head. Maybe not so safe.

"It's all yours." Caleb moved the dog then slid off the bed. "I have to go."

"Okay." Becca bit her lip. "Thanks. Again. For, um, everything."

She looked as confused as he felt.

No matter. Time to get out of here before he changed his mind and did something really stupid, like trying to kiss the confusion out of her eyes.

Caleb patted the dog then slipped on his shoes. He tried to ignore how sexy Becca looked right now. "I need to put in extra hours at Fair Face with the dog show this weekend."

"You don't have to go." The words rushed out of her mouth faster than the rapids on the Snake River. "I can handle the show on my own."

She didn't want him to go. "I know, but I want to see about the products and my grandmother wants me there."

"Gertie is a worrywart when it comes to her dogs."

And when it came to Becca, too. Caleb was torn. As appealing as a weekend away from work sounded, spending more time alone with Becca wasn't smart. But he couldn't forget about his grandmother's wishes. "I'd rather not disappoint Grams."

"Gertie will understand if you're busy and have other plans." Becca's mouth tightened. "Say a date or something."

She'd baited the hook and cast the line. He didn't mind biting, if only to see her reaction and appeasing her curiosity about his going out with anyone. "No date. Work."

The lines around her mouth disappeared. "It's not a problem if you stay in Boise. Really."

"Well, since you don't mind…"

"I don't."

"I'll talk to Grams."

"Do."

She seemed too adamant about his not going. Maybe he'd misread her curiosity. Maybe she didn't want him to go to see what she'd be up to at the dog show. "I won't be around as much the next few days, possibly the entire week."

"Good. I mean…it'll be good to have time away. At Fair Face."

Becca sounded nervous. Flustered. She seemed so natural and unstudied and artless. Maybe he hadn't misread her after all.

A smile tugged at his lips. "Call me if you have any questions about the business plan."

"Will do. Thanks again for taking care of Maurice."

As if on cue, the dog jumped off the bed. He nudged Becca's hand with his nose so she'd give him attention.

Too bad that trick didn't work for Caleb. "You're welcome."

She bit her lip again. "You were on your way out?"

"Yes." Caleb grabbed his jacket and forced his feet to move in the direction of the front door. He'd better get going or he could end up staying here all morning. "Have a great day."

"Wait," she called out.

He stopped, hoping she was going to ask him to stay. A long shot, but this was as good a day as any to try being an optimist.

Becca handed him a lint roller. "Take this."

This was the last thing he expected. So much for optimism. Caleb laughed. "You need it."

"I have more than one, including two in my car."

"Always prepared."

"I never want to find myself unprepared again."

"I feel the same." He wasn't prepared for how much he wanted to stay with her now. Time to put some distance between him and the oh-so-appealing Becca Taylor "If I don't talk to you before the weekend, good luck at the dog show."

More than once after Caleb left the guest cottage, Becca picked up her cellphone to call Caleb. More than once she put away her cellphone.

That afternoon, she worked with Dozer on obedience training. The little guy needed to learn to behave and obey if he was ever going to find a forever home. Gertie would adopt him before sending him to live at the rescue shelter, but she and Becca agreed he'd do better with a family.

"Sit."

The dog sat.

"Stay."

She walked to the end of the leash, approximately six feet away, and hit the timer on her cellphone.

Dozer remained in place. Now to see if he sat for the full sixty seconds, a long sit in obedience training.

The seconds ticked off.

Becca wondered what Caleb was doing. He'd been on her mind since he'd left. She had questions about the business plan. As soon as she figured out one thing, that raised a bunch more questions. But she could find the answers herself if she searched on-line. The reason she wanted to call Caleb was to hear his voice.

Pathetic.

Hadn't she learned anything?

Even if Caleb was handsome, polite, hardworking, liked dogs, getting involved, at whatever level, with a man who had money was a bad idea. Like dumping water on an oil fire.

Explosive. She'd been burned once. No reason to repeat that experiment.

Stop thinking about him.

Becca needed to forget about Caleb and focus on getting ready to leave for the dog show on Thursday. She'd gotten her wish. She was going alone. If she needed a hand with the dogs, she could ask one of the Junior Showmanship kids to help her. Most of them were eager to help and learn more. She'd been that way.

Dozer rose to all fours and trotted toward her, as happy as a dog could be.

She glanced at the stopwatch. Forty-five seconds. Fifteen seconds too short. She gave him a pat. "We'll have to try this again.

Her cellphone buzzed. A new text message arrived. She glanced at the screen. From Caleb. Her hands tightened around the phone with excitement.

How's Maurice?

A ball of heat ignited deep within Becca. Caleb might have some faults, but he cared about the elkhound. She typed out a quick reply.

Good as new. Hungry again.

Maybe Caleb would find some spare time to stop by to see the dog. Maurice would like that. She would, too.

Becca waited for a reply. And waited. And waited.

She didn't hear from him. No texts. No phone calls. Nothing.

Tuesday gave way to Wednesday. Becca packed her suitcase and readied the RV for the trip to Central Oregon.

She tried not to think about Caleb. Or ask Gertie if she'd heard from him. He'd told Becca he wasn't going and would be busy. No. Big. Deal.

Thursday arrived. She packed everything she needed for the next three days in the RV.

Gertie said goodbye to each dog. "Don't cause Becca any trouble."

"They'll be fine," she said.

Gertie hugged her. The woman smelled like flowers and sunshine and the color pink. "Call me when you get there."

Becca loaded the dogs into their crates. "I will."

"I'm sorry you have to go alone."

"Caleb's a busy man." That was what she kept telling herself.

Concern filled Gertie's gaze. "Too busy. He's going to wake up one day and not have anything to show for it."

Becca thought a huge checking account balance would show for a lot, but she'd never had any money so what did she know?

Having so much responsibility thrust upon him at a young age had to have taken its toll. She wasn't going to add to his burdens. "Caleb will figure things out when he's ready. He's been spending more time with you."

"Last week, yes. This week, not so much. But you're right. Any time is an improvement. I just wish…"

"What?"

"I hate to think of you being alone this weekend."

"I'm not alone. I have the dogs to keep me company," Becca said. "I'll be fine."

The worry from Gertie's eyes didn't disappear. "I know. You're quite capable, but humor an old woman."

Becca's parents loved her. But they didn't have the luxury to sit around and worry about her the way Gertie did. Becca had been on her own from a young age because they'd worked multiple jobs. Knowing Gertie cared so much gave Becca a true sense of belonging. Something she hadn't found outside the trailer park or dog shows or the animal clinic where she worked. "How about I text you each time I stop to let the dogs out? I'll let you know what's going on during the show, too."

Gertie's features relaxed. "That would make me feel better."

Now, if Becca could stop thinking about Caleb and what he would be doing while she was away, she might feel better, too.

What the hell was Caleb doing here?

He glanced around the fairgrounds in Redmond, Oregon. White fenced outdoor show rings, dogs of every color and size, bright sunshine and green grass.

He was supposed to be working today, Saturday, not at a dog show. But Grams had said between showing the dogs and passing out samples of their dog products Becca had sounded exhausted and she still had two more days to go.

Caleb was responsible for so much. Now he had to take on his grandmother's dog consultant?

He could have said no to Grams insisting he attend. He could have sent someone else. But he'd wanted to see Becca.

If only Caleb could find her among the RVs, dogs, crates, grooming tables, rings and people. He'd tried calling and texting her, but couldn't reach her. He walked along the row of show rings.

On his left, vendors sold everything from dog-imprinted tea towels to doggy massage services. One booth had a dog treadmill for owners who couldn't—didn't want to, perhaps?—take their animals for a walk. People passed out samples of food and treats. Seeing all these products first hand made one thing clear…Grams's skin care line didn't stand a chance against all the edible wares and dog-inspired tchotchkes.

He didn't see Becca anywhere.

Women and men dressed in business attire scurried around with combs, brushes, spray bottles and raced from the grooming stands to the ten show rings set up at the county fairgrounds.

Two big dogs barked at a group of smaller black-and-white papillions. Others from the show ring next to them joined in. Annoying, but they were dogs. Dogs barked and shed.

Outside the fenced area of Ring Six stood Becca. She wore a lime-green suit that showed off her curves nicely. She looked professional, as she had in his office on Monday night. But today she appeared more confident.

A puff of white stood at her side. Snowy must have spent his morning being bathed and primped to look like a cotton ball.

He walked toward her. Snowy saw him first and barked.

Becca turned. Smiled.

Her eyes widened. Twinkled.

Caleb's heart slammed against his ribs. He hadn't expected her to be so excited to see him. He'd thought she wanted him to be at the show, but her reaction told him otherwise. Maybe coming here hadn't been such a waste of time. "Hello."

"What are you doing here?" she asked, a breathless qual-ity to her voice.

"Gertie said you sounded exhausted on the phone last night."

"What?"

"Grams said you were totally overwhelmed passing out samples and showing dogs and needed help."

Becca inhaled sharply. "So she sent you to the rescue."

He gave a mock bow. "At your service, milady."

"Thanks, but I have no idea why Gertie said what she did. I'm not overwhelmed or tired. Things are going well. I've passed out samples and feedback fliers. The interest has been high. Eighty percent of the people I've spoken with have taken the packages. I only have a few left."

"Then why am I here?" Though seeing Becca felt good. Thoughts of her had distracted him all week. He'd forced himself not to call her each day.

Becca scrunched her nose. "Gertie must have a reason."

But what? Grams never did anything without a reason. Well, except shopping. "Did my grandmother say anything to you?"

"Just that she hated the thought of my being here alone."

Alone. Alone. Alone.

The word echoed in his mind.

She didn't want Becca alone. Grams didn't want Caleb alone. She wanted them…

Together.

That would explain everything going on recently. "My grandmother's up to her old tricks."

"That's a relief," Becca said. "For a minute I was worried Gertie didn't trust me."

"That's not the case at all."

"So what's going on?

"Matchmaking."

"Matchmaking?" Lines creased Becca's forehead. Her mouth gaped. "With us?"

"It's the only thing that makes sense."

"I really don't think—"

"Can you come up with a better reason?"

"I…Well…" The startled look in her eyes matched the way he felt. "No, I can't."

"Grams has been vocal about wanting great-grandchildren, but I never thought she'd stoop to matchmaking." Caleb had to give Grams credit. She'd picked a woman who was the polar opposite of Cassandra. "But she created a line of baby products, so who knows how far she'd go?"

Snowy pulled away to sniff a small terrier, but Becca tugged on the leash stopping him.

"I don't think Gertie is playing matchmaker." Becca motioned to herself. "I'm not corporate trophy wife material."

Caleb took a long, hard look. "Don't sell yourself short. I like what I see."

"I'm not talking physical appearance." Her mouth slanted. "Imagine me schmoozing at a client party. Think about my past. I'm not the kind of woman you take home to meet your mother."

"My grandmother thinks you're amazing."

Becca straightened. A satisfied smile lit her face. "The feeling's mutual. But your grandmother is a special person."

"That's true." Becca's lack of pretense was far more appealing than the pretentious poise of his ex-fiancée and mother. "But you should know you're in a class so high above my mother it's not even funny."

Becca gave him a confused look. "Gertie said your mother died."

"She did, but if she were alive I would never want to introduce you to her. My mother married my father for his money. She ran off with her personal trainer. Once the divorce was finalized, we never saw or heard from her again."

Becca touched his arm. "What a horrible thing for a mother to do to her kids."

He shrugged. "Even before my mother deserted us, my grandparents were the ones raising us. It was them or a team of nannies."

"Sounds like you were better off with your grandparents."

He nodded, but this conversation was getting too personal. He'd never told anyone except Ty about his mom. Caleb wasn't sure why he'd shared the story with Becca. Maybe because she'd been so self-deprecating when she shouldn't have been. She was also easy to talk with.

Dogs continued barking. People milled about. Applause filled Ring Seven.

"When do you go?" he asked, changing the subject.

"After the Tibetan terriers."

"Snowy looks like a puffball."

"It takes time for him to be whitened, washed, volumized, combed, teased and sprayed."

"Do you do that with every dog?"

"Each breed is different," she said. "I have a schedule. I know who to work on when. Snowy's grooming is intensive, but he loves going in the ring, so he's more patient than some others. Maurice hates being on the grooming table. Blue doesn't mind it much."

A man in a suit and red striped tie approached. "Rebecca, isn't it?"

She nodded. "Hi, Dennis."

Caleb moved closer to her, unsure who this fellow was or why he seemed so interested in Becca.

Dennis smiled. "Nice job with the elkhound this morning. I thought you'd get Best of Breed."

"Thanks, but Gertie's happy with Select," Becca said. "This is Gertie's grandson, Caleb Fairchild."

"I'm Dennis Johnson." The man shook his hand, then looked right back at Becca. "Nice looking bichon. What products are you using on him?"

"Prototypes Gertie developed using all-natural, organic ingredients. I've been using them on all her dogs." Becca didn't miss a beat. "Would you like samples to try?"

The man looked as if he'd hit three sevens on a slot machine. "Yes, please."

"Find me at my RV. I have a package with the products and a form for you to give us your feedback."

"I'll be by later," the man said. "Good luck in the ring."

Caleb found the exchange interesting. The man recognized something different about the products Becca was using on her dogs. "Giving away samples with a feedback form is a good start, but maybe a little soon since you're not ready to manufacture products."

"Not on a large scale. But we can do something smaller in the interim."

"Sounds like Grams talking."

Becca nodded. "She's eager."

"More like a runaway train."

Which was why Grams playing matchmaker would mean trouble. Not only for Caleb, but Becca.

A woman in a purple apron walked past at a fast clip with an angry expression on her face. "That bitch didn't want to free stack."

Caleb waited for the woman to pass then looked at Becca. "That's…"

"Dog speak." Laughter filled her bright eyes. "I'm assuming you know that a bitch is a female dog. Stack means placing a dog in a position that shows off the breed standards. Hand stacking is when a handler manually positions the dog's paws.

Free stacking is when the handler uses bait, calls or signs to get the dog to position himself."

Dog showing didn't only have it's own vocabulary. A sociologist could have a field day studying these people and their interactions with each other and their dogs. But this was the most comfortable he'd ever seen Becca. Except at the kennel.

She adjusted the chain collar around Snowy's neck. "It's our turn."

A tall, thin man with a beard and in a three-piece suit called her number. Becca entered the ring with the dog. Three other handlers and their dogs, replicas of powder puff Snowy, followed them. The judge studied each of the dogs.

The dogs all looked the same to Caleb, but he couldn't take his eyes off Becca. She ran around the ring with Snowy, then positioned him in front of the judge. Caleb assumed that was hand stacking. They ran diagonally across the ring and back. One by one the other handlers did the same until all circled the ring in a line once again.

The judge pointed. Snowy won and was awarded a ribbon.

A few minutes later, Becca and Snowy returned to the ring and went through the same routine. Snowy was named Best of Breed, BOB for short, and Becca received a large ribbon.

Becca skipped out of the ring. "Gertie is going to be thrilled. I need to get Snowy in his crate so he can rest before Group, then I'll call…"

Caleb didn't know why her voice trailed off. "What?"

"Would you mind holding Snowy for a minute?"

He had no idea what was going on, but took Snowy's lead, a black leather leash with silver beads.

Becca walked twenty feet away to a little girl, who looked to be around seven or eight. The child sat on a folding chair. She held the leash of an Irish setter puppy with both hands and wiped tears from her face with her arm.

"Hello, I'm Becca." She knelt at the girl's side and put her hand in front of the dog nose. "What's your name?"

"Gianna."

"You have a pretty dog."

Gianna hiccupped. "Thank you."

Caleb had no idea what Becca was doing, but moved closer so he could find out.

The dog sniffed her hand. "What's your puppy's name?"

"P-Princess."

"Is Princess going to be shown today?"

"No." Gianna sniffled. "My mommy twisted her ankle, so can't show her. This would've been Princess's first time in the ring."

Becca looked around. "Where is your mommy?"

"Getting ice for her foot."

"When your mom gets back, why don't we ask if she'd let me show Princess for you."

Gianna's tears stopped flowing. Her mouth formed a perfect O. "You're a handler?"

Becca petted the dog, and Gianna scooted closer to her. "I'm a dog handler and I'd be happy to show Princess."

Caleb knew Becca had a full schedule, especially with Snowy continuing on, yet she wanted to help this little girl.

Becca's action filled him with warmth. How many people had walked past the crying child without noticing or pretending not to see her? But she'd done something about it. The woman was...special. He couldn't believe he'd doubted her motivations and accused her of being a scam artist.

A thirtysomething woman with her hair in a bun and wearing a purple suit hobbled toward them. She carried a plastic bag full of ice. "Gianna?"

The girl leaped out of her chair. She bounced from foot to foot, her ponytails flying up and down. "Mommy, Mommy, this lady can show Princess for us. She's a handler."

Becca rose and held out her hand. "My name is Becca Taylor. Your daughter told me about your ankle. I'd be happy to show your puppy for you."

"Oh, thanks." The woman's gaze flitted from Becca to her

daughter and the dog. "That's nice of you to offer, but I can't afford to pay for a handler."

"No charge," Becca said without any hesitation. "I wouldn't want Princess to miss her first time in the ring."

Caleb's chest tightened, a mix of affection and respect, at her generosity. One more attribute to add to Becca's growing list. But she wasn't being a smart businesswoman, given her first priorities were Grams's dogs and the product samples. He assumed Grams wouldn't mind, given her kind heart, but even if she did, Caleb wasn't about to say a word. Becca was doing exactly the right thing.

Gianna tugged at her mother's arm. "Please, Mommy. Please, oh, please, oh please."

The woman looked stunned. Relief quickly took over. "Th-that would be great. Thank you."

Becca glanced back at Caleb. "Do you mind holding unto Snowy a little longer so I can work with Princess?"

"Happy to." He would do whatever she asked. She was so genuine he wanted to help her, not make things harder. "I'll put him into his crate."

"That would be great."

"Come on, Snowy." If Caleb hurried, he might make it back to watch her in the ring. "I don't want to miss this."

But whether Becca Taylor was in the ring or out of it, she was a very special woman. There was no other place he'd rather be this weekend than right here with her.

CHAPTER EIGHT

BECCA STOOD OUTSIDE the ring where Best in Show, aka BIS, would be held in a few minutes. She wiggled her toes inside her black flats. The dogs, including Princess, had all placed in their events and Snowy had won his group. The buzz surrounding Gertie's dog-care samples kept increasing. Gertie was beside herself with pride. Win or lose in the next few minutes, the day couldn't get much better.

"You look so calm and cool." Caleb stood next to Becca. "Not the least bit nervous."

She glanced his way. Her stomach did a somersault. She was so happy he was here.

"I'm more excited than anything else." Becca wanted to pinch herself to make sure her eyes were open and she wasn't dreaming. She adjusted Snowy's lead in her hand. "No matter how Snowy does, we've already won. People are very interested in Gertie's new line of dog products."

"It can't hurt your reputation, either."

"Or Snowy's. He's on his way to Grand Champion," she said. "But he's never won BIS."

"Today could be the day."

Caleb's words, spoken with sincerity, pierced her heart like an arrow. She double-checked Snowy to make sure he looked his best, then rerolled his lead. "I hope so."

"Good luck." The tender look in his eyes made her feel as

if they were the only two people at the fairground. Her breath caught. Her temperature rose. "Not that you need luck."

Her heart melted. If only he'd wished her luck with a kiss the way he had when she took Maurice to the vet on Monday night.

Caleb's gaze lingered, tenderness turning to something resembling desire.

Her pulse skittered. He might want to kiss her again.

Please, oh, please. She realized she was acting like a little girl, like Gianna.

Becca didn't care. She parted her lips, in case he was looking for an invitation.

Then she realized…they weren't alone. Hundreds of people stood and sat ringside, many who knew Gertie. Going down this path with Caleb was fruitless and dangerous. He might have decided Becca wasn't a scam artist, but a kiss would mean nothing to him. A kiss would mean more to her. Kissing him, even if she might want that, wasn't right or smart or even sane.

She was about to go in for Best of Breed. She needed to concentrate on Snowy, not think about Caleb.

Becca pressed her lips together.

The ring steward announced the competition.

She took a deep breath and raised her chin.

"You're going to kill them," Caleb whispered, his warm breath against her ear. "No one stands a chance against you and Snowy."

His words provided an extra jolt of confidence. Not needed, but nice. Very nice, actually.

She fell in line with the six other handlers and their dogs.

With a grateful smile in his direction, Becca squared her shoulders, then stepped into the ring with Snowy.

It was show time!

Best in Show!

Snowy—registered name White Christmas in Sunny July— had been awarded Best in Show.

Pride flowed through Caleb. His chest expanded with each breath. A satisfied smile settled on his lips.

The crowd applauded and cheered.

He videotaped the award ceremony. Snowy pranced around as if he knew he was top dog, but Becca's wide smile and joy-filled eyes defined the moment for Caleb. A photographer snapped official winner pictures with the judge. Handlers shook Becca's hand. She juggled the gift basket, flowers and three feet long ribbon she'd been awarded.

Caleb stood back, away from the entrance to the ring, and waited. He wanted to watch Becca savor the win.

People congratulated her on the way out of the ring, but she gave all the credit to Snowy, who soaked up the attention as if he knew he'd be getting extra doggy treats tonight. Little Gianna and her mom hugged Becca.

The crowd dispersed.

Becca made her way to him, her arms extended outward with the basket and flowers and Snowy's leash and ribbon in the other. "Best in Show!"

"Congratulations." Caleb wrapped his arms around her. Her breasts pressed against his chest. The feeling of rightness nearly knocked him back a step. Holding her felt good, natural. He didn't want to let go. He chalked it up to working too hard on the baby product launch and not going out on many dates. He forced himself to drop his arms. "You killed it."

She blushed, a charming shade of pink. "Thanks, but Snowy did all the work."

Becca was too modest. But that was something he liked about her. "We need to celebrate. Bend has some nice restaurants."

"Thanks, but I don't want to leave the dogs alone in the RV."

The dogs. He'd forgotten about them even though he couldn't look anywhere without seeing one dog or twelve. "We can find a place that delivers."

"I'm all set for food for the weekend. I never leave the grounds of a show once I arrive," Becca said. "I'm positive

Gertie will want to celebrate when we're home. She's never had a dog win Best in Show. She'll probably throw a party."

"Sounds like Grams." But Caleb didn't want to wait. He wanted to make tonight special for Becca. "But we can still celebrate here."

"I thought you were going to fly home tonight. Don't you have to get to the airport?"

"I was…am." But Caleb wasn't sure he wanted to leave now. "Unless you want me to stay."

"Don't waste your entire weekend here. Fly home so you and your sister can have brunch with Gertie."

Caleb did that every Sunday. He would rather have brunch with Becca. Preferably after spending the night together. The idea of having a fling with her had been floating around his head since he saw her standing next to the bed Tuesday morning.

She juggled the items in her arms.

He took the basket and flowers from her. "I've got these."

"Thanks." A smile brightened her face. She walked with a playful bounce to her step. Neither of which he had anything to do with.

He wanted to be the reason she was so happy, but only dogs got that honor. He was at a disadvantage without four legs and fur.

The light fragrance of the flowers tickled his nose, teasing him, as if the blossoms knew he wouldn't be around in the morning, but they would be.

People streamed out of the fairgrounds. Engines roared to life. Horns honked. Dogs barked. People were clearing out, returning to their hotels off-site. Others returned to their RVs parked in a special area at the fairgrounds.

Becca placed Snowy into his pen under the shade of an awning then checked the other dogs. "Want a drink or a snack before you head to the airport?"

"What makes you think I'm leaving now?"

Her eyes widened. "I assumed you'd want to get home."

"Home is a three-thousand-square-foot loft in downtown Boise." A quiet place—a lonely place—compared to the activity and noise here. He breathed in the fresh air. "This is a nice change. No need to rush back."

"You're more than welcome to join me for dinner. I'm grilling hot dogs."

He did a double take. "Hot dogs."

"Does wiener dogs work better? Or how about Dachshund dogs?" she teased. "We're at a dog show. A themed meal makes sense."

"What else is on the menu?"

Laughter filled her eyes. "Saluki Slaw, Bloodhound Beans and Pekinese Potato Chips. Oh, and Corgi Cookies for dessert."

"Corgi cookies, huh?"

"There's also Bernese Brownies."

A quick thinker. He liked that. "Not a bad job coming up with those names on the fly."

And turning a meal into fun. He needed to have more fun.

"Not bad." A corner of her mouth slid upward. "Darn good if you ask me."

"You've convinced me to stay. I'll fly back to Boise after dinner so I can still have brunch with Grams in the morning."

Panic replaced the laughter in Becca's eyes. She shot him a what-have-I-gotten-myself-into smile. She tugged her bottom lip with her teeth. "Win-win."

She was a good sport. "Those are the games I like."

Except he wasn't sure what he was doing with Becca right at this moment. There was no reason for him to stay and every reason in the world to go. Hot dogs weren't his typical Saturday night dinner fare, but he was more interested in the company, Becca's company. And, how could he turn down a Corgi cookie?

Win-win any way he looked at it.

After dinner, Becca stood at the RV's sink. She placed the paper plates and plastic utensils from dinner in the garbage.

She kept a smile on her face, but tension wreaked havoc inside her. Awareness of Caleb flowed down her spine and pooled at her feet. She slanted a glance over her shoulder. "I'm almost finished."

Caleb sat in one of the leather lounge chairs. His legs were extended and crossed at the ankles. His gaze on her. "You'd be finished if you'd let me help."

Cleaning up after dinner gave her something to do with her hands other than combing her fingers through her hair and straightening her clothes. Being around Caleb made Becca self-conscious about her appearance, about everything. It wasn't anything he did—he offered to help prepare the meal and clean up. Or anything he said—he was easy to speak with and complimentary. It was just…him.

She placed the now-dried pans in the cabinet above. "There wasn't much to do."

"Maybe not in the kitchen," he said. "What about the dogs?"

She checked the clock on the microwave. "I need to take them for walks."

Caleb rose. "I'll go with you."

"What about your flight?"

He took a step toward Becca. His tall, athletic frame made the spacious and luxurious RV feel like a pop-up trailer. "It's Grams's jet. There's no set departure time until I tell them I'm ready."

"Must be nice." Becca was still trying to get used to Gertie's top-of-the-line RV, purchased specifically for dog shows. She held out a plastic container containing the leftover cookies. "Want more?"

"If I eat another bite, I'll need a crane to get me out of here." He patted his flat stomach. "I forgot how good hot dogs tasted."

"Must be a big change from the haute cuisine you eat."

"Prime rib is about as fancy as I get," he said. "I take after my grandfather when it comes to food. Gramps was a meat-and-potatoes man. Much to the chagrin of Grams, who liked to experiment in the kitchen the way she does in the lab. We usually ended up with two dinners when I was a kid. One for Gramps that our cook made and one for the more adventurous appetites that Grams provided."

"Which did you eat?"

"Both. I took one bite of whatever Grams cooked. Sometimes more. Only once did I spit it out. I made her promise never to tell me what it was."

"Growing up with Gertie must have been interesting."

"It was never boring. But no matter how busy my grandparents were with Fair Face, we always ate dinner together. That was our special time."

"Sounds nice." She felt a twinge of envy, even though she knew she'd been loved. "My parents worked multiple jobs so eating meals together didn't happen much."

"That had to have been rough."

"It's all I knew." She put the lid on the cookies, then set the container on the counter. "My folks worked hard to make ends meet so it was difficult for me to complain."

"You get your work ethic from your parents."

She nodded. "I wish things were easier for them. Maybe someday…"

"Invite them to visit you at Grams's house."

"Gertie suggested that, but my parents don't have the same days off," Becca said. "I emailed them pictures. They thought the estate looked like something from a TV show. The grounds impressed my dad. His dream is to have a lawn to mow."

"We've always had gardeners to take care of that, but I thought the rider mower looked fun."

"I take it your loft doesn't have a yard."

"No. There's a terrace with planters and a lap spa. Grass would be impractical."

She exited the RV. Caleb followed her out. The sun had disappeared beneath the horizon. Street lamps along the roads that now doubled as walkways around all the RVs lit up the area.

"Well, if you ever want a lawn up there, there's always Astroturf"

He gave her a look. "You can't mow Astroturf."

"Vacuum it."

"Vacuuming doesn't sound like fun."

"Let me guess—you've never vacuumed."

"I haven't."

Their lives were so different. Too different. She couldn't forget that even if she liked talking and being with him and wondering what kissing him would feel like. "Try it sometime. Vacuuming is a good way to clear your mind."

"Maybe I will."

She locked the RV door. "Maybe means you won't."

A sheepish grin spread across his face. "Wouldn't want to offend the team that cleans my place."

Whoa. He lived in a completely different universe than her. "You have a team of cleaners?"

"Doing my part to stimulate the economy."

Okay, that was funny. She liked his sense of humor. With a smile, she shook her head. "Working for Gertie sure has given me a glimpse into how the other half lives."

"What do you think so far?"

His question didn't sound flippant, but why would he care what she thought? Few people except her parents and Gertie did.

"That bad, huh?" he asked.

"No, not at all."

"So…"

He sounded genuinely interested in knowing Becca's opinion. "Honestly, it's been nice," Becca said. "Gertie is eccentric and loves luxurious things, but she's more grounded than I imagined someone as wealthy as her to be. It'll be hard to leave behind."

His gaze narrowed. "Planning on going somewhere?"

"Not in the near future, but I want to be a full-time handler. Care for the dogs in between shows. Teach handling classes to kids and dog owners."

"You can make a living doing that?"

His disbelief didn't surprise her. "The top handlers in the country make over six figures a year."

"I had no idea people did this as a full-time job."

"A few do," she said. "Most work other jobs and handle part-time or as a hobby. Some save money so they can take time off."

"Saving for a rainy day."

She couldn't believe he remembered their conversation in his office. "Yes."

"You realize you could have a lucrative career working for Grams, especially if the dog-care products take off. You'd earn more than you'd make as a dog handler."

Becca shrugged. "I never set out to be a business person."

"You care about what you do. You're not just out to make a buck."

"No, but having a few bucks in the bank doesn't hurt."

He smiled. "You belong here. In this dog-show world."

"I think so." She hoped this was where she belonged. "I appreciate Gertie giving me the opportunity to show her dogs."

Becca attached Maurice's leash to his collar and released him from the pen. The dog ran straight to Caleb.

"You have a new friend," she said.

He rubbed the dog's head. "It's only because I have no dog hair on me. Maurice needs to mark his territory."

"As long as he's not marking it another way."

Caleb gave her a look. "Don't give Maurice any ideas."

Becca peeked in on Snowy. The dog slept soundly, his back leg jerking as if dreaming. She would take him out later.

"Come on, Blue." She removed the gray eighteen-month-old puppy from his pen. "Time for your walk, boy."

Caleb walked next to her with the dogs out in front, leading the way.

A man, a well-known handler from California, walking four beagles, greeted them with a nod and a hello.

Caleb looked back at the dogs. "Some people show the

same type of dogs. Why doesn't my grandmother stick to one breed?"

"Gertie loves all dogs, not a particular breed. She also owns dogs others weren't sure about or gave up on. She could have the pick of most litters, but she'd rather choose a dog who needs a second chance."

"Why would they need a second chance? They're pure-breds."

"Yes, but not every purebred meets the breed standard. Reputable breeders have those dogs neutered or spayed and placed in homes as pets." Becca pointed to Blue. "This guy was the runt of the litter. No one expected him to be show quality, but your grandmother saw something in him and took a chance. Now he's on his way to being a champion."

"I'm not surprised," Caleb said. "Grams has always been fond of strays."

"No kidding. She took me in."

"My sister and me, too."

"You weren't strays," Becca countered. "You're family."

Caleb shrugged.

"Gertie treats her rescue and foster dogs the same as her show dogs." Becca could tell he didn't want to talk about this. "Your grandmother has a big heart."

"So do you."

His words meant more than they should. Becca tried to down play the fluttery feeling in her stomach. "It's easy with dogs."

"There was that little girl Gianna today."

"Just trying to be nice."

"Is that what you're doing now? Being nice to me when you wish I'd left hours ago?"

Becca didn't know what she was doing. Feeling. But she didn't like how Caleb saw right through her, as if her every thought and emotion were on display especially for him. They were too much in sync, able to understand each other even though they were in very different places in life.

He made her feel vulnerable, a way she'd felt for three long years in prison. A way she never wanted to feel again. She tightened her grip on the leash and looked up at the sky full of twinkling dots of lights. "Lots of stars out tonight."

"You're changing the subject."

"You're supposed to pretend you don't notice and play along."

He stopped walking to allow Maurice to sniff the grass. "What if I don't want to do that?"

"You're the kind of guy who plays by the rules."

"Normally, yes." He moved closer to her until she could feel the heat of him. "But this isn't normal."

She fought the urge to step back. "Being at the dog show?"

Caleb stopped inches away from her. "Being here with you."

The light from the streetlamp cast shadows on his face. He looked dark and dangerous and oh-so-sexy. Becca swallowed. Last time she'd thought that about a guy she'd ended up in jail. That might not be what would happen to her next, but she shouldn't take any unnecessary chances and do something stupid again.

His gaze locked on hers. "Do you want to keep playing by the rules?"

Her heart slammed against her ribs. She should step back. Way back. Put distance between them. For her own good. And his.

But her feet wouldn't move. She remained rooted in place, waiting, hoping, anticipating.

Caleb tilted his head down, bringing his lips close to hers.

Becca rose up and leaned forward.

Their lips touched.

So much for rules.

He wrapped his arms around her, pulled her close and kissed her hard.

Hot, salty, raw.

His lips moved across her, skillfully. His kiss possessed, as if staking a claim and declaring she was his.

Becca had never felt that way before. She shouldn't like it, either. She was independent. She didn't need a man to give her value. But at the moment, with tingles reaching to the tips of her toes and fingers, possession seemed a small price to pay.

Pleasurable sensations pulsed through her, heating her from the inside out. He deepened the kiss. She followed willingly, arching toward him.

Ruff.

Caleb jerked backward. His arms let go of her.

Becca stumbled to the right.

Grrrrowl.

Maurice and Blue lunged toward two teeth-baring Pekingese with satin bows on their ears.

She yanked on the leash. "Heel!"

Caleb grabbed Maurice by his collar.

The other two dogs didn't back down. Their owner, a petite woman with spiky white hair, a shimmery short robe and flower-trimmed flip-flops, frowned. "Next time get a room."

Becca's cheeks burned. Her lips throbbed.

Oh, no. She'd been so wrapped up in Caleb she had forgotten about the dogs. What if they'd gotten into a fight and been hurt? Not acceptable.

The woman marched away, dragging her wannabe fighters behind her. The dogs looked back and growled.

"That didn't turn out like I expected. Maybe Grams knows something we didn't." Desire flared in his eyes. "We should try that again."

Oh, yes. Becca would love another kiss. Make that kisses. But she couldn't. She glanced at Blue, who sniffed the grass as if nothing had happened. If only she could forget…The past. Who Caleb was. Who she was. "I can't."

"Can't or won't?"

"Does it matter?

His jaw was set, tense. "If not for those bow-toting dogs—"

"If it weren't for them, I'd still be kissing you."

A sinfully charming grin lit up his face. "Then let's pick up where we left off."

Temptation flared. "Kissing you was…amazing. But I forgot everything, including the dogs. They could have been hurt. They're my responsibility. I can't be distracted."

Approval tempered the desire in his gaze. "I understand and respect that."

Respect was all she'd wanted. Until this moment. Now she wanted more of his kisses. Uh-oh.

"Thanks." She tried to remember all the reasons Caleb and more kisses weren't good for her. "I appreciate it."

"Just know when you're back in Boise and the dogs aren't around, I want to kiss you again. If that's what you want, too."

Her heart lodged in her throat. She couldn't breathe, let alone speak.

Heaven help her, but Becca couldn't wait to get back to Boise.

CHAPTER NINE

TWO NIGHTS LATER, the party at Grams's place was going strong when Caleb arrived. He handed his keys to a parking valet.

A big crowd for a Monday.

But when Gertie Fairchild issued an invitation, few sent regrets.

Inside the house, Caleb greeted people he'd known his entire life and made his way toward the patio.

Leave it to Grams to pull together an impromptu gathering for two hundred of her closest friends in honor of Snowy winning Best in Show. On the patio, a DJ spun music in the backyard. Bartenders fixed drinks. Uniformed servers carried trays of delicious smelling appetizers.

Caleb searched for the two women he wanted to see most—his grandmother and Becca. He caught a glimpse of Grams, wearing pink capris and a sparkly blouse, and wove his way over through the crowd.

"Caleb!" Grams hugged him. "I've been wondering when you'd arrive."

"I had a few things to finish up at the office."

"Take off your jacket and tie," she said with a smile. "Get a drink. And relax."

He glanced around.

"Looking for Becca?" Grams asked.

"Yes."

"She's here. Courtney, too."

His sister never turned down a party invitation, even if the average age of the guest list was twice hers. "I hope Courtney's staying out of trouble."

"Probably not." Grams waved at someone who'd stepped out onto the patio. "You should find Becca and see if you can get yourself into trouble."

"Grams!"

"What?" She feigned innocence. "Thirty-one is too young to be so serious about everything. Becca would be good for you. Help you to lighten up and enjoy life."

Maybe in the short term. He'd enjoyed their time together at the dog show. Talking, laughing, kissing. Best not let Grams know or she'd be hiring a wedding planner to come up with the perfect proposal, one that would go viral on YouTube. "Becca and I figured out you've been playing matchmaker."

Grams pointed to herself. *"Moi?"*

"Oui, Grandmère."

"Speak French to Becca," Grams said. "Women like that."

Caleb shook his head, but made a mental note to give speaking French a try.

"Becca is a special woman." Grams lowered her voice. "But it's going to take a special man to break through her hard shell."

"Becca and I are friends." Friends who had shared a passionate kiss before being rudely interrupted by a pair of Pekingese dogs. He might want more of Becca's kisses, but he wasn't that "special man." The last thing he needed was a girlfriend. He didn't want to be responsible for one more person. "Nothing more."

"Your loss is another man's gain."

The thought of Becca kissing another man made Caleb's shoes feel too tight. He stretched his toes. "I'm going to see if I can find Courtney."

"Have fun." Grams flitted toward the house, taking on her role as Boise's most gracious hostess.

Caleb grabbed a bottle of beer from the bar. He took a long

swig. Just what he needed after a long day at the office. Now, if he could find Becca.

"Hey, bro." The scent of his sister's perfume surrounded him. Her ruffled miniskirt barely hid her underwear. Her two tanks showed as much skin as a string bikini top. Her blonde hair was clipped on top of her head with tendrils artfully placed around her face. Her make up was magazine layout perfect. Typical Courtney. Somewhat disturbing for a brother who worried about his younger sister. "I met your new girlfriend."

He nearly spit out his beer. He forced himself to swallow. "I don't have a girlfriend."

"Becca."

"She's not...What has Grams been telling you?"

"Only that she found the perfect woman for you." Courtney took a flute of champagne from the tray of a passing waiter. "Becca is cute. With a wardrobe makeover, some highlights and makeup she could be totally hot. I'm happy to assist—"

"Becca is fine the way she is."

"You like her."

"I don't..." He lowered his voice. "Becca is sweet. She doesn't need to be pulled into Grams's matchmaking scheme."

"Better her than me." Courtney sipped her champagne. "The alarm on Grams'a great-grandbaby clock is ringing louder and louder."

"Don't look at me. I do enough as it is."

"Well, I'm not ready to be a mom. I've never dated a guy longer than a month."

Caleb stared at her over the top of his beer bottle. "Considering your choice in men, that's a good thing. Maybe you should have Grams fix you up. Bet she'd pick a winner for you."

"Yeah, right. Someone totally respectable, proper and boring like you." Courtney shook her head. "Don't forget I lose everything. Imagine if I misplaced a kid. That would be bad."

"Very bad," he agreed. "No worries. Grams will get over the idea of great-grandchildren eventually."

"I hope so, but I think we should be proactive about this," Courtney said. "Let's buy Grams a kitten."

"Grams is a dog person."

"That doesn't mean she can't be a crazy cat lady, too. Kittens are cute and cuddly. Kind of like a baby, but you don't have to deal with diapers, only litter boxes."

Caleb wasn't in the mood to try to understand his sister's twisted logic, especially after she'd called him boring. He downed what remained of his beer. "Hold off on the kitten for a while. And stay out of trouble tonight."

Courtney stuck her tongue out at him. "You're no fun."

Walking away, he realized Courtney was correct. He used to be fun. When he was younger, he and Ty had had nothing but fun. After Caleb took over Fair Face for his grandfather, life revolved around the company and family. Nothing else.

He followed the path past the guest cottage—only the porch light was on—to the kennel.

A dog barked from inside.

Caleb couldn't see which one, but he recognized the sound. Maurice.

Caleb entered the kennel. More barks erupted, drowning out the pop music playing from an iPod docking station.

"Quiet." Becca faced Dozer's door. Her floral skirt fell two inches above her knees. The green sleeveless shirt showed off toned arms. Her white sandals accentuated thin ankles. "We don't want Gertie's guests to hear you."

The dogs stopped barking. Maurice stood with his front paws on his door.

"What's gotten into you?" Becca asked the dog.

Caleb stopped two feet behind her. "So this is where you've been hiding."

She gasped and whirled around.

The hem of her skirt flared, giving him a glimpse of her lower thighs. Much more enticing than a super short skirt that left nothing to the imagination.

Her eyes were wide, her cheeks pink. She placed her hand over her heart. "Caleb."

"I didn't mean to startle you."

She peered around him, as if to see if anyone else was behind him. "What are you doing here?"

"I was going to ask you the same question." Seeing her felt good. He couldn't believe they'd only been apart two days. It seemed longer. "The party's up on the patio. But you're down here. Alone."

She motioned to the dogs, watching them intently from their individual stalls. "I'm not alone."

"You know what I mean."

She nodded. "It's a bit…overwhelming."

"The party?"

"And all the people. Guests, servers, bartenders, DJ, parking valets," she said. "Gertie introduced me to about a hundred people tonight. No way can I keep the faces and names straight."

"So you escaped here."

Another nod. "This is my favorite place at the estate. It's where I'm…"

"Comfortable," he finished for her.

"Yes. It's where I fit."

The way he knew her, understood her was…unsettling to him.

He cut the distance between them in half with one step. "You love the kennel and the dogs, but you also fit in up at the house with everybody else."

She ground the toe of her sandal against the floor. "I don't know about that."

"I do." Caleb used his finger to raise her chin. "You're smart, beautiful, kind."

The pink on her cheeks darkened. "You don't have to stop."

"I don't plan on stopping unless you want me to stop." He didn't want to frighten her off "I'd like to pick up right where we left off."

Her lips parted.

He grinned. "I'm going to take that as an invitation."

"Please."

Caleb kissed her. Something he'd been thinking about doing since he drove away from the fairgrounds on Saturday night. But he never expected her to melt into his arms as if she'd been looking forward to this moment as much as him.

He pressed his lips against hers, soaking up the feel and taste of her.

So sweet. Warm. His.

He wrapped his arms around her, pulling her close. She went eagerly. Her soft curves molded against him.

So right.

His temperature shot up, fueled by the heat pulsing through him.

Her hands were on his back, in his hair, all over.

His tongue explored her mouth, tangled with her tongue. He couldn't get enough of her.

Caleb's hand dropped to her skirt. He lifted the hem and touched her thigh, the skin as soft and smoothed as he imagined. His hand inched up, with anticipation, with desire.

"Well, I'll be damned."

Grams.

He jerked his hand from underneath Becca's skirt. He jumped back totally turned on, his breathing ragged. Becca's flushed face and swollen lips were sexy as hell and exactly the last thing he wanted his grandmother to see.

Too late now. He faced the woman who had raised him. Courtney stood next to his grandmother.

Grams had her hands clasped together. She looked giddy, as if she'd been granted three wishes from a magic lamp. She needed only one, because the silly grin on her face told him exactly what she was thinking—great-grandbabies.

Her eyes twinkled. "Nothing more than friends, huh?"

"So this is how it feels not to be the one in trouble." Courtney smirked. "I kind of like it."

Caleb positioned himself between his family and Becca. "It's not what you think."

"Yes, it is." Grams rubbed her palms together. "And I couldn't be more delighted."

Becca's heart pounded in her chest, a mixture of embarrassment, passion and pride. The way Caleb shielded her from his family like a knight in gray pinstripes made her feel special.

He might be everything she didn't want in a guy, but at this moment she wouldn't want to be with anyone else.

Her lips throbbed. Her breathing wouldn't settle. Her insides ached for more kisses.

She'd experienced those same reactions in Redmond. But something felt different, awakened, as if she'd finally met a man who saw beyond her past and could accept her for who she was today. No guy had ever made her feel like that.

Becca longed to reach forward and lace her fingers with Caleb's in support and solidarity. But that would only fuel Gertie's speculations.

It's not what you think.

But it could be. And the possibility gave Becca hope. Strength. She stepped forward and took her place next to Caleb.

Gertie rose up on her tiptoes, acting more like an excited child than the creative genius of a skin-care empire.

Courtney's snicker turned into a smile, transforming the beautiful young woman from a life-size cardboard cutout of the latest fashion trends to someone more real and genuine.

"People want to see Snowy," Grams said.

Becca glanced back at the dog that stood at his door all fluffed and ready to go. "He's ready."

"We'll bring Snowy up there in a few minutes," Caleb added.

Gertie winked. "Don't take too long."

Her suggestive tone sent heat rushing up Becca's neck.

A vein twitched at Caleb's jaw. "We won't."

Gertie and Courtney, looking as if they were about to burst out laughing, exited the kennel.

As soon as the door shut, Caleb looked down at the ground, shaking his head.

Becca touched his shoulder. "I'm sorry."

His gaze met hers. Softened. "You have nothing to be sorry about."

"But Gertie's going to think—"

Caleb kissed Becca, a gentle whisper of a kiss. The tender brush of his lips made her feel even more cherished, as if she was meant to be treasured. Her chest swelled with affection for this man. He backed away from her slowly, as if he didn't want to end the kiss.

Becca swallowed a sigh. She wished he could keep on kissing her…forever.

"Don't worry about my grandmother or my sister." He touched her face again, lightly tracing her jawline with his thumb. "It doesn't matter what they think is going on between us."

Becca nodded, but she was worried. All they'd done was kiss. But something was happening between her and Caleb, something big. At least, it felt that way to her. If he didn't feel the same…

"I'm happy I finally got to kiss you from beginning to end— even if we were interrupted again. Now that we've finished that, we can go from here."

His words swirled around her and squeezed tight, like a vise grip around her heart. Her breath hitched. Her throat burned.

Caleb wasn't talking about kisses. He wanted more. A hookup. A one-night stand. That was why he'd said what he had to Gertie. The kisses hadn't meant the same thing to him.

Becca's shoulders sagged. At least she'd found out before any real damage had been done. She straightened and raised her chin. "I need to get Snowy."

Caleb's eyes darkened. "What's wrong?"

A "nothing" sat on the tip of her tongue. But "nothing" wouldn't keep her stomach from knotting a thousand different ways. "Nothing" wouldn't keep her from staying up all night analyzing the situation until exhaustion took over.

She'd been there before. She wasn't eager for a return trip.

With a deep breath, she mustered her courage. "So now that we've finished—"

"We—" he twirled a short strand of her hair with his fingertip "—are going on a date."

Hope exploded inside her—short-lived, as caution shouted a warning. "A date?"

"Dinner at Pacifica."

Pacifica was a new restaurant in town. "I've heard Pacifica's incredible, but impossible to get a reservation."

"I'll get us a table."

His confidence attracted her as much as it repelled. Less than a minute ago she was ready to write his kiss and him off. Now she was going on a date with him. The tennis-match-worthy back and forth was enough to make her light-headed.

Becca wasn't interested in his money or power. She liked the way he cared about people and took care of them. But she was pleased he was trying to do something special to make her feel important. She found it endearingly silly because she would be happy going out for hot dogs. "Sounds great."

"Are you free Wednesday?" he asked.

That was only two days away. No worries. He'd never get a table. "I am."

He typed on his smartphone. "This shouldn't take long."

"What are you doing?"

"Making a reservation." His phone buzzed. He stared at the screen. "Wednesday at eight. It's a date."

"How did you manage that?"

"I grew up here." He looked so pleased with himself. "I have a few connections."

And now she had a date with Caleb Fairchild.

The realization of what she'd agreed to hit her like a two-hundred-pound Newfoundland dog wanting a hug. Hope turned to an impending sense of dread. Her sandals felt more like cement blocks. Becca trudged to Snowy.

A date with Caleb Fairchild.

She opened the door and attached Snowy's leash to his collar. She would need something nice to wear, nicer than one of her dog-show suits.

Snowy trotted out.

She would need to know what utensils to use when. Was the saying from the outside in or was it the inside out? She would need to look up rules of etiquette and table manners on the Internet.

She would need to figure out what to say or not say to Gertie about going out with Caleb.

"Snowy looks like a champion," Caleb said.

Becca nodded, but she couldn't relax.

Her muscles bunched. Her stomach clenched.

A date with Caleb Fairchild.

A man who could get a table at the hottest restaurant in town with a simple text was the last guy she should ever want to date. Or kiss. Or…

No falling for him. A date was one thing. A kiss another. Anything more could be…disastrous.

On the patio, Caleb stood back while Gertie, Becca and Snowy took the spotlight. Becca's confidence blossomed around the dog. He wished she exuded the same confidence when she wasn't with one of the dogs.

Courtney sidled up next to him. "Not what you think. Really?"

"Drop it."

"No." She leaned closer, sending a whiff of expensive perfume up his nostrils. "I saw the direction of your hand. Becca didn't seem to mind one bit. You like her."

"I enjoy spending time with her."

"You like her."

Becca stacked Snowy, the way she had in the ring. The dog ate up applause and attention as if it were beef jerky.

"How long have you been dating?" Courtney asked.

"You're not going to let this go."

"You dating someone takes pressure off me."

She flipped her hair behind her shoulder with a practice move rumored to have cut men to their knees. Not any man Caleb would want to know.

"So spill," she said.

"We're not dating, but I'm taking Becca to Pacifica on Wednesday."

"Fancy-schmancy." Courtney used her favorite saying since childhood. The words described his sister's lifestyle perfectly. "You're out to impress Becca."

"I want her to enjoy the evening." But Caleb realized he did want to impress Becca. "I want her to feel comfortable, not intimidated."

Courtney grinned as if she'd been handed a platinum Visa card with no spending limit. "Leave it to me, bro."

Two women couldn't have been more different. He eyed his sister warily. "What do you have in mind?"

Wednesday morning, Becca released the dogs into their run. She cleaned the kennel from top to bottom—sweeping, scrubbing, disinfecting. The entire time she thought about Caleb. Tonight was their date.

She ran through all the things she'd been learning online about eating at an expensive fancy restaurant. Use flatware from the outside in. Napkins are for dabbing, never wiping. Bread should be torn, not cut with a knife. Her parents had taught her a few of the rules like no elbows on the table, don't take a bite until everyone had been served and don't slurp soup or drinks. Maybe she would be able to pull this off.

If not, it was only one date. No big deal.

Yeah, right.

This was the biggest deal since Gertie had hired her.

Mopping the floor outside the dog stalls, Becca pictured the outfit she was going to wear. She'd gone through every piece of clothing she owned and settled on a slim black skirt, white blouse and a pair of black pumps. A scarf would add a burst of color. Silver hoop earrings and a bracelet would be her jewelry.

She wanted to look elegant. Most likely she would be dressed too plainly for a place as trendy and hip as Pacifica.

Maybe she should cancel.

Becca rested against the mop.

You could take a mutt into the show ring, but no matter what she wore or how she acted, the maître d' would know she was a mixed breed, not a purebred. No sense pretending otherwise.

Her cellphone rang. "Hello."

"Please come to the house right now."

The urgency in Gertie's voice made Becca drop the mop. "On my way."

She ran to the house. The family room was empty. The kitchen, too. "Gertie?"

"Upstairs."

Becca climbed the stairs two at a time, her heart racing, worried about Gertie. She entered Gertie's bedroom, her gaze scanning the room. Unique antiques. Luxurious textiles. Exotic treasures.

On the bed was something new. A pile of clothing. Shoes, too.

Gertie stood with a beaming smile on her face and a familiar twinkle in her eyes. Courtney was next to Gertie. Mrs. Harris and Maura were there, too.

"What's going on?" Becca asked.

Courtney motioned to the bed with a pile of clothing and shoes on top. "I have a bunch of stuff that isn't the right color or style. We're about the same size. Maura, too. I thought the two of you might want to see if there's anything you like."

Becca imagined her not unsuitable but not perfect outfit for tonight. She couldn't believe her luck or Courtney's generosity. A lump of gratitude clogged Becca's throat. Tears stung her eyes. She covered her face with her hands.

Gertie put her arm around Becca. "What's wrong, dear?"

"This is so nice. The timing is perfect," Becca sniffled. "I have a date tonight, but I don't have anything nice enough to wear, so I've been thinking about canceling."

"Don't fret," Gertie said in a voice that made it seem as if the world could end and everything would still be okay.

"And please don't cancel," Courtney said. "We'll find you a knockout outfit to wear. Some of the clothes still have the tags on them."

Becca rubbed her eyes. She didn't understand rich people.

"Courtney is a shopaholic. Something she may have inherited from me," Gertie said to Maura and Becca. "It's about time others benefited from my granddaughter's addiction."

Maura stepped forward. "I'd love some new clothes. Tags or not."

Most of Becca's clothes came from thrift stores or consignment shops. She had no issue with hand-me-downs. "Me, too."

"Where are you going tonight?" Gertie asked.

As soon as Becca told them where, they would know she was going with Caleb. But she couldn't lie. "Pacifica."

Both Mrs. Harris and Maura gasped.

A snug smile formed on Courtney's lips.

"A lovely restaurant." Beaming, Gertie led Becca toward the bed. "Let's find something that'll make Caleb's eyes bug out and want to go straight to dessert."

CHAPTER TEN

DINNER AT PACIFICA was a hundred times better than Caleb had expected. It wasn't the mouthwatering Northwest cuisine from the award-winning chef. It wasn't the all-star service from the waiter dressed in black. It wasn't the romantic atmosphere with flickering votive candles and fresh flowers atop a linen-covered table for two. It was the woman sitting across from him who made the night memorable.

Caleb squeezed Becca's hand. "Have I told you how stunning you look tonight?"

Her smile meant only for him made Caleb feel seven feet tall. "About ten times. But I don't mind."

"Then I'll keep saying it." She wore a one-shoulder floral dress with a tantalizing asymmetrical hem. The heels of her strappy sandals accentuated her long legs. She'd glossed her lips and wore makeup. "You're the most beautiful women in Boise."

Her cheeks flushed, a pale pink that made her more attractive. "Only because I had your sister to help me."

"You don't need makeup and clothes to be beautiful." He pointed to her heart. "It's all right there. The rest are optional accessories."

Gratitude shone in the depths of her eyes. "Thank you."

"You're welcome." Caleb didn't have room in his life for a girlfriend. But he liked being with Becca. Maybe she'd be up for a casual relationship. Time permitting. He kissed the top of her hand. "But even though your dress is spectacular, I kind of miss seeing you covered in dog hair."

Her laughter, as melodic as a song, caressed his heart.

"I doubt they would have let me in with a speck of hair or lint on me." She glanced around, then lowered her voice. "I'm so relieved I made it through dinner. I kept thinking if I made a mistake, used the wrong fork or something, they'd kick me out."

"You didn't make any mistakes."

She kissed his hand. "It wasn't as hard as I thought it would be."

Their waiter, dressed in a black tuxedo with a gleaming bald head and an equally bright smile, dropped off the leather case containing Caleb's credit card and the bill.

Becca rubbed his hand with her thumb. "Thank you for tonight. I'll never forget this evening."

He wouldn't, either. "We'll have to do it again."

"I'd like that, but…"

"What?"

Mischief filled her eyes. "You've given me a peek into your world. If we do this again, I want to show you mine."

"Not if, when. That sounds like fun."

She shimmied her shoulders, as if excited.

Caleb wanted to lean across the table and kiss her bare shoulder, then trail more kisses up her neck until he reached her lips.

"How does Friday sound?" he asked.

"This Friday?"

He might not want a girlfriend, but a few dates didn't mean anything. He liked hanging out with Becca. No big deal. He could walk away any time. But for now he would enjoy her. "Yes."

On Thursday, Becca printed out a stack of emails for Gertie. "These are product orders. Too bad we don't have any products to sell."

Gertie's smile kept widening as she thumbed through the pages. "We can make up some batches in the lab. Sell those."

"Is that legal?"

"We're using natural, known ingredients, so we shouldn't have a problem." Gertie looked at Becca. "But double-check with Caleb to be on the safe side."

Becca would love to hear his voice. His good-night kiss in the parking lot had tempted her, but common sense won out over raging hormones. She was growing fonder of him each time she saw him. Still no sense taking a swan dive into an empty pool. "I'll text him."

She didn't really need to hear his voice.

Gertie tapped her chin. "We should pick a show, set up a booth and debut the products."

"Stumptown is in July, but that's too soon. The Enumclaw show is a couple weeks later in August. That one draws people from all over and has lots of breed specialties going on, too."

"Sounds good. Mark your calendar."

August wasn't that far way. "It's going to be a busy summer with all the dog shows we've entered."

"Have Caleb go with you."

Thinking about spending the summer at dog shows with Caleb made her pulse race faster than a Greyhound chasing a rabbit. But Becca could never ask him to do that. She couldn't lower her guard that much and open herself up to more heartache. "We're not…"

"Friends? I've seen the way he looks at you." Gertie raised a white eyebrow. "He's never looked at another woman like that. Not even his ex-fiancée."

Becca had heard about his ex from Courtney the other night doing Becca's makeup for her date. Becca realized how much Caleb and she had in common with their past romances. No wonder he hadn't trusted her when he first met her. It would be hard to trust anyone after almost being scammed by someone who claimed to love you. At least they were past that now.

"That makes you happy." Gertie said.

Yes, very much so. But Becca didn't dare admit that aloud.

A little voice inside her head whispered a warning. The caution reverberated through her. Getting her hopes up too high could mean a long, hurtful drop. The last thing she wanted—needed—was for her heart to go splat. But there was something she could say. "Caleb is a nice guy."

"Yes, but my grandson is still a man," Gertie said. "They'll take whatever you offer and try to keep the status quo as long as possible."

"I don't understand."

"Don't sleep with Caleb until there's a wedding band on your finger."

Becca's cheeks burned. "We've only kissed a few times."

"Some pretty hot kisses from what I saw."

She covered her mouth with her hand, unable to believe Gertie talked so openly about kissing and…sex.

"Don't be embarrassed. I might be old, but I was young once," Gertie said. "Remember the adage about the cow and getting milk for free is as true today as it was when I was your age."

Becca knew her boss had only her best interest at heart, but this was awkward. "I'll remember."

Not that she and Caleb were even close to…that. Taking things to the next level would be a game changer.

What had Caleb said?

Win-win.

She'd always come out on the losing side before. She didn't see that changing, even if a part of her wished it would.

But Becca knew one thing. She wasn't sure she was ready to trust her heart again. Or if she ever could.

Friday evening, Caleb arrived at what looked to be an Old West saloon for his date with Becca. He hadn't seen her in two days, two of the longest days of his life.

If he wasn't thinking about her, he was texting her. If he wasn't texting her, he was figuring out the best time to call her.

If he wasn't calling her, he was back to thinking about her. A vicious cycle. One that left him distracted and behind at work. One he wasn't used to and wanted to stop.

No matter. This wasn't some serious relationship. They shared a few interests and sizzling chemistry. That was what drew him to her, nothing more.

Becca stood outside the restaurant, waiting for him. She wore jean shorts, a red lace-trimmed camisole with a red gingham button-down shirt over it.

His heart tripped over itself at the sight of her. His temperature skyrocketed at the tan, toned skin showing.

"You came straight from the office," she said.

"I got stuck in a meeting." He kissed her cheek. She smelled sweet like strawberries. "I'm overdressed."

"Take off your jacket and tie."

"It's fine."

She tugged on his tie. "I'm serious. You need to take this off now."

"Don't worry."

"You're going to regret not—"

He touched his finger to his lips. "Shhh."

"Your loss."

Caleb had no idea what she was talking about. "How was your day?"

"Good. I reviewed our new website and made a list of changes for the web designer."

"Text me the URL. I can't wait to see it."

"Courtney came up with the name. Gertie's Top Dog Products."

He opened the door to the restaurant. "I'm surprised Grams dragged my sister into this."

Becca entered. "Courtney wanted to help."

"She must have an ulterior motive."

"Being nice isn't enough?"

"Not for my sister." Inside, he took a step. Something

crunched beneath his shoe. He looked down. Peanut shells. "Interesting floor covering."

The entire place was interesting. The hole-in-the-wall grill was a far cry from Pacifica. The smell of hops and grease filled the air. The din of customer's conversations and cussing rose above the honky-tonk music playing from speakers.

Becca pointed to a No Ties sign. "You should take yours off."

"No one cares what I wear here."

She dragged two fingers over her mouth, zipping her lips. "Won't mention it again."

The hostess wore supertight, short jean shorts, a spaghetti-strap top and a ponytail. She led them to a table.

Caleb sat across from Becca. A tin pail full of shelled peanuts sat in the center of the table next to a roll of paper towels.

The hostess handed them menus. "Your server will be right with you."

He looked around. Customers had engraved their names on the wood planks covering the walls. He doubted they used a butter knife. That told him a lot about the clientele. He would have to bring Ty here the next time his friend was home. "Come here often?"

"No, but it's one of my favorite places in town."

"I've never heard of it."

"It's time you discovered one of Boise's hidden gems."

Hidden, yes. A gem? Becca would have to convince Caleb. But he had no doubt Ty would love this place.

Caleb read the menu. Lots of red meat and potatoes. Fried, French, mashed, baked. Okay, maybe this place was okay.

"Howdy, partners. I'm Jackie, your server." A perky, voluptuous woman with equally puffy big hair stood at their table. She wore tight jean shorts and a T-shirt two sizes too small. "I see we have a new visitor to our fine establishment. Welcome, fine sir. I take it you did not see the sign."

"What sign?"

Becca shook her head.

"The No Ties sign," Jackie said.

"I saw it," he admitted.

"Then there's only one thing left for me to do." She pulled out a pair of scissors from her back pocket, leaned toward him giving him a bird's-eye view of her breasts and cut off his tie right above one side of the knot.

"What the…" He stared at where his tie used to hang. The spot was empty. "That was a silk tie."

An expensive one.

"I told you," Becca said. "More than once, if you remember."

"You never said they'd vandalize my tie."

Jackie shrugged. "You saw the sign. You disobeyed the sign. You pay the price."

This was unbelievable. "What happens to the tie now?"

"It becomes part of our decor," Jackie said. "Look up."

Caleb did. Hundreds of colorful ties hung from the ceiling.

"You should have listened to me," Becca said. "But I didn't try that hard to convince you. I've never been all that fond of your yellow tie. No big loss, if you want my opinion."

"Red is a power color." Jackie tucked the tie into her bra. A good thing they had a use for it, because he wasn't going to want it back now. "Yellow is too…"

"Understated," Becca said.

Unbelievable. His grandmother had said the same things. He half laughed.

"You've got your peanuts and menus and sense of humor," Jackie said. "I'll be back in a jiff to take your drink orders."

With that, the server walked away.

"I hope you're not too upset about your tie?" Becca asked.

"Not upset," he admitted. "It's my fault. You warned me. I chose not to listen to you. Lesson learned."

With a smile, Becca grabbed a handful of peanuts. "Dig in."

He took one from the pail. "You just toss the shells on the floor?"

"You've led a sheltered life. Watch." She illustrated what to do. "Your turn."

Caleb took another peanut. Opened it. Removed the peanut. Tossed the shell on the ground.

"Easy-peasy." She dumped a handful of peanuts in front of him, then pointed to a target painted on the aisle between the tables. "Now we can get serious. High point wins."

That sounded fun. "What's the prize?"

She shrugged. "What do you want it to be?"

You. In the horizontal position. But he didn't think she was up for that. At least not yet. Maybe later tonight. "I don't care."

"Then I'll have to think of something—until then…go for it."

With each peanut shell he tossed, the stress of his day spent working at Fair Face and attending meetings slipped away. Nothing mattered, not Grams or Courtney. There was only here and now. And Becca.

He threw another peanut. "This is more fun than I thought it would be."

"Fun is the name of the game here."

Caleb saw that. He liked it, too. "I like having fun."

Becca had brought fun back into his life. The kind of fun Grams said he needed. And Caleb knew one thing.

He didn't want it to end.

At least not anytime soon.

Becca didn't want the night to end. Delicious food. Interesting conversation. A handsome date who made her think of slow, hot kisses.

Charmed by Caleb, yes. Totally enchanted by him—she was on her way.

Time to pull back. Though that was hard to do when he held her hand in the restaurant's parking lot.

"I had a great time tonight," Caleb said. "Want to get together tomorrow and go tie shopping?"

Her heart leaped. Common sense frowned. She laughed, not knowing if he were serious or not.

"I mean it."

Okay, he was serious. She bit her lip.

The list of reasons she shouldn't want to see him again was long. But those things were easy to forget when Caleb's gaze made her feel like the only woman in the world. His world, at least. That could be oh-so-dangerous. "You should ask your sister to go. I know nothing about ties."

He brushed his lips over Becca's hair, making her knees want to melt. "Courtney might know fashion, but you know me."

Her heart bumped. The thought of spending more time with Caleb made her want to cancel her plans. But she couldn't. "I would love to go tie shopping, but I'm driving down to see my parents tomorrow."

"Overnight?"

"A day trip," she said. "I need to be back for the dogs."

"Ah, yes, the dogs."

He sounded funny. "What do you mean by the dogs?"

"I never thought I'd be jealous of some pups."

"Jealous, huh?"

"You're at their beck and call."

"It's my job."

"Admit it," he said lightheartedly. "You like the dogs better than you like me."

He was teasing, but there was some truth to his words. Becca liked dogs better than most people. But better than Caleb?

"It's a different kind of like," she said. "Dogs are loyal, protective and think I'm the center of their universe. That's pretty appealing."

"True, but a dog can't do this."

Caleb dipped his head, touching his mouth to Becca's. Electric. His lips moved over hers, sending pleasurable tingles shooting through her. She savored the feel and the taste of him. Forget the dinner they'd eaten, this was all she needed for nourishment. He drew the kiss to an end much to soon.

"You're right." She rubbed her throbbing lips together. "A dog can't to that."

His chest expanded. "Damn straight they can't."

She laughed. "Thanks for dinner. It's been a lovely evening."

"We don't have to call it a night."

Oh, Becca was tempted. But keeping her heart under lock and key was becoming more difficult each time they were together.

Thanks to Caleb, she felt more confident, competent, sexy.

She liked it. Liked him. And felt herself growing closer to him. But she wasn't sure she could trust her feelings. Or his. He didn't seem eager to get into a relationship. She had avoided them herself. "There's no reason to rush into anything, right?"

"No," he said. "But I would like to see you tomorrow. How about I go with you to your parents' house?"

She stared at him in disbelief. "Seriously?"

He nodded. "You know Grams. Seems fair I should meet your parents."

"Sure." Becca wiggled her toes. "That would be great."

On Saturday afternoon, Caleb drove into the trailer park outside Twin Falls. He wasn't sure what to expect, but so far seemed stereotypical. Singlewides, doublewides and RVs filled the various lots. Cars and trucks were parked haphazardly on the narrow streets. Cats lounged in the sun. Dogs barked at his car.

"Turn left at the Statue of Liberty. You can't miss it," Becca said.

"I'm looking forward to meeting your parents."

"They can't wait to meet you."

A six-foot replica of the Statue of Liberty stood like a sentry at an intersection. Nearby, two men with handlebar mustaches and tattooed arms eyed his sports car. An elderly woman sat in a rocking chair with a Chihuahua on her lap on the porch of another trailer.

Becca pointed out the windshield. "My parents live in the trailer with the chicken wire fencing and the Jolly Roger flag."

O-kay. Caleb gripped his steering wheel and parked. Not only was there chicken fencing, but also live chickens. Was that even legal in the city limits? He turned off the ignition.

"My parents are normal folks, so don't be nervous," she said.

A couple thoughts ran through his mind. One, this was going to be interesting, if not enlightening. Two, he doubted he'd ever see the hubcaps on his car again. At least he had insurance. "I'm not nervous."

Not much anyway.

"Good, because I am."

Caleb fought the urge to kiss her nerves away. He squeezed her hand. "No reason to be nervous. They're your parents."

"Exactly." She rewarded him with a grin. "If my father wants to show you his gun and knife collection, say no. Otherwise, he'll try to intimidate you."

Caleb knew from what Becca had told him as well as the private investigator's report that her father had been arrested and jailed for fighting, so this didn't surprise him. "Good to know."

"If my mom mentions UFOs and government conspiracies, smile and nod. Whatever you do, don't mention Roswell or Flight 800."

"Maybe I should have brought a tinfoil hat."

"If you had, you would endear yourself to her forever." Becca moistened her lips. "I'm not kidding."

Her serious tone told him she wasn't.

If Becca considered this "normal folks," he wondered what her version of not-so-normal would be like. Given the Taylors' daughter had grown up to be such a lovely, caring and hardworking woman, he shouldn't rush to judgment. He'd made that mistake with Becca. "Let's go meet your folks."

A man and a woman in their early forties stood on the porch and waved.

"That's my mom and dad, Debbie and Rob," Becca said.

The woman had the same brown hair as Becca, only longer,

and a similar smile. The man had lighter brown hair and the same blue eyes as his daughter. "They look so young."

More like an older brother and sister, not her parents.

"My mom was seventeen and my dad eighteen when they got married. I arrived a week before her eighteenth birthday."

"Kids having kids."

"They thought they were grown up enough at the time, but both told me I should wait until I was older, maybe even in my thirties, to get married."

He opened the gate for Becca. "Good advice."

"Make sure none of the chickens escape."

Caleb closed the gate behind him and double-checked the latch was secure.

Introductions were made. Becca's parents were friendly. He received a handshake from Rob and a hug from Debbie. The four of them entered the house. Their trailer was small, tidy and welcoming. Pictures hung on the walls. Knick-knacks covered shelves. But no pets. Not a dog or a cat in sight. That surprised him given Becca's love of animals.

Caleb studied the photographs of a young Becca riding a tricycle and one of her winning a ribbon at a 4-H dog show.

He motioned to her high school graduation picture. "You used to have long hair like your mom's."

She nodded. "I'm not that same person anymore. I like my hair shorter."

"I like it, too," Caleb said, noticing her parents watching the exchange with interest.

"Why don't you help your mother with dinner," Rob said to Becca. "I'll keep Caleb company."

Becca followed Debbie into the kitchen.

Rob slapped him on the back. "So Caleb, you into guns and hunting?"

He remembered what Becca had told him, but he wasn't about to be intimidated. "My grandfather used to take my best friend and me elk hunting. Crossbows, not guns."

"Bag anything?"

"A buck." Caleb remembered his surprise when he'd hit the animal. He'd felt a burst of excitement at making the shot and a rush of sadness at seeing the elk fall. "He was so much bigger than me. Had a helluva time getting him back to camp."

Bob looked toward the kitchen. "I've done some bear hunting."

Caleb expected to be invited to see the gun collection next.

Bob leaned closer. "Never could bring anything I shot home or Becca would cry. You might not want to mention that elk. She's fond of animals. Might hold it against you."

So much for being intimidated. "Thanks for the advice."

"You're welcome." Bob's gaze drifted to the kitchen again. He lowered his voice. "My daughter's caught some bad breaks."

"Becca told me."

"She works hard. Sends us money, even when she doesn't have much herself." Rob's gaze met Caleb's in understanding. "I don't want to see my little girl hurt."

"Me, either. She's a special woman."

"Good to hear you say that," Rob said. "Becca's never brought a man, or a boy for that matter, home before."

Caleb straightened. That surprised him. But she hadn't asked him home to meet her parents. He'd invited himself. She must be taking her parents' advice about waiting to get married until she was older. She had goals and dreams. The last thing she needed was a boyfriend to get in the way. The same way he didn't need a girlfriend. This would make life easier for both of them.

They wouldn't have to worry about things getting serious and complicated. They could keep having fun together and enjoying each other's company.

Yes, this was going to work out well.

In the kitchen, Becca put the tray of biscuits into the preheated oven. She set the timer. "Dinner smells good."

"Meatloaf with mashed potatoes and pie for dessert," her mother said. "Caleb's handsome."

"He's got the prettiest eyes and the nicest smile."

"You really like him."

"We haven't been seeing each other long."

"That doesn't mean you can't have feelings for him." Her mother stirred the gravy simmering on the stove. "I knew your father was the one a week after we met."

Becca had heard the story of how they met at a local burger joint over chocolate milk shakes and French fries many times. "How did you know?"

"It was a feeling." Her mother tilted her head. "We fit from that very first day. When we were apart it wasn't awful like the world was ending or someone had died, but when we were together things were better. We were a team. We complemented each other. If that makes sense."

That was how Becca felt with Caleb. "It does."

"Do you think you and Caleb might turn into something serious?"

Yes! She was afraid to voice her desire aloud. Afraid to believe in a happily ever after with him. "Maybe."

Her mother removed a bottle of salad dressing from the refrigerator. "How does he make you feel?"

"Special. Important. Like I can do anything." Her breath caught. "I think I'm falling for him."

"You think?"

Becca laughed. "Okay, I'm falling. I may have already fallen. It feels scary."

"Falling for someone is very scary. That's a normal feeling. But good, too." Her mother touched her shoulder. "You can't live stuck in the past. Afraid. Caleb isn't Whitley. If you like Caleb, give him a chance."

"I always thought all I needed in my life were dogs, but after meeting Caleb…"

Kissing him…

"You want more," her mom said.

"Yes." Becca not only wanted more, she needed more. That terrified her. The last time she wanted more, she'd ended up heartbroken and in jail. She hated to think that could happen with Caleb, too. "But we're so different. I'm not sure it can work. Do you think I can really fit into Caleb's world?"

"Yes. Just be yourself. If who you are doesn't fit, then he's not the right man for you."

"Mom."

"I'm serious." Her mother wrapped her arms around Becca. "You are a sweet, generous, smart woman with so much love to give the right man."

"I think Caleb might be the right man for me."

"Only time will tell."

Caleb wouldn't waste hours to drive to her parents' house if she didn't mean something to him. He acted as if he accepted her and her past. He called, texted and wanted to spend time with her. He had feelings for her. The only question was what kind of feelings. "I hope it doesn't take long."

"Patience is a virtue," her mother said.

Becca checked the biscuits. "I spent three years being patient. You'd think I'd get a break this time."

"Sorry to say, baby, but there aren't many breaks when it comes to love."

Love.

Becca liked the sound of that, liked it a lot.

She only hoped Caleb would, too.

And this time wouldn't turn out to be another big mistake.

CHAPTER ELEVEN

FOUR HOURS LATER, the headlights of Caleb's car cut through the darkness. Becca sat in the passenger seat, cocooned in the comfy, leather seats. Looking at his handsome profile, warmth flowed through her. "I thought the visit went well."

He glanced her way. "I had fun. Your parents are great."

"They like you."

"I like them." Caleb maneuvered the car around an orange semi-truck. "Your dad didn't pull out any guns or knives."

"Lucky," she teased. "He'd threatened to do that if you turned out to be a bozo or an idiot."

"Good to know I'm neither of those things." He readjusted his hands on the steering wheel. "Your mom is a kick. She should have been a lawyer. She had me almost convinced we never landed on the moon."

Becca laughed. "My mom can argue with the best of them."

"But I'm glad she had you instead of going on to college."

The pitter-patter of her heart tripled. "Me, too."

"What's your week like?" he asked.

"Busy. There's a local dog show on Saturday and Sunday. I'm going to be driving back and forth each day. We're too busy producing products in the lab for me to be away."

"It's going to be a busy week for me, too."

Bummer, but she wasn't about to complain after spending today with him. "Maybe we can see each other online."

"We'll figure something out."

The perfect end to a perfect day. Well that, and Caleb's toe-curling good-night kiss.

After he left, Becca brought the dogs to the guest cottage. "I'm in such a good mood you guys can sleep with me tonight."

She changed into a pair of flannel shorts and T-shirt and closed the blinds.

With two dogs on the bed with her, another three on the floor and a laptop in front of her, she answered emails about the products, a result of the samples she'd been handing out at dog shows and word of mouth. The lab had been turned into a mini-manufacturing plant, but Gertie's research assistants were taking the temporary change in job responsibilities in stride.

Becca's cellphone rang.

She glanced at the clock on the nightstand—11:28 p.m. Late for a call. Unless it was Caleb.

Adrenaline surged. She grabbed the phone. The name on the screen read Courtney Fairchild.

Becca hit answer. "Courtney?"

"Sorry to call so late." Courtney sniffled. "I'm in a bit of a jam."

The words came out stilted. Something was wrong. "What's going on?"

"My, um, car's in the Boise River."

Concern ricocheted through Becca. "Are you hurt?"

Her sharp voice woke the dogs. Maurice tried to climb on her lap. Hunter jumped off the bed.

"I'm…I think I'm okay." Courtney's voice quivered. "My car is ruined. Caleb's going to kill me. That's why I called you and not him or Grams. You won't be mad at me."

"Of course I'm not mad." Becca changed out of her pajamas and into clothes. "Where are you?"

Courtney gave her the crossroads. "Just follow the flashing lights. I'm going to need a ride home. If I don't end up going to the hospital. There's a cute firefighter who thinks I should go."

"Listen to him."

"Okay. I'll do whatever he says." Courtney sounded strange,

mixed up, in shock. "I can't believe I ruined another car. Caleb's going to…"

"Don't worry about your brother." Becca slipped on her sandals. "I'm going to put the dogs in the kennel, then drive over. If you're not at the river, I'll drive to the nearest hospital, okay?"

"Thanks. I appreciate this."

Becca hoped Caleb wouldn't be upset for not calling him immediately. But she'd been in a similar spot. Calling anyone was difficult. She was happy to be there for Courtney, and as soon as Becca knew more she'd contact Caleb. "See you soon."

Hours later, Becca dozed in the waiting room of the hospital. She'd been sitting with Courtney until they took her for more tests due to the nasty bump on her head.

"What are you doing here?"

She opened her eyes to see a not-so-happy-looking Caleb standing in front of her. His gaze was narrowed. His mouth set in a firm, thin line. No wonder Courtney didn't want to call him.

"Courtney called me. She was hurting," Becca said. "Scared."

"My sister should be terrified." He shifted his weight from foot to foot. "Texting while driving. She could have been killed or killed somebody else."

"Thankfully, she wasn't, and she didn't."

"Her car is ruined."

"The airbag saved her life."

Caleb looked tense like a spring ready to pop open. His jaw was as rigid as a steel girder.

Becca touched his arm. His muscles bunched beneath her palm. "Courtney's going to be okay."

"This time. Like the last time." He exhaled slowly. "One of these times she won't be. That will kill Grams."

And him.

Becca could tell this was tearing Caleb up inside. She put her arm around him.

His body stiffened tightly—she might as well be hugging

a tree. He backed out of her embrace. "You shouldn't butt into my family's business."

Where had that come from? He was upset. She realized that, but his words were like a slap to her cheek. She took a breath. And another. "I'm not butting in. I told you Courtney called me."

Suspicion filled his gaze. Something she hadn't seen since they first met. "Why didn't you call me?"

"Courtney wasn't ready to see you."

"And you didn't think I should know what happened to my sister."

Becca tried not to take his anger personal. "It was late. If her injuries had been more serious—"

"The police thought it was serious enough to call me."

"The police?"

"I'm co-owner of the car. But that's the last time I do that." He brushed his hand through his hair. "Courtney needs to deal with the consequences of her actions. Clean up her messes. Not have others do it for her."

"She's still young."

"Only a year younger than you."

That surprised Becca. "She seems younger."

"That's because Courtney still acts like a spoiled little girl. She's too much like our father. My grandmother bailed him out of so many jams he never learned from his mistakes. Courtney's the same way."

"Learning from mistakes isn't always easy," Becca said. "Sometimes the lessons are so in your face it's hard to miss them. But other times it's not as clear."

He studied her for a moment, the anger clearing from his eyes. "You learned."

"I had three years to think about what I did."

But right now she wondered if she'd learned anything during that time. One thing was clear tonight. Caleb didn't want her here. He wanted to keep family stuff private. She ignored the sting in her heart. She needed to focus on Courtney right now.

Becca took a deep breath. "The point is everyone makes mistakes."

Including Caleb.

"Courtney makes more mistakes than most."

"You're her big brother." Becca softened her tone. If only he could see that he was making a big mistake with his younger sister. "Help Courtney figure out what she should be doing instead of getting into so much trouble."

"I've tried."

The anguish in his voice hurt Becca's heart. She touched his back. This time he didn't tense. "Try harder. You have a lot on your plate, but Courtney is your sister. I just met her, but it's clear she's bored out of her mind. She hates her job at Fair Face."

"She's never in the office."

"Why not?"

"She's off shopping or sleeping in late."

"So Gertie isn't the only one who lets Courtney get away with stuff."

"My sister is a handful."

"Yes, but threatening to kill her or cut her off from her trust fund if she messes up isn't helping matters."

"I don't want her to end up like our dad."

"No one does, but she's not happy. You can't force her to work at a job she doesn't want. She might be better off working in a different department or even another company," Becca said. "Getting Courtney pointed in the right direction isn't enabling her. It's supporting her. Helping her. That's what family does for one another."

"I'm being a jerk."

"Courtney will understand."

"I meant with you." He touched Becca's face. His gaze softened. "I wasn't expecting to see you here. It caught me off-guard."

"I understand."

And Becca did. She might want to let Caleb into her life

and heart, but he wasn't there yet. For all she knew, he might never be there.

And that realization sucked.

The week dragged for Caleb. He hadn't seen Becca since the night at the hospital. He'd been a jerk to her. But he couldn't help himself.

Grams adored Becca. Courtney turned to Becca in her time of need. Caleb wanted to spend all his free time with Becca.

She'd become a pivotal person in his family. Something no one, not even Cassandra, had managed to do.

That bothered him. Immensely.

She'd gotten under his skin, but he couldn't allow her into his heart. He wasn't ready to get into something too deep. Not that she was pushing him into a relationship. Or had mentioned the word.

Maybe all he needed was distance.

So he didn't call her the rest of the week. Didn't text her.

But that didn't stop him from thinking about her.

He'd tried focusing on work, but thinking about her interfered with him accomplishing much. Sitting through one boring meeting after another hadn't taken his mind off her.

And here he was again in another meeting on a Friday afternoon.

To make matters worse, there was a weird vibe in the conference room. He looked around the table, pen between his fingers.

Glen, the vice president of Sales and Marketing, checked his watch for the twelfth time in the past fifteen minutes. Ed, the usually messy director of advertising, played housekeeper—wiping off the table, pushing in unused chairs and straightening papers. Julie, the new head of PR, kept sneaking peeks at the door as if HGTV were about to burst in and award her a dream house.

People were ready to kick off their weekends, but that didn't explain why the three of them were acting so strange.

Caleb tapped his pen against the table. "Anything else we need to discuss?"

Glances passed between them. Glen to Ed. Ed to Julie. Julie to Glen. All over Caleb's head. They might as well have been tossing a ball back and forth for their lack of subtlety.

"What's going on?" Caleb asked.

"Nothing."

"Nada."

"Not a thing."

The three spoke at the same time, their words falling on top of each other.

Something was definitely going on. He might be the CEO, the closest thing to a puppet master Fair Face had, but right now he felt as if someone else was manipulating the strings. He didn't like it.

"Talk to me," he said, using his hard-as-nails-don't-mess-with-me CEO voice he'd perfected for use in conference calls with suppliers.

Another shared glance passed among the three.

Glen cleared his throat. "Just a little anxious."

Caleb understood wanting to go home. He hadn't made plans to see Becca tonight, but maybe it wasn't too late. "Let's call it, then."

Julie jumped to her feet, her brown eyes widening and her gaze darting to the door. "Wait!"

Both Glen and Ed nodded furiously like Buster Bronco–the Boise State mascot—bobble-head dolls.

"I thought you wanted to get out of here," Caleb said.

"There's one more thing." Julie practically skipped away from the table, her shoulder-length red hair swinging behind her. She opened the door.

A bright light shone into the conference room.

Caleb dropped his pen. "What's—"

An attractive woman dressed in a maroon suit burst into the room. She held a microphone in one hand and a bottle of champagne in the other. Her straight, bleached teeth were as blinding as the camera light behind her.

"I'm Savannah Martin with *Good Day Boise*." The woman pronounced each word with precision. "Congratulations, Caleb Fairchild, you've been named Boise's Bachelor of the Year."

What the…

With lightning-quick moves that would make a ninja in high heels proud, Savannah thrust the champagne into his hands and shoved the microphone into his face. "Exciting news, isn't it?"

Caleb's gut churned, as if the gyro he'd eaten for lunch was waging war on his internal organs. He had no idea what being Bachelor of the Year entailed, but he doubted any of the hoopla would include Becca.

A predatory gleam filled the reporter's eyes, making him think she'd eat her young to get a story.

Not having a clue what to say, he stood. After all, that was the polite thing to do. Sweat dampened the back of his neck under his lightly starched collar. "Thank you."

The words rushed out faster than he'd intended. But he hadn't planned on being ambushed by the media and his own people.

Where was Ty when Caleb needed him? No one had his six here.

He glanced at the champagne and composed himself with a breath. "This is quite…an honor."

"Indeed." Savannah batted her eyelashes. Predator or flirt? "You had several nominations."

Who would have nominated him for Bachelor of the Year?

Not Grams's style, but Caleb wouldn't put it past Courtney with her odd sense of humor.

Caleb now knew why his coworkers had been acting so strangely during the meeting. The three stood together grinning like fools, as if year-end bonuses were going to arrive five months early. No doubt they'd had a hand in a few of the nominations. But…why?

"This is unexpected." He wished they had picked some

other bachelor in town, someone who cared about this sort of thing. "I'm…stunned."

"I'm not." Savannah gave him a look that would make Jack Frost blush. "Trust me, ladies, this is one bachelor you most definitely want to get to know better. He's a hot one."

Hot, yes. Because of the damn light in his face.

Caleb didn't know how to respond, so he kept smiling instead, a tight smile that hurt the muscles all the way to his toes.

The reporter failed to sense his discomfort or his plastic smile. She seemed more interested in the camera than in him. "This is Savannah Martin with Fair Face CEO, Caleb Fairchild, Boise's Bachelor of the Year."

The light went off. The camera lowered.

He could see again. And breathe. But that didn't loosen the bunched muscles in his shoulders or the fist-sized knot in his stomach.

A twentysomething man with a goatee and wearing faded jeans with a green T-shirt walked out of the meeting room carrying the camera.

Savannah's smile dimmed, as if her on switch connected to the camera's power button. "See you on Tuesday."

"Tuesday?" Caleb asked. Did he look as dazed as he felt?

"At the studio." The reporter's gaze ran the length of him— slow, methodical, appreciative.

She needed to stop looking at him like that. Becca wouldn't like it.

Whoa. Shock reverberated through him. He'd never worried about other women sizing him up when he was engaged to Cassandra. He shouldn't care now. Becca didn't own him. They weren't serious or exclusive. Had he gotten in deeper than he realized?

Julie skipped forward still looking as if she was in a hazy, dreamy mode. "You're being interviewed by *Good Day Boise*. I have all the details."

This was totally insane. There'd better be a good reason for the insanity, or three people would be looking for new jobs come Monday.

"See you on Tuesday, then." Caleb tried to keep his voice pleasant. Savannah left the room, closing the door behind her. "Sit."

His three employees took their places. Caleb sat, placed the champagne bottle on the table and let his smile drop. "What the hell was that all about?"

Ed and Julie looked at Glen, who twirled his pen like a baton. The pen rotated faster and faster.

Caleb's annoyance increased at the same rate of spin. He shot his vice president a tell-me-now-if-you-know-what's-good-for-you look. "Glen."

"My wife told me about the contest," he said. "I thought it would be good publicity for Fair Face."

"I agreed," Ed said.

"Me, too," Julie added. "It's a fantastic opportunity."

"Boise's Bachelor of the Year?" The words tasted bitter in Caleb's mouth. He picked up his pen and tapped it against the table. "Sure about this?"

Because he wasn't.

Two months ago, he would have popped open the champagne to celebrate. Two months ago, he would have phoned his grandmother to share the news. Two months ago, he would have texted Ty to rub it in.

Two months ago, Caleb hadn't known Becca Taylor.

He couldn't stop thinking about her melodic laughter and her hot kisses and when he could see her.

Even if seeing her again didn't make sense.

He didn't know what to think. Do. Say.

"This is a no brainer," Ed said. "Rave reviews about the baby line products are pouring in. Mothers are calling asking for samples. This is perfect timing."

"You can't buy this kind of PR," Glen said. "That's why we nominated you."

"The three of you?" Caleb asked.

"Our staffs," Glen admitted.

"And a few other employees." Ed made it sound like no big deal, but for all Caleb knew the entire company had nominated him. "This is a win-win situation for everyone involved."

It was lose-lose for him. Someone—okay, Becca—would be upset. That would make him unhappy.

Ed rested his elbows on the table. "We need you to play this right to maximize our exposure."

It sounded so calculated. Business often was, especially with advertising, and Caleb's job was to be the perfect CEO and present the correct image to the public. His grandfather had instilled that into him. "Tell me the slant."

Julie opened a manila folder. "Play up being single, but how you're looking to settle down."

Caleb drew back. "Whoa. Settle down?"

"And have a family," Julie said.

His empty hand slapped the table. The harsh sound echoed in the room. "What?"

"Mentioning you want a family will be the perfect segue to Fair Face's new baby products. The whole reason Gertie created the line is because she wants great-grandchildren, right?"

Caleb shifted in his chair. "Ri-i-i-ight."

"But you don't want to mention Gertie. This is about you, not your grandmother." The strategic glint in Glen's eye made him look more like a shark wearing a tie than a business executive. "Say you can't wait to use the new organic, all-natural baby products on your kids."

Caleb imagined Becca, her stomach round with their child. What the hell? He shook the image from his head. "I'm not married. Having kids is years off."

Julie's excited eyes and flushed face made her look as if she were about to bounce out of her chair. "That's where the contest comes in."

Ed nodded. "*Good Day Boise* wants to run a contest on their website."

"What's the prize?" Caleb asked.

Glen smiled. "A date with you."

Caleb stared in disbelief. "Please tell me you're kidding."

"This isn't any old date," Julie said, as if he hadn't said a word. "A dream date. Limousine. Romantic dinner for two at Pacifica. A dance club."

That was where he'd taken Becca on their first date. He couldn't take another woman—make that the contest winner—there.

"You can also do whatever else you want once the official date is over," Glen said with a wink-wink, nudge-nudge to his voice.

Caleb slunk in his chair. Becca was not going to like this.

Not that she had a claim on him, but just the fact he was putting her feeling first was out of character for him. He didn't understand it. He wanted it to stop.

"We'll do a billboard to promote the contest somewhere visible where most of Boise can see," Ed said. "We'll put it on the Facebook page. Take it national if we can. Offer a plane ticket and hotel accommodations if the winner isn't from Boise."

"Who picks the winner?" Caleb asked.

Julie rubbed her palms together as if she were trying to spark a fire. "A modern-day matchmaker."

Dream dates. Matchmaker. "This has to be a joke."

"Do I look like I'm joking?" Glen looked ultra-serious, as if the fate of the company were riding on this. "Your qualities for the perfect woman will be listed on *Good Day Boise*'s website. Viewers who believe they qualify can fill out a profile and see if they're a match."

He tossed his pen. It skidded across the table. "That's…"

"Marketing genius," Ed said. "If you end up dating the winner—"

"Imagine if you marry her," Julie said, her voice rising with each word as if Caleb was such a grand prize.

His stomach roiled. He was going to be sick. And it had nothing to do with what he'd eaten for lunch.

He needed to speak up, put an end to the craziness. "I'm seeing someone."

"Seeing?" Glen asked. "Or dating?"

Caleb hesitated. "It's not that serious."

It wasn't. So why was Becca branded on his brain? Affecting his working life? His family? Why was he putting her feelings ahead of what was best for Fair Face?

"Then it shouldn't be a problem," Glen said.

Caleb wished he had that much confidence. He didn't want to hurt Becca's feelings. They might not be that serious, but he didn't want to do anything to push her away. At least not that far away. "Put yourself in my shoes."

"A pair or two of new shoes might soothe any hurt feelings," Julie suggested.

Becca couldn't care less about fancy shoes. But she might like a new pair of grooming scissors. So not enough to smooth out this fiasco.

"This isn't personal. It's a business decision," Ed said. "Remember when we featured Gertie and Courtney in that series of ads for the moisturizing lotion. Sales shot through the roof."

How could Caleb forget? That campaign's success had floored everyone, including himself, and driven the company's brand recognition to new highs. Profits, too. "One in five women in the United States has tried a Fair Face product. You think we can achieve the same results here?"

"I do," Ed said. "As Bachelor of the Year you'll be the Grand Marshal of parades, do interviews and cut ribbons at grand openings. By the time we milk the last drop out of your title, two in five moms will be using our new products on their babies."

"Those numbers would make you happy," Glen said.

"I'd be thrilled." And Caleb would be.

He thought about the numbers. The exposure. The profits.

Face it. The website contest wasn't that big a deal in the grand scheme of things. One date. With a stranger. No big commitment.

Except for Becca.

Becca.

What was he worried about?

He liked her. They weren't exactly dating. They had fun together. Getting seriously involved with her would be too complicated and only add to his list of responsibilities. Becca. Her parents, Debbie and Rob. All the dogs.

That would be too much with everything else on Caleb's plate.

This Bachelor of the Year award would be the perfect reason for him to refocus on work and get Becca out of his heart—make that head. He was blowing a few dates—uh, get-togethers—out of proportion. He wasn't about to fall in love with her.

No worries at all.

Besides, Becca was one of the most practical women he knew. She would understand that he was doing this for Fair Face. She wouldn't care.

At least she shouldn't.

They weren't boyfriend and girlfriend. They hadn't made any type of commitment to one another. He wasn't going down that path again any time soon. If ever.

"Okay," Caleb said. "Let's make this work."

CHAPTER TWELVE

AT AN ITALIAN café in downtown Boise, Becca sat across from Caleb. "Thanks for inviting me out to dinner tonight. I didn't expect this at all."

"I'm glad you didn't have other plans."

She couldn't think of a better way to spend a Friday evening. "Well, I must admit it was a tough choice. Going out to dinner with you or getting ready for the dog show tomorrow."

He glanced up from his menu. "I'm honored you picked me."

Her heartstrings played a romantic tune that matched the violin music playing in the restaurant.

Romantic, indeed, with a lit candle stuck into a wax covered bottle of Chianti. A single red rosebud sat in a small glass vase, looking so perfect she'd wondered if the flower were real. One sniff of the sweet fragrance answered that question.

Real.

Just like tonight.

Becca looked over her menu at Caleb. He wore a navy suit, white button-down collared shirt and a colorful red tie with swirly patterns.

Proper CEO, definitely.

Handsome, oh yes. Swoonworthy, no doubt.

Becca swallowed a sigh. She liked spending time with him. It didn't matter what they did, either. His company and his kisses were more than enough. A good thing he seemed to agree.

She'd worried what happened at the hospital with Courtney had changed things between them. He hadn't called or texted. But Becca knew he had to be busy like her. "I wanted you to know Courtney is working on the labels for the dog products. She has an eye for design."

"Wait until you see the finished product."

"Caleb…"

"Okay, that wasn't nice of me." He looked over the top of his menu. "You'll be happy to know Courtney's going to be doing four-week rotations through various departments to see what type of jobs are available at Fair Face."

"That's wonderful."

"We'll see how it goes."

"Have faith."

"You haven't been through this with Courtney before."

"No, but I've been through it," Becca said. "Imagine if Gertie hadn't taken a chance on me. We wouldn't be here to-night."

The thought sent a chill down her spine. Becca expected Caleb to say something funny or sincere. She wanted him to smile or laugh. Instead he returned to reading his menu.

That was…odd. Maybe he'd had a rough day at the office. "Good day at work?"

"Typical."

His one-word answer was atypical. Usually he told her about something he'd done, a story from a meeting or an office anec-dote. She wondered if something had happened that he didn't want to talk about.

"Know what you're going to order?" she asked.

He perused the menu. "The salmon looks good. You?"

"The halibut special sounds tasty."

"It does."

Standard dinner conversation, except it wasn't standard for them. Each word made her want to squirm in her seat. Maybe she was being paranoid. Overly analytical. Or maybe some-thing was really going on.

She crinkled the edges of the menu. The words blurred. She couldn't stand it. "Is something wrong?"

"I wouldn't say wrong."

Okay, she wasn't paranoid. But that didn't make the churning of her stomach any better.

"What's going on?" Becca tried to sound nonchalant. She wasn't sure if she succeeded. She took a sip of water, hoping to wash away the lump in her throat.

"I was named Boise's Bachelor of the Year today."

Becca choked on the water in her mouth, coughed, but managed not to spit the liquid out. She swallowed instead.

"Wow." She tried to think of something to say other than *But aren't you going out with me?* "You must be…excited."

"I wouldn't say excited."

That made her feel a little better. She bit the inside of her cheek. "So this isn't that big a deal?"

He set his menu on the table. "Everyone at Fair Face is calling it a PR coup."

"A coup?"

"I'm being interviewed on *Good Day Boise* next week."

"Wow." Oops. She'd already said that. But her mind was reeling. "A TV interview is huge."

"I've done interviews before."

Caleb was downplaying this. Maybe Bachelor of Year was like the Sexiest Man Alive award, more of an honorary title than anything else. No reason for her to freak out. They might be dating, but technically he was still a bachelor.

Becca needed to be supportive, not act like a shrew. She raised her glass in the air. "Congrats."

He studied her with an odd expression. "You don't…mind."

"Why would I mind?" She asked the question as much for her benefit as his. "I don't see a ring on your finger."

Or one on hers.

But even though she knew better, even though his harsh words at the hospital had stung, she could imagine a tuxedo-clad Caleb sliding a shiny gold wedding band on her finger.

Her insides twisted. She took another sip of water. It didn't help.

He picked up his menu. "Thanks for being so understanding about this."

"Why wouldn't I be understanding?" She asked herself aloud. "It's an honor."

"You're really great, you know that."

So that was what being understanding got her. She would take it. "Thanks. Though I have no doubt women are going to be throwing themselves at you wanting to capture the Bachelor of the Year's heart."

His smile returned, reaching all the way to his eyes. "They can try, but they won't succeed."

Caleb's words put her at ease. His heart wasn't up for grabs because it was spoken for...by her. Even Becca's fingernails felt as if they were smiling. "Good to know."

"Don't worry about any of this," he said. "It'll be a big infomercial for Fair Face's new organic baby product line."

"Bachelor and babies. Not the usual combination."

"It's how things are done these days."

Business, she reminded herself. Nothing personal. How many times had she heard that since meeting Caleb?

More times than she could remember. Except...

Something niggled at her. Something she couldn't quite explain.

The feeling was familiar, like a little voice of caution whispering inside her head. The voice she should have listened to before going out with Whit and his friends that fateful night.

Crazy. She was thinking crazy thoughts now. Going overboard with the paranoia.

Caleb Fairchild was nothing like those rich kids back in high school. He might wear designer labels, drive an expensive car and have a ton of money, but he cared about her.

Everything he'd done, everything he was doing, proved that.

Maybe he hadn't fallen for her as she'd fallen for him. But he liked her. She should enjoy this time with Caleb, not borrow trouble. Things would only get better between them. A satisfied smile settled on her lips.

"You look happy," he said.

"I am."

"You've put me in a much better mood."

That pleased her. "Being with you makes me happy."

"I want you to be happy."

Becca's heart sang with joy. He did care. She knew it.

Ever since Caleb had entered her life, things had gotten better, not worse. The words *I love you* sat on the tip of her tongue. They would be so easy to say.

But she wanted the timing to be right. She wanted the place to be perfect. She wanted him to say the words back to her.

Becca needed to wait. Just a little while. Let this bachelor thing blow over. Give them more time to make memories together.

But soon. Very, very soon.

Tuesday morning at the television studio, the lights beat down on Caleb. Sweat streamed down his back, a mix of heat and nerves.

The red light on the two cameras reminded him the show was being shown live. He needed to at least act like he'd rather be here than at the dentist for a root canal.

But sitting on the couch with Savannah and Thad, the hosts of *Good Day Boise*, was the height of awkwardness. The two looked like pictures from a plastic surgeon's office with their bleached smiles, pouty fish lips and straight, proportioned noses. They droned on about this year's bachelor candidates and why Caleb had been chosen number one.

He kept a smile super-glued on his face and nodded when he thought appropriate.

Savannah leaned toward him with a coquettish grin. The V-neckline of her dress gaped, showing her cleavage. Caleb looked away.

Thad laughed, though Caleb had no idea at what. "The big questions our female viewers want to know—"

"Single female viewers," Savannah interrupted. "Though there may be a couple married ones, too."

Thad guffawed. Or maybe it was another of his fake laughs. "Is there a special woman in your life, Caleb?"

Becca. An image of her appeared front and center in his mind. Her sweet smile made his day. Her beautiful eyes lit up each time she saw him. Her hot kisses turned him on. She was special, more special than any other woman he'd dated.

Saying Becca's name would be easy. Saying Becca's name felt right. Saying Becca's name wasn't part of the script he was supposed to follow.

It didn't matter anyway. She understood. She'd said so herself on Friday night. She wouldn't care or be upset. They weren't serious.

Caleb took a deep breath. "No one special. Which is too bad."

"Why is that?" Thad asked.

The hosts gobbled the bait, exactly the way Ed had said they would. Time to reel them in with the money shot. Or in this case the perfect sound bite. Caleb straightened. "Because I want to start a family."

Savannah and Thad exchanged glances. Excitement danced in their eyes. "Boise's Bachelor of the Year wants a family?"

They spoke in unison, in a creepy kind of singsong voice.

The image of Becca remained front and center in mind, calling to Caleb.

Speak up, his heart cried.

Why the hell was his heart involved in this? It shouldn't be. No woman could touch his heart. Not even...

Get with the program, Fairchild.

Caleb swallowed around the lump in his throat. He pushed the image of Becca from his mind. He needed to follow the script. "Yes, I want a family. Having one is important to me."

Savannah touched his sleeve with her bright red painted

nails, making him think of a spider, the kind who eats their mates. "What is a handsome, rich industrialist looking for in his perfect woman?"

Perfect woman.

The two words made his stomach turn.

Caleb knew what he wanted. Who he wanted. But the PR department had dreamed up a list for him. A list that technically fit his position and roughly reflected his interests for a woman who Caleb would have, up to this point, considered an ideal spouse. "Educated, a keen sense of humor, stylish, fit, well-traveled, social, a little sophisticated, a foodie, a discriminating ear when it comes to music and plays tennis."

Each word rang hollow.

Such a woman was safe, dull, orderly.

Like his life.

Becca was so much more than the sum of all those items on the list. Fun, energetic, nurturing.

He wanted to tell the hosts and the audience about Becca, about her amazing qualities. But Fair Face was counting on him. It didn't matter what he thought. It didn't matter what he wanted.

Ty was downrange fighting bad guys to keep their country safe. Caleb was stuck on a couch lying his ass off because safe and dull had made his family company successful.

"Sounds like there might be a woman or two in Boise who share some of those characteristics," Savannah said.

Yes, but he wanted only one woman.

No, he didn't.

Caleb was getting in too deep. The fact that Becca kept coming up told him that. He'd lowered his guard too much and let her into his heart. Bad move. He couldn't trust romantic relationships. Being involved in a serious relationship was too difficult. Too much work and responsibility. He'd had enough of that already. "I hope so."

Except being with Becca hadn't been work, his heart countered. She made him happy.

He wanted his heart to shut up.

He'd tried getting married. That relationship had been a disaster. Becca wasn't trying to scam him. As special as she was, as much as she hadn't been a burden, he didn't want to fall in love with her. He couldn't do that to himself. Or her.

Caleb had gotten too close to her, too fast. He needed to pull back, stop seeing her, focus on Fair Face.

The expectations of the marketing and PR departments were riding on Caleb's every word, weighing him down and making him sweat. He always did what was expected of him. This was no different.

Stick with the script.

"I'd hate to think I'd never be able to use Fair Face's new line of organic baby products on my own children."

Savannah sighed along with the audience full of smiling women. "Baby products."

He'd elicited the right response from her and the audience. Good, except his victory felt empty.

"My grandmother's ready to be a great-grandmother. She created the products as a not-so-subtle hint to me. All I'm missing is…"

"A wife," Savannah said with glee.

"Perhaps we can help you find her," Thad said.

Savannah nodded enthusiastically. "We're going to hold a contest on our website to find Boise's Bachelor of the Year's perfect woman."

"She could be sitting in our studio audience. Or maybe she's watching at home," Thad said. "Go to our website and find out if you have the qualities to be Caleb's perfect woman. The prize is a dream date with Boise's Bachelor of the Year. Who knows? The date could turn into something more!"

"Thanks." The word felt as if Caleb was eating tar. "I could use all the help I can get finding her!"

One thought ran through Caleb's head. Too bad he couldn't have been voted the second most eligible bachelor in Boise this year.

At least this would be over soon. He would go on the stupid date, then get on with his life. Alone, the way he liked it.

Win-win, right?

Becca stared at the television set in the guest cottage. She held on to two dogs, Dozer and Hunter, one on each side of her. Each breath took concerted effort. Her throat burned. Tears filled her eyes.

Don't cry. Don't cry. Do not cry.

She blinked back the tears.

She'd set the DVR to record the interview. She never wanted to watch it again. Not ever.

Her heart ached, a painful, squeezing kind of hurt. Disappointment. Betrayal.

Caleb had made her think this bachelor-of-the-year thing was no big deal. That it was business.

PR opportunity or not, his words on this morning's interview stung. More than she ever thought possible.

So much for protecting her heart.

Becca hadn't. It had splintered into a million razor sharp shards. And now…

Women all over Boise, likely northern Idaho and eastern Oregon, were going to be vying to be Caleb's perfect woman and go on a dream date with him in hopes of being his wife.

Thank goodness she hadn't told him she loved him.

She wanted to throw up.

It was clear she wasn't his perfect woman.

Tears continued to sting her eyes.

Judging by the list of qualities, he was looking for a woman with a similar background and upbringing. She might be able to write a business report, but an AA degree didn't count as educated. Preferring hot dogs to fancy food meant she couldn't call herself a foodie. She'd never travelled outside the Pacific Northwest.

Hurt sliced through her stomach. All her insecurities rushed to the surface.

The dogs squirmed out of her arms. She let them go.

Why had Gertie played matchmaker when Becca was so wrong for Caleb?

Becca wrapped her arms around her stomach.

Gertie should never have chosen some fish out of water to put in the rich, corporate aquarium for her grandson. Dating might not influence Fair Face's bottom line, but there was intrinsic value to the woman Caleb...married.

Becca rocked back and forth.

Caleb had shown his practical side during the interview. He didn't need someone who preferred the company of dogs, not dressing up and eating hot dogs. He needed a corporate wife. Someone who could entertain, dress the part and play hostess. A trophy wife.

The vise tightened around Becca's heart, pressing and squeezing out the blood. She sniffled.

How had she completely misread the man? Maybe she'd ignored signs because she enjoyed being with him. The same way she'd ignored the signs with Whit.

It hadn't felt the same, but she could have been fooling herself. She had to have been fooling herself.

Caleb hadn't told her about the dream date contest, only being named Bachelor of the Year and doing an interview. He'd lied by omission, making her wonder if he'd lied about other things. Lied or...been practical?

She'd told him she wouldn't pretend to be someone she wasn't after what happened with Whit. If she wasn't what Caleb wanted, was this his way of breaking up with her?

Becca couldn't answer that question herself, but she intended to find out the answer.

If not for the time of day, champagne would have been flowing at Fair Face. Interest in the new baby line had skyrocketed following Caleb's interview. Whatever issues he'd had about saying he wanted to settle down had disappeared.

Genius. Brilliant. Smart move.

The words described how wonderfully they'd pulled off the PR coup on *Good Day Boise*. There was only one loose end to tie up, and he could relax.

Becca.

His assistant buzzed him. "Ms. Taylor is here to see you."

Okay, that was weird. He hadn't expected her to come to him. But he might as well get this over quickly so he could attend the celebration in the company's cafeteria in honor of his award and interview. "Send her in."

Becca entered his office. She was dressed casually in a pair of plain khakis, a blue blouse and canvas tennis shoes. She looked neat, fit and very pretty. But she wasn't smiling

He didn't blame her.

As she walked in, the others in his office walked out.

"See you in the cafeteria," Ed said.

Caleb nodded. "Be down shortly."

The door closed. He walked around to the front of his desk and leaned against it. "You saw the interview."

"I did." She raised her chin. "I'm sure the show's servers are going to overload with all the women wanting to win a dream date with you."

Her sarcastic tone matched the expression on her face. "It's a contest. A promotion."

She pursed her lips. "Then why didn't you tell me about it?"

"I didn't think it mattered. It's just business."

"Business?" Disbelief filled her voice. "You listed all the qualities you're looking for in the perfect woman. None of which I have."

"The PR department provided the list. It was a publicity stunt. Nothing more."

"It hurt hearing you say all those things you were looking for and imagining the perfect corporate trophy wife who fits the list. A woman who wasn't me."

"I told you it wasn't my list," he said. "But it's not like we're seriously dating."

"Ouch." She stared at him as if he'd grown a third eye and horns. "At least I have bruises on both cheeks now."

"I never wanted to hurt you." But Caleb had, and he couldn't take it back.

Her bottom lip quivered.

It was all he could do not to take her in his arms so she would feel better. But he couldn't.

This was the best. For Becca and for him.

"So what happens next?" she asked. "And I don't mean your dream date. I'm talking about you and me."

You and me. Not us. That had to be a good sign. "I'm not in a place to have a serious relationship."

"I figured that much."

"You have a lot going on with the dog products and developing a handling career."

Her gaze narrowed. "Don't put any of this on me."

Guilt coated his throat. Okay, bad move. "It's me."

"Yes, it is." She wet her lips. "I want to know why you went out with me."

"Being with you was fun."

"Fun," she repeated twice. "I thought things were more serious than that."

"No. I can't. I'm sorry. I've been distracted. I need to get back to work."

"So this is about Fair Face?"

"After my father died, my grandparents' hopes and dreams for him were transferred onto me. I've spent my life trying to do everything my father didn't do. For my family and for Fair Face. I can't take anything else on."

"You mean me."

"Yes."

"I don't want to be your responsibility. I'm doing fine on my own."

Becca was. And she was cutting through his reasons like a skilled surgeon. He would try again.

"I'm not ready to make an emotional commitment." The

last time he did that it blew up in his face. Desire had a way of turning him inside out. He couldn't screw up again. "I can't risk the indulgence of a relationship right now."

Flames ignited in Becca's eyes. Her jaw tensed. "Indulgence of a relationship?"

"Perhaps that's the wrong word." He was bungling this up. He wasn't usually so clumsy and the hurt in Becca's eyes was killing him. He couldn't think straight. Not when she was around him. Even more proof he needed her out of his life. "I need to focus my attention on Fair Face. Nothing else. Not even the dog care products."

His words slammed into him, as if he'd punched himself in the gut. But he'd had no other choice than to say them. He couldn't keep seeing her.

Becca swallowed, but said nothing. Hurt dulled her eyes.

He reached for her, then drew his arm back. If he touched her, he might not want to let go. "Look, I could have gone about this differently. But I didn't. We had some good times together. Let's not have this blow up into something awful."

"That's the first thing you've said that I agree with." She met his gaze. "Thanks for opening my eyes to the truth."

"The truth?"

"You don't deserve me."

"Becca—"

"You act responsible and practical, but you're not." Her voice rose. "I'm guessing you went out with me to appease Gertie and keep her happy. You could make sure I wasn't trying to scam your grandmother and you could have a little fun at the same time."

"No." Her words hit him like a dagger to the heart. "I went out with you because I wanted to be with you. No other reason."

"But once things turned into something real, where you would have to take risk, you decided it was over between us. You could have spoken up, but that would have been too scary, so you followed someone else's script, the way you've done your entire life."

"That's not true." But his words didn't have a strong conviction behind them. He would try again. "Not true at all."

"It is true, because I was once there myself. But I'm over the wariness of my past. In part, thanks to you. But you're not because of your mother, your father and Cassandra. I'm not sure you ever will be, either." Squaring her shoulders, Becca met his gaze. "I never thought I'd say this, but I feel sorry for you, Caleb Fairchild."

She turned and walked to the door.

He stood, his heart pounding in his chest. "You have no idea what you're talking about."

Becca didn't glance back. She kept walking out of his office and out of his life.

Which was exactly what he'd wanted to happen.

So why did it hurt so badly?

CHAPTER THIRTEEN

BECCA FOUGHT THE urge to run out of Caleb's office. She made a conscious effort not to slam the door to his office behind her. She wasn't going to make a scene.

Or cry.

Her anger spiraled.

She knew her worth. She wasn't going to forget that or become someone else to make Caleb love her.

Screw him.

Becca should have seen through his BS, through the sweet words and tender smiles and hot kisses. Caleb couldn't accept her for who she was. He wanted someone more suited to his world. He wasn't willing to take a risk on her.

On them.

She marched to the elevator.

Caleb could blame his job at Fair Face or his family or a hundred other things, but bottom line…he wasn't capable of loving her as she was.

That was what Becca deserved.

What she wanted.

The elevator dinged. The doors opened.

Becca stepped inside. She poked the button for the lobby, nearly breaking one of her already short fingernails.

How could she have been so stupid again?

She'd been trying to fit in and prove herself in order to gain Caleb's acceptance. But the people who truly loved her and knew her accepted her fully, the way the dogs did. People like Gertie and her parents. Anything Becca accomplished was the proverbial icing on the cake.

She hadn't needed to earn their love.

Love was unconditional. And if it wasn't, she wasn't interested. Period.

The weeks ran into each other. Caleb tried to focus on work, but thinking about Becca distracted him as much as when she was a part of his life. He kept telling himself things had worked out for the best. Breaking it off now had saved them both from suffering any real hurt. It was time to move on.

But tonight, on his dream date at Pacifica, he had to wonder if moving on had been for the best.

Sweat dripped down the back of Caleb's neck due to the heat of the camera light and nerves.

A cameraman stood next to the table for two, filming every moment Caleb spent with a beautiful blonde thirty-year-old woman named Madeline Stevens. He had to give the matchmaker credit. Madeline met all the PR department's qualifications and then some. She'd graduated from Yale, studied in Paris and owned an art gallery. She sat on the board of two local nonprofits. She had a centerfold-worthy body and wore a sexy little black cocktail dress that showed off her curves. She was everything a man in his position should want in a girlfriend, a wife even.

Except she wasn't…Becca.

Madeline glanced at the camera. "I had no idea tonight would be a threesome."

Sense of humor, check. He'd been crossing off the qualities she met from his mental list. "No one mentioned we'd have a chaperone and everything would be on camera."

He would never have agreed to this if he'd known a follow-up story, complete with film footage, would be shown on *Good Day Boise*.

"Well, I guess we're getting a taste of what being on a reality TV show would be like," she said.

"I'll pass."

"Me, too." She stared up through her mascara-covered eyelashes at him and lowered her voice. "Maybe we can ditch him and find some place private where we can...talk."

The suggestive tone of her voice told him talking wasn't what she had in mind. But strangely, Caleb wasn't the least bit interested in doing anything other than calling it a night.

He didn't want Madeline to feel uncomfortable, though he sure did. He hated being here. Hated having to pretend to be interested in such a lovely woman when he'd rather be eating hot dogs at home by himself or peanuts with Becca.

The cameraman moved in closer, then adjusted the microphone.

Caleb needed to keep the conversation flowing, something he'd struggled to do with Madeline. Unlike with Becca. If she were here, the discussion would flow, uninterrupted, from topic to topic.

He didn't understand why he was out with a stunningly attractive woman and thinking about Becca, especially after what she'd said to him. But he couldn't get her out of his head. "So, do you have any pets?"

"No," Madeline said. "I work long hours. I don't think it would be fair to a dog or cat to leave them alone."

Good answer. One that Becca—make that Grams—would approve of. "I don't have any pets or plants for the same reason."

She leaned forward. Her face puckered in distaste. "There are silk plants. But at least live plants don't shed dog hair."

Caleb remembered Maurice and Becca's lint roller. "My grandmother has a couple of dogs that leave hair everywhere. It's not that bad. Unless you're wearing black."

Madeline's eyes narrowed. She wet her lips. "Oh, no. I never meant that it was bad. I'm an animal lover. Dogs are the sweetest things. One of these days, I'll adopt one from a rescue group."

Her backtracking reminded him of Cassandra, who'd said whatever she thought he wanted to hear. The total opposite of Becca, who spoke her mind, whether he wanted to hear it or not.

He remembered being at the dog show with her. "Dogs are a lot of work."

"That's why people use doggy day cares."

The words made him cringe. Becca would never take a dog to a place like that. She would rather care for them herself.

The way she'd taken care of Grams's dogs and Grams and Courtney and...

Him.

His mouth went dry. He picked up his water glass and drank. It didn't help. He took another sip. The funny feeling in the pit of his stomach only worsened.

What had he done?

He'd been so worried about taking on one more responsibility, but he shouldn't have been. Becca had been taking care of all of them, especially him, from the day he met her.

He'd been wrong about her past.

He was wrong about her.

But he couldn't see that until sitting here with a woman who on paper should have been perfect for him, but wasn't.

Not Madeline's fault. She was too much like Cassandra and totally different from...

Becca.

Tomorrow he would go to her. Apologize. Ask for a second chance.

All he had to do was survive the camera and the rest of his dream date. He hoped that the rest of the evening didn't turn into a nightmare.

The next morning Caleb arrived at the estate and rang the doorbell.

Mrs. Harrison opened the door. "Your grandmother is in her bedroom."

"What about Becca?"

"I believe she's on her way to a dog show."

Damn. That would complicate talking with her. He entered Grams's room to find her packing. "Where are you going?"

"Enumclaw, Washington." She folded a pink T-shirt. "Big dog show. We have a vendor booth for our products."

"Is Becca going to be there?"

"She left yesterday in the RV with the dogs and her parents. I'm meeting her there later today." Grams stopped packing. "How was your dream date last night? Did you find your perfect woman?"

The sarcasm in Grams's voice was clear. Caleb took a deep breath. "I won't be asking the winner out again, if that's what you're asking."

"At least you haven't lost all your brain cells." Grams returned to packing. "Before I forget, I need you to schedule a week's vacation. I'll give a range of dates to your assistant before I head out."

"Why?"

"Your birthday present."

"My birthday isn't until January."

"With your schedule, I need to plan ahead."

"Where am I going?"

"A navy SEAL training camp."

His heart skipped two beats. He could barely breathe. He'd always wanted to attend one. He had the money, but not the time. He'd also never told anyone he wanted to go, not even Ty. "How did you…?"

"I buy your gift in the summer, since your birthday is close to Christmas. That way I make sure it's different. Special."

"But SEAL training?" he forced the question from his dry throat.

"Becca. It was her idea, " Grams said. "I wasn't sure about it."

"It's the perfect gift."

"That's what Becca said."

Becca.

Of course she would be the one to suggest the gift. She knew him, really and truly knew him.

And she was exactly the woman he needed.

He'd been such a fool. An idiot.

I learned my lesson. I'm not going to try to be someone I'm not ever again.

No wonder hearing that list had hurt Becca so much. Caleb had known what she'd gone through with Whit, but he'd been thinking only about Fair Face and himself. Not how hearing the list of his perfect qualifications would affect and hurt Becca. She was correct, he didn't deserve her.

But he loved her. He wanted her back.

His chest tightened with regret.

Becca was the one for him.

He should have screamed her name during his interview, not gone along with someone else's script for his life and taken another woman on a dream date. He should have held on to Becca with both hands, not let her walk out of his office and out of his life. He should have told her she was his perfect woman, not let her think she wasn't.

"Grams…"

She walked to his side and touched his face. "You're pale as a ghost."

He was so used to taking care of everyone, but he hadn't taken care of Becca. Not the way she'd taken care of him. "I've made a big mistake. The biggest mistake of my life."

"With Becca?"

Caleb nodded. He had always done what was expected of him. He'd put his own dreams aside. He'd put his life on hold. He'd hurt someone he cared about because that was what everyone expected him to do.

No longer.

Becca had been right. He'd been following a script. That was easier than risking his heart only to be hurt again.

He was in the doghouse, but he was willing to beg, to perform tricks, to do whatever was needed to be a part of her life. She didn't need him. But he needed her. Her smile, her sense of humor, her love.

Grams smiled. "So how do you intend on fixing it?"

Becca walked out of Ring Five with Hunter's leash in one hand and a Best of Winners—the prize for a dog still working on his championship ribbon—in the other. The sun beat down, but the beagle didn't seem to mind. She couldn't wait to remove her suit jacket.

Gertie stood, her hands clasped together and a bright smile on her face.

Becca handed off the ribbon. "He needs one more major and he's a champion."

"So proud of both of you."

"Thanks." The word sounded flat. Becca couldn't help it. Normally she would be thrilled with the win, bouncing on her toes and tingling with excitement, but it was all she could do to keep her feet moving and not retreat to the RV to nap.

Maybe some caffeine would help. She'd been living off coffee lately.

Heaven knew she needed something to get her out of this funk. She couldn't quite shake her sadness. She'd tried pushing Caleb out of her thoughts. She'd succeeded somewhat, but she couldn't get him out of her heart.

At least not yet.

The feeling would pass. Someday. Someday soon she hoped.

But she was better off having met Caleb. He'd shown her what she wanted and didn't want.

"Let's go see how your parents are doing at the booth." Gertie had hired Becca's parents to sell the products at dog shows and fill online orders. "I also want to show off Hunter's ribbon."

They walked along the row of vendor booths, tables and displays set up under pop-up canopies that provided shade.

"Your parents have company at the booth," Gertie said.

Becca was pleased by how much her parents enjoyed talking to dog owners about the products. Gertie called them "natural salespeople." Maybe so, but Becca also knew they were friendly hard workers who didn't want to disappoint Gertie or their daughter. "Customers are a good thing."

"I don't think this one is interested in dog products."

Becca looked over and froze.

Caleb.

Her heart tumbled. She couldn't breathe.

"What's he doing here?" she asked, her voice shaking as much as her insides.

"Let's find out."

"No." Becca's feet were rooted to the pavement. She couldn't have moved. Even if she were being chased by vampires or brain-eating zombies or ax-wielding murderers, she would be eaten or slain where she stood. "You go."

She stared at him in his khakis and polo shirt. She could only see his backside, but every nerve ending tingled as if she'd touched a live wire and sent a jolt of electricity through her.

Gertie pulled on Becca's arm. "Come on. You're no coward."

"Yes, I am."

Gertie gave a not-so-gentle shove. "Chin up and move those feet, girlie."

Becca moved. It was either that or fall over. With each step, an imaginary boom, like a timpani, echoed through her. "I can't—"

"Yes, you can," Gertie encouraged. "One step in front of the other."

Becca crossed the aisle toward their booth. Lightheaded and stomach churning, she thought passing out was a distinct possibility. At least in that case, she wouldn't have to face him.

"Caleb," Gertie said.

He turned. Smiled.

Becca went numb.

"Hello," he said, as if his being at a dog show in a different state was to be expected.

She opened her mouth to speak, but no words came out.

He looked at Becca with warm, clear eyes. "I missed you."

Her heart slammed against her ribs. Anger surged. "Is this some kind of joke?"

"No joke." Caleb motioned to the booth. "Looks like the products are selling thanks to your top-notch sales force."

Becca's parents smiled at her.

She stared at Caleb, her temper spiraling out of control. "You discard me like garbage. Hurt my feelings worse than anyone, which is saying a lot. Then show up here as if nothing had happened. Unbelievable."

Tension sizzled in the air. People glanced her way, but kept walking. Two dogs barked at each other.

"You're right." He sounded contrite, but that didn't make her feel any better. "You've always been right."

Okay, she hadn't been expecting that.

"I am here. I don't blame you if you don't want to talk to me, but I hope you'll hear me out."

A beat passed. And another. "Five minutes."

He pulled her to one side and glanced at his watch. "I was getting too attached to you. I was distracted at work. I was happier with you than my own family. That scared me. You scared me. I was too afraid to take a risk. Too afraid you might be the one to break me. So I played it safe. Too safe. And I lost the one person I need most in my life. The one person who understands me. The one person who makes me stronger. You took care of me in a way no one else had. I miss that. I miss you."

The air rushed from her lungs. A lump burned in her throat. Tears stung her eyes. She couldn't think. She couldn't speak.

"You're amazing, unique and everything I didn't realize I wanted until you came into my life, and then I stupidly let you go," he continued. "I'm sorry for the crappy way I treated you. I was no better than that idiot Whit. But I apologize. For doing the asinine interview and agreeing to the contest. For not telling you and then breaking up the way that I did. I don't blame you for not loving me after all I've done, but I love you. And if there's any way you could find it in your heart to forgive me, I'll make it up to you. I want to spend the rest of my life making it up to you."

She forced herself to breathe. "That's why you came here?"

He nodded. "I was going to go crazy if I had to spend another day without seeing you."

Her heart melted. She knew better, but it didn't matter.

"I think I have at least another two minutes. Maybe three." His eyes were earnest, his voice sincere. "Do I stand a chance?"

She wanted to say no. She wanted to tell him to go. She wanted to move on without him.

His smile practically caressed her.

But her heart wanted something different. Wanted him.

"For as long as I can remember I've been trying to prove myself. If I did that, then I thought I could be accepted." Becca took a deep breath. "But Gertie encouraged me. Then you. I realized I didn't have to do anything special. I had to accept who I was and the rest would happen."

"It's happening."

Becca could feel it. Acceptance. Joy. Love.

"I forgive you." The way she'd finally forgiven herself for her past mistakes. "I'm ready to try a relationship, but I want the man beneath the pinstripes. The guy who grew up wanting to be a navy SEAL."

"He's yours." Caleb kissed her forehead. "But I don't want to try anything. I know the right woman, the perfect woman, for me."

He dropped down on one knee.

Becca gasped.

Caleb held her hand. "Will you marry me, Becca? Be my wife and partner and dog whisperer?"

Maurice trotted toward Becca. Her father held one end of the long leash. The dog came closer. A white ribbon was tied to his collar. Hanging from the ribbon was a…ring.

Her throat tightened. "You're serious."

Caleb nodded. "I asked your dad's permission."

Based on her parents' beaming faces, Caleb had no doubt received approval and been offered help with the proposal.

"So what do you say?" he said.

"I come with baggage."

"You also come with lint brushes," he said. "A fair trade-off in my book."

That was all she needed to hear. Know.

"Yes." Happiness flowed through her. "Yes, I'll marry you."

He removed the ring from Maurice's collar. The entire gold band was inlaid with tiny diamonds. In the center were bigger diamonds in the shape of a dog's paw. "I thought a large diamond would get in the way of all the things you have to do with the dogs. If you'd rather have—"

"This is perfect. I can't tell you how perfect."

He slid the ring onto her finger. "I love you."

"I love you."

He kissed her gently on the lips.

Maurice barked.

"Think he's jealous?" Caleb asked.

She glanced at the sparkling ring, then back at him. "No, that's his bark of approval."

"Let's give him more to approve of."

Caleb lowered his mouth to hers and kissed her. Hard.

Joy flowed through Becca, from the top of her head to the tip of her toes. The Boise Bachelor of the Year was off the market and would be ineligible to win ever again. But his kiss definitely deserved the prize for Best in Show. The first of many.

* * * * *

FALLING FOR
MR MYSTERIOUS

BY
BARBARA HANNAY

Reading and writing have always been a big part of **Barbara Hannay**'s life. She wrote her first short story at the age of eight for the Brownies' writer's badge. It was about a girl who was devastated when her family had to move from the city to the Australian Outback.

Since then, a love of both city and country lifestyles has been a continuing theme in Barbara's books and in her life. Although she has mostly lived in cities, now that her family has grown up and she's a full-time writer she's enjoying a country lifestyle.

Barbara and her husband live on a misty hillside in Far North Queensland's Atherton Tableland. When she's not lost in the world of her stories she's enjoying farmers' markets, gardening clubs and writing groups, or preparing for visits from family and friends.

Barbara records her country life in her blog, *Barbwired*, and her website is: www.barbarahannay.com.

CHAPTER ONE

When the train drew in to Roma Street Station, Emily checked her phone messages one more time. There was still nothing from Alex, so now she was officially worried—not only about Alex's twenty-four-hour silence, but also about her own fate. She had no idea what she'd do if he wasn't in Brisbane.

She'd rushed to the city in blind despair. She needed to see Alex, to stay with him and, yes, to pour out her heart to him. Of all her family, Alex would understand, and Emily had been so very desperate to get away from Wandabilla that she'd jumped on the train in the vain hope that Alex would return her call before she arrived.

Now, the train came to a stop with a wheezing sigh of brakes and, all around Emily, passengers were rising from their seats, gathering their belongings in a businesslike fashion, pulling on jackets and coats and heading for the carriage doors, eager to be out on the platform and gone.

They, of course, had somewhere to go.

Emily did not.

If Alex was away, she would have to find a hotel. She certainly wasn't going to turn tail and head home to Wandabilla, to face the music, with everyone in the small country town knowing what had happened to her.

Besides, Emily told herself, there was still a slim chance

that Alex was home. He might have a problem with his phone, or perhaps he'd let the battery run down, or he'd bought a new phone and changed his number and hadn't got around to telling her.

Although her doubts about the wisdom of rushing to Brisbane were mounting fast, she rolled the magazine she'd been trying unsuccessfully to read and stowed it in her shoulder bag, then retrieved her suitcase from the luggage rack.

It was an unusually cold August afternoon, and a biting westerly wind whistled callously along the platform. Shivering, Emily buttoned her coat and turned up its collar, then she lugged her suitcase behind her and headed for the warmth of the pedestrian tunnel.

As luck would have it, she was in the depths of the tunnel, jostling with crowds of shoppers and commuters, when she heard the soft *quack-quack*, which was the silly ringtone she used to distinguish social from business calls. She grabbed her phone from her bag. It was a text message.

Em, sorry I missed you, and very sorry to hear about that @#$%$# of a boyfriend. Wish I could be with you now, but I'm in Frankfurt at a Book Fair. Please use the apartment tho. Stay as long as you like and use my room. I've checked with Jude and he's cool, so he's expecting you.
Hugs,
Alex xxx

Emily had to read this twice, standing rock still in the tunnel while commuters steered somewhat irritably around her. She needed a moment to take the message in, to deal with her see-sawing emotions of relief that Alex was OK, and her disappointment that he was so far away.

Very quickly, overriding these initial reactions, rushed a flurry of questions. Who was this Jude person? When had he arrived in Alex's life? And…would he really be as cool as her cousin suggested about her sudden appearance on his doorstep?

She felt awkward about imposing on a stranger and she wondered, briefly, if she should continue up the coast to her grandmother's instead. Granny Silver was as understanding and welcoming as Alex, but she preferred to see the world through rose-coloured glasses, so Emily rarely burdened her with her problems.

Also, if this Jude fellow was expecting her, and if he was anything like Alex—which he probably was, remembering Alex's former housemates—he'd probably already jumped into host mode.

Jude could well be whipping up something delicious for their dinner right now, so it would be rude to simply not turn up. Emily headed to a nearby bottle shop, bought a good quality red as well as a white, because she didn't know Jude's tastes, then went to the taxi rank. But as the taxi sped towards West End, crossing a bridge over the wide Brisbane River, her impulsive dash to the city began to feel more foolish than ever.

She'd been so self-absorbed, so totally desperate to get away from prying eyes, that she'd seen her cousin Alex as her one safe haven. She'd had visions of crying on his shoulder, of sitting with him on his balcony, looking out over the river and the city skyline, drinking wine together while she told him all about the whole sorry mess with Michael.

Alex was such a wonderful listener, way better than her mum. He never trotted out *I told you so*, or kindly but firmly pointed out her mistakes. Best of all, once he'd sympathised and mopped her tears, he always made her laugh.

Man, she could do with a laugh right now, but she couldn't expect sympathy, wine and cheering up from Alex's new flatmate. As the taxi drew up outside the apartment block, she told herself that the best she could hope for was friendly tolerance from this perfect stranger, and a little privacy in which to nurse her wounded feelings.

At any rate, it was reassuring to know that she wouldn't have to negotiate any of the bothersome boy-meets-girl nonsense. She'd had enough trouble with men to last her a lifetime, but she could rely on the fact that any man living with Alex would be gay and totally safe to live with.

Jude Marlowe was still typing at his laptop when the doorbell rang. He was in the midst of a thought, a decent thought, one of the few he'd come up with that day. He was trying to get it onto the page so he continued typing, despite the doorbell, knowing that if he stopped, the precious words would be lost, never to be recalled.

The bell rang again, with a slight air of desperation. Fortunately, the last sentence was captured and Jude saved his work and pushed away from the desk. Taking off his reading glasses, he rubbed at the bridge of his nose, then stood unhurriedly and stretched, rolling his shoulders in a bid to ease the tension that always locked in when he became too absorbed in his writing.

The caller would be Alex's young cousin. Jude had received a garbled message that she needed a bed for a few nights and so he'd manfully hidden his reluctance to socialise and assured Alex that he'd oblige. Apparently, she'd had boyfriend trouble and was suffering from a broken heart.

Another of Alex's lame ducks, Jude thought wryly, knowing he was one, too.

He was in the hallway, blinking at the darkness—was it really that late?—before he gave a thought to his appearance. Still in the clothes he'd dragged on in the morning, he was wearing old, badly ripped jeans and a baggy, ancient football jersey, stained at the neck and worn at the elbows. Not exactly suitable for receiving Alex's houseguest, but it was too late to do anything about it. The girl at the door would be getting impatient.

Jude turned on the light as he pulled the door open and a yellow glow spilled, golden and honey-warm, over the chilled figure outside. At first sight of her, he felt deprived of oxygen.

Later, he asked himself what he'd been expecting, and he realised that if he'd given Alex's lovelorn country cousin any thought at all, he'd mentally classified her as frumpy and miserable. An unfashionable, possibly plain, country mouse.

How wrong he was.

The girl standing before Jude in a stylish white wool coat and knee-high brown leather boots was a stunner. Her red-gold hair flowed softly over her white lapels, making him think of fire on snow. Her face was delicate yet full of character.

And while there was a hint of sadness about her blue eyes, her skin showed no sign of country mouse freckles. Her complexion was fair and smooth, her chin neat, her mouth curving and smiley.

She looked, at first glance, like all Jude's female fantasies rolled into one hot package.

He found himself silenced to the point of stupidity.

'You must be Jude?' she enquired, tilting her head to one side and smiling cautiously.

'Sure.' Somehow, he remembered his manners. 'And you must be Emily.'

'Yes. Emily Silver, Alex's cousin.' She held out her hand. 'How do you do, Jude? Alex said he'd warned you about me.'

'Yes, he rang.' But the warning had been totally inadequate, Jude realised now. He'd planned to offer the barest courtesies as a host and then leave Emily Silver to mend her heart in whichever way she needed to. He still planned to do that, but already he knew she wouldn't be easy to ignore.

'I must say it's very kind of you to take me in at such short notice.' She shook his hand, and it was a ridiculously electrifying experience.

'You're very welcome.' Jude spoke gruffly to cover his dazed dismay. Then he noticed her suitcase. 'I'll get that for you.'

'Oh, thanks. And I've brought wine.' With a dazzling smile, she held up a brown paper bag. 'A bottle of each.'

There was a slight shuffle in the doorway as he stepped forward to reach for the luggage while Emily came inside. Their bodies brushed briefly. *Damn.* Jude couldn't believe he was reacting this way. He'd had more than his fair share of girlfriends, but this evening his body was reacting as if he'd been cast away on a desert island and Emily was the first woman he'd seen in two decades.

'Oh, it's lovely and warm inside,' she was saying.

Jude nodded, adding grouchily, 'Alex's room is down the hall, as I'm sure you remember. First on the left.'

In the doorway to the master bedroom, Emily paused and sent a dimpling smile back to him over her shoulder. 'Wow. I've never stayed in this room. I'll be able to enjoy the amazing view of the river from Alex's bed.'

'No doubt.' Jude set the suitcase on the floor just inside

the doorway, angry that the mere mention of the word *bed* set his mind diving into fantasy land. Refusing to meet her animated gaze, he said tersely, 'You settle in. I'll… ah…be in the kitchen.'

In the kitchen, he stared disconsolately at the contents of the refrigerator while he rated himself as several versions of a fool. It made absolutely no sense that he'd been sideswiped by Alex's country cousin.

Sure, she was a looker. But her beauty was irrelevant in this situation. She'd come to the city to escape from a low-lying jerk of a boyfriend, while Jude had problems of his own. He was in the city for medical tests that freaked the hell out of him.

And yet, when he'd seen Emily on the doorstep, there'd been an out-of-this-world moment when he'd forgotten all of this. Now, he'd plummeted back to earth. And to common sense.

Emily was sharing this apartment, and yes, he'd promised Alex that he would keep an eye on her. But that could be covered by token exchanges. A few courteous words. Now and again. Nothing more than the most superficial hospitality was required.

He was grateful to have that sorted. He need show no more than cursory interest in this guest, which was just as well, considering everything that lay ahead of him.

Emily wondered if she'd made a terrible mistake as she sank onto the edge of Alex's king-size bed.

She was imposing on Alex's flatmate, and she could tell from the moment she'd first seen Jude that he wasn't thrilled about her sudden arrival. Now cold hopelessness washed over her as she saw her flight to Brisbane as just another mistake among the many mistakes she'd made lately.

She would have to reassure Jude that she wouldn't stay. Problem was, she wasn't ready to go back to Wandabilla, either. So, in the morning, she would have to check out accommodation options.

In the meantime…she would try to be as little trouble as possible for Jude.

He was very different from Alex. She'd seen this immediately. Physically, the two men were poles apart. Her cousin shared her auburn colouring and he was slim and scholarly-looking, while Jude was tall and dark, with the broad-shouldered, lean-hipped build of a man of action. Not too rugged or too chiselled, his looks were nicely in between.

But, of course, Alex always had good taste in men.

After taking off her coat, but not bothering to unpack, Emily went through to the kitchen and discovered another difference from Alex. Jude was no cook.

There was absolutely no action at the stove. In fact, Jude was standing in the middle of the kitchen, staring at the open pantry cupboard and scratching his head.

When he saw her, he gave an offhand shrug. 'I'm afraid I never think much about food when I'm caught up with my work.'

'Please, don't worry about feeding me,' she assured him. 'I'm happy to look after myself.' The last thing she wanted was to be any bother, but curiosity prompted her to ask, 'What sort of work do you do?'

Jude frowned, then spoke with obvious reluctance. 'I'm a writer, so I work from home, but I'm totally disorganized when it comes to meals. Sometimes I heat up a tin of soup for my dinner, but since I've been here in West End, I've mostly eaten takeaway.'

Emily guessed he was missing Alex's gourmet cooking. 'Honestly, I'm happy with takeaway,' she insisted. 'I know there's a host of great restaurants here. I could pop out now, if you like, and get something for both of us.'

She smiled, hoping to show Alex's flatmate that she really wanted to fit in as smoothly as possible. But smiling didn't seem to work with this man. His gaze darted away.

'I'll come with you,' he said.

'Are you sure?'

'I promised Alex I'd look after you.'

She almost told him not to bother. She was perfectly capable of walking a block or two to the shops, but she didn't want to start off on a bad footing. 'OK. I'll grab my coat and a scarf.'

They met again in the hallway, and Emily saw that Jude had changed lightning-fast into less tattered jeans as well as outdoor boots and a thick black woollen sweater.

Gosh—he was actually rather good-looking. Lucky Alex. Under other circumstances—circumstances in which she wasn't totally 'over men' and Jude Marlowe wasn't gay and standoffish—she might have taken second or third looks at him. And more, right now, she would have been far happier if he'd been less attractive, but empathetic and warm, like Alex.

Clearly this wasn't the case, and she would have to nurse her sorrows on her own. At any rate, she was relieved to be in the company of a man she could trust not to make a move on her.

Outside on the footpath, the wind made their cheeks pink, but Emily was snug in her coat and the air was invigorating—a beautiful clear and crisp winter's night in the city.

She was starting to feel a tiny bit better already. Of course, there was still a sickening ache in her chest whenever she thought about her former boyfriend, Michael, and a stomach-churning twist of appalling guilt whenever she thought about the wife and children he'd conveniently forgotten to mention. But just getting away from Wandabilla had helped. At least no one knew her here in Brisbane and she didn't have to face the gossip and curious glances.

The restaurants were filled with diners, talking and laughing and generally having a good time, and as Emily passed each doorway, she caught snatches of music and chatter and sensational appetising smells.

She came to a stop outside an Indian takeaway.

'Is this what you fancy?' Jude asked.

'I would love a curry. We only have Chinese in Wandabilla, and I adore Indian.'

'Indian it is then,' he said, stepping inside. 'Too easy.'

'Are you going out of your way to oblige me, or are you always this easy about meals?'

Jude's eyes shimmered. 'When it comes to food, I'm a pushover.'

They ordered two kinds of curries—one meat and one vegetarian, as well as steamed rice and naan bread.

'And samosas,' said Jude. 'For entrée.'

Heading back to the apartment with their mouth-watering packages, he suddenly took a left-hand dive into a supermarket and emerged moments later with an armful of bright yellow daffodils.

'Wow—' Emily swallowed her surprise as he handed the sunshiny blooms to her '—what are these for?'

'I've heard you need cheering up.'

'Oh.' It was the lovely sort of thing Alex would have done. Perhaps Alex had given his housemate instructions.

'That's so sweet,' she told him, feeling suddenly, unexpectedly grateful, and just a tiny bit weepy. Impulsively, she stood on tiptoe and gave Jude a kiss on the cheek. To her surprise, a dark tide of colour stained his neck.

Afraid that she'd embarrassed him, she quickly changed

the subject. 'Should we get something for breakfast while we're out?'

'Of course. Sorry. I've been a bit distracted lately.'

For the briefest moment, Emily saw something else in Jude's grey eyes—just a flash of a darker emotion that might have been anxiety or fear. It was gone almost as soon as it arrived, but it made her wonder if he'd been distracted by more than his work.

She couldn't exactly quiz him about it, so she turned her attention to their shopping, choosing food she thought a guy might like—eggs and bacon, and then a punnet of blueberries, a tub of yoghurt and a bag of good quality coffee. At the cash register, Jude insisted on paying, warding off her protests with a grim fierceness that was hard to fight.

A slight awkwardness descended as they hurried back to the apartment, laden with their purchases.

In the kitchen, Jude set the takeaway tubs on the table, then found cutlery and plates.

'Where do you normally eat?' Emily asked, not at all surprised when he frowned again. She'd already decided that his thoughtful purchase of flowers had been an aberration, and from now on she should probably expect frowns and grimness.

She half expected Jude to tell her that he preferred to eat on his own, hidden away in his room in front of his computer.

But he said, 'Here's OK, isn't it?'

'Of course.' Emily tried not to look too surprised or pleased, but she couldn't deny that she would prefer his company to being left alone with her own unhappy thoughts. She shot him a cautious smile. 'What about wine? Would you rather red or white?'

'Actually…I'm not drinking alcohol.'

'Oh?'

'I've given it up. Temporarily.'

Once again, she thought she caught a flash of emotion, as if there was something else, a deeper worry that haunted Jude. For a second she thought he was going to say more but, if that was his plan, he quickly changed his mind.

'I won't have wine, either, then,' she said. 'It's not a great idea to drink alone.'

'But you're not alone.' Jude was insistent. 'Go on. Have a glass. It'll do you good. You want to drown your sorrows, don't you?'

If only she could just drown her sorrows and be rid of them. But the pain would still be there when the effects of the wine wore off. Just the same, as Jude peeled silver foil from the wonderfully aromatic tubs of curry, Emily poured herself a glass of white and gratefully flopped down in a seat.

'That smells amazing. I didn't eat lunch.'

'Neither did I. I'm starving.'

At first they were both too ravenous to bother with conversation, but there were plenty of appreciative groans and nods of approval as they helped themselves to the food. Emily, however, hadn't been able to eat much since she'd found out about Michael, and it wasn't long before she had to call a halt.

'My eyes were bigger than my stomach,' she said as she watched Jude help himself to more curry. She sipped her wine instead, then because he was starting to look more relaxed, she gave in to her growing curiosity. 'I hope you don't mind my asking, but how long have you known Alex?'

He looked surprised. 'Why would I mind? I've known him for about five years. As I said earlier, I'm a writer. Alex is my agent.'

'Oh? Really?' So they had a business relationship as well as a personal one. 'That's a handy arrangement.'

Jude frowned at her, as if, yet again, he found her comment puzzling. 'Yes, it is. Very handy.'

'What do you write?'

'Thrillers.'

She gaped at him. 'As in thriller novels?'

'Afraid so.'

'How amazing.' Now it was her turn to be surprised, and she stared at her mysterious host with new respect. 'Should I have heard of you?'

'Not unless you like reading thrillers.'

Emily liked reading crime novels, and she didn't mind a thriller plot, but she mostly read books written by women writers because they had more female characters in their stories. 'I'm not keen on the really blokesy books,' she said.

Jude actually smiled at that. 'To be honest, neither am I. In fact, I always include at least one major female character in every story.'

'Well—' her respect for him was growing by the second '—I should be reading your books then, shouldn't I?'

His head dipped in a mock bow.

Before Emily could ask anything else, he held up a hand as if to stop her. 'I think that's enough questions about me.'

'Ah…' Emily pulled a face. 'So now we talk about Alex? Or world affairs?'

'Or you.'

'Believe me,' she warned him darkly, 'you don't want to go there.'

While she'd come rushing to the city to tell Alex *everything* about Michael, she couldn't imagine ever confessing her personal problems to Jude. The very thought of telling him about her cheating boyfriend made her face burn. She took a swift and, hopefully, cooling gulp of wine.

As if he'd sensed her sudden panic, he said, 'I was wondering what sort of work you do.'

This, at least, was easy to answer. 'I work in a bank.'

'As a teller?'

'As a manager.'

'I beg your pardon?' His intelligent grey eyes narrowed. 'Do you mean you're a *bank* manager?'

'I do.'

Jude blinked at her.

'Don't you believe me?'

His smile was sheepish. 'I'm very sorry if I looked surprised, Emily. It's just—' Pausing, he took a breath and clearly made an effort to stifle another urge to smile. 'I'm fascinated, to be honest.'

'Most men find my work boring.' *Or threatening.*

'Perhaps you've been talking to the wrong men.'

Well, yes, Emily had discovered this the hard way, but she wasn't prepared to admit it now.

'I'd love to hear how you've done so well so quickly,' Jude prompted.

'By a rather roundabout route, to be honest.'

'The best stories are never straightforward.'

He managed to look genuinely interested, and Emily decided that Alex would be very pleased with his housemate's efforts to play the attentive host. At least talking about her job distracted her from other thoughts.

'The thing is, I never planned to work in a bank,' she said. 'I was always going to be a famous ballerina. After high school I went straight to Melbourne, to study ballet.'

'A dancer. That explains…' His voice tapered off.

'Explains what?'

'Why you're so graceful,' he said simply, but he looked unhappy, as if he wished he hadn't said that.

'I certainly loved everything about ballet. I loved the discipline, the music and the opportunities to perform. But—' she twisted the stem of her almost empty wine glass '—after a couple of years, I ran into problems with a choreographer.'

'A male choreographer?'

'Yes.' Looking up, her eyes met Jude's and she saw that he was watching her with another thoughtful frown.

'Let's just say I have bad luck with men.'

She let out a sigh. Just being here in Alex's kitchen reminded her of all the other times she'd been here, confiding in Alex. There was something about this setting, and the warm, exotic food and relaxing wine that seemed to encourage confidences.

And the man sitting opposite her might not be Alex, but he had the loveliest smoky-grey eyes. Right now they looked soulful and understanding, almost as sympathetic as Alex's. Poor fellow. He felt obliged to fill Alex's shoes.

With a shrug, she found herself saying, 'When it comes to men, I make really bad choices. Or they make the bad choices. I don't know. I just know I always end up miserable and running away.'

'Is that what you're doing now?' Jude asked with surprising gentleness.

'Of course.' She lifted the glass and drained the last of her wine.

Then she jumped to her feet. 'Now, let me clean this up, seeing as you so kindly paid.'

'I won't argue with that.' He was on his feet, probably relieved to escape.

'And, Jude,' Emily said, as he turned to head out of the kitchen.

He turned back to her.

'I'll head off in the morning.'

His eyes grew cautious and he frowned again. 'Do you have somewhere to go?'

'I can easily find somewhere. I'll be fine. Coming here was a spur of the moment thing. I had no idea Alex wasn't home. Tomorrow I'll leave you in peace.'

After a beat, he said, 'If you're sure.'

'I am, truly.'

It was totally silly of her to be disappointed when Jude nodded, then retreated, wishing her goodnight and muttering something about checking his emails.

Shortly afterwards, with the kitchen tidied, Emily went to Alex's room and, out of habit, she retrieved her phone from her bag. Almost immediately, she wished she hadn't bothered.

The first message was a text from a girlfriend in Wandabilla.

Is it really true about Michael? OMG. How awful.

Already, the gossip was spreading.

Emily's mind flashed to the photo she'd seen on Facebook just yesterday, a shot of Michael, her boyfriend of twelve months, with his pretty wife and two cute children, a little boy who looked just like him and a baby girl with golden curls.

Pain washed through her, an appalling tide of anguish and grief. How could he do that? She'd given him a whole year of her life, and she'd been ready to spend the rest of her life with him.

How could she have been such a fool?

CHAPTER TWO

NIGHTS were the worst for Jude. During the day, he could keep his thoughts under control and he wouldn't allow himself to worry. At night, however, the shadowy fears returned to haunt him, jumping out to snare him when he was almost asleep, or sneaking by the back door, sliding into his dreams.

Tonight, he came awake, shaking and drenched in a cold sweat, and he sat up quickly, hating the fact that waking brought very little comfort. His real life was almost as frightening as his dreams. His increasingly frequent headaches pointed to something serious, especially as lately his vision had begun to blur at the edges.

Alone at night, with no distractions, he found it so much harder to stop himself from worrying. This damn problem was dominating his life right now—even though he tried to hide it as best he could. All his life he'd viewed any illness as weakness—a bad habit he'd no doubt learned from his father, who'd never had any sympathy for their childhood illnesses. Measles, flu, grazed knees…his dad had always made his irritation very apparent.

Once, when Jude was about ten, he'd broken his leg playing football.

'This will be a test of your manhood,' his father had said. 'Nobody likes a whinger.'

It was a message Jude had taken to heart.

Now, he noted the time—three-thirty a.m.—which wasn't too bad. He'd already had several hours' sleep, and he only had to manage for a few more hours before it would be daylight again.

Rolling over, he closed his eyes and willed himself to relax, but in the perfect stillness he heard noises coming from down the hall.

Soft sounds of crying.

From Emily's room.

Any lingering thoughts about his own problems vanished. Jude sat up, listening intently through the darkness. Emily's sobs were muffled, no doubt by her pillow, but, even so, the crying went on and on in an uncontrollable outpouring of misery.

The sounds were like hammer blows to Jude's conscience. He knew damn well that if Alex were here Emily wouldn't be crying like this. He'd promised Alex he'd keep an eye on her.

His feet hit the floor and he was halfway across the room before his head caught up with his chivalrous impulses.

OK. What, exactly, was he planning to do? Go to Emily? Offer her a shoulder to cry on?

Brilliant. If she'd broken her heart over a good-for-nothing boyfriend, she was hardly going to welcome another lusty bloke offering to hold her in his arms.

Sinking back onto the edge of his bed, Jude remembered the way she'd looked at dinner as she'd talked about her unhappy track record with men. She'd seemed so fragile, with shadows beneath her eyes and a trembling droop to her soft pink mouth. It was hard to believe she was the same tough cookie who managed an entire district's bank accounts.

Obviously, the louse of a boyfriend had struck a cruel blow, and she'd come here to recuperate. To be consoled by Alex.

Alex would have known how to help her. Alex would have listened and encouraged her to talk and he would have known, instinctively, what she needed. Whereas Jude felt utterly helpless and totally inadequate. To make matters worse, he'd more or less accepted her offer to leave, which was tantamount to booting her out of the door.

How lousy was that after he'd promised to look out for her?

At last the crying settled down, but Jude couldn't get back to sleep. He was in the kitchen quite early, brewing coffee, when Emily came into the room. In her nightgown.

Far out. He almost dropped the coffee pot. What was she thinking?

Her nightdress wasn't deliberately provocative or see-through, but the frothy concoction of cream and lace frills hinted at her nakedness underneath. And, with her red-gold hair tumbling about her pale shoulders, she looked like an old-fashioned princess, a young Elizabeth the First. An appealing but tired princess who'd spent a troubled and anguished night.

Jude tried his best not to stare at the delightful hints of her breasts and bottom. He wondered if Emily assumed he was immune—gay, like Alex. He knew he should probably explain that this wasn't the case, but he wasn't sure how he could introduce the subject without tying himself in knots and embarrassing them both.

Instead, he tried to cover his reaction with an attempt at cheerfulness. 'Are you hungry?' he asked brightly. 'In the mood for pancakes? Or bacon and eggs?'

To his surprise, Emily made a shooing gesture. 'Don't

worry about breakfast. I can look after it. You need to start your writing.'

'What are you? A slave-driver?' He smiled to indicate this was an attempt at humour.

Emily merely blinked. 'I thought you wrote madly all day and didn't bother about meals.'

Well, yes, he had given that impression last night, hadn't he? Truth was, he'd been writing since four a.m., and his hunger pangs had steadily mounted. For hours now he'd been fantasising about the breakfast ingredients they'd bought last night.

About to grab a frying pan, he saw, again, the red-rimmed despair in Emily's eyes, lingering traces of her midnight tears. She would probably find cheery chatter at breakfast painful. Perhaps the kindest thing he could offer was to stay clear and hide behind his work.

'I'll head off then,' he said quickly. 'But, before I go, I've been thinking about your plan to leave. You know there's no need.'

He couldn't quite believe he'd said that. The words had jumped out of nowhere.

Emily looked surprised, too. Her eyes widened and Jude almost back-pedalled. His life over the next week would be so much easier without her here.

'Are you sure, Jude?'

'Of course. You're Alex's cousin, and he wants to make his home welcome to you. You've more right to be here than I have.'

Her blue eyes sparkled with a suspicious sheen. 'That's very kind of you.'

Jude was quite sure he hadn't been half as kind as Alex had hoped. He cleared his throat. 'And if you need to talk…'

To his dismay, Emily flushed brightly.

'I don't mean to pry,' he added awkwardly. 'I'm not Alex, but if there's any way I can help…'

'That's sweet of you, Jude, but I couldn't dump my problems onto you.'

He shrugged, unsure what to say. Counselling was so *not* his forte.

Then Emily gave a helpless flap of her hands. 'Oh, heck. Perhaps I should tell you what happened. Just to clear the air.'

He waited, leaning against the door jamb, trying to look as if he had all the time in the world.

'I've been seeing a geologist for over a year,' she said quietly but steadily. 'His name's Michael and he came to Wandabilla regularly as part of his work. Exploratory prospecting—that sort of thing. And—' she gave a hopeless little shrug '—he was charming and sexy and I fell in love…'

On the word *love* her voice cracked and she took another deep breath while her gaze was fixed on the jug of yellow daffodils on the kitchen counter.

'This week, Michael and I were supposed to go away on holiday together. I'd taken my annual leave. Everything was planned.'

Again Emily paused, paying serious attention to the daffodils. 'We were due to fly to Fiji, but on the night before our flight, a friend sent me a link to a Facebook page. Actually, it was a link to Michael's *wife's* Facebook page.'

Suddenly, her mouth twisted out of shape.

Jude's throat tightened. 'You're absolutely sure it was him?' he asked, keeping any hint of reproach from his voice.

Emily nodded. 'Michael admitted it. He could hardly deny it when the photo was there on the screen. There he was with his lovely wife and two beautiful children. They live in South Australia and his name's not even Michael. It's Mark.'

Jude's hands fisted, itching to land a punch on the rat's nose.

'So that's my sad little story.' Emily's lips tilted in a travesty of a smile. 'But please don't worry. I'm OK. Heartbreak's not fatal. I'll get over it.'

'But you must stay here as long as you need to,' Jude said. 'Try not to take any notice of me. Just treat this place as your own.'

'Well, if you're sure…thanks.'

He raised his coffee mug in a salute, and managed to smile. 'I'll be off to the salt mines, but I might sneak back later to make some toast.'

'Oh, I can make toast for you.' Suddenly she was eager, as if to make amends. 'What would you like on it? Marmalade? A slice of bacon?'

'Ah—bacon would be great. Thank you.'

'Actually,' she said with a hopeful look, 'I make a great bacon sandwich.'

'Sounds terrific.'

As Jude retreated to his room, he told himself that keeping his distance from Emily was, truly, his wisest option. She needed privacy to get over her heartache, and he had plenty of reasons to keep to himself.

Reasons he preferred not to think about now. But the appointment at the hospital was looming towards him like headlights on a speeding freight train. Every time he thought about the tests and the possible outcome, he was flooded by a rush of anxiety.

Shaking those thoughts aside, he opened his work in progress, and he prayed that his muse would be friendly, letting him escape into a world of fantasy.

* * *

The words did not flow.

Not the right words, at any rate. Jude's morning commenced poorly and came to a grinding halt when Emily, still in her nightdress, appeared at his door with a tray.

'Breakfast,' she said softly, as if she were afraid to interrupt a genius at work.

The tray held the promised bacon sandwich, which smelled amazing, as well as a glass of freshly squeezed orange juice and another pot of coffee.

'My ministering angel,' he told her and she gave a self-conscious laugh.

'Hardly.'

'Well, in that get-up, you look like some kind of angel.'

She blushed and looked upset and Jude immediately wished he could take the words back. Too late, she was already whirling away and he found himself watching her retreating heels, flashing pink beneath the frilled hem of her nightdress.

He didn't see her again for the rest of the day. Which was, he decided, a very good thing.

Naturally he was grateful that he'd been left in peace. Except…the afternoon's writing fared as badly as the morning's. Ideas wouldn't come. Words evaded Jude and when he emerged from his room at the end of the day, he felt particularly irritable and sluggish. And mad with himself for wasting precious hours.

Usually, when he felt like this, he went for a long, brisk walk to shake out the cobwebs. This evening, however, he was distracted by enticing aromas wafting from the kitchen.

Following his nose, he discovered Emily wrapped in one of Alex's gaudy aprons, and looking especially fetching with her bright hair pinned up in a loose knot from which fiery tendrils escaped.

'That smells amazing.'

She turned to him and she was a bit pink and flushed, but much happier than she'd been when she'd left his office this morning. In fact, she sent him a bright-eyed smile. 'It's coq au vin. I hope you like it.'

'I'm sure I'll love it, but I don't expect you to cook for me, Emily.'

'I don't mind. I like cooking, and it's my way of repaying you for last night's dinner.' She shot him a quick enquiring glance. 'Or were you planning to go out?'

It occurred to Jude that he should have called one of his mates and planned an evening out. Surely that was a wiser plan than spending another night at home with this far too attractive girl.

However, he found himself saying, 'I don't have any plans.' And he helped himself to a glass of iced water from the fridge. 'That dinner smells sensational.'

'So speaks a self-confessed pushover when it comes to food.'

'Sprung,' he admitted with a rueful smile.

Emily smiled, too, and he thought he could stare at her smile for ever...

'I've tried to keep quiet,' she said. 'Have you had a productive day?'

'Not very.'

For a moment she looked worried, but then her eyes widened with unmistakable excitement. 'I bought one of your novels this afternoon. It's called *Thorn in the Flesh* and I've started reading it. It's fabulous, Jude. Totally gripping. I'm hooked, and it's exactly what I needed to stop me from dwelling...on...everything.'

'I'm glad it hit the spot.'

To his surprise, she folded her arms and leant a shapely hip against a kitchen cupboard with the air of someone settling in for a discussion. 'Morgan, the heroine, is really tough,' she said. 'Mentally tough. And I like the way she guards her heart.' Emily rolled her eyes. 'I should be more like her.'

Jude shrugged. 'Perhaps you're too hard on yourself. Fictional characters are always larger than life.'

'That's true, I guess.'

'I could never live up to my hero's standards.'

She nodded. 'Raff's a very cool customer, isn't he?'

'Of course.'

Of course... Jude thought. His heroes had always been very cool and very tough, ever since he'd first created them for the stories he told to his little sister, Charlotte. At the age of eight he'd been trying to drown out the nightly ordeal of their parents' rowdy arguments.

These days, with new enemies, Jude wished it was as easy to escape from reality.

Emily had turned to the stove and was adjusting the flame beneath the fragrantly simmering pot. 'Have you heard from Alex?' she asked casually.

'Not today.'

'Do you miss him?' She gave the pot a stir.

Finishing his iced water, Jude shrugged. 'Not especially. He'll only be away for three weeks or so.'

Then he saw the way Emily was watching him, her blue eyes soft and round with obvious sympathy, and he realised with a slam of dismay that she'd decided he was Alex's lover.

He should deny it now. Tell her the truth. Hell, just looking at her in her simple jeans and Alex's striped apron, Jude was fighting off desire so strong that it startled him. He was surprised that Emily could stand there in the same room and not be aware of his screaming lust.

Thing was, it should have been dead easy to set her

straight. How hard was it to make a simple statement? *By the way, Emily, I'm not gay.*

All things being equal, he would have told her. Immediately. No problem.

Except…there were other factors at play here. Emily was enjoying a kind of immunity in this apartment, but if she knew the truth about him, she was likely to pick up on the attraction he felt. For all kinds of reasons, that was a bad idea.

Her trust in men had taken a severe hammering and she'd come here seeking sanctuary. Feeling safe was very important to her right now, and Jude didn't want to upset that. This apartment offered her time-out. From men. Time to pick up the pieces after her recent relationship disaster. The last thing she needed was an awareness of a new guy with the hots for her.

Just as importantly, Jude knew he was totally crazy to entertain randy thoughts when he'd come to the city to find out what the hell was wrong with him. He needed a medical diagnosis, not a romantic entanglement with the first gorgeous girl who walked through the door.

All things considered, it was much easier and safer to simply let Emily assume that he was gay. After all, she wouldn't be here for long, and he—

Hell. He had his life on hold until he knew what the future had in store for him.

When Emily woke the next morning she felt marginally happier. She'd slept quite well during the night, no doubt because she'd gone to bed feeling thoroughly relaxed after a pleasant evening at home with Jude.

They'd enjoyed a leisurely meal, which Jude had complimented lavishly, and then they'd sunk into comfy armchairs and read novels in the pleasantly heated lounge room while CDs played softly in the background. It had been rather cosy and undemanding, the kind of evening she'd often spent with Alex.

Now, having dressed in jeans and a sweater because she didn't want another comment about angels and nightgowns, she wandered into the kitchen at almost nine o'clock. It was the longest sleep she'd had in ages. No wonder she felt better.

To her surprise, there were no signs that Jude was up. The kettle was cold, which meant he'd either made his cuppa long ago, or he hadn't bothered.

She made coffee and blueberry pancakes and assembled a breakfast tray, as she had on the previous day, then knocked softly on Jude's door. After all, bringing him breakfast was the least she could do when he was hard at work and generously sharing his living space with her.

He didn't answer to her knock, which was another surprise. She wondered if he was in some kind of artistic frenzy, typing madly as the clever words flowed straight from his imagination through his fingertips and onto the keyboard. He might be very angry if she interrupted.

Then again…he'd welcomed the breakfast she'd prepared yesterday. She knocked again, less cautiously this time.

There was a muffled growl from inside.

'Jude, would you like coffee and pancakes?'

At first he didn't answer, but then the door opened slowly and Jude leant a bulky shoulder against the door frame. He was wearing black boxer shorts and a holey grey T-shirt that hugged his muscly arms and chest. His eyes were squinted as if the muted light in the hallway was too bright.

His dark hair was tousled into rough spikes, his jaw covered in a thin layer of dark stubble, but it was the glassy strain in his eyes that told Emily he was in pain.

'I won't bother with breakfast this morning,' he said dully. Then, added as an afterthought, 'Thanks, those pancakes look great, but I'm not hungry.'

'Are you unwell?'

'Headache.'

'Oh, gosh, I'm sorry. Is there anything I can get you? Do you need aspirin? Camomile tea?'

A ghost of a smile flitted over his face and he started to shake his head, then grimaced, as if the movement was too painful. 'I have medication. Don't worry, I'm used to this. I'll hit the sack for an hour or so and then I should be fine.'

Clearly, Jude didn't want to be bothered by any more questions, so Emily tiptoed away, leaving him to rest, but she felt disturbed and worried. She'd experienced guys with hangovers, but Jude hadn't been drinking, and he'd said he was used to these headaches. How awful for him.

A pool of morning sunlight on the balcony beckoned, so, feeling unaccountably subdued, she ate her breakfast at a little wrought-iron-and-glass table, with *Thorn in the Flesh* propped against a pot plant. She finished the last two chapters while she ate.

Jude's story was wonderful. Not only was there a fabulously thrilling chase at the end to catch the bad guys, but there was also a lovely and poignant romantic finale for the deserving hero and heroine. She marvelled that a gay man could portray the male-female emotions so perfectly.

There was only one problem. When Emily put the book down, she came back to earth with an abrupt and unhappy thud. Her own romances had never finished happily. Every one of them had ended suddenly and miserably, leaving her to feel like The World's Greatest Romantic Loser.

She couldn't help wondering if there was something crucially wrong with her personality. Some genetic defect that caused her to always fall for the wrong man.

All she wanted, really, was to be like her parents, to find one person to love, one relationship to feel safe inside. She'd grown up watching their warmth and affection and she'd listened many times to their story of how they'd met at a country dance and married young, never regretting their decision.

Even her brother Jack had been lucky in love. He'd married his high school sweetheart, Kelly, a girl from a nearby farm. There'd only ever been one girl for Jack, and now he and Kelly were ridiculously happy.

Emily's family made finding love look easy, and yet she'd tried so many times and failed. Now, she punished herself with memories, starting with Dimitri, the dark and ruggedly handsome Russian choreographer at the ballet school in Melbourne.

Having taken advantage of her youth and naivety, Dimitri had promptly dropped her overnight when he took up with one of the stars of the Australian Ballet. Emily had taken almost a year to recover from that heartbreak.

Back home in the Wandabilla district, she'd met Dave, a nice, safe farmer, and this time she was sure she'd struck gold. She would marry and live on a farm near her family, and she could envision her happy future so easily.

Dave had been as different from Dimitri as possible—practical and rough around the edges, and not the slightest bit interested in 'culture'. She'd been happy to swap satin pointe shoes and the barre for tractors and cow manure.

But Dave's first love was rodeos and, eventually, he'd taken off on the competition circuit, travelling to all the outback events. He'd expected Emily to throw up her job and follow him, but she wasn't prepared to do that, she'd realised, much to her own surprise.

In western New South Wales, Dave had discovered Annie, a camp-drafting champion who shared his passion, and his phone calls to Emily had stopped.

After that, Emily had thrown herself into her work. She'd attended workshops on customer relations and marketing, and any other professional development programmes that could boost her up the corporate ladder.

When she'd dived into the dating pool—unsurprisingly, it was rather shallow in Wandabilla—she'd set herself strict rules. No longer would she be so trusting and open, and she wouldn't allow herself to fall in love again until she met a man who ticked all the right boxes. Following her new plan, she'd never gone out with any one fellow more than a few times, and she was determined from then on that *she* would be the one who ended her relationships.

She had been feeling quite confident again. Before Michael had arrived in town.

Conservatively good-looking, intelligent and charming, Michael had been perfect. Emily had learned from her mistakes, however, and she'd resisted his attention at first. Michael had chased her with flattering persistence and, in the end, she'd decided he was genuine in his admiration.

And surely he was safe? He wasn't a foreign artist or an outback drifter. He wasn't even a local. He was a geologist from South Australia, prospecting in the Wandabilla district for a mining company.

Admittedly, Michael was only in her district for six weeks at a time, but he flew back regularly, and he always wrote to her or phoned her while he was away.

In time she was confident that he was *The One*.

After all, weren't geologists clever and educated, and as solid and dependable as the rocks they studied?

What a joke.

Emily let out a long groan of frustration. And pain.

Losing Michael hurt. So much. Her pain went way beyond disappointment. She felt betrayed, used and foolish, as if she hadn't gained one single jot of wisdom since Dimitri. And, even though she was the innocent party, she felt guilty that she'd slept with someone else's husband and father.

She could too easily imagine how deeply Michael—no, *Mark's*—wife loved him, could imagine how hurt the other woman would be if she ever found out.

Emily's sense of gloom dived even deeper when she returned to the kitchen and saw the blinking light on her mobile phone.

Wincing at the possibilities, she clicked on her message bank and discovered five—count them, *five*—new text messages from people in Wandabilla.

Normally, she would try to reply, to at least thank these people for their concern, even though they weren't genuinely close friends but mainly curious gossipers.

Today, however, there were also three voice messages from Michael-slash-Mark, and his first message was full of apologies and entreaties, begging her to ring him back.

Hearing his voice brought a fresh slug of misery and anger, and Emily almost hurled the phone across the room.

She might have done that, actually, if she wasn't worried that the crash would wake Jude. Her gaze flashed to his novel, *Thorn in the Flesh*, sitting on the breakfast tray, and she remembered Morgan, Jude's tough heroine.

Emily needed to be like her. From now on.

Smiling, she picked up the phone and deleted every single message without responding.

It felt good.

Very good, actually.

CHAPTER THREE

Mid-afternoon...

EMILY had been out to a bookshop, where she'd bought two more of Jude's books, and she was stretched out on the sofa, deeply absorbed in a thrilling mystery set in the wilds of The Kimberley Coast when she heard Jude's door open. Shortly after, she heard the sound of the shower in the bathroom.

Good. He must be feeling better. She was surprised by how pleased she felt about this. She even found her attention wandering from the book as she waited for Jude to emerge from the bathroom. It was suddenly important to make sure that he really was OK.

When he finally came into the living room, freshly shaved, hair damp from the shower and smelling pleasantly of lemon-scented soap, he was no longer frowning or squinting with pain, and it was almost impossible to tell that he'd been unwell.

'Feeling better?' Emily asked with a jolly-nurse smile.

'Much better, thanks.' He seemed keen to shrug her concern aside. 'Actually, I'm heading out now.'

It was crazy to be instantly disappointed. Why should she miss Jude? She'd never been a person who was needy for company.

Annoyed with herself, she held up the book she was reading. 'I'm really enjoying this, by the way.'

Jude saw the cover and his eyes glinted with amusement. 'Don't tell me I've acquired a fan?'

'Perhaps,' she said airily. 'You've done a good job with Ellie. She has hang-ups like the rest of us, but she wouldn't dare let them show. I like that about her. She's classy. And I love that she's blonde and leggy and carries a pistol in her handbag.'

'Glad you approve.' Hands sunk deep in the pockets of his jeans, Jude bowed with mock solemnity, then turned and headed for the door. 'Don't worry about dinner,' he called over his shoulder. 'It's my turn to cook tonight.'

Emily was about to remind him that he didn't like to cook when he looked back and she caught the ghost of a twinkle in his eye.

'How about I bring home Thai?' he said, then quickly disappeared before she could answer.

The front door closed behind him, and the apartment felt weirdly empty.

It was quite late, almost dark, when Jude arrived back bearing the promised tubs of takeaway Thai. They ate on the balcony, watching the last of the sunset over distant Mount Coot-tha.

'I was wondering if you'd like to see a movie tonight,' he asked as they ate. 'It'll cheer us both up.'

'Do we need cheering up?'

He sent her a measuring glance. 'Isn't that why you're here?'

'Well, yes,' she admitted. 'But I'm not your responsibility, Jude. Don't feel obliged to entertain me.'

'I could do with cheering, too. That blasted headache left me feeling a bit out of sorts.'

'That's not surprising.' Emily couldn't shake off the lingering suspicion that there was something else, something more deeply serious that was troubling him. She didn't know him well enough to ask, so she said instead, 'I suppose you'd prefer to see a thriller?'

'Would you mind?' He offered her an apologetic shrug. 'I've never been much good with chick flicks.'

'That surprises me, actually. I thought you must watch them and study them. You write such lovely romantic scenes in your books.'

'Do I?' He looked suddenly caught out, almost guilty.

'But don't worry,' Emily assured him. 'I'm happy to watch a thriller. I'm certainly not in the mood for romance.'

This time when their gazes met, she thought she caught a different expression—a momentary flash in Jude's handsome grey eyes that caught her completely on the back foot. Not at all what she'd expected from a gay man. For a moment, she'd gained the unlikely impression that he was very much aware of her—as a woman.

Heaven knew she'd read that message in men's eyes often enough in the past. But surely she was being fanciful now? Of all the guys she'd spent time with, Jude was safe.

To her relief, he said simply, 'A thriller it is then. There's a really good one that just came out last week. And it will be my shout. After all, I get to count it as research.'

It was certainly pleasant to get out of the house, to wrap up and walk the frosty streets, and it was nice to know she could enjoy a man's company without any danger of breaking her heart.

The movie, as Jude had predicted, was an exciting, edge-of-the-seat thriller, and it soon worked its magic. For close to two hours Emily almost stopped thinking about Michael.

Joy.

'I definitely feel better for having seen that,' she said as they left the cinema.

Jude raised a questioning eyebrow. 'Do you want to prolong the fun? Are you in a rush to get home, or would you like to find somewhere for coffee?'

Going back to the apartment would mean returning to her solitary bedroom and her solitary one-track thoughts.

'I'd love to stay out for a bit longer,' she admitted. 'I'm glad you seem to have completely recovered.'

'So am I.' He smiled, but the effect was spoiled by the flicker of a shadow in his eyes. 'I'm fine now.'

Emily wished she hadn't seen that flicker. For a fanciful second it had looked like the shadow of a falling axe. She wished she could shake off the sense that something was really troubling Jude, and she wondered if he was trying to distract himself, just as she was. It was probably a good thing she'd agreed to stay out.

They found a snug table in the back corner of a crowded coffee shop. Emily ordered hot chocolate, which came with tiny pink and white marshmallows for melting, and Jude ordered tea—Lapsang Souchong, which arrived in a ruby-glass pot, smelling smoky and inexplicably masculine.

'You drink the same tea as your hero, Raff,' she teased as she scooped a sticky blob of marshmallow from her mug.

Jude smiled. 'Strange coincidence, isn't it?'

As they sipped their warm drinks, they talked about the movie, debating the significance of some of the plot twists.

'The scriptwriters certainly knew all about crime and the underbelly of society,' Emily suggested. Across the lamplit table, she narrowed her eyes at Jude. 'So do you, actually. It shows in your books. How do you do it? How do you get inside the mind of a hardened criminal?'

'I research,' he answered simply.

'Yes, I guessed that, but *how*? Who do you talk to?'

'Hardened criminals.'

He said this so dryly and with such a poker face that, momentarily, she almost fell for it.

Then, matching his dry tone, she replied. 'So you're telling me it's not safe to associate with you.'

This time his eyes twinkled. 'Touché. Of course, you're safe.'

There was a moment, as their gazes met across the table, when Emily felt a kind of woozy warmth that was totally unfitting.

'Seriously,' she said abruptly, shaking off the feeling. 'I'm interested in how you make your stories so real.'

'Seriously,' Jude said, 'I have contacts with the police and in the military. I've grilled them mercilessly about their work. I've spent full days with a firearms instructor, and another day observing Army commando training. I've even taken part, so I know what it feels like to be cuffed, down on the ground and immobile while a tactical unit performs a mock hostage rescue.'

With a smile, he said, 'And now I've met a bank manager, and that could be very handy, too. I can imagine all sorts of scenarios involving a heist and a beautiful banking boss.'

Heat flamed in Emily's cheeks, and she pressed her hands against the patches of warmth, hoping to hide them. She couldn't believe she was blushing simply because Jude had implied she was beautiful. Of all the ridiculous reactions.

Why should she blush over this man's completely non-sexual assessment of her looks?

To cover her silly reaction, she made a joke against herself. 'Just my luck, one of the robbers will turn out to be a former boyfriend.' Then, quickly, she steered the subject safely away from herself. 'What about your current book? Where's it set?'

'The Gold Coast. But I'm beginning to think it's a bit too close to home. I prefer more distant settings.'

'Why? Does your imagination work better at a distance?'

He looked at her with surprise. 'Yes, I think it does.' Then he frowned. 'Are you pretending to be interested, or are you genuinely curious?'

'I'm genuine. Honestly. Why do you ask?'

Jude shook his head. 'I was just wondering… I wouldn't have expected a bank manager to be interested in fiction.'

'You're stereotyping,' she accused with rather more iciness than she actually felt.

'Yeah. It's a failing.' Jude's unrepentant gaze flickered over her and then swept around the crowded café and the chattering customers gathered in the booths. 'I know it's not polite to mention this, but your clothes seem very—or should I say—*extremely* fashionable. Not quite what I'd expected from a little place like Wandabilla.'

'Is this another example of your narrow views?'

'I'm afraid it is.' He confessed this without a hint of remorse. 'But I'm genuinely curious. Is it a status thing?'

'I…I suppose it might be.' Emily hadn't been asked this question before, but there were a lot of wealthy farmers who conducted their business at her bank and classy clothes had become her armour. For a young woman to hang on to a position of power, she had to win respect any way she could.

At least, this was what she'd told herself, but she sometimes wondered if her efforts to acquire a perfect career and a perfect wardrobe were compensation for her lack of a perfect relationship.

'So where do you shop?' Jude asked. 'Do you travel to the city?'

'Not often. I do almost all my shopping online.' She gave a little laugh. 'I love the Internet. If I ever give up my current job, I think I'll develop some kind of business I can run online.'

Thinking about the Internet, however, brought back sickening memories of Michael-slash-Mark.

Emily wasn't sure how long she sat there, sunk in miserable memories.

Eventually, she heard Jude's voice.

'Are you OK?'

He asked this solicitously, just as Alex might have, and she couldn't help answering honestly. 'I'm very mad with myself for wasting a whole year on a relationship that was never going anywhere.'

'It's not easy to see through a practised conman. They're usually consummate charmers.' Jude's face was surprisingly fierce. 'My father was like that—having affairs all over the place.'

His hands were clenched into fists on the tabletop. 'And then my mother punished him by having revenge affairs.'

He looked so upset, Emily stopped thinking about her own worries. She was imagining Jude growing up with unhappy parents. At least her problems hadn't started until she'd left home.

Their conversation, she realised, had suddenly gone deeper. Jude's grey eyes were as hard as granite, as if just thinking about his parents changed him completely.

'Have you ever talked to Alex about this?' she asked.

Jude looked startled. 'No.'

'It's just that he's very good at laying ghosts to rest.'

'Yes, I can imagine he would be.' Then Jude gave a shake, as if ridding himself of unwanted memories.

They lapsed into silence and Emily finished off her chocolate. 'I'm sure I have a moustache.' With an embarrassed smile, she reached for a paper napkin.

'Here, let me.'

To her surprise, Jude took the napkin from her and dabbed at her upper lip. The pressure of his fingers so close to her mouth felt strangely intimate and he was looking at her with an intensity that stole her breath.

After what felt like an age, he blinked like someone coming out of a trance, then dropped the napkin onto his saucer. 'What were we talking about?'

Emily's mind had gone blank. To her dismay, she found herself thinking how attractive he was, and how the message in his grey eyes had made her feel strangely knife-edgy and weightless. And there was a vibe between them, an impossible awareness that was very confusing.

Surely her imagination was playing tricks on her? There must be something wrong with her. After her debacle with Michael, she couldn't possibly be interested in *any* man for ages. Right now, a life of celibacy had huge appeal and, anyway, Jude wasn't even available.

She made a flustered, helpless gesture, hoping to break the strange spell that seemed to have fallen over her, and promptly knocked the pepper pot. Next moment she was sneezing, then floundering in her bag for tissues.

Fortunately, after she'd finished blowing her nose, Jude suggested it was time to leave. Emily gratefully agreed.

Outside, it was chillier than ever. She turned up her collar and sunk her hands deep into her warm coat pockets, and hoped that the cold night air would clear her head of nonsense. She walked beside Jude in sober silence, wondering what on earth he was thinking. Had he noticed her silly reaction?

They didn't talk on the way back, for which she was grateful, and when she stole glimpses in Jude's direction, he seemed to be frowning and thoughtful. So it was a surprise when they reached the apartment that he turned to her with a warm smile.

'Thanks for a great night.'

'Thank *you*,' she said politely. 'It was a good idea to go out tonight. Just what I needed.'

'Same here.'

Despite the formality of their exchange, they stood in the hallway, neither one moving, as if they were trapped again by a mysterious spell. But the last thing—the *very last thing*—Emily expected was that Jude would lean in and kiss her.

On the lips.

And yet he did just that.

Before she had time to think, he was holding her by the shoulders and he was kissing her effortlessly and expertly. So expertly that she forgot to be shocked at first. She was seduced by the enticing smell of him and the warm, blissful pressure of his lips. Instinctively, she closed her eyes and gave in to the deliciousness of the moment.

An inappropriate stretch of time elapsed before she remembered that this kiss was wrong.

Wrong, wrong, wrong, wrong, wrong!

For heaven's sake.

She sprang back in shocked horror.

How had this happened? Had her brain short-circuited? Stunned, she pressed her fingers to her tingling lips. 'That was…unexpected.'

Understatement of the year.

'I'm sorry,' Jude said. 'I couldn't help it. You're so lovely.'

'And...' She gasped as the bald truth became obvious. 'And you're not gay.'

'No,' he said softly. 'I'm not.'

Gathering her dignity and her anger about her like a protective cape, she glared at him. 'You conned me, Jude. You pretended to be safe and uninterested in women. You let me assume you were like Alex, so I was lulled into a false sense of security.'

'I'm sorry, Emily. I—'

She cut him off with an angry cry, then stamped her foot. 'I should have known that every male on this planet is a scheming, cheating rat.'

Anger and despair swept through her. She was reliving Michael's deception. She'd trusted Michael utterly.

Now, she'd trusted Jude to be a safe, uncomplicated friend, but he was as bad as every other man.

Beyond furious, she raised her hand and slapped him hard.

Whirling around, she marched down the hallway to her room, kicking the door savagely behind her. *Bang! Slam!*

Jude winced as Emily's door crashed shut.

Good one, Marlowe.

What on earth had possessed him to kiss Emily? Had a kind of madness overcome him?

It was his only explanation.

He'd spent an entire evening in her company and she'd been lovely and amusing and interesting—in other words, utterly enchanting. On the walk home, the crisp night air had heightened her loveliness even further, adding stars to her eyes and colour to her cheeks and lips, and he'd been spellbound. Totally. He hadn't been able to resist stealing one little kiss.

He hadn't meant to shock her. He'd imagined that at some stage during this evening she'd guessed that he found her impossibly attractive.

That wasn't a good enough excuse, was it?

Damn.

Emily had come here for security and, while he hadn't actually lied to her, he'd held back the truth that he and Alex were nothing more than friends and business associates. And *of course* he should have shown more restraint just now. He should have known that Emily's sense of trust was too fragile to mess with. For goodness' sake, she was only a few days out of another relationship!

Problem was—he'd been looking for a distraction tonight, looking for anything to help him forget the barrage of tests he'd undergone at the hospital this afternoon. Tomorrow morning he would find out the results of these procedures and he would no doubt learn the cause of the headaches and vision problems that had plagued him over the past few months.

Truth be told, he was horrified. His career and, possibly, his life hung on the edge of a precipice.

Tonight had been all about forgetting—warding off fear, holding back the future.

But he'd been selfish. Of course he had.

He knew what Emily had been through. He knew she had trust issues—and, in all honesty, he'd known she'd thought he was gay. His health issues weren't a good enough excuse for helping himself to a kiss that hadn't been on offer.

Nor was the fact that he found her loveliness irresistible. He wasn't the first guy who'd had that problem.

* * *

Emily lay awake for ages, stewing over men's dishonesty.

The knowledge that she'd once again been hoodwinked was almost more than she could bear.

But, despite her anger, she was beginning to suspect that perhaps she shouldn't have hit Jude. She felt rather guilty remembering the way her hand had stung, which meant his face must have stung even more.

He'd been rather manly about it, not even flinching, even though he must have seen the slap coming.

He'd taken it on the cheek and, at the time, she'd thought, *Good. Serve him right.*

Now she was beginning to suspect that she'd hadn't really been hitting out at Jude, but at Michael. Michael-slash-Mark. So, along with her anger, she now had to deal with guilt, too. Heavens, she was Jude's guest, and she couldn't start a habit of slapping every guy who tried to kiss her.

It was ages before she drifted off to sleep, but in the end she slept deeply and woke quite late.

She took her time getting up, thinking at first that Jude could get his own breakfast this morning. But when she tried to resurrect the previous night's anger, she found that it had weakened. Granny Silver had always told her that things looked different after a good night's sleep and, more than once, her grandmother had been right.

Now, Emily felt guiltier than ever about her over-the-top reaction to Jude's kiss. It hadn't been a demanding kiss, after all, even though it had felt surprisingly intimate. Surely, she could have handled it more wisely and coolly?

She knew very well that a girl who didn't want to be kissed shouldn't stand in a hallway, smiling dreamily into smouldering grey eyes.

In the clear light of morning, she decided that there was no point in sulking. Jude had been very good about sharing this apartment with her and she just had to remember to be ultra-cautious in future. More head than heart—like Jude's heroines.

At least, after last night's carry-on, Jude wouldn't want to repeat the kiss, so hopefully they could resume their friendship without any drama. She would suggest something to that effect at breakfast.

By the time Emily had showered and dressed, however, she discovered that Jude had long gone. The door to his room was wide open and she could see that his bed was made, his laptop closed and his desk was uncharacteristically tidy.

In the kitchen the kettle was lukewarm, as if it had been boiled some time ago, and there was a mug with a coffee ring and a plate with a smattering of toast crumbs in the sink.

It was rather frustrating. Emily had been ready to talk to Jude, to clear the air. Disappointed, she went back to her room to switch on her phone and check for messages. Even a nosy text from Wandabilla would be welcome right now, but there was something better—a voice message from her grandmother.

It was wonderful to hear her granny's familiar musical voice and Emily rang straight back. 'Granny, I'm sorry I missed your call.'

'That's all right, dear. I was just ringing to let you know that I'm coming down to Brisbane today. I have an appointment at the hospital.'

'Not for anything serious, I hope.'

'No, thank goodness. It's my six-month check-up after my cataract operation.'

'Oh, that's all right then. What time's your appointment? I can meet you at the hospital, then take you to lunch.'

'Oh, Emily, I'd love that. Thank you.'

'Me, too. I'm looking forward to it already.'

Emily didn't like hospitals—they were so huge and clin-
ical and grim. When she arrived at the ophthalmology
department, she was told that her grandmother was still
being attended to, so she sat in the waiting area thumbing
through a very out-of-date magazine. She wished she'd
remembered to bring Jude's book to read.

There was plenty of action about the place, of course,
plenty of people in white coats and always someone coming or going. Emily passed the time by people-watching,
which she'd always found fascinating, although she'd
learned not to trust first impressions.

In her job, many, many people walked into her office,
and she knew very well that their exterior appearance was
not always a true indicator of the health of their bank accounts, or the strength of their character.

Pity she never remembered this when it came to her
love life.

She was mulling this over and flipping idly through the
magazine when firm footsteps on the polished linoleum
caught her attention. She looked up to see, of all people,
Jude.

He was striding down the corridor, looking pale and
worried. When he saw Emily, he stopped abruptly, and
looked as shocked to see her as she was to see him.

'What are you doing here?' His expression was one of
worry, mingled with something close to horror. 'Are you
following me? This is none of your business, Emily.'

'I've come to collect my grandmother. She's having her
eyes checked.'

'Oh, right.' The furrows in Jude's brow lessened marginally, as did the anguish in his eyes.

'But what about you, Jude? You seem upset.'

His throat rippled as he swallowed, and for a moment he looked as if he didn't want to answer her. He looked away, and his jaw squared and tightened as he stared hard at something down the corridor.

Remembering his awful headache yesterday, Emily was pierced by a nasty suspicion, but then his expression eased back into his usual good humour.

'I'm fine.' He gave her a disarming smile. 'I've been having my eyes tested, too. I need a new prescription for my reading glasses, for working at the computer.'

'Oh, is that all?' She found herself releasing a huff of relief. 'For a minute there you had me worried that it was something serious. That headache yesterday really knocked you out.'

'No doubt because I need the new glasses,' he said with a casual shrug. 'But thanks for your concern.' With a cautious smile, he added, 'Does this mean you're no longer mad at me?'

At the memory of last night's kiss and its aftermath, Emily blushed, much to her consternation.

'I guess not.' She spoke frostily to counteract the blush but, in truth, she *was* more than a little ashamed of last night's overreaction. 'I'm prepared to call a truce.'

'A truce?' Jude's right eyebrow hiked high. 'Does that involve terms and conditions?'

'Most definitely.' Emily shot a quick glance about her and was dismayed to discover that several people in the waiting area were watching them with acute interest. 'We can sort out the details later,' she said, lowering her voice.

'I'll look forward to it,' Jude replied in a low rumbling tone that set unacceptable vibrations thrumming inside her.

Perhaps it was just as well that her grandmother appeared then, full of smiles.

'Granny, how'd you go?'

'Wonderfully.' Granny Silver beamed at them. 'My eyes are better than they've been in a decade.'

'How fabulous.' Emily gave her a hug, but as soon as she released her grandmother, the elderly woman turned her attention to Jude. Introductions were necessary, and then explanations. 'Jude is a writer, Granny. He writes under his own name—Jude Marlowe—and Alex is his agent.'

'And I'm very pleased to meet you, Mrs Silver. Both Emily and Alex have spoken so highly of you.'

'Have they really?' Granny laughed and sent Jude a flirtatious sideways smile. 'Now, I do hope you're going to join us for lunch, Jude.'

'Sorry. I'd love to, but not today.'

'What a pity. I assumed you came here to meet up with Emily. Are you terribly busy?'

Emily had been watching Jude during this exchange and she thought she'd caught an underlying tension beneath the surface warmth and politeness. She was sure he was still worried about something, but trying to hide it.

'Why don't you join us?' she asked him on an impulse she didn't quite understand. No doubt it was her conscience urging her to make up for slapping him last night. 'Lunch won't take up too much of your time, and you'll still have all the afternoon for your writing.'

Jude's eyes shimmered with an unreadable emotion. 'Is this part of your truce deal?'

'It might as well be.'

'It's very kind, Emily, but I—'

'Oh, come on,' urged Granny as she sensed Jude's hesitation. 'It's not often that I have the chance to enjoy lunch in the company of a handsome young man.'

'How could I refuse such a flattering invitation?' he replied gallantly. 'In any case, I have my car here, so I can offer you a lift.'

'Wonderful,' said Granny.

They dined at Granny's favourite Italian restaurant overlooking the Brisbane River. There was no problem arranging for an extra place to be set at their table in a sunny corner with a view. Granny was charming company, as always, and Jude seemed to relax as he basked in the warmth of her smile.

He even turned on the charm as they ate their delicious meals—veal Marsala for Granny, mushroom risotto for Emily and gnocchi Gorgonzola for Jude. As soon as he discovered that Granny Silver was a great bird-lover, he chatted animatedly about sightings of terns and honey-eaters, parrots and bowerbirds. The old lady was delighted.

For Emily, it was all very pleasant, sitting in a stream of gentle winter sunshine, joining in the agreeable conversation while looking out at the boats on the river and the elegant houses lining the far bank. She was reminded of the many happy times she and Alex had dined with their granny. Pleasant memories were important—they helped counteract all the bad ones.

As they were finishing their coffee, Jude rose and excused himself. Moments later, Emily saw him talking to the cashier and realised that he was already paying the bill.

'This was supposed to be my shout,' she protested, rising from her seat.

She was stopped by a bony hand on her arm. 'Don't fret, Emily. If it bothers you, you can always talk to Jude about it later.'

'I guess...'

'Why not let your grandmother enjoy a little old-fashioned largesse from a nice-looking man?'

As Emily sat down again, both women watched the tall, dark figure on the far side of the room while he shared a smiling exchange with the girl at the till.

'He's just the kind of man you need,' Granny Silver said in a confiding tone.

'No. Don't start that, Granny.'

For long seconds her grandmother studied her, a shrewdly measuring light gleaming in her lively blue eyes. To Emily's relief, she didn't ask questions.

'It's a lonely life,' was all she said.

Yes, Emily knew the loneliness of singlehood all too well, but she was resigning herself to a life on her own. It seemed to be her destiny.

'Look at you,' she told her grandmother. 'All the years I've known you, you've lived alone and you've always been the happiest, most stable person I know.'

'I didn't live alone from choice.' Her grandmother looked at her with a wistful smile. 'I've missed Jim every day of these past thirty years.'

'I'm sorry.' Emily was instantly filled with remorse. 'Of course you have.'

Perhaps it was just as well that Jude returned then and they finished that particular conversation.

Playing the gentleman to the hilt, he helped Granny Silver out of her chair. 'Now, where can I take you?' he asked.

'Granny needs to get to the station to catch the train, if that's not too much trouble.'

'My pleasure.'

Perhaps Emily shouldn't have been surprised that Jude accompanied her as she saw her grandmother off at the station. After all, he'd been at his most gallant from the moment he met Granny.

'I can see why you're so fond of her,' he told Emily as

the carriage bearing the small white-haired figure in a lavender suit disappeared. 'She's charming.'

Emily nodded. 'She's always been super-understanding and ahead of her time, really. I think I valued her true worth when Alex came out. She was so sensitive and supportive.' She shot Jude a smile. 'You were a hit.'

'Talking of hits...' he said.

'Yes,' Emily said quickly. 'I'm sorry. I've been meaning to apologise for last night.'

'So have I, Emily. I didn't mean to deceive you, but I was worried that I might embarrass you if I tried to explain. It's not all that easy to tell a girl you've just met that you're not gay so she'd better watch out!'

'I might have hit you for that as well,' Emily admitted with a small smile. But at least the subject was out in the open now, and she felt much better as they headed back to the apartment.

Jude, on the other hand, was subdued again. To make matters worse, clouds had arrived to block out the sun and the city looked grey and depressing and cold. Emily tried to make light conversation. They squabbled mildly over the restaurant bill and Jude insisted that he didn't want to be reimbursed.

All the way home, however, she wondered about the problem that was troubling him. 'Are you sure you're OK?' she asked.

Jude's eyelids lowered as if he found her question tiresome. 'I'm fine, Emily,' he said in a bored tone, which made her feel like a fusspot rather than a concerned friend.

When they arrived at the apartment, he spoke almost sharply. 'Right. I need to get to work.'

Without another word, or the suggestion of a smile, he

disappeared into his room, shutting the door firmly behind him.

Emily's feeling of rejection made no sense at all.

CHAPTER FOUR

Jude let out a soft groan as he leant back against his closed door. He hoped Emily hadn't guessed that the pain had come back with a vengeance on the way home.

After a couple of calming breaths, he crossed his room, opened the drawer in his bedside table and snatched up the bottle of pills, downing two tablets swiftly, grimacing.

He sank onto the edge of his bed and felt the facade he'd worn all afternoon peel away. He'd enjoyed the company of Emily and her grandmother. In fact, he'd been somewhat stunned by how very much he'd enjoyed lunching with them. No doubt he'd been grateful for the diversion.

But now he allowed himself, for the first time since he'd left the doctor's office, to consider his fate.

There'd been good news and bad.

The doctor had been quite cheerful as he delivered the good news that a growth on Jude's pituitary gland was not malignant. Apparently these tumours were relatively common and could be removed by simple, but necessary, surgery via the nose. The gland was not secreting excess hormones, so Jude was lucky in that respect. The complications should be minimal.

Then had come the bad news—and even the doctor couldn't smile about the fact that the growth was pressing on Jude's optic nerve, meaning that he would go blind if he didn't have the operation. The surgeons would do everything possible to save his sight, but there was still a significant risk that the surgery might cause irreparable damage.

Significant risk. Bloody hell. Was that medico speak for *we don't like your chances, mate*?

Jude had challenged the doctor. 'Give me figures, man. What aren't you telling me? Do I have a fifty-fifty chance of blindness? Worse?'

The fact that the doctor wouldn't commit to a figure freaked the hell out of Jude.

Nausea rolled in his stomach now as he allowed himself, finally, to contemplate the full impact of going blind.

How could he possibly cope? Reading and writing were his life. He'd built his dream home in the mountains with spectacular views over the rainforest. His hobbies included observing the forest wildlife and hiking the rocky and difficult skyline. If he couldn't see, his life as he knew it would end.

Under the surgeon's knife.

Sure, there was Braille and there were talking books and voice activated software for his computer, but Jude's independent spirit ranted and rebelled at the thought of using them.

He hated the idea of being reliant on others for support or help. He couldn't bear it. Independence was in his blood and his bones. He'd learned it at his father's knee. He mustn't lose it. He mustn't.

And there was so much more to lose than mere self-sufficiency...

He would never again see the face of a beautiful woman like Emily. He would never savour that moment of opening a brand-new book and turning to the first page, seeing the shape of the words on the crisp white paper, encountering the magic of the first tempting sentence.

He would never watch a Broncos footy game, or see a sunset or the fresh perfection of an apple, would never see rain scudding across a city street.

Right now, he couldn't even be grateful for his imagination, which would continue to see these things even if his eyes could not. It was too soon to be thinking like flaming Pollyanna.

Yes, he knew he had to man up about this. He had to think positively and deal with whatever came his way, but for one afternoon he wanted to shut out the world. And, yeah, maybe feel more than a little sorry for himself.

The tablets had begun to ease the wretched ache that gripped his skull when he heard a gentle tap on his door.

At his grunted response, the door opened and Emily stuck her head through the gap, her sunset hair glowing like a candle flame in the twilight darkness of his room.

'Sorry. I thought you were working,' she said.

'Taking a break.'

Her expression suggested that she didn't believe him, and no doubt her deductions were aided by the fact that he was lying in the dark and hadn't opened his laptop.

'I've made a light supper,' she said. 'Scrambled eggs and toast, and a pot of tea.'

'Wonderful, thanks.'

'I'll put the tray on the desk here, shall I?' Emily spoke in the soothing tone of a nanny talking to a sick child. Having set the tray down, she stood in the middle of the room, twisting her hands nervously, as if she was waiting for him to explain what had happened.

He contemplated telling her the truth. He'd kept one truth from her already and she'd made it very clear that she hadn't appreciated the deception. But illness was different, surely? Why burden her with his personal worries when she had enough of her own?

'Is there anything else you'd like?' she asked at last.

'No, this is perfect. Thank you.'

With visible reluctance, she left him, closing the door behind her with a soft click. A few minutes later, he heard the TV come on in the living room—with a loud burst at first and then turned low. He imagined Emily eating her supper on her lap, watching the television alone, and he felt more depressed than ever.

When morning arrived, slanting sunlight through the blinds, Jude blinked awake and was relieved to discover that he was feeling fine. In fact, he felt so good it was hard to believe that he needed an operation in a week's time.

Seven days' grace.

He drew a deep breath. He wouldn't think beyond this week. Not yet. For now, he wanted to consider the best way to spend the precious time he had left.

A conscientious writer would tackle the ending of the book he was working on—get it finished and out of the way, in case there were any dreaded complications.

Jude shot a glance to his laptop, still lying closed on his desk. Normally, he looked forward to opening it each morning and starting work. Each new day gave him the chance to play creator and there were always surprises and fresh challenges, and occasional moments of deep satisfaction. As far as he was concerned, he had the best job in the world.

But now…

Everything was different this morning.

This next week could be his last week as a sighted man. He smashed that thought almost as soon as it arrived. He couldn't bear to think about trying to manage his writing career if he couldn't see.

Even so, he felt a burning compulsion to make the most of this week. He wanted to take time out to see all the things he loved one more—hopefully not for the last—time. Art galleries and museums, the botanical gardens, a ferry ride on the river. A day on Stradbroke Island. Lots of movies.

Books.

Girls…

Yeah…if only he could spend entire days sitting on a park bench watching beautiful women saunter by.

After showering and dressing, he took last night's supper tray to the kitchen and stashed the rinsed crockery in the dishwasher. Then he filled a mug with coffee from a freshly made pot that Emily had left on the bench and went in search of her. He needed to let her know that at least he was fine again. He found her on the balcony, drinking her coffee in a patch of sunlight.

Even when she was wearing a simple white blouse and jeans she looked lovely enough to cause a catch in his throat. Her face, when she saw him, was an instant picture of concern.

'I'm OK,' he told her before she could ask.

Her eyes narrowed in an assessing gaze that clearly said she thought he was lying. But Jude was determined to keep his health problems to himself. It would be bad enough when he had to ring his sister in Sydney to tell her his news.

'Just the same, I am taking a few days off,' he admitted, pulling out one of the balcony chairs and sitting with his legs stretched in front of him while he feasted his gaze on the Brisbane River as it sparkled in the morning sunlight. 'I need a few days away from the computer to give my eyes a rest. I thought I might do a bit of sightseeing to refill the well.'

'What well?' Emily frowned in obvious puzzlement.

'The well of inspiration.' He shot her a smile. 'Finding fresh sights and experiences to keep the muse happy.'

'Oh, yes, I can see how that would help.' Emily looked as if she'd like to quiz him further, but she said instead, 'I'm sure food helps, too. What would you like for breakfast?'

'Emily, you don't have to keep feeding me.'

'I've told you I'm happy to.'

'I know you are.' He rose again, struck by a new restlessness. 'But if we're going to eat breakfast together, we might as well find a café down the street. Broaden our horizons.'

'OK. That sounds good.'

On a wave of generosity, Jude added, 'Afterwards, I'm going on a sightseeing jaunt. You're welcome to join me.'

This time Emily frowned. 'Jude, this isn't a date, is it?'

'Not at all,' he hurried to reassure her. 'I only asked because I know you're at a loose end.'

She didn't respond straight away. She seemed to be weighing up everything in her mind, and Jude was already wishing he'd done the same before jumping in with his rash invitation.

He'd been avoiding his friends because he didn't want them to discover his health problems and start offering sympathy. He should have been equally cautious with Emily. Then again, she'd witnessed two rounds of his headaches now without getting too nosy, and she *was* good company. And he *had* told Alex that he'd keep an eye on her.

On the plus side, if Emily accompanied him, he would

be able to look at her as often and as long as he wanted to. Surely, given his future, getting an eyeful of Emily was the best justification of all.

'All right,' she announced, after frowning out at the view for several long seconds. 'I'll come but on one condition.'

'Ah, yes…your conditions.' Jude nodded. 'We still haven't discussed the terms of your truce, have we?'

'No, we haven't.' She eyed him sternly. 'Obviously, there'll be no more kissing, Jude.'

'Obviously,' he repeated dryly, even though the very thought of kissing her sent a jolt of desire firing low and hot. 'Is that all?'

'I'll keep you informed if I think of anything else.'

'So you're making up the rules as you go?'

'Absolutely.' Her serious expression morphed into an arch smile. 'A girl can't be too careful.'

Nor can a guy, Jude reminded himself.

There was method in her madness, Emily decided. She was worried that Jude was hiding something, that he hadn't told the truth about his trip to the hospital yesterday.

She hoped she was mistaken and that he was fine. It was almost impossible to imagine that such a vital man with the physique of an athlete could be unwell. But after two bouts of terrible headaches, there was clearly something wrong. If for no other reason, she should accompany him for his own good. If he had another bad spell while he was out, he might need her help.

By the end of the morning, she was pleased for other reasons that she'd come along with Jude. It was genuinely fun to visit the museum and the art galleries with such an interesting companion. Jude seemed to know so much, but he shared his knowledge in a way that was entertaining, without arrogance or obvious showing off.

One thing that surprised her was the way he sometimes stopped and just stared at things. It was predictable enough behaviour in art galleries or at the museum, but at other times his attention would be captured by the most unexpected things like branches of a winter-bare tree silhouetted against the noon sky. Sunlight slanting on an ancient carved church door. The sight of a striped deckchair on a rooftop.

Jude seemed to be soaking these scenes in.

He was stopping to stare again now as they walked through a stretch of parkland after a picnic lunch. A white heron was wading in the shallows of a pretty reed-fringed pond and Jude came to a halt to watch it, which might have been fine if his expression hadn't been so disturbingly sad.

Emily wanted to ask him if he was all right, but she knew that would probably annoy him. To distract herself from worrying, she decided that he was imagining a scene for his current story.

'Are you thinking that this bird might be booby-trapped and that it's about to blow up?' she asked.

Jude blinked and looked at her strangely, as if he feared she'd lost her marbles.

'You were staring so hard, Jude. I thought the heron must be inspiring your imagination, and you were thinking up a scene for your book.'

He laughed. *Oh, wow.* He looked so amazingly handsome when he laughed.

'That hadn't occurred to me,' he said and his smiling gaze lingered on her. 'It's not a bad idea. But, as a bird-lover, I've a strict code of ethics. No birds are harmed during the writing of my books.'

Emily grinned. 'Then perhaps there's a beautiful woman trapped inside the body of a heron.'

This time she was rewarded by an extra gleam of appreciation in his eyes, a bright sparkle in the grey depths.

'You're the one with the fabulous imagination, Emily. Perhaps you should be making up stories, too.'

'Not a chance.' There were limits to her imagination.

'Perhaps the heron could be an alien sent to Earth to observe humans,' Jude suggested.

'Yes, or it might have a surveillance device attached.'

He stopped again. The tall white bird was standing on a flat shelf of rock in the middle of the pond. Tall and dignified, its feathers gleamed pure white.

'Or it might just be a beautiful bird fishing in the winter sunshine,' Jude said quietly. 'And we're mere humans admiring the perfect simplicity of nature.'

Something about the way he said this brought a lump to Emily's throat. She felt as if he'd shared an incredibly meaningful moment with her, and she had an absurd impulse to give him a hug, or to slip her arm through his and walk companionably close to his side.

Thank heavens she'd resisted the impulse. Not only would she have shocked Jude, she would have broken her new resolution to toughen up. For a moment there, she'd been carried away by her feelings. She'd felt a deep emotional connection with Jude. But feelings and emotions were highly dangerous. She'd learned the hard way that she couldn't trust them.

All her decisions from now on had to be made with her head, not her heart.

'So what happens first?' Jude asked much later, coming to stand beside Emily at the kitchen bench.

She'd offered to teach him how to cook a stir-fry, as a simple alternative to tinned soup.

This close, however, Emily could smell his aftershave. Fortunately, she resisted the temptation to lean in to the woodsy, masculine scent.

'First we cut the vegetables into thin, even strips.' She wished she felt calmer as she handed him a carrot. Jude, with a knife in one hand and a carrot in the other, looked more attractive than any man should in such a domesticated setting.

She turned her attention to her own chopping board and asked crisply, 'Why don't you tell me about the women in your life?' She needed a reality check. *Now.*

'Why would you want to know about them?'

'I've told you about my disastrous love life, so it's only fair you spill about yours. Is there anyone special?'

Jude didn't answer at first, and Emily began to slice mushrooms with the care of an artist.

Standing beside her, Jude said, 'If I was seeing someone else I wouldn't have kissed you the other night.'

Her knife slipped, almost cutting her thumb. Memories of his kiss flooded her—the taste of his lips, the strength of his arms, the woozy, warm sensation that had flowered inside her.

'It's reassuring to hear that not every man is as sleazy as my two-timing ex,' she said tightly. 'By the way, you need the oil to be really hot before you add the meat.'

She added strips of grain-fed beef to the hot oil in the wok and began to stir them briskly. 'And on that other matter, I'm sure you've had a string of girlfriends, Jude.'

He stopped slicing a capsicum and stood watching her, eyes flashing unreadable sparks. 'Sure, we've established I like girls.'

Emily drew a sharp breath. 'Let me guess. But you're not the marrying kind.'

'That pretty much sums it up.'

'Do you have any special reason for dodging the altar?' Heavens, she couldn't believe she was being so nosy.

Jude's eyebrows lifted as he considered this. 'Perhaps I'm attracted to the wrong kind of girl.'

What a cop-out.

Her lips parted, ready to let fly with a smart retort, but her eyes met Jude's again. Locked in his grey gaze, she felt an unsettling tremor skip down her spine and her desire to be a smart mouth disappeared. Her heart beat strangely fast.

Dismayed by her reaction, she concentrated on adding onion and garlic to the wok. But as she recovered her wits, she felt compelled to ask, 'So what kind of girl is the wrong type for you?'

'You certainly like asking the hard questions.'

'I'm congenitally curious.'

Jude pursed his lips. His grey eyes shimmered. 'OK. My problem is I tend to go for professional women with an independent streak.'

Emily's jaw dropped. 'And that's a problem?'

'Sure.'

'What's wrong with women who are professional and independent?' She prided herself on having both these qualities. Not that her interests were relevant.

Jude was smiling now, as if he knew Emily was digging a very deep hole that she might very soon fall into. He reached for a stick of raw carrot from the pile he'd made. 'In theory, dating career women is fine. But I have a house at Mount Tamborine, and that's rather inconvenient for girlfriends with really important and demanding careers.'

'Such as?'

Good grief. She was asking *way* too many questions, but now she'd started she couldn't stop. It was like trying to stop eating a chocolate bar after just one bite.

Jude's raised eyebrows signalled his amused disbelief. 'You want a list of my girlfriends' careers? Well…let's see. There was Suze, who was an airline pilot, and Keira was an Army doctor, and Gina was a research scientist—'

'OK. I see what you mean,' Emily cut in, suddenly unwilling to listen to his entire list of lovers, even though she most certainly wasn't jealous. 'I guess I can see your problem. Women with those careers would appeal to a thriller writer, but they wouldn't suit a lifestyle tucked away in the mountains and far from a city.'

'That's it in a nutshell.'

Something in his voice made her look up. He was watching her with a mixture of amusement and thoughtfulness that sent her cheeks flaming.

Flustered, she tossed the sliced carrot and capsicum into the stir-fry and refrained from asking any more questions. After she'd added a generous dollop of sweet chilli sauce and stirred it through, their dinner was ready.

A girl with any sense would drop the questions, Emily told herself as they sat down. But she found her mind veering back like a boomerang to the subject of Jude's girlfriends. After her own problems with finding the right partner, she found Jude's apparent lack of success intriguing. He had everything going for him—brains *plus* looks. He was a great kisser, and he was even nice to grandmothers.

What was his fatal flaw?

'I know it's none of my business, Jude.'

'But you're going to ask anyway.'

'Do you mind?'

He shrugged. 'I become quite tolerant with food in my stomach. What do you want to know?'

'I was wondering if you've ever considered moving to the city to fit in with a girlfriend's career.'

It was some time before he spoke. 'I haven't given that serious thought,' he admitted at last. 'But I might, if I found the right girl.'

Emily thought how lucky that right girl would be.

'Then again,' Jude added, 'I might never find her. And who knows how any of us will feel in the future?'

Once again, she caught a shadowy flicker in his eyes. What was it that bothered him? She wished she could ask him about it, but she'd already asked far too many questions.

She drank some wine and said with a rueful smile, 'It seems we have something in common. I'm forever finding myself attracted to the wrong kind of man.'

Leaning back in his chair, Jude watched her through narrowed eyes. 'Have you worked out why?'

'If only I could. I'd give anything to understand why I choose men who'll hurt me.'

'Hurt you?' He looked shocked. 'But surely that doesn't happen every time?'

'Too many times, I'm afraid.'

She sighed, and suddenly she found herself needing to explain. Perhaps it was the relaxing glass of wine, or perhaps she felt more comfortable with Jude now that he'd revealed something about his own dating issues.

She found herself spilling the entire sorry story of her relationship disasters, starting with Dimitri in Melbourne and then Dave on the rodeo circuit.

Surprisingly, Jude was very good at listening—every bit as good as Alex was. Emily went on to tell him about her attempts to take control of her dating.

'You know your problem, don't you?' said Jude.

Unsure how to respond, she simply stared at him.

His mouth quirked into a lopsided smile. 'You're such a stunner, Emily, guys can't help themselves. And on top of that, your job puts you in a position of power, so you attract men with big egos who see you as a trophy.'

'So they didn't really care about *me*, just the way I looked?'

He shrugged his shoulders. 'It happens.'

Jude was probably right, Emily realised, thinking about Michael.

Oh, help. Michael.

For large chunks of today, she'd managed to push him out of her thoughts, but now she was remembering everything. The whole picture of their relationship unrolled in her mind like a tragic movie—the way he'd courted her so persuasively, the lavish gifts he'd bought for her, the late-night phone calls from Adelaide, the South Pacific holiday they'd planned together...

Then the Facebook page...

It was only when Jude reached across the table and squeezed her hand that Emily realised she'd been sitting silent for too long, a glum statue, wrapped in her unhappy memories.

Now, the pressure of Jude's strong, warm fingers wrapped around hers was incredibly comforting.

Perhaps it was a little too comforting. Without warning, all the pain and emotion she'd been holding inside seemed to swell and burst up through her.

Her mouth pulled out of shape as she tried to explain. 'He said he loved me.' It was almost a wail. 'He *told* me he loved me.' Her voice broke on a choking sob.

And then, as if she'd cracked wide open, she began to weep without any hope of stopping.

In a heartbeat, Jude was out of his chair and beside her, wrapping his strong arms around her shaking shoulders.

'I'm s-s-sorry,' she spluttered against his neck.

'Don't be,' he murmured. 'You need to let it out.'

Then he was hugging her and she was out of her chair and clinging to him with her face pressed into his shirt-front, while his arms supported her and he murmured soothing noises into her hair.

It was some time before Emily's sobbing subsided and she was aware of Jude's fingers stroking the back of her neck…gently…so wonderfully gently. Beneath her cheek, his chest was a solid wall of strength, and she thought that being in his arms might very well be the most comforting sensation she'd ever experienced.

She couldn't remember ever weeping all over a man before. She'd always done her weeping after they'd left her.

Now, with some reluctance, but feeling strangely calmer, she lifted her head. 'Thank you,' she said softly, taking a step back out of Jude's embrace. 'I seem to be stretching your hosting duties way beyond reasonable bounds.'

'Emily, holding you in my arms is hardly a chore.'

For a moment she thought he was going to kiss her again. She certainly wouldn't slap him if he did, and when she looked into his eyes she saw a dark grey heat that suggested he knew this.

The air was practically crackling with electricity.

Surely that was dangerous.

They'd both agreed that another kiss mustn't happen. It would be like jumping from the fire back into the frying pan.

She gave a shaky laugh. 'Isn't a crying woman a man's worst nightmare?'

To her surprise, Jude touched her cheek and wiped a

damp tear track with the pad of his thumb. His eyes were serious as he smiled. 'You've been meeting the wrong men.'

'Well, yes, I think we've established that.'

She took a deep, necessary breath, grateful for his understanding, and especially grateful that neither of them had undermined this healing moment with another kissing mistake.

Why let attraction ruin a promising friendship?

'Thanks, Jude. I think it was cathartic to let that out. I must admit I feel much better.'

Quite miraculously better, Emily realised as they carried their dishes to the sink. She could think of Michael now without an accompanying surge of anger and shame. For the first time she could see him clearly for what he was—a silly, weak man who hadn't deserved her love, and who certainly didn't deserve his nice wife and family.

Thank heavens she'd been strong enough to tell him off and to send him packing. She was especially grateful that Michael was fully aware of her disdain for his behaviour.

She felt a new confidence now, a sense that in time she would be able to move on.

Much later, in bed, Emily thought about all of this again calmly. It was rather amazing that she'd come to Brisbane to seek comfort and understanding from Alex, only to receive it from a totally unexpected quarter—her cousin's temporary houseguest.

Jude was such a surprise package. A bit of a tall, dark, handsome mystery, really.

She thought again about the odd moments when she'd caught him looking worried, and she wondered if there was any way she could help, or whether, in fact, it was time for her to leave. She could go and visit Granny Silver for a bit. Perhaps she should suggest it to Jude in the morning? She didn't want to outstay her welcome.

not necessary, but she did guess, what almost made it worse, for a long time she should be dragged to Jude in the recurrent. She only wanted to cement her embryon.

CHAPTER FIVE

EMILY wasn't given the chance to make this suggestion the next morning. Jude jumped the gun.

By the time she came into the kitchen he'd already made breakfast for both of them. A coffee pot was ready on the table, and there were bowls of pink grapefruit sprinkled with brown sugar, with boiled eggs and buttered toast to follow.

'I'm seriously impressed,' she told him. 'Seems you're a man with hidden talents.'

'Needs must,' he countered. 'I've decided to drive home to the mountains today. I have quite a few things to do there, so I wanted an early start.'

'Oh, right. Good idea.' Emily hoped she didn't sound as disappointed as she suddenly felt. Really, this reliance on Jude for company was a worrying trend. For heaven's sake, hadn't she been thinking of moving out today?

As if he'd sensed her disappointment and felt responsible, Jude said, 'You could come with me if you like.'

Emily gulped on the piece of grapefruit she was eating, shocked by the leap of pleasure his suggestion triggered. Not only would she enjoy a drive into the mountains, but she was also curious about Jude's home. And the prospect of another full day in his company was very attractive.

That, however, was the danger.

The more time she spent with Jude, the more she liked him.

She was increasingly confused about her feelings, actually. After Michael, she'd been relieved to meet a man she could be friends with, without the threat of romance. Jude's kiss had been a stumbling block. He'd been on his best behaviour ever since then, yet she was still worried.

Yesterday, she and Jude had drawn quite a lot closer. She'd never experienced anything quite like that conversation in the park, watching the heron. Or the comfort of his hug when she'd had the Michael meltdown.

But there'd also been tummy-tingling thrills that bothered her with mounting frequency, and this was a problem Emily couldn't ignore.

Apart from the slip with the kiss, Jude hadn't made any attempt to attract or seduce her, and yet she was plagued by a sense of building excitement whenever she was with him.

It was quite different from anything she'd experienced before.

She was quite sure that travelling to his mountain retreat would only add to her problems. It was a step too close. Too intimate. She should be pulling back from this man, not drawing closer.

Besides, Jude was probably just being polite with his belated invitation.

'I'm afraid I can't come,' she said carefully. 'I've already made plans for today.'

There was a flash in Jude's eyes that might have been disappointment, or relief.

But his response was cheerful enough. 'That's OK.'

Fortunately, he was too polite to ask what her plans for the day were. She would have been hard pressed to answer him. Perhaps he understood her wariness about getting too close. No doubt he shared her caution.

She wondered if she should mention her plan to leave, but he was keen to be on his way so she decided to leave it till his return.

'Don't hang about here, Jude. I can tidy the kitchen. I might give the apartment a once-over as well.'

'There's no need. I could never keep this apartment up to Alex's spotless standards so I've hired a woman to take care of it. Today's her day. She'll be here about nine.'

With a quick smile, he grabbed an apple for the road. 'I'll see you later then.'

It was the weirdest day for Emily. She knew it was madness to feel so fidgety and *lost* simply because Jude was away for the day. She'd been quite pleased with her idea to clean the apartment as a thank-you present, but if a cleaning woman was on her way there was no point. So, at a total loose end, she caught a bus into the city for a little retail therapy.

By mid-morning, however, she'd only bought another of Jude's books and a beautiful scarf for Granny Silver's birthday. After that, she wandered aimlessly up and down the Queen Street Mall, unable to dredge any further interest in shopping.

In a coffee shop she ordered a latte and sat in a booth by a window, nursing her mug, savouring the coffee's smoothness and its soothing rich flavour. Staring out at the passing faces in the street, she allowed herself, for a fanciful moment, to imagine what it would be like to live with a writer, like Jude, in a secluded mountain hideaway.

Would she miss her job at the bank, or would she jump at the chance to follow her secret yearning to start her own online business?

Her happiness would depend on whether the writer in question had been honest with his feelings and truly loved her.

Whoa. Emily almost spilled her coffee. She couldn't believe she'd allowed her mind to wander into such crazy territory. It was so utterly pathetic.

Clearly, being on leave from work was not good for her.

When her phone rang with a friendly *quack*, she grabbed it from her bag, grateful for the distraction, although a part of her silly brain was instantly hoping that the call was from Jude.

It was from Alex.

'Hi, Emily.' His voice, coming all the way from Germany, sounded wonderfully clear and near. 'How are you?'

'I'm fine, thanks. How lovely to hear from you. How's Frankfurt?'

'Mad. Fascinating. Inspiring.'

'Sounds exciting.'

'It is. Listen, I'm ringing quickly between appointments to find out how Jude is. I could only get a cleaning woman at home.'

'Jude's fine. He's gone home to Mount Tamborine for the day.'

'Really? That's fantastic. So it's nothing serious?'

'Sorry, Alex. I don't know what you mean.' Tendrils of alarm snaked through Emily's insides. She gripped the phone so tightly she almost crushed it. 'What are you talking about?'

Jude stood on the deck at the back of his house, drawing deep lungfuls of fresh, sparkling air as he stared at the breathtaking view of lush rainforest-covered mountains.

He was glad he'd come home. There'd been a risk of another headache attack on the winding roads, but he actually felt fine, and now he took a long soul-wrenching look at the place where he'd made his home. He never failed to be uplifted by this majestic scenery.

There was something almost spiritual about its beauty. So much grandeur in the tumbling steepness of the hillsides. So many shades of green in the tree canopies and the undergrowth of lianas and ferns and palms. Even now, in the middle of the day, a wispy veil of white mist drifted around the tallest peaks.

At the thought that he might never see any of this beauty again he felt...*gutted.*

Gutted in the worst sense of the word. Empty. Bleeding. Dead.

Hell.

What would you think of me now, Dad?

His father had always been so stoical about illness. Jude would never forget the day his barrister dad collapsed after being away in Sydney all week for an important court case.

Quite late on a Friday evening, Max Marlowe had come into the living room, tossed his leather briefcase onto a chair, turned to the sideboard to pour a Scotch, then pitched forward onto the Oriental carpet. It turned out that he'd burst his appendix and nearly died.

Later, the family learned that Max had been in pain all week, but he wouldn't allow anything to interfere with winning his court case. He was damned if he'd complain about a bit of bellyache.

'Silly old fool,' Jude's mother had said.

Jude had searched her eyes for a glimmer of fondness, anything to counter her scoffing tone, and he'd been mortified when he hadn't found it.

A groan broke from him now. He knew it didn't really make sense but, more than ever now, it felt important to be as tough as his old man. He had to shake off his negative thinking.

Closing his eyes, he centred his thoughts on the sounds around him, focusing on each bird call that came to him. Some were delicate and bell-like, others sharp and strident—the calls of the whipbird, the catbird, the rifle bird and the trillers…the overhead screech of a flight of rainbow lorikeets. And, way below in the valley, the distant sound of a creek cascading over rocks.

He tried to take comfort from this… Even if he couldn't see, he would still be able to hear. All of this. Every musical note.

But somehow…

It wasn't enough…

Damn. He was being morbid again. No doubt, he'd be in a better mood if Emily were here to cheer him up.

At the thought of Emily, Jude's grip on the railing tightened. Against reason, against his best intentions, there was a very good chance he was falling for her. Seemed crazy, really, that he could feel this way on the strength of one brief kiss.

Well…one kiss and several days of her company and of feeling at ease to a degree that was quite extraordinary. Then again, perhaps he'd simply been intoxicated—as had others before him—by her smile and her dancing blue eyes and the fiery silk of her hair.

It was a miracle that he hadn't kissed her again last night. As he'd held her in his arms while she wept over that lowlife ex, Jude had drawn on willpower he hadn't known he possessed. Which suggested that there was more going on than his physical need for her.

Emotions were involved.

A jagged sigh escaped him. He couldn't have chosen a worse time for emotional entanglement. There was no way it could work. Given Emily's history with men, she was sensibly avoiding new relationships, so even if he was totally well she wouldn't want to get involved.

Bottom line...he wasn't well, so the option for involvement wasn't even there.

Besides, with his lifestyle he had nothing to offer a career-focused bank manager. Which meant he was facing his old problem, with a whole new set of health problems on top of it.

The reality was—and here was the biggie—if he lost his sight he would not tie himself to any woman. He'd buy a tape recorder and the dreaded voice recognition software and he'd spend his days dictating his books into a machine.

The thought chilled him.

He loved writing, loved it with a passion that he rarely admitted to anyone, and he'd fought hard to make this career his.

His parents had been dead against it. They were determined that he would study Law, but while Jude was fascinated by the cause and effects of crime, he had no desire to follow in his parents' footsteps.

No chance of happiness there.

Naturally, they believed he'd wasted his university years, studying Arts with no clear career path, and they'd given him little support during his years of hard slog and rejection while he was trying to find a publisher—writing long into the night and working as a newspaper reporter by day.

His satisfaction had come from loving his work, but could he still love it if he had to dictate his stories?

He hated the idea. He was a writer, not a speaker, and while some writers were also great oral storytellers, Jude knew he didn't share that talent.

Hell, how would he cope if the writing dried up?

Another chill crept over his skin like so many spiders. Giving the railing an angry thump, he turned and went inside the house.

Later, in a calmer mood, he made a final tour of his home, taking mental snapshots of favourite items and rooms. He wondered if he should tell Emily, when he got back, about his impending operation. If she was going to stay on in Alex's apartment, it was only fair that she understood what was going on.

Perhaps he should suggest that she move somewhere else—to her grandmother's beach house maybe.

But when he imagined trying to tell her—trying to introduce the subject of hospitals and operations and the possibility of personal disaster—he recoiled from dumping all that doom and gloom on her when the poor girl was struggling with her own problems.

Why talk of hospitals and illness when all he really wanted was to make virile, wild, *healthy* love to her?

And, knowing what he did of Emily, she would probably feel involved in his problems. She would want to help him, to play nursemaid or hold his hand.

Hell. He would never want that. His masculine pride bucked and roared at the very thought.

Emily was on tenterhooks as she waited for Jude to come back that evening. She'd been totally rattled after Alex's phone call and his news that Jude was having medical tests for a potentially serious problem.

Obviously, Jude had avoided telling her the truth about his headaches. Which was fair enough—his health was his private business—but if he was in trouble, Emily wanted to help in any way she could.

She decided she needed to appear calm and unconcerned—Jude would hate any sign of fuss—so she'd gone to a fair amount of trouble to set the stage for his return.

Now, at six-thirty, he was due at any moment and she was dressed in a soft grey tunic over black leggings and sitting curled in an armchair, trying to look serene, with a book in her lap, although she was too keyed up to actually read it. She'd turned all the lamps on to show off the apartment at its gleaming, newly cleaned best, and she'd arranged a bunch of sunflowers in a tall vase on the coffee table to help the place to look extra cheerful. Upbeat mood music played softly.

Best of all, she'd found a wonderful recipe for Greek roast chicken and potatoes with masses of lemon and mustard and garlic, and now wonderful, tummy-tempting aromas wafted from the kitchen.

Emily thought she was waiting patiently enough, but when the phone rang her heart almost flew out of her chest. She jumped to her feet.

Calm down, she warned herself. It was probably just Alex ringing back, wanting an update on Jude, but she wouldn't have news until Jude arrived. She took a steadying breath as she picked up the receiver.

'Emily.' It was Jude's voice. 'How are you?'

'I…I'm fine.' Why was he telephoning? She'd been expecting him to walk through the door at any moment. 'Where are you?'

'I'm still at my place at Mount Tamborine. I'm afraid something's come up, and I need to stay on here for a few days to sort it out.'

A few days!

A flood of disappointment swamped Emily. She'd been so on edge, so waiting for his return, so anxious to have everything perfect for him. He'd been incredibly understanding and kind to her, and if he was in trouble she'd wanted to return the favour.

Clearly, he had other ideas.

'Emily, are you there?'

'Yes.' She gave a little shake, trying to throw off her disappointment. 'I'm sorry to hear that something's come up. I hope you're all right, Jude.'

'Yes, I'm fine.'

Yes, well, she now knew that this was a lie. 'You might need to ring Alex then,' she said a shade too crisply. 'It would be good if you could reassure him. He called here today because he's worried about you.'

'Really? All right. I'll give him a call.'

'Jude, I'm worried, too,' she couldn't help adding. 'Alex said you were having medical tests to find out what's causing your headaches.'

She thought she heard a sigh on the other end of the line. 'I realise it's none of my business…'

'I don't want to bother you with that stuff, Emily.' Jude said this firmly, as if to ward off any argument. 'You're on holiday and you should be having fun. Honestly, I'm OK. I have everything under control.'

She knew it was unreasonable to view this as another rejection. Jude wasn't a close friend. She couldn't expect him to confide in her or share his troubles, even though she'd done exactly that with him. But she didn't enjoy having her wonderful plans to support him come to nothing.

'Let me know if there's anything I can do to help,' she said glumly. 'Anything at all.'

'I will, Emily. If I need you, I'll be in touch. I have your mobile number, but hopefully you won't hear from me until it's all over.'

All over. That had to mean some kind of medical procedure, surely? An operation? Clearly, Jude was distancing himself from her, and Emily couldn't believe she felt so bad. It was ridiculous to feel rejected by Jude Marlowe when she'd only known him for...how long? Five? Six days?

She had to toughen up, had to show the grit that Jude's heroines had in spades. She cranked her features into a wobbly smile. 'You're certainly going to miss a darn good meal tonight, Jude. Speaking of which, I'd better go. Don't want to let it burn.'

Then, because she had to, she added more gently, 'Take care, won't you?'

After she hung up, she went to the kitchen and turned the oven off, her enthusiasm for the new recipe having fizzled to nil.

Jude was tucking a water bottle into a side pocket in his backpack when he heard the sound of a car in his driveway. Crossing to the window, he scowled at the vehicle, a bright red sedan he didn't recognise. The last thing he wanted was to play host right now, when he was about to set out on a hiking trip.

From his vantage point, he had a clear view through the car's windscreen, and a familiar shimmer of red-gold made his heart thud. Hard. His throat constricted. What was Emily doing here?

He watched her climb out of the driver's seat and then lean in to haul out a cooler bag. She was wearing a longish grey top over black leggings and slim-fitting knee-high black leather boots. She looked stunning, as if she'd just stepped off a plane from Milan or Paris.

Damn. Jude hadn't picked her for a busybody or, worse, a stalker. He wasn't sure he could handle this.

Her footsteps sounded on the stone path and he set his mouth into a grim scowl as he went to open the door.

'Hi, Jude.' Emily looked up from beneath long lashes and no doubt caught the surliness in his expression. Her face tightened. 'Before you get mad, Alex asked me to come to see you.'

Jude found this hard to believe. When he'd returned Alex's call, he'd instructed his agent to keep his condition confidential. He'd always believed that Alex was trustworthy, which was why he was one of the very few people Jude felt he could open up to.

'Alex kept his word to you,' Emily said next, as if she could read his mind. 'He hasn't told me anything he shouldn't have. I still have no idea what your problem is, and that's fair enough. I don't want to pry.'

Lifting her face, she met his gaze directly. 'But Alex is worried, Jude. He's very worried about you being up here on your own and…well…he asked me…actually, he more or less begged me to pop by, to check.'

Jude hadn't shifted from the doorway and Emily was still standing on the top step, fiddling with the strap of the cooler bag.

'As you can see, I'm perfectly fine.' He gave a bored shrug. 'I'm sorry, you've come all this way for nothing.'

Her blue eyes narrowed. Tipping her head slightly to one side, she regarded him with a surprisingly cool and measuring stare. Jude wondered if this was the look she gave her clients when they came to her bank, hoping to pull the wool over her eyes.

'Jude Marlowe,' she said in a quiet, no nonsense tone, 'you and I both know you're not fine. Alex believes your problem is quite serious, so forget the tough-guy act.'

Squaring her shoulders, she looked as serious as a hanging judge. 'Alex is your close friend and the poor fellow's stuck on the other side of the world, worried and helpless. Apart from that, it's only common sense that you shouldn't be alone. If you have one of your headaches, you'd be in-capacitated up here.'

Jude flinched at the word *incapacitated*. 'I'm not that bad.'

Emily let out a noisy sigh. 'Why do you have to be so stubborn?'

He was certain she was about to deliver a lecture but, without warning, her face seemed to crumple and the hard glare in her eyes softened to concern. 'I'm worried about you, too,' she said in a small voice.

Jude struggled to resist. He'd been determined to keep Emily well clear of his troubles, although, in truth, he wanted nothing more than to haul her into his arms and to kiss her soft trembling mouth. Kiss her for a month. He'd been thinking of little else for days. Right now, he was imagining her long slim legs wrapped around his waist.

With a huge mental effort, he pushed his crazy desires where they belonged—clear out of his head.

But that still left him torn between two difficult choices. He could play the jerk and send Emily packing—or he could put himself through hell by inviting her into his home, *without* following through on his lustful urges.

He found himself apologising. 'I'm sorry. I don't want everyone worrying.' And then he took two steps back and stifled a sigh. 'You'd better come inside.'

'Thank you,' she said with dignity. She held up the cooler bag. 'By the way, I've brought you that chicken dinner you missed out on last night.'

Emily drew a deep, shaky breath as she followed Jude into his house.

Alex had warned her that Jude was fiercely indepen-dent and that she might have a battle on her hands. He was dead right. But she had to admit Jude didn't *look* as if there was anything badly wrong with him. He was as strong and sexy-looking as ever, and it was very easy to believe he was fine, especially here against the backdrop of his incredibly beautiful home.

He led her into a large open-plan area with acres of polished timber floors and massive uncurtained walls of glass that looked out into the rainforest. At one end of the space a sitting area held sleek leather couches grouped around an open fire.

The dining area was defined by a long Viking-style table, and beyond that the kitchen comprised solid timber benches and gleaming top-of-the-range stainless steel appliances.

Jude was certainly not a writer who starved in a garret, and he clearly had very good taste, or at least he'd employed someone with very good taste to design his home and to decorate its interior.

'This house is amazing,' Emily told him. 'It's absolutely gorgeous.'

'Thanks. I'm glad you like it.' He spoke politely and he was no longer scowling, but he wasn't quite his usual relaxed self. 'Can I make you a cuppa?' he asked, already heading for the kitchen.

'Only if you're having one. I hope I haven't interrupted anything important.'

He shook his head, not quite meeting her gaze, then turned on the kettle. 'Tea? Coffee?'

'I'll have tea, please. Do you mind if I take a look around?'

'Feel free.'

As Jude dropped teabags into mugs, Emily wandered. There were piles of books, magazines and newspapers scattered about the place, so it wasn't as tidy as Alex's apartment, and she guessed that Jude's freezer was stacked to the brim with frozen store-bought dinners, while his pantry would be crowded with tins of soup.

But, as a living space, his home had *wonderful* vibes. She loved all the natural timber and the huge walls of glass letting the forest in. It was like living in a tree house, looking out at the tall, straight trunks of massive trees, at fallen logs covered in moss and native orchids, and beautiful lush tree ferns.

This wonderful environment was also home to the birds Jude loved. Right now, Emily could see a flock of gloriously coloured rainbow lorikeets feeding on rainforest berries.

She stood, drinking in the beauty, thinking how creatively inspiring it must be for Jude to wake up each morning to this. Meeting him in the city, she would never have guessed…

'Here's your tea.'

She turned to find him standing behind her with their mugs.

'Thank you.' She sent him a smile as she took the red-and-white-striped mug he offered. 'I'm in awe, Jude. This is so beautiful, I feel like whispering, as if I'm in church.'

He smiled—for the first time, a proper, skin crinkling around his eyes smile. 'I know what you mean. It still gets me that way.'

As they headed for the sofas, her attention was caught by groupings of photos on a wall. A happy group shot of family or friends, a couple of beach holiday snaps, and another, obviously taken in an alpine region with people in bright-coloured mountaineering gear and parkas standing around several international flags.

'I can pick you out easily, in all of them,' she said.

Jude looked a bit younger and leaner and more suntanned, but it was impossible to mistake his dark hair, broad shoulders and arresting smile. In the alpine shot, he had his arm looped around the shoulders of an attractive athletic-looking woman with long dark hair.

'Are you a mountain climber?' Emily asked.

'Strictly an amateur, but I've climbed quite a few interesting peaks around the world.'

She bit down on her lip to stop herself from asking about the girl, who was none of her business.

About to turn away from the photos, her attention was caught by a framed photo of a young couple smiling and posing with what looked, from the equipment, like a rescue team. Again, Jude was included and there was a printed caption beneath the photo.

To our rescuers...we will never forget...from Tim and Jill Martin.

Emily blinked in surprise. 'So you not only climb mountains, but you're a rescuer as well.'

Wow. She was looking at Jude and his house with new eyes, which was possibly why, when she glanced back to the kitchen, she now noticed a backpack on the floor, propped against a cupboard. And then she realised Jude was wearing hiking boots.

'You don't have to stand about,' he said, waving his mug of tea towards the sofas. 'Come and sit down.'

Frowning, Emily disregarded the invitation. 'Were you about to set off now? Up the mountain?'

He shrugged and looked away. 'It's no big deal.'

'But were you?' she persisted. 'You've got your backpack ready and you're wearing boots. Were you planning to hike?'

He looked down at the mug cradled in his big hands. 'I was about to head off to Sunset Ridge. It's something I'd like to do before—' his throat rippled '—before I go into hospital.'

Emily gulped as she heard the word *hospital*. A hundred questions clamoured to be answered but she pushed them down. He would tell her if and when he wanted to.

'So the walk is really important to you?' she suggested.

Instead of answering her directly, Jude pointed to the view through one of the huge picture windows. 'See that ridge up there?'

Emily looked up to the outline of the mountains, solid and dark against the pale afternoon sky.

'Best view of the sunset you'll ever see is from up there,' Jude said quietly. 'One of the main reasons I bought this land is because it's the closest freehold to that ridge.'

'I guess that answers my question.' Following his gaze, Emily gave a slow nod. 'This walk is definitely important to you.' Her sideways glance met Jude's. 'But is it wise to go up there on your own?'

He was staring at her now, his grey eyes faintly amused and yet also challenging. 'Are you offering to join me?'

A pulse beat at the base of her throat. 'Are you inviting me to join you?'

'I guess I am,' he said with a slow, cautious smile.

CHAPTER SIX

EMILY'S first reaction to Jude's invitation was excitement, but she had to be practical. 'We wouldn't get back till dark, would we?' She was returning to Brisbane tonight, and she didn't like the idea of having to drive back down the unfamiliar mountain road in the dark.

'You'd need to stay the night, of course,' Jude said deadpan.

Talk about a turnaround. Five minutes earlier, he'd been determined to throw her out. Now, a cautious, untrusting voice whispered a warning to Emily. She found Jude far too attractive for her own good. Now, in this setting, he was more attractive than ever.

Problem was, she'd promised Alex she would keep an eye on him. How could she let him go traipsing up a mountain alone?

'I brought a pair of jeans and a sweater with me, but I don't think I have any suitable shoes,' she told him. She also wasn't sure she'd be able to keep up with an experienced mountain climber.

Jude ran an assessing gaze over her fashionable boots. 'I might have walking boots that'll fit you.'

'From an old girlfriend?'

His response was a slow tilted smile. 'Yes. The Army

doctor, Keira, comes up here sometimes when she's on leave, but she wouldn't mind if you borrowed her shoes.'

Emily couldn't help feeling curious about what appeared to be an ongoing relationship with this former girlfriend. Not that it was any of her business.

They finished their tea, and then went downstairs to the garage where a couple of mountain bikes were stacked against a wall and a large green canoe was suspended from the roof. Jude opened a side door to reveal shelves stacked with backpacks, coiled ropes and other camping and outdoor gear. There was also a pair of women's hiking boots, which he handed to Emily.

'Try these, Cinderella.'

Conscious that he was watching her every movement, she sat on the stairs, took off her black boots and tried on the ones belonging to his girlfriend.

She reserved judgement until she'd tied up the laces and was standing, wriggling her toes. 'They feel fine.' She took a few steps. 'They're a good fit, actually.'

She sent him a surprised smile and Jude smiled back. It was their first shared smile since she'd arrived and it made her feel much happier than it should have.

But then she remembered the boots' owner. Obviously, Jude and this Keira were still quite close, and for a fanciful moment Emily imagined the boots were beginning to pinch her.

But they were fine, really, an uncannily good fit—and the hike wasn't long or particularly demanding. Although it was rather dark inside the rainforest and there was the occasional slippery patch on the track, the undergrowth wasn't thick, so, apart from dodging buttress roots and the occasional wait-a-while vine, it was fairly easy-going.

Jude made it look easy, of course, and Emily suspected that he'd slowed down for her. If there was a rocky creek to be crossed, or a mossy log to clamber over, he was always ready with a strong hand to help her. She wished she didn't enjoy those brief moments of contact quite so much.

Even discounting the pleasure of Jude's company, she genuinely enjoyed the hike. As a former dancer, she was fit and she loved any form of physical exercise that didn't involve throwing or catching a ball. And who didn't love a rainforest? Beauty abounded every step of the way, and always in the background there was the music of endless bird calls. Looking up, she was rewarded by bright glimpses of blue sky or golden sunlight streaming through the dense green canopy.

As they neared the top, the thick forest gradually opened out into sparser eucalypt trees, and then finally they were on a ridge.

Emily stood, breathing in the pure, clean mountain air. She opened her mouth to speak, but then she changed her mind as she realised that *wow* was totally inadequate. In fact, there wasn't any word she could think of that would do justice to this spectacular view to the west, with descending mountains and ridges as far as the eye could see.

After a bit, she said simply, 'Thanks for letting me come, Jude.'

He smiled, and there was a heart-stopping softness in his eyes that made her feel, in that moment, that they might have been the only two people on the planet.

'There's a seat along here.' His voice brought her back to earth and she followed him along the ridge till they reached a shelf of rock.

Indeed it made a very comfortable seat, smooth and warmed by the sun, with another smooth rock wall behind it forming a backrest.

'Definitely dress-circle seats for a sunset,' she said, looking out at the sky, already growing pink in the west, while a pair of huge wedge-tailed eagles circled and rolled on the air currents above the valley.

Jude handed her a water bottle and they sat quenching their thirst and taking in the spectacle. Emily asked him about his climbing experiences and he told her about his skyliner friends—fellow bush-walkers who added an extra challenge to their hiking by not sticking to the easy routes.

'We follow the tops of the ridges,' he explained. 'Any obstacles like gorges and fast-running mountain streams or cliff faces are simply part of the fun.'

She thought it was a very fitting activity for a somewhat reclusive thriller writer. The more she discovered about Jude, the more she was fascinated by him, and she was surprised that at least one of his former girlfriends hadn't been tempted into adjusting her lifestyle to blend more easily with his.

Or hadn't that been an option?

Then she forgot about his social life as the sun began to bleed liquid colour across the western sky. They stopped talking and simply watched in hushed awe as the heavens were stained with pink and orange deepening to crimson, and clouds were rimmed with bright shimmering gold.

It was so beautiful, they watched until the light began to fade. Emily stole a glance in Jude's direction, wondering if they should leave before it got too dark. Then she saw how unbearably sad he looked.

It was the same lost look she'd seen when he was watching the heron.

Perhaps worse. Such a depth of despair that she was shocked to the soles of her borrowed boots.

She wasn't sure if he was in pain again, or if he was worrying about his future. And then—oh, God—she almost fell off the rock as a worse thought struck. Had the doctors given him really terrible news?

'Jude,' she said softly. 'Are you OK?'

He blinked and the sadness evaporated. 'I'm fine,' he said. 'Why?'

'You were looking a bit grim.' She tried to make her voice light.

He sighed, then let out a soft chuckle. 'One way or another, you're going to get it out of me, aren't you?'

'Only if you really want to tell me.' She hugged her knees. 'I know we only met a week ago, but I think we've become pretty good friends in that short time. I know you've really helped me, and I'd like to think that I could be there for you, if you needed a friend.'

His gaze was fixed on the water bottle he was holding. 'I do appreciate your concern, Emily.' He continued to stare at the bottle, then he closed its lid with an emphatic snap, and took a deep breath as if he'd made a decision.

'I have to have an operation,' he told her flatly. 'There's a benign tumour pressing on my optic nerve, so there's a chance that I may lose my sight.'

No.

Oh, God, no.

Never in her wildest dreams had Emily imagined anything this awful.

Her throat was choked by a knot of pain. Her eyes stung. She wanted to cry—except that crying was the very worst thing she could do in front of Jude. He'd probably held back from telling her because he didn't want a sobfest making everything worse.

Jude…might go blind.

How truly frightening for him.

Suddenly, the more puzzling aspects of his recent behaviour began to make sense—the trips to the art galleries, and those unexpected moments when he'd stopped and simply stared at a tree or a bird—and now, at this sunset.

He'd been trying to capture those images, to hold them in his memory. All this time he'd been dealing with the terrifying prospect of blindness, and yet he'd said nothing to her. Instead, he'd listened to *her* silly problems with an ex-boyfriend and offered her comfort.

Oh, Jude...

Emily had never felt such a storm of emotions. Her desire to be careful was drowned by the overwhelming force of her feelings. All of which centred on Jude. Feelings deep and profound, and more genuine than anything she'd felt before.

She wanted to take him into her arms, to hold him against her heart. Wanted to be with him. For him. In any way he wanted.

Gulping back her tears, she slipped an arm around his shoulders. 'I'm sure there's a very good chance that everything will be fine.'

'Yeah. I'm thinking positively.' He gave her hand a squeeze. 'But this will get you into trouble.'

'Trouble?'

'Or it will get *me* into trouble.' He slanted her a smile. 'Just warning you. If you stay this close, I'll end up kissing you.'

Emily felt a jolt so strong she almost flew off the mountaintop. In this setting...with the sunset and the emotional wallop of his sad news...a kiss had never felt more necessary.

'If you do kiss me, I promise not to hit you.'

To her relief, Jude didn't stop to ask for further clarification. He gathered her in and the next moment they were kissing. They simply flowed together, as if their bodies had minds of their own. As if this was meant to happen.

She'd never known a kiss quite like it, hadn't known a kiss could be so moving. So sad. So blistering and sweet and healing. So full of heart and soul. Earthy, and filled with hungry need. She wound her arms around Jude's neck, needing to press closer, craving contact with every inch of him. Her insides caught fire, and she might have burned to ashes in his arms.

He suddenly went very still.

She heard him draw a deep shuddering breath.

'Oh, God, Emily.' He was breathing rapidly. 'This is crazy. I'm so sorry.'

'I'm not.'

'Emily.' Her name was uttered softly—half rebuke, half prayer.

'Don't start talking about mistakes, Jude. It was an emotional moment.' *Life-changing.*

'No doubt about that.' He touched her cheek just once, then pulled his hand away quickly. 'But this is my problem. You mustn't get too involved.'

Too late. I'm involved. So deeply it's scary.

Already Jude was reaching for the backpack, and his face was hidden in the gathering darkness. 'There's always going to be temptation when a man and a woman are alone, but this is the very worst time for either of us to get involved.'

So sensible. Now he sounded like a parent.

Worse…he was right. He was about to undergo surgery, touch-and-go surgery with potentially disastrous results. And Emily had made so many mistakes with men she ought to know better. She certainly shouldn't have made a rule about no kissing and then promptly broken it.

But wasn't this also a time when Jude really needed a caring and loving someone in his life?

'I hope you'll at least allow me to be a friend,' she said,

flashing a brave smile. 'If nothing else, I could be Alex's stand-in.'

He looked at her for the longest time, as if he was giving this serious thought. But all he said was, 'We should be getting back.'

True. It was getting darker and colder by the minute, and this was neither the time nor the place to try to persuade Jude that he needed her, especially when she'd come to the mountains uninvited and invaded his privacy.

'Will we be able to find our way back to the house in the dark?'

'Sure.' From his pack, Jude produced little torches for them to strap around their heads, rather like miners' lights. As they set off, the narrow beams proved wonderfully effective, leaving their hands free to push vines out of the way, or for Jude to take Emily's hand to help her over rough bits, which he needed to do frequently.

The constant contact didn't help her to calm down.

It was quite cold by the time they reached the house and Jude was pleased to hurry inside and busy himself with lighting the fire, while Emily reheated her chicken dish. In no time the flames were crackling in the grate and the rich aroma of lemon-infused chicken and potatoes was wafting from the oven.

Jude drew the curtains, making the dark forest retreat, and the house became warm and cosy. And intimate. Dangerously so.

Obviously he had very poor self-control when Emily was around. The merest glimpse of her set his heart leaping. He wanted to stare and stare at her. To touch. And to taste her. Wanted to lose himself in her.

He'd almost kissed her senseless on the mountain this evening. It was a miracle he'd found the strength to pull back. If only he hadn't weakened and invited her to stay here overnight. They needed the no kissing rule more than ever now.

He didn't want his name added to the list of men who'd hurt her.

Apart from enjoying the Greek chicken, Jude seemed rather distracted. After dinner, when he and Emily sat on the sofa in front of the fire, he was careful to keep his distance.

And a very good thing, too. Emily knew she'd been carried away by the sunset and the flood of emotions that had come with hearing Jude's diagnosis. Now that she was calmer, she knew he'd been sensible to re-establish their boundaries. Friendships were so much clearer and safer than romantic entanglements.

If they stuck to friendship, hearts wouldn't be broken, lives wouldn't be turned upside down and everyone would remain happy. It was actually a relief to have this sorted in her head.

It left her free to concentrate on practical considerations, like Jude's impending trip to hospital.

'Who's going to look after you, after you leave hospital?' she asked him now. 'Do you have family you can call on? Are your parents still alive?'

'My folks were both killed in a plane crash in China ten years ago.'

'Gosh. How awful.'

'It was terrible,' Jude agreed. 'But in some ways I think my father wouldn't have minded going quickly like that. He couldn't stand being ill. Saw it as a character flaw. I know he would have hated growing weak or decrepit with old age.'

A log on the fire made a loud popping sound, and Emily

watched a little spray of sparks as she digested what Jude had just told her. Perhaps his father's attitude explained why Jude was so stoical about his condition.

'Is there anyone else in your family?'

'My sister, Charlotte, in Sydney.' As soon as he mentioned her name his face softened. 'I've told her what's happening, of course, and she wants to help, but she has three young children, so I don't think she'll be able to get away for long.'

'So you—'

'I have plenty of friends. But I don't expect I'll need help. I'm sure I'll be fine.'

'It's such a pity Alex is away. He's never happier than when he's looking after someone.'

Jude smiled. 'That's why he's such a great agent.'

'You'll let me help, won't you?'

His smile faded. 'I'd rather you didn't.'

'Why?' It was impossible to keep the hurt from her voice.

'I'd rather get through this on my own.'

She bit down hard on her lip to stop herself from pleading. After all, a girl had her pride.

Quickly, she changed the subject. 'This must be the worst part—waiting for it all to be over.'

'If Alex had his way, I would have kept busy working— writing right up until they wheeled me into Theatre.'

She sent an eye-rolling smile towards the ceiling. 'This is one occasion where I can't agree with Alex.'

'So how do you think I should be spending my time?'

'Doing exactly what you've been doing. Seeking out your favourite sights, storing up memories.'

Jude's eyes widened. 'You've seen through my scheme?'

'Well…I assume you've been taking another look at your favourite things, like the art galleries and that heron in the park, and the sunset.' She hurried to add, 'Not that I think you'll need the memories, Jude. I'm sure you're going to be fine, but it's like having—' She paused, hunting for words.

'An insurance policy?'

'Exactly. Or backup for your computer.'

She wondered if Jude had included pretty women on his list of favourite things. But it wasn't a question she could ask, especially now, when his smile morphed into thin-lipped grimness and he kept his gaze fixed on the fire.

At midnight, Jude lay alone in the dark with his eyes closed, thinking about Emily.

Emily, Emily, Emily...

She was becoming a dangerous obsession.

He let his mind drift back to the first time he'd seen her when he'd opened the door to Alex's apartment and he'd found her standing there, dressed in her lovely white coat and long, sexy boots. Her bright red hair had tumbled about her shoulders like a fiery river and her blue eyes had sparkled and he'd forgotten how to breathe.

Her loveliness eclipsed any masterpiece in an art gallery, was more exciting than any magnificent sunset. And this evening when he'd kissed her he'd been consumed by disastrous longing.

Now, the longing wouldn't leave him. Emily was lying in another room, mere metres away, and he was torturing himself with fantasies of going to her.

He couldn't.

He mustn't.

He had too many freaking question marks hanging over his future.

* * *

They drove back to Brisbane in separate vehicles. Emily had offered to drive Jude in her hire care because she was worried he might develop a headache on the way down the mountain, but he'd politely refused and she knew she'd offended his masculine pride. She played the radio the whole way to distract herself from worrying.

As soon as they were back at the apartment, he promptly told her he was heading out. 'Just grabbing a few things for the hospital stay,' he called over his shoulder.

'Don't forget to put pyjamas on your shopping list.'

He turned back to her. 'Pyjamas?'

'Sleepwear, Jude. A two-piece garment. Top and bottom, usually matching.'

'Why are you suddenly worried about my sleepwear?'

His amused and glittering gaze held her trapped, and she had to swallow before she could answer.

'I'm not normally interested in what you wear to bed.' *Liar.* 'But I thought your holey T-shirts might frighten the nurses.'

He responded with a huffing sigh. 'Of course. Thanks for reminding me.'

After Jude had gone, Emily rang Granny Silver. She just had to talk to someone, and she knew her grandmother wasn't a gossip.

'Darling,' her granny soothed. 'I'm so sorry to hear such bad news, but the doctors are so clever these days. I'm sure Jude will be fine.'

'I know. I keep telling myself that. I just wish I was like you or Alex. You're so good at helping people in difficult times.'

There was an unexpected chuckle on the end of the line.

'What's so funny?'

'I'm sure Jude would much rather have your company, than either mine or Alex's.'

'I've already told you, Granny. Jude and I are just friends. Quite new friends at that.' Emily had been working hard to remind herself of this, and it helped to say it out loud.

'Well, yes...I'm sure that's sensible, Emily, given everything that Jude has ahead of him.'

'But I feel so helpless. I wish I could think of wise and comforting things to say, or really practical ways to help.'

'You worry too much, dear. You have oodles of empathy. You put it into practice every day in your work. That's why you make such sound decisions for your clients. You just need to put yourself in Jude's shoes. Follow your instincts and I'm sure you'll work out the best way to keep his spirits up.'

'All right. Thanks. Follow my instincts. I'll hold that thought.'

CHAPTER SEVEN

FOR Jude's last night at home he invited Emily to join him at one of Brisbane's classiest restaurants.

This didn't surprise her as much as it would have a week ago. She and Jude had spent a great deal of time together in the past few days and she couldn't help feeling secretly pleased that he sought her company, even though many of his friends had rung him after they'd received urgent but cryptic messages from Alex.

It appeared, however, that Jude was more comfortable spending time with a relative stranger during these pre-surgery days than with old friends. He seemed to hate having to discuss his illness with these people when they rang.

Emily wasn't quite sure what to make of this. She guessed that Jude saw illness as a weakness, just as his father had. He would rather hide than accept people's sympathy. So he was happy just to spend time with her, no doubt because she was already in the know and didn't need to ask more questions.

Together, they'd spent a day on Stradbroke Island and they'd stood on Point Lookout, watching whales frolic; they'd been to a couple of movies, spent an afternoon scouring Alex's bookshelves and reading sections of books aloud to each other, spent a rainy afternoon making an elaborately layered lasagne.

There'd been no more kissing, which Emily knew was wise, given what loomed ahead for Jude. But they'd become quite close in an amazingly short time. There was something very *simpatico* about their tastes. If Emily ignored the silly tugs of longing that kept getting in the way, she very much enjoyed just being Jude's friend.

Tonight, however, she was very tense. She particularly wanted this final hospital-eve to be special. Hoping to look her best, she'd bought a very expensive dress in deep-chocolate silk.

'Good heavens,' Jude said when he saw her. 'Now *that* is a sight for sore eyes.'

Emily almost cried. 'How can you joke about it?'

'I'm not joking,' he said with a dry smile. 'The dress is gorgeous.'

Just the same, his half-joking comment about sights for sore eyes lit a tiny light-bulb idea. All week, she'd been thinking about her grandmother's comment. *You just need to put yourself in Jude's shoes.* Emily had been trying to think of a really unique and fun surprise that he'd like.

No, I couldn't. I couldn't possibly.

Just the same, a daunting but intriguing idea simmered at the back of her thoughts while they took their time over their delicious three-course meal, savouring the food and never once talking about hospitals or illness. Or relationships.

It was surprising how many other topics they could find—Jude's theories about space travel, Emily's thoughts on the global financial crisis, his ideas for future books, her dream of an online retail business.

Throughout the meal, Jude hardly noticed the restaurant's famous view of the city's lights. He was too busy watching the subtle play of lamplight on Emily's face, or watching her lips as she talked and the expressive way she used her slim, pale hands to elaborate a point.

He watched her hair and wished he could study it more intimately. He needed to understand how the red and gold blended. Were some strands darker than others?

So many things he needed to know…about Emily…

He longed to feast his eyes, and yes…to touch and to taste her. Wanted to rediscover the magic they'd started on the mountain. That one kiss had been so tantalising. He hadn't been able to get it out of his head, and there were times when he thought he might go mad from holding back. But sex with Emily was out of the question.

He knew that. A thousand times he'd told himself that he was grateful she'd been the perfect companion this week—warm with her smiles, ready with her wit, careful to keep her distance.

But he felt as if he was wasting precious time. He'd wasted days and nights in Emily's company, holding back while every cell in his body screamed at him to make sweet, wild love to her.

And now the hours were slipping away.

Soon there would only be minutes left.

Of course, despite their leisurely dining, the evening flew all too quickly. In no time they were back in the apartment, where the only sane action for Jude to take was to head straight to his bed. Alone.

'Thanks for your company.' He spoke with necessary formality. 'It was…fun.'

Fun was such an inadequate way to describe the depth of his pleasure in Emily's company. Given the circumstances, it was the best he could come up with.

He longed to close the gap between them. *Just one night, Emily.*

He turned to leave.

'Hey, hang on a sec,' she called after him. 'I want you to see something.'

Jude turned. 'What is it?'

'Put some music on,' she said enigmatically. 'Something with a good slow beat.'

'Why?'

'You're asking too many questions. Just take a seat and I'll be back in a moment.' Already she was off, down the hallway to her room.

Intrigued, he obeyed. He found a CD with a slow, sultry beat and he chose an armchair by the door and sat casually, with an ankle propped on a knee, tapping his fingers to the music as he waited.

And waited…

'Hello,' he called after five bemused minutes. 'What's going on? How long is this going to take?'

'Not much longer. Sorry. Coming soon.'

He wondered if Emily had lost whatever she'd planned to show him, but hell, he had nothing better to do. He waited a little longer. Told himself that no, he couldn't go to her room. That was madness.

He was about to call again when he caught a movement—a brief flicker of a shadow on the wall at the end of the hallway.

A sixth sense made his heart thud.

He dropped his relaxed pose and was instantly tense with anticipation.

And then…a leg appeared…a slim and shapely leg, spellbinding in sheer black stockings and black patent high heels.

Jude's jaw dropped so hard he was sure it must have dislocated. Transfixed, he watched as Emily gave a little dancer's kick and stepped into the room in a slinky short coppery silk dress.

The fabric was the colour of her hair and it hugged her curves divinely. Little black buttons ran down the front. Buttons and loops…

His heart began to thunder. What was going on? He couldn't believe this, but he sure as hell hoped it wouldn't stop.

A double bass pulsed, slow and sexy and deep.

A soft blush warmed Emily's cheeks and she smiled shyly and began to move forward in a smooth, hip-swaying dance, before kicking off one shoe…

And then the other…

Surely not?

Jude's blood pounded as Emily's hands fluttered to the hem of her dress. Then she pushed the silk aside, undid a suspender belt and began to peel down a stocking to reveal smooth pale skin that gleamed softly in the lamplight.

He couldn't believe it. Far out, she was going to strip…

It was quite possible that he'd stopped breathing.

Emily, for heaven's sake…you crazy, gorgeous girl.

She looked so beautiful, so desirable…but vulnerable, too.

Yes, vulnerable and brave, as if, deep down, she was scared…

And suddenly Jude got it. He guessed why she was doing this… He was almost certain that she wasn't aiming for seduction. This was a gift to add to his repertoire of memories.

Oh, Emily.

Couldn't she tell this was killing him?

But he couldn't have stopped her now even if he'd wanted to, which he didn't. He was nailed to the chair. Electrified.

She began to undo the buttons at the neckline of her dress. Slowly, with a grave little smile directed at a spot on the wall above his head. With the tiniest fumble of fingers on slippery silk...one button popped open to reveal a tempting glimpse of soft pale skin...

Somehow, Jude bit back a groan.

She performed a neat pirouette, and then she was facing him again, releasing a second button. Her dance continued—a sensual sway here, a bobbing kick there, and more buttons popped.

Three...

Four...

The copper silk fell away to reveal the creamy tops of her rounded breasts. Through delicate skin-toned lace, he could see their pink tips.

He rose out of his chair, his body on fire. She was so gut-wrenchingly beautiful...even lovelier than he'd imagined.

But his throat felt as if he'd swallowed shards of glass. He knew that beneath Emily's saucy bravado she was still...

Scared...

He wanted to tell her that she didn't have to do this, but he couldn't get the words past the sharp ache in his throat.

Tense as a bow string, he dragged in deep breaths. Then he realised that Emily had stopped dancing.

She was standing absolutely still in the middle of the room, watching him with round, worried eyes...

Then she flushed deeply and looked away, grabbing at the silken halves of her dress and pulling them over her lace-covered breasts. 'I'm so sorry.'

Hell.

'Don't be.' Jude forced the words past the burning log-jam in his throat.

Emily was shaking her head, keeping her eyes averted. 'I…I've never done anything like this before. I don't know why I thought it was a good idea.'

'It's a fabulous idea, Emily. Amazing. Best idea you've ever had…'

'It was supposed to be a bit of fun, Jude. But…' Her lips trembled. 'But you looked so sad.'

'Did I?' Distraught, Jude stepped closer, touched a trembling hand to her chin and turned her face towards him. Tears glittered in her eyes.

He wanted to kiss the tears away, wanted to kiss her all over—the lobe of her ear, the palms of her hands, the hollows behind her knees, her pink-and-white breasts, wanted his lips on every sweet inch of her. Wanted to carry her to his room and stay there with her till the end of next summer…

But Emily was turning her back to him, and already she'd begun to do up her buttons. 'It was a stupid idea.' Her voice was high and tight. 'You probably think I'm a brazen hussy and that it's no wonder I can't keep a boyfriend for long.'

No, damn it. Now his eyes were stinging as well as his throat. 'Believe me, Emily, that thought did not cross my mind.' He spoke quietly, trying to calm her. 'I'm only thinking how beautiful you are—and how thoughtful.'

Just in time, he stopped himself from adding—*and how badly I want you.* 'I think I know why you did this.'

Her head jerked up and she stared at him in surprise.

'I'm guessing you thought this might be my last chance to see a beautiful woman…taking her clothes off.'

For a moment she continued to stare at him, then she looked away and her face crumpled. 'I'm sorry. I was trying to imagine what a man might want, but it was silly. I don't know why I thought it was a good idea.'

'Emily.' There was a rough tremor in his voice. 'It's a *great* idea. The best idea in history. Greater than discovering the wheel, or that the Earth is round, or putting beer into cans.'

She smiled weakly.

'My only complaint is that you stopped.'

Standing before him, looking utterly delightful as she clutched at her dress to protect her modesty, she stared at him, her mouth a perfect circle of surprise.

Perhaps she was coming to terms with what he was telling her. Eventually, the worry in her eyes lightened. 'So I should have kept going? I couldn't get that right, either?'

A strangled laugh broke from Jude as tenderness and desire waged war with his reasoning and common sense. 'I think I may be the one who's made the biggest mistake.'

'You?'

'For reinstating that crazy kissing ban.'

'Oh.' The word bounced softly into the space between them. Still clutching at her dress, Emily frowned. 'But this was meant to be purely for fun. I wasn't trying to—' She blushed. 'You don't want more complications in your life.'

'That's true,' he agreed reluctantly. 'And I don't want to mess up *your* life, either.'

He took a step closer, knowing it wasn't wise, and Emily seemed to melt towards him. Their fingers brushed and he was zapped by fire. He heard her soft gasp.

'I'd rather not risk joining the list of males who've hurt you,' he said.

She shook her head. 'Maybe that's a risk worth taking.'

CHAPTER EIGHT

A RISK worth taking? Emily couldn't believe she'd said that. If Jude kissed her now—

Too late. Jude was already kissing her—and from the moment his lips touched hers, her fears no longer made any kind of sense. He kissed her slow and easy, calming her and soothing her scampering heartbeat.

She'd become so scared during the strip, starting out gamely and confidently, then beginning to think she'd made the hugest blunder of her life.

Now, with his strong arms holding her, warm and secure, Jude's lips worked a special magic, sending golden heat through her, down her arms, pooling low in her stomach.

Relaxed and dreamy, she gave up worrying about risks and simply sank into this bliss—savouring the strength of his arms about her, revelling in the manly texture of his jaw against hers.

He'd turned the tables on her this evening. She'd started out trying to surprise him, but now he was the one taking control. With a hand buried in her hair, he held her just where he wanted her and took the kiss deeper.

Oh, man. Her knees almost gave way. They were like two notes blending in perfect harmony, building to a joint crescendo.

Her dress fell apart and his touch on her breasts through their thin covering of lace was so sexy their kiss turned molten.

She thought fleetingly of Michael and a flash of panic flared. Then she leant back and looked into Jude's sexy grey eyes, and she saw gravity and tenderness mixed with his desire.

Her panic subsided. This was OK. It really was OK. Their passion was fuelled by so much more than simple lust. Yes, her heart was involved, but she was quite clear-headed. This night was all about hope and courage, and the soul-deep need for two human beings to connect.

Against her ear, Jude murmured, 'You know I can't make promises about the future.'

'Shh.' She pressed a finger to his lips. 'I understand, Jude, and I'm not asking for promises.'

She couldn't deny she was in love with him. Painfully, wonderfully in love. But Jude had put his life on hold, and she would, too. For the first time, she was offering her love without an accompanying dream of ever after. It was such a relief to simply be with him without the weight of expectation.

Winding her arms around his neck, she kissed the underside of his jaw. 'I vote we make this a night to remember.'

It was all the invitation Jude needed. Scooping her effortlessly into his arms, he carried her down the hallway to the big double bed.

At last.

They'd been dancing around this for days, trying to resist, but now it felt so good to let the barriers fall. So right to let the world retreat, to allow their emotions to swell and their longing to build, till just the two of them existed.

Now. Here. This.
Sweet journey of discovery.

As they lay close together in the darkness, Jude was tormented by questions.

Why did I find her now?
Why her?
Why now?

He'd been falling hard and fast for Emily from the moment he set eyes on her. Within no time he'd become addicted, needing to watch her at work in the kitchen, to chat with her about his books, to chat with her about anything, really, share his favourite view…

And now, after loving him with a passion and honesty that utterly enslaved him, she was lying beside him in the darkness, with her round little rump settled against his hip, her foot hooked possessively over his calf, her breathing soft and even…

And he wanted more. Wanted to make her his own, to keep her by his side.

Emily had asked him once if he would give up his lifestyle for the right woman. Now, he was beginning to suspect she was that woman, and he was quite sure he would do anything. He wanted to offer her the world…

But all he had to offer was a gaping black hole filled with question marks.

With a heavy sigh, he tried to fight off his thoughts of what lay ahead of him. To counter them, he replayed precious images in his mind. The fall of lamplight on Emily's soft white curves. The fiery shimmer of her hair on the pillow. The adorable perfection of her pale pink-tipped breasts.

The other gifts she offered for his senses, the wildflower scent of her skin, her silky softness, the intoxicating sweetness of her kisses, her heartbeats knocking against his.

He wanted it all.

Morning sunlight filtered softly through the curtains.

Emily lay on her side, not wanting to disturb Jude, not wanting to think how rash she'd been to sleep with this man.

She had no regrets. Last night had been beyond wonderful, and today was all about Jude. She mustn't spoil it by worrying about where this would take her.

For now, she was very happy to feast her eyes on him, and there was much to admire. Even when he was asleep, his face was strong, with a largish nose, not too pointy or too fleshy, dark eyebrows and a long jaw, now covered in morning stubble.

The duvet had slipped and she let her gaze drift over his bare torso—over his wide muscled shoulders and solid chest, his flat stomach, no doubt toned from all that hiking he did.

She thought about the day ahead of him, and a wave of fear eddied through her. She couldn't bear to think of Jude's precious, clever brain being interfered with by surgeons' scalpels. Quickly, she pushed those thoughts aside and dwelled instead on the amazing night they'd shared.

Amidst the emotion and dizzying passion, there'd been sweet moments of intimate connection, so beautiful and tender that she'd almost wept. Thank heavens she'd held back on the tears, for Jude's sake. She wanted only happy memories for him.

Now, also for Jude's sake, her task was to stay upbeat today, *all day*, even though she was as scared as she'd ever been.

It helped to remember her grandmother's words. *You*

just need to put yourself in Jude's shoes. Follow your in-stincts and I'm sure you'll work out the best way to keep his spirits up.

Emily smiled at this. She wondered what Granny Silver would think if she knew her advice had led her grand-daughter to attempt a striptease. Truth was, there'd been a double benefit. Not just for Jude but for her as well. For the first time she'd taken an impulsive risk, and wow, hadn't it been worth it?

In the past, she'd always been a bit inhibited in her rela-tionships. She'd been aware of *something* holding her back and, deep down, she'd known that she'd disappointed her boyfriends—even Michael.

Given this history, it was quite amazing that she'd at-tempted something as bold as a striptease for Jude. Perhaps the secret was that she'd been totally focused on his needs. Her own disappointments with boyfriends had made her ultra-careful, but last night she'd thought only of Jude, and she'd been determined to give him something fun to remember.

Now that she thought about it, she supposed the strip-tease was the kind of challenge Jude's heroines might have taken on.

How about that?

And look at the result—the most wonderful night of her life. She might even be able to think of herself as a winner at last.

Slipping out of bed, she pulled on her nightgown, the old-fashioned cream and lace frills one that Jude had said made her look like an angel, and she padded out to the kitchen to make breakfast.

He was awake when she returned with a tray, and he greeted her with a happy grin. 'Ah, my favourite nightgown. This morning with that tray, you make me think of Florence Nightingale.'

'I don't have a lamp.'

'No, you have a coffee pot, which is even better.'

Indeed it was. They sat in bed propped against a bank of pillows, sipping big mugs of coffee and munching on blueberry pancakes topped with lightly fried sliced bananas.

Emily had drawn the curtains wide to give them a clear view of the morning sky and the Brisbane River wandering slowly between forests of skyscrapers. They felt rather smug as they listened to the sounds of the city traffic and the poor workers hurrying to their offices, which was ironic considering what lay ahead for Jude. But he seemed quite relaxed.

Emily wondered if he was faking this calmness. For her own part, she was finding it increasingly hard to keep up a brave face. Every time she looked at the clock and saw the time creeping closer to the fateful hour of three o'clock, the time Jude was to be admitted, she felt a fresh download of dread.

After breakfast, Jude wandered down to the shops to buy a newspaper or two, and Emily tried to keep busy, washing the breakfast things by hand, even though there was a dishwasher. She also dried the dishes and put them away, and wiped down the benches and polished them until they shone. Still feeling restless, she swept the floor.

Several times, she wanted to ask Jude if there was anything she could do for him, but she knew he'd packed everything he needed for the hospital, including his laptop.

'You never know, I might get some writing done. Better to be optimistic than the alternative.' He'd said this with a cheeky wink that made her throat ache.

For lunch Emily made toasted cheese sandwiches and

heated one of Jude's collection of tinned soups—rich to-mato and basil. Afterwards, she was standing at the sink, once again rinsing plates, when Jude came up behind her.

Looping his arms about her, he hugged her, holding her against his chest—and Emily loved it.

She could remember when she was a child, watching her dad come up and hug her mum this way. Her mum would be tired, with no make-up or fancy clothes, but he'd kiss her neck and ask fondly, 'How's my favourite girl?'

Her mum, who'd also worked as hard on their farm as her dad, used to pretend to be too busy and brush him off. But she'd give him a quick kiss, and she'd smile to herself and hum happily under her breath as she peeled potatoes or sliced beans.

Emily had grown up wanting a husband like that, some-one who liked to hug her at any old time of the day.

Now, as Jude pressed his lips to the nape of her neck, she closed her eyes, relishing the reassuring warmth of his arms about her and the familiar intimacy of the gesture.

'I want you to do me a favour this afternoon,' he said, still with his arms around her waist.

Emily nodded, eager to please. 'Of course. How can I help?'

'I want you to go to your grandmother's and stay there for the next few days.'

No!

She went cold all over, and only remembered just in time to bite back a wailing protest. She didn't want to do or say anything to upset Jude today, but crikey, he was upsetting her. She thought he'd given up on this desire to keep her away, but he was asking her to step out of his life at this most crucial time. It was hard not to panic.

She drew a deep breath, praying for calm. 'I can't just

drop you off at the hospital and walk away as if I don't care.'

Jude's arms tensed, and then they dropped to his sides as he stepped away. Fighting panic, Emily turned to face him and her heart trembled when she saw the resolve in his eyes and the determined set of his mouth. He was serious.

'I don't want you hanging around the hospital, Emily. I couldn't bear to think of you sitting around in some dreary waiting room tomorrow, while I'm in the theatre. I'll give the staff your name as a contact, and you can ring when it's all over to see how I'm doing.'

'But I don't mind waiting.' A pleading note crept into her voice. But she sensed that wouldn't work with Jude, so she forced a smile and tried another tack. 'Honestly, I have a couple of fabulous books to read. I've found this fantastic thriller writer, you see, and he keeps me glued to the page and—'

'Emily, listen.' Stepping forward again, Jude grasped her shoulders and his eyes were storm-grey serious. Then his expression softened and he said gently, 'I'll feel so much better if I know you're away from there.'

'But I won't feel better.'

'You will,' he insisted in that same quiet voice. 'Do this for me.' The ghost of a smile crept into his eyes. 'I want to picture you sitting on a beach, watching the waves roll in, or going for walks beside the water with your hair blowing in the wind.'

His big hands squeezed her shoulders. 'Granny Silver will be much better company tomorrow than a hospital waiting room. And tonight I want to think of you going to sleep listening to the sea.'

But couldn't he understand that, for her, leaving him

alone felt like the worst kind of desertion? Yet another rejection?

Admittedly, she hadn't been looking forward to waiting at the hospital—she hated it at the best of times—but she'd been determined to be there for Jude.

But perhaps she should have expected this reaction from Jude. He was behaving the way his father had, not wanting others to see him weakened or helpless.

He hadn't told any of his friends about his health problems until Alex had sent them prompting text messages. And it made sense that a man as independent as Jude was would hate the idea of a woman hanging about the hospital ward, feeling sorry for him.

He was probably also worried that she'd consider them a couple after last night, but he'd offered no promises and she'd pledged to respect his wishes.

Blinking to banish the threat of tears, she managed to smile. 'OK, I'll stay away from the hospital, on one condition.'

'Not another condition?' A silvery light glistened in Jude's grey eyes. 'What is it?'

Stepping closer, she linked her arms around his neck. 'One last kiss. For luck.'

'Emily.'

Her name was a whispered prayer as he drew her into his arms and his warm, pliant lips met hers in a perfect kiss—tender and beautiful and utterly close-your-eyes-and-go-to-heaven blissful.

She could feel his heart thundering against her and she wished, more than anything, that they could simply skip over these next twenty-four hours. She was gripped by a terrible feeling of powerlessness and she pressed her cheek against Jude's chest and hugged him close.

There were so many things she wanted to tell him—that

he was a truly wonderful man, that he was going to come through this just fine, that no matter what happened, she would be there waiting for him.

But she kept these thoughts to herself. She wasn't sure he wanted to hear promises that sounded suspiciously like love.

They left early for the hospital, driving in Jude's car, which he insisted Emily use when she continued on to her grandmother's.

Their route took them past the park, and Emily wondered aloud if the heron was there again today.

Jude grinned. 'We have time. Why don't we take a look?'

They were in luck, finding a parking spot close to the gates, so it was no time before they were following the path that wound through a grove of jacarandas.

But as they rounded the bend, the pond was disappointingly empty of herons.

There were ducks on the water and a few children throwing food to them, but no long-legged white bird wading in the shallows.

'Maybe he's turned back into an alien?' Emily said to lighten the moment. She knew it was silly to feel disappointed. There was nothing symbolic about the heron. It wasn't as if he was a good omen or anything, but now she wished she hadn't suggested looking for him.

She was turning away when Jude said, 'Look.'

He was smiling as he pointed—and, sure enough, emerging from a clump of reeds, appearing quite dazzling in the sunlight, came the heron.

'He's like you,' Emily said.

Jude looked at her in surprise. 'Really? How?'

'He's bit of a loner.'

He laughed and a smile lingered as they walked back to the car. For some reason she couldn't quite explain, Emily felt just a little braver.

She was very proud that she didn't cry when she said goodbye at the hospital entrance. It was all over in a moment. Jude hugged her so tightly she could hardly breathe, then he grabbed his leather overnight bag and flashed a quick smile.

'See you in a while.'

With a final cheeky wink that just about broke her heart, he turned and strode through the swinging glass doors.

On the expressway to the Sunshine Coast there were very few places for Emily to pull over, so she couldn't allow herself to cry. She wouldn't help Jude by blinding herself with tears and having an accident, so she listened to music on the radio and tried not to think about him.

Having rung her grandmother earlier, she was expected, and at the first available shopping centre she bought a bunch of flowers and ingredients for a few meals.

She would enjoy cooking, and it would give Granny Silver a break. She bought chocolates, too, and a bottle of Granny's favourite sherry, and then she drove on, looking forward to the moment she crested the final rise and saw her first glimpse of the sea.

This last leg of the journey had always excited her. But today when she saw the curling blue waves, she could only think about Jude and her spirits refused to lift. Even the sight of her grandmother's cottage hunkering beneath a big old cassia tree brought only the tiniest sense of relief.

As soon as she parked in the driveway, the cottage door opened and Granny Silver was there waiting, arms ready to hug her. Emily's eyes filled with tears, but she still had to stay strong. She couldn't dissolve into tears on the footpath in full view of her grandmother's neighbours.

Taking a deep breath, she climbed out, hauled her bags and her shopping from the back seat and closed the car doors with her hip before walking with her arms full up the crazy-paving path.

'You're weighed down, there,' Granny said. 'Can I help with anything?'

Emily shook her head. 'I've got it all balanced, thanks. I'll take the shopping straight through to the kitchen. OK?'

'Of course, dear.'

Stepping through the doorway into the dearly loved front room, Emily saw its deep chintz-covered armchairs and lush pot plants and dozens of family photographs. She caught the faint smell of dried lavender and the lump in her throat swelled to the size of a grapefruit.

Here she was, surrounded by so much that she loved, while Jude was alone in Brisbane in a hospital ward… waiting…

She managed to dump the groceries on the kitchen counter before her tears fell.

In torrents.

'I'm so sorry,' she spluttered to her concerned grandmother, but she couldn't explain. All she could do was collapse into an armchair and weep… For Jude, for herself… and for the unknown future…

CHAPTER NINE

'So it seems that your friendship with Jude is rather special after all,' Granny Silver said gently.

'It is and it isn't.' Emily released a slow sigh, not sure how she could explain now that she'd apologised for her tears and washed her face, and was leaning back against her grandmother's embroidered cushions.

They were drinking a post-tears cup of tea and she knew an explanation was expected.

'Jude's a really wonderful guy, so of course I really like him, Granny. But this is a very scary thing that's happening to him, and he's determined to deal with it on his own.'

'That's hard on you.'

'Yes. I hoped I'd be stronger.'

'Try not to worry too much, Emily. A friend of mine had a similar operation at the same hospital and apparently the neurosurgeons there are all wonderful. I don't think you should be too concerned.'

'That's good to know. Jude doesn't say much, but I know he's freaked about the possibility of blindness.' Emily looked at her grandmother with a shaky smile. 'But if the surgeon's excellent, Jude should be fine, shouldn't he?'

'Exactly, my dear.'

* * *

The next morning, the day of Jude's operation, Emily was far too restless and tense to hang about the house. She needed to take a really long walk, and she needed to be alone.

'Of course, I understand,' Granny Silver assured her. 'Off you go. I'll say a prayer for Jude.'

It was a beautiful day with a brilliant, cloudless blue sky and rolling, sunlit surf. Emily walked along the sand to the far end of Sunshine Beach and then climbed the track over the headland into Noosa National Park. It felt somehow appropriate to be climbing on this particular day. The ascent was fairly sedate and she stayed on the beaten track, but she felt as if she were climbing for Jude.

From the top of the headland she caught sight of porpoises leaping and frolicking in clear green waves, and they looked so lively and cheerful she couldn't help smiling.

She continued on to Hell's Gates, a steep narrow canyon of rocks where the sea rushed in, wild and rough and foaming. Usually she was fascinated by the crashing waves and the shooting spray. Today the sense of danger made her skin crawl and she turned away, choosing a sandy track that wound away from the sea through friendly bushland.

Always, with every step, she thought of Jude.

It was so awful to think of him lying on an operating table, beneath bright lights and surrounded by people in masks, holding scalpels. Each time an image from the operating theatre flashed through her mind, she was sluiced by hot fear.

Hastily, she substituted happier memories. Jude striding purposefully up the track to Sunset Ridge. Jude laughing with her as they invented crazy theories about the white heron. The silvery warmth in his eyes just before he kissed her.

It was impossible to pretend that she wasn't in love with him. She'd tried walking around that fact and dressing it up in other names, telling herself that as far as Jude was concerned, she was a stand-in for Alex, or a caring friend, or simply…a female distraction.

Once again, she'd actively tried to resist falling in love. It was way too soon. She'd just run away from a disastrous relationship and she knew all too well that, for her, romance was a shortcut to misery. The very words *in love* brought every one of her trust issues bursting to the surface.

Not that she had a good reason to mistrust Jude. He'd gone out of his way to make his position crystal clear. He wasn't available for a new relationship, and even if he had been available, he'd intimated that he had a history of avoiding long-term commitment.

In her head, Emily was totally OK with this. She certainly wasn't looking at Jude as future husband material. She'd archived that dream where it belonged—with the Tooth Fairy and Santa Claus. *And* she'd tried her best to keep her heart strong and safe but, whether she liked it or not, she'd become emotionally involved with Jude. On all kinds of levels.

Small wonder he'd sent her away yesterday.

He probably hoped that distance would bring her to her senses.

Just as she reached this miserable conclusion, the track emerged out of bushland into a burst of sunshine and a view of a gorgeous cove. Emily found a flat rock to sit on and looked down at the rocky cliffs, the pale yellow sand and the clear, clear water in three shades of aquamarine.

She'd worn a long-sleeved shirt to protect her from the sun, and now she peeled the cuff back to check her watch.

It was eleven-thirty, and Jude's operation should be almost over.

Sickening fear churned in her stomach. *Please, let him be OK.*

Worries crowded in, and she found herself imagining what his life would be like if his optic nerve was damaged and he lost his sight. So many things he wouldn't see—sunsets, wading herons, mountain views, words on a page…or on a computer screen…

Closing her eyes, she hugged her knees. 'Hang in there, Jude. You're going to be fine. You'll be better than ever when this is over.'

Taking a deep breath, she opened her eyes and saw a white-breasted eagle swooping down from the heights, curving in a majestic pure loop, right in front of her.

Jude loved birds and, although Emily wasn't normally superstitious, she couldn't help hoping that this eagle was a sign that all was well.

Bending down, she picked a wild flower from a clump growing at the base of the rock she was sitting on. The flower was a small daisy, nondescript and pale brown, but she threaded it through the band of her sunhat and set off again, her heart once more hopeful.

'Good afternoon. I'm ringing to enquire about Jude Marlowe. He had surgery this morning.'

'Jude Marlowe,' a young woman's voice repeated. 'And your name is?'

'Emily Silver. I believe Jude left my name as a contact.'

'We have Charlotte Kenney listed here as Mr Marlowe's next of kin.'

'Yes, that's Jude's sister.' Despite her nerves, Emily tried to speak calmly. 'But I understand he was also going to leave my name.'

'Let me see… Can you hold the line, please? I'll be back in one moment.'

Emily felt sick as she waited, clutching the phone, while a thousand scenarios flashed through her head. She wondered if Jude had forgotten to leave her name. Or, worse, that he'd changed his mind and no longer wanted her to be informed about him. Or the very worst possibility— something awful had happened and the nurse needed permission to tell Emily about it.

'Hello, this is Dr Keira Arnold.'

A doctor? Fear exploded in Emily's face. *Was this bad news? Please, no.*

'I believe you'd like an update on Jude Marlowe's condition,' the doctor said.

'Yes.' Emily's throat was so tight she could barely squeeze the word out. 'Please.'

'So you're Emily Silver?'

'That's right.'

'It's good to speak to you, Emily. I'm an old friend of Jude's.'

'A friend?' Emily gulped. Her first thought was that Jude must be OK. Surely this doctor wouldn't be chatting about friendships if there was a problem. Then another thought clicked.

Was she speaking to the owner of the hiking boots? 'Are you Keira, the Army doctor?'

'Yes, that's right. I'm actually Major Arnold, but pulling rank doesn't go down too well in a civilian hospital.'

So this was the attractive dark-haired woman in Jude's alpine photo, the former girlfriend who regularly returned to his home.

Keira Arnold said, 'Fortunately, my leave has coincided with Jude's op, so I've been able to keep a friendly eye on him from the wings, so to speak.'

Emily's head was buzzing with a gazillion questions, but there was only one that really mattered. 'How is he?'

'The operation went very well. The neurosurgeon is exceptionally experienced, for which I'm grateful. Jude came out of the recovery room a short while ago and he's in good spirits.'

Emily let out a shuddering whoosh of relief. 'That's wonderful. What about his vision? Is that OK?'

'I'm afraid it's too early to tell.'

'Oh...I see.'

There were so many questions Emily wanted to ask, but she'd sensed a subtle vibe coming from this other woman. Despite the surface friendliness, there was an atmosphere that smacked of power play. Emily had experienced plenty of this in the course of her work at the bank but, under these circumstances, she wasn't quite sure what to make of it.

Opting for caution, she said simply, 'Thanks for telling me. I'm very relieved and if you're speaking to Jude, please tell him I called and give him my...my love.'

'Of course.'

'And I'd appreciate hearing—if there's any more news.'

'All right. We'll keep in touch. Oh, and by the way—' the doctor's voice dropped to a confidential purr '—congratulations on your engagement. I'm pleased that Jude's finally taking the plunge.'

She promptly hung up.

And Emily almost dropped her phone.

Engagement? What engagement?

How on earth had the doctor arrived at that crazy conclusion? Jude would never have suggested such a thing.

It was downright *weird*. And unsettling.

Emily was shaking her head as she went through to the

kitchen where her grandmother was adding fresh water to a vase of flowers.

Granny turned, her eyes cautious, yet eager for news.

'Jude seems to be fine,' Emily said.

'Oh, darling, what a relief.' It wasn't long, however, before her grandmother was frowning. 'You don't look happy. Is there something else?'

'I'm very happy. Truly, I'm thrilled.' Emily gave a dazed shake of her head. 'But, for some reason I don't under-stand, the people at the hospital think I'm Jude's fiancée.'

'How interesting.'

'It's rubbish, of course. We've only known each other for about two weeks.'

'A lot can happen in two weeks.' Granny straightened an iris, then stood back to admire the arrangement Emily had bought for her yesterday.

'Jude and I haven't had a whirlwind romance, if that's what you're thinking.' Emily stooped to pick up a fallen petal from the floor. The action helped to hide her guilty flush from her granny's searching gaze. 'It's possible that the hospital wouldn't pass on any news unless I was a wife or a fiancée, so perhaps Jude fudged the truth.'

'Yes, that might be the story. Or perhaps it's wishful thinking on his part?'

'Granny—' Emily sent her a withering look '—when did you become such a hopeless romantic?'

'A few decades before you did, my dear. I'm afraid I may have passed on the gene.'

They shared a rueful smile.

'Actually, that's a sore point,' Emily admitted. Pulling out a kitchen stool, she plumped down on it, resting her elbows on the bench. 'I fall in love far too easily, and then I leave myself wide open to be hurt.'

'Are you saying that you don't trust your own feelings?'

'Maybe. I certainly don't understand how love happens so easily for everyone else and I find it so hard. Even when I'm convinced I've found someone perfect, he can turn out to be a dud.'

Lifting her gloomy gaze, Emily saw her grandmother's shocked face. 'I don't mean Jude. There was…someone else.'

Granny accepted this with a thoughtful nod. Then she asked carefully, 'How would you feel about Jude if he did lose his sight?'

The most awful ache bloomed in Emily's heart. 'I'd be devastated for him,' she said softly. 'But it wouldn't change how I feel about him.'

No matter what happened to Jude, she would feel this same deep emotional bond with him. And if this sense of connection and caring wasn't love, Emily didn't know what it was.

'But Jude's a loner, Granny. Even if he was perfectly well, he wouldn't be looking for a long-term relationship.'

'A loner?' Granny Silver's eyes widened. 'That surprises me. He has such a warm and engaging personality. Are you sure he's a true loner?'

'He has a definite reclusive streak, although I must admit he was a very hospitable host, in spite of everything else going on in his life.'

'Perhaps he's just waiting for the right woman, dear.'

Emily rolled her eyes to the ceiling. 'That's what he says.'

But I'm not holding out hope that I could be her.

Despite that last wonderful night together, Jude had sent her away, as if he was already preparing her for an eventual permanent separation.

Once again she'd fallen too quickly and too easily for

a man who was, ultimately, no more suitable for her than
Michael had been—or Dave, or Dimitri, for that matter.

Climbing from the stool, she went to the pantry. 'I think
I'll make a bacon-and-macaroni casserole.'

Granny's eyes met hers and they shared another smile.
They both knew very well that since Emily's early childhood, whenever she was anxious or disappointed or hurt,
this dish was her number one comfort food.

It was the middle of the next morning when Jude rang.
Emily saw his name on her screen and her heart leapt like
a kite in a wind gust.

'Hi, Jude.' Her voice was all fluttery. 'How are you?'

'Not too bad, thanks.'

It was so-o-o good to hear his voice and to know he really was OK. She held the phone close to her ear, as if it
could somehow strengthen the contact. 'So everything's
going well?'

'Apparently I'm on track. The physio's just taken me
for a walk, and I wasn't too doddery.'

'Fantastic. How are your eyes?'

There was a beat before he answered. 'Hard to say. I've
been told to be patient. How are you?'

'I…I'm absolutely fine.' *Missing you.*

'*Where* are you?'

'On the beach, actually.'

'Sunbathing in a bikini?'

He asked this in such a hopeful, boyish tone that Emily
laughed.

'No, Jude. I'm a redhead, remember? I don't sunbathe.
I'm lying on the sand, reading one of your books, but I'm
in the shade and I'm wearing a boring sunhat and a long-
sleeved top.'

'Very wise of you,' he said warmly. 'It'd be a crime to burn your lovely complexion.'

Encouraged by this, Emily said, 'I rang the hospital yesterday and I spoke to Dr Keira Arnold.'

'Yes, Keira mentioned you'd called. I hope she set your mind at rest.'

'She told me your surgeon was top-notch and that everything went well, so of course I was incredibly relieved. But one thing was odd, Jude. Keira thinks we're engaged.'

'Ah…yes. Sorry about that.' There was a small throat-clearing noise. 'I told a white lie to the front desk. They're nervous about giving patient information to anyone outside the family. But don't worry; I've now set Keira straight.'

'Right.' Emily ignored the sinking feeling in her stomach. 'Glad to hear it.' She wondered if Keira Arnold had already known this and had been playing with her.

'So when can I come to visit you?' Emily asked.

There was an unsettling silence.

'Can you hold off for a day or so?' Jude said at last.

'It…it's up to you, of course.' She hoped he couldn't hear her disappointment. 'I'll call you tomorrow, OK?'

'Yes, do that. I'll look forward to it.'

After she disconnected, Emily sat staring out at the sea, watching wave after wave roll in and crash in a fringe of frothing foam. She told herself she should be glad Jude was well. That was all that mattered.

But even though his recovery was the only thing that really mattered, it couldn't quite heal her niggling unease over Keira Arnold. The woman had a carte blanche invitation to stay at Jude's home any time she fancied *and* she was, apparently, at his bedside night and day, holding his hand, mopping his brow, doing the whole Florence Nightingale act while Emily had been sent into exile.

Exactly what kind of ex-girlfriend was this Keira? Was she still angling to become Jude's *Mrs Right*?

Hospitals, Jude decided, were the least private places in the world. There was always someone coming through his doorway—a tea lady, an orderly, a nurse, a doctor...

He barely got five minutes to string his thoughts together. Although that was possibly a good thing. Left alone, he'd spend far too much time thinking about Emily.

Even with the interruptions, he still found himself replaying snatches of their many conversations in his head, remembering the delightful sparkle in her eyes when she talked.

The more intimate memories damn near broke his heart.

Every moment he'd spent with Emily—in the apartment, or downtown, or in the mountains—seemed to be lit up in neon lights. His life was divided into two parts: before and after meeting Emily.

And now *this*...

This frustrating, humiliating illness.

It was all very well for the doctors to assure him that he'd be fine. In time. Right now, his head was a field of pain and his sight was scarily blurred. He had to wait six weeks for an MRI to determine the true success of the op.

Was it too long to expect Emily to wait?

The next day, gently encouraged by Granny Silver, Emily rang Jude and adopted the assertive tones she used in her office on a daily basis.

'I'm bringing Granny to Brisbane to collect her new glasses, so I'll call in and see you while I'm nearby.' Without giving Jude a chance to object, she went on, 'It would be silly to come all that way and not say hello.'

Jude agreed, but with less enthusiasm than she would

have liked, and she arrived early in the afternoon, heart thumping unnecessarily hard as she reached the door to his private room.

A grey-haired man and woman were just leaving.

Somehow, Emily hadn't expected this. Slightly bewildered, she nodded to them and they smiled and nodded back.

As she rounded the doorway, she saw Jude sitting in a chair in the corner, dressed not in pyjamas but in jeans and a white shirt, open at the neck, sleeves rolled up, looking very much his usual hunky self, except that he was wearing dark glasses.

There was a young woman in a chair next to him. Her hair was a mass of dark shiny curls and she was leaning close, holding Jude's hand.

Emily told herself she didn't care if this was another of Jude's ex-girlfriends. Just the same, her knees began to shake.

Then the other woman saw her. She dropped Jude's hand and smiled. 'Here's another visitor. You're popular today, Jude.'

He tensed, turning his head to the door.

Emily had no idea if he could see her. 'Hello, Jude.' Her voice was as shaky as her knees.

'Emily.' He stood quickly, but he wasn't smiling.

'I'm Charlotte,' the woman next to him said, stepping forward and smiling as she held out her hand. 'Jude's sister.'

His sister? Of course. Why hadn't she thought of that? Pumped with relief, Emily grinned at them both. 'Nice to meet you, Charlotte.'

'I'm so glad to meet you,' Charlotte responded. 'Jude's been telling me how much he's enjoyed your company.'

'Has he?' Emily almost floated into the room and

her grin was probably ridiculously wide as she shook Charlotte's hand. Then she kissed Jude's cheek, catching a quick heady whiff of his delicious aftershave.

'You look really well,' she told him. 'You look fantastic.'

'Thanks.' His mouth tilted, not quite making a smile.

Clearly, he wasn't as thrilled to see her as his sister was.

'I wasn't sure what to bring,' Emily said, trying not to sound too easily deflated by Jude's grimness. 'I settled for grapes and dark chocolate.' She turned to put them on the bedside table. 'Oh, I see you already have grapes *and* chocolate.'

'Sid Johnson brought them,' Charlotte said. 'The old police friend of Jude's who's just left.' And then she smiled, defusing the awkward moment. 'Great minds think alike.'

'Can't have too much of grapes and chocolate,' Jude added gallantly. And then, politely, 'Emily, take a seat.'

'No, I'm fine, thanks.' Jude was the patient—she couldn't take his seat.

'I'll hop back on the bed.' Already Jude was walking over to the bed, but his movements were super-careful and, when he sat, he grimaced slightly as he swung his legs up and settled against the pillows.

It was unsettling to see him moving so cautiously when just a few days ago he'd climbed a mountain with effortless ease. Emily realised she'd been holding her breath as she watched him. Her gaze met Charlotte's and she could see that his sister shared her disquiet.

Charlotte was warm and friendly, however, drawing Emily into the conversation, and the three of them were soon chatting quite congenially.

Charlotte filled Jude in on her family's news. Her eldest, Sophie, had started ballet lessons. Oliver skinned his knee falling off his trike. Daisy would soon be walking.

Jude was much more relaxed and smiling as he listened to her, and his questions about his nieces and nephew revealed genuine interest rather than mere politeness.

Emily told him about her walk through the Noosa National Park, how she'd seen porpoises and an eagle.

'A white-breasted sea eagle?'

'Probably. I'm not great on identification, but it was certainly white and it was beautiful. I decided it was a good omen.'

'I'm sure it was,' said Charlotte warmly, but Jude made no comment.

'I've also had a brilliant idea for an online business,' Emily said, too excited to keep this news to herself.

Jude turned to her, clearly interested. 'Come on, tell us.'

'The idea hit me yesterday while I was watching mothers and children playing on the beach—'

'Well, what's this?' interrupted a voice from the doorway. 'The Jude Marlowe fan club?'

Emily turned as yet another young woman entered the room. Tall as a model, and wearing a neat navy trouser suit, she wore her dark hair pulled back from her intelligently attractive face. Emily instantly recognised her as the woman in the photo at Jude's place—Dr Keira Arnold.

Keira didn't wait for Jude's introduction. 'I'm guessing you must be Emily,' she said, breezing into the room. 'I'm Keira. We met over the phone.'

As she shook Emily's hand she let her keen dark gaze linger for a shade too long, as if she were sizing her up. Then she turned to Jude, smiling.

'Move over,' she ordered him and she sat on his bed, nudging his legs with her bottom, very much at ease.

Emily hung on to her smile—*just*—and she thought she heard a small huff that might have been reproach from

Jude's sister. Shooting a quick glance Charlotte's way, she caught her fleeting raised-eyebrow look of sympathy.

Apparently she had an ally, which was interesting. Grateful for small mercies, Emily took a deep breath and secured her smile more firmly. But there was an awkward atmosphere in the room now that hadn't been there before.

'Emily was telling us about a new business idea,' Charlotte told Keira.

'Oh? Do tell…'

'It's OK,' Emily said uneasily. 'I can fill Jude in with the details some other time.'

Similarly, Charlotte's chatter about her family seemed to have dried up and Jude, for his part, looked tired.

Their conversation was reduced to unexciting small talk about the traffic on the freeway, the length of Charlotte's stay in Brisbane and the weather. After less than five minutes, Charlotte looked at her watch, then jumped to her feet.

'If you'll excuse me, I really must hurry to make a phone call. I've just remembered something I need to remind my babysitter about.' She kissed Jude and gave him a gentle hug. 'See you later, big brother.'

She sent Emily a warm smile. 'Lovely to meet you.' Impulsively, she gave Emily a hug, too. 'I might not see you again before I leave tomorrow, so let me thank you now for taking such great care of Jude.'

Surprised, Emily wondered what Jude had told his sister. Judging by Keira's dark expression, she may have been pondering the same question.

After Charlotte left, the conversation might have become really awkward if Jude hadn't yawned.

Emily took this as her cue. 'You need to rest, Jude, and I should be on my way. Granny Silver is probably ready and waiting for me.'

Jude smiled. 'How is Granny?'

'As sprightly as ever. She sends her best wishes.'

This time, when she kissed Jude's cheek, she was uncomfortably aware of Keira watching them.

'Take care,' she told him softly.

'You, too,' Jude murmured.

Before she could draw away, his hand closed around her wrist, holding her close to him. His lips brushed her cheek again in a deliberate unhurried caress. 'Thanks for coming,' he murmured. 'You're a breath of fresh air.'

It was ridiculous that such brief, sweet contact with him could set Emily's skin flaming. Unfortunately, the knowledge that she was being watched by his ex made the flames even hotter.

Gamely, she flashed Keira a brilliant smile. 'Bye, and nice to meet you.'

Outside in the hallway, she let out her breath in a whoosh of relief. Visiting Jude had been so much harder than she'd expected.

His remoteness had been disconcerting, but she'd also been puzzled by his relationship with Keira Arnold. What was this woman's role, exactly? Control freak, or extremely close and caring friend?

Or was she still in love with Jude?

'Emily?'

Keira's voice sounded behind her. *Talk of the devil.* Emily took a quick breath before she turned.

'Can I have a word?' the doctor asked.

Emily gulped. What was this about? She smiled. 'Yes, of course.'

'We can talk in here.' Keira pushed open a door, revealing a small, surprisingly empty sitting room with vinyl seats, a rack of tattered magazines and a coffee machine in the corner.

Emily's stomach tightened. Why the seclusion? Was Keira going to grill her about her connection to Jude? Would she quiz her about the fake engagement?

'Would you like a coffee?' Keira asked.

Emily shook her head. 'I don't have long. My grandmother's waiting.'

'Of course.' Keira sat, crossing her long athletic legs, and she indicated for Emily to take a chair opposite. 'This won't take a moment, but I wanted to talk to you about Jude's recovery.'

Instantly alarmed, Emily sat forward. 'Is there a problem? He'll be OK, won't he?'

'Physically, he's on track to make a fine recovery,' Keira began with a watchful smile. 'It would help, though, if he didn't feel compelled to play the tough guy. In the Army, I deal with men like Jude all the time. They keep their problems, particularly their medical problems, to themselves. It's part of the masculine thing. To bottle it up.'

Emily nodded, and wondered again where this was leading.

'Believe me,' Keira continued, 'I've seen a lot of hardened men serving in dangerous situations and it's the guys who play it cool who often suffer the greatest emotional pain when they're suddenly helpless. They *hate* to lose control.'

'I know Jude's very worried about his eyesight.'

'Of course he is. The risk of going blind is a huge deal for him. It would be for anyone.'

'Is there still a risk?' Emily pressed her hands over the sudden painful ache in her chest.

'To be honest, I don't think there's a huge risk now. His vision's still very blurry, but that should settle down, if he takes it easy. I see my role as trying to keep him calm, which is important.'

With a self-satisfied smile, Keira said, 'I'm just so glad I took leave this week. I usually stay at Jude's mountain retreat, clearing my head in the fresh air and the rainforest, but I'm so pleased I can keep a professional eye on him now. I don't have to be back with my unit for another ten days.'

Ten days?

Just in time, Emily stifled a gasp of dismay. 'I thought he'd be out of hospital in a day or two.'

'He will, but he'll need ongoing professional care.'

Emily had planned to do any necessary caring. She could stay on at Alex's apartment for at least another week, and she'd imagined cooking for Jude and possibly reading the paper to him until his vision cleared. She could take him to the park and they'd go for walks together. Each day they'd walk a little further and he'd grow stronger.

'My plan,' said Keira, 'is to get him out of hospital as soon as possible. I've already spoken to his surgeon and he agrees that Jude will do much better in familiar surroundings. The mountain is a bit isolated in terms of any post-op problems, though, so I think your cousin's place is the best option. I'll stay on until things have fully stabilised.'

But there are only two bedrooms in Alex's apartment.

'I'm used to kipping down on stretchers,' Keira added, as if she'd already guessed the direction of Emily's thoughts. 'I'll monitor the severity of Jude's headaches and make sure that he either wears his dark glasses or stays in a semi-darkened room.'

These tasks didn't sound particularly difficult to Emily, certainly not matters that required the skills of a fully qualified Army surgeon. But if she questioned Keira's generous offer, she would imply that she hadn't Jude's best interests at heart.

She tried to imagine staying on in Alex's apartment while Keira set up camp on a stretcher in the living room. Keira would be constantly caring for Jude. Keira would always be there as a buffer between herself and Jude.

It was selfish of her to resent this, of course. She knew Jude should have the best possible medical supervision—and she'd known all along that her future with Jude was unclear at best.

If only he hadn't grasped her wrist and kissed her as she'd said goodbye. There'd been something so very intimate in the heat of his handgrip and the brush of his lips, almost as if he'd been staking a claim. In front of Keira.

Walking away from him had been so painful.

But how much worse would it be to try to hang around like a fifth wheel, becoming more and more aware each day that she wasn't really wanted?

'You shouldn't have to camp on a stretcher,' she told Keira, covering her disappointment with a tremulous smile. 'I'll move my things out so you can be comfortable.'

The other woman frowned. 'But where will you go?'

Emily hesitated. She wasn't ready to go home to Wandabilla yet. 'I can stay on at my grandmother's at Sunshine Beach.'

'The beach? Lucky you.' Keira couldn't quite hide the flash of triumph in her eyes. 'That's perfect then, isn't it?'

CHAPTER TEN

JUDE dropped his overnight bag in his bedroom, set his laptop on the desk, but left it unopened. His eyes were gradually improving, thank goodness, but it would be a while yet before he was reading a computer screen.

Just the same, he was relieved to be back in the apartment, the next best thing to his own home.

He went to the kitchen, which seemed strangely empty without Emily. Not that he thought of her as a 'kitchen' kind of woman, but they'd had some great times in here, just hanging out, preparing meals, eating, washing up.

As he continued on to the living room, he realised the whole damn apartment felt empty without Emily.

He wondered where Keira had got to. No doubt he should offer her tea or coffee before she headed off.

To his surprise, he heard noises coming from Alex's bedroom. He headed down the hall, turning at the doorway, remembering the last time he'd been in this room. In bed with Emily.

Now, the white sheets that he and Emily had tangled in were in a heap on the floor, and Keira was smoothing a new navy-blue sheet over the king-size mattress.

'I didn't expect you to start on the laundry,' Jude said, surprised.

Keira shrugged and pulled a coy face. 'Call me fussy, but I like clean sheets.'

'*You* like them?' Jude frowned at her. 'I'm sorry. Have I missed something? You're not planning to stay here, are you?'

'Naturally, Jude. How else can I look after you?'

'I don't need looking after.'

'Don't be stubborn. Of course you do. You're just out of hospital.'

Jude scowled. How had he not seen this possibility? Why hadn't he guessed that Keira would be in her element when a man was in a weakened state?

He suppressed a sigh, which she might have interpreted as tiredness. 'I've been released from hospital because I'm fine, Keira. I've been told what to watch for. I have a phone if I need help. Apart from that, I can manage just as I always have. On my own.'

'But why put yourself to all that trouble when I'm perfectly willing to help?'

Jude knew there was no point in repeating the obvious—that he didn't need help. It would only lead to an argument and that was the last thing he wanted today.

Just the same, he didn't want Keira supervising his every move, taking his blood pressure half a dozen times a day, asking questions about his headaches or the colour of his urine, for crying out loud.

More to the point, if Keira was moving into *this* room, where would Emily sleep?

Jude's frown deepened. 'It's a bit rich of you to move in before I check with Emily.'

'Oh, that's not a problem. I sorted it with her.' Keira smiled at him as she stuffed a pillow into a navy-blue case.

'Sorted? How?'

'We had a nice little chat yesterday, at the hospital.'

That was quick work. Jude's temper stirred. Why hadn't he been included in this discussion?

Keira stuffed another pillow into its case and set it neatly on the bed.

Jude watched her with mounting irritation. 'I assumed you were dropping me off here and then heading on to Mount Tamborine.'

'Good heavens, no. I couldn't desert you, Jude. You're more important than my recreation.'

'Now hang on. I've already told you I don't need a nurse. I certainly don't need you to give up your precious leave from Afghanistan. You know the mountains clear your head and get you centred again.'

At any rate, that was the line Keira had always spun him.

Truth was, he didn't want her here now. He didn't want any woman fussing over him. That was why he'd sent Emily away. He needed to deal with this recovery on his own, and he didn't want to see anyone until he felt confident within himself that he was going to be OK.

Now, without warning, a wave of dizziness made him sway a little. He gripped the doorframe, hoping Keira didn't notice.

'Listen,' he told her, 'I don't want to be rude, or to sound unappreciative of your efforts, but I'd like to have a little time on my own.'

The bed was made now and Keira was bundling up the dirty linen—the linen Jude and Emily had slept in. He wondered if she'd guessed.

'I think you're being very foolish, Jude. Stubborn and foolish. I'm sure Dr Stanley wouldn't approve.'

'First sign of a problem, I'll be in touch with Stanley.'

Keira stood clutching the sheets against her stomach,

lips clamped together in a scowl. She was making it clear that she thought he was crazy. 'Are you certain?'

'Absolutely.'

'Then be it on your head,' she said in a tight, hurt voice and, letting the sheets drop to the floor, she pushed past him out of the room.

In the hallway, she whirled around to send him a parting scowl. 'There's something you should realise, Jude Marlowe. This need of yours to hide your imperfections is *not* a strength. It's a failing.'

Jude sighed. All he'd wanted was a little peace and quiet.

With an overnight bag in one hand and a heavy supermarket bag in the other, Emily climbed the stairs to the apartment.

She'd changed her mind about retreating to her grandmother's place and letting Keira Arnold take over caring for Jude, and she'd switched tack for two very good reasons. First—Jude, in his weakened state, might actually need shielding from Keira's bossiness. Second—staying away was wimpy, passive behaviour.

Emily was tired of being a loser in love.

Ever since her teens, she'd been hoping that love would fall into her lap, the way it had apparently done for her parents and her brother. Finally—and yes, finding the nerve to try that striptease had helped—she was beginning to understand that love wasn't a gift that arrived from above. It required a little risk-taking. Winning took courage.

She certainly needed courage now. Coming hot on the heels of her break-up, she hadn't wanted to believe she might be in love again so soon. But she loved Jude with a depth she'd never experienced before. She felt truly connected to him on so many levels.

Just two weeks with him had shown her how totally superficial her previous relationships had been. Now she believed she could be best mates with Jude as well as his lover. It was exactly the kind of relationship her parents had, and it was too special to let slip away.

This time she was determined to win.

She straightened her shoulders as she reached the top of the steps, but had to take a step back when the apartment's door flew open and a women's figure stormed out, letting the door slam behind her.

Keira Arnold glared at Emily. 'What are you doing here?'

Emily's stomach clenched. 'I changed my mind.' It sounded hopelessly lame. Not a good start. She held up the supermarket bag. 'I'll take care of the cooking. It's not exactly Jude's forte.'

'Jude's forte is pigheadedness,' Keira spat. 'Watch out.'

Then she rushed down the steps, pushing past Emily so roughly that her large shoulder bag banged against her, knocking the shopping bag to the floor. Apples spilled from the bag and bounced down the concrete steps. A packet split, seeping white flour.

'Bloody hell,' groaned Keira.

She didn't apologise, but she did chase after the apples and dump them into the bag, while Emily did her best to seal up the flour packet.

'They're not too bruised,' Keira said, referring to the apples. She cocked her head towards the door. 'Good luck in there, but I don't like your chances.'

Open-mouthed with surprise, Emily watched as she hurried down the steps and disappeared into the car park.

Shaken, she set the shopping down while she extracted the spare key she'd kept, then opened the door and let herself inside.

'Hello, Jude?' she called softly, standing in the hallway, clutching her bags.

It was several moments before he appeared at the doorway to his room. Just the sight of him set small flames inside Emily, but she could see that behind his sunglasses he was scowling as fiercely as Keira.

'What are you doing here?' he demanded.

Not quite the greeting she'd hoped for. He sounded tired. Fed up. Angry.

'I brought some groceries.' She was almost apologetic.

Jude sighed, rubbing at his forehead.

'You look tired,' she said, knowing she probably sounded as worried as she suddenly felt. Why had Keira left? Wasn't she supposed to be supervising Jude's post-operative care?

'Please, go and rest,' she said. 'I'll just pop these things in the kitchen. I won't disturb you.'

Jude didn't bother with thanks. He gave a slight nod, then shut his door.

Emily gulped. Just as well she hadn't expected this to be easy.

Jude lay with the curtains drawn and his eyes closed. He'd been drained by the argument with Keira, and he simply had no energy to deal with Emily as well.

He'd almost wept when he'd seen her, standing in the hallway looking like a Renaissance angel with her arms full of twenty-first century groceries.

But she shouldn't have come. He hated her seeing him like this. He'd tried to keep her at a distance, but she'd come to the hospital anyhow and it had nearly killed him to see her yesterday, sitting on the far side of the room like any run-of-the-mill visitor.

What was he going to do about her?

Was he in love with her?

He'd never felt this intensity of confusion and distraction over any other woman. He'd never felt so lonely as when he was apart from her. He'd never spent hours reliving every memory of the way a woman moved or smiled. He'd never felt so incomplete in a woman's absence.

But, in his current state, a future with Emily seemed too much to hope for.

His sister, Charlotte, thought otherwise. She'd told him so this morning when she'd said goodbye before retuning to Sydney.

'Hang on to this one,' she'd said, hugging him with tears in her eyes. 'Don't push Emily away, Jude. I know she's right for you.'

'How can you know?' He was desperate to hear her answer.

'Don't be a deadbeat,' she'd gently chided. 'You're my brother. I know these things. I've known you all my life, and I've met most of your girlfriends, and I—'

Charlotte had given a shrugging little laugh. 'OK, maybe it's only a hunch, and I don't know where the hunch comes from. Call it sisterly intuition or wishful thinking, but there's something about Emily that feels very in tune with you, Jude.'

In tune. In harmony.

It was such a simplistic concept, but Charlotte had hit straight on the truth. When Jude remembered everything he and Emily had shared together, from watching movies to breakfast in bed, there'd been many, many harmonious moments and next to no discord.

That in itself was interesting. He usually ended up arguing with his girlfriends, or disappointing them, just as his father had argued with or disappointed his mother. Jude had assumed that he'd inherited the failing.

Perhaps he was reading too much into his sister's comments, but he couldn't deny that he'd loved having Emily in his life. *Loved?* There ought to be a stronger word. The thought that he might lose her horrified him. But after the disappointments she'd had with boyfriends, he had no intention of offering her false hope.

Until his vision cleared and his headaches eased, he had nothing to offer her except uncertainty and poorly suppressed fears.

She deserved so much more.

At the very least she deserved a whole man.

Jude grimaced as Keira's final accusation pounded in his head. Was she right? Was his need to hide his imperfections a failing rather than a strength?

Probably.

But his desire to keep his weaknesses hidden was so ingrained that he couldn't imagine living any other way. He'd learned as a child to cope on his own and to paper over any visible cracks in the image he presented to the world.

This warped version of coping probably came from having parents who arrived home every night, tired from the Court House and preferring to drink expensive wine and to argue with each other than to take more than a cursory interest in their children. Jude had spent many evenings entertaining Charlotte with bedtime stories. It was how he'd discovered and nurtured his writing talent.

Their nanny had been kindness personified and Jude had adored her but, under his father's watchful eye, even she had been instructed to offer minimum pampering when the children were sick or hurt.

Charlotte had reacted quite differently to their upbringing. She'd taken up nursing and thrown herself into caring for others. After she'd married, she'd become a perfect wife and mother, devoted to her family.

Jude had chosen fierce independence. He could totally lose himself in his writing, so he'd been more or less happy with his life as a semi-recluse. Before Emily.

Could he change? Or was he fooling himself to think he might ever be right for her, even if he was fully recovered?

The question was too hard to answer, certainly now... when his head was aching and he needed to sleep...

Jude slept for hours, and Emily couldn't believe how disconcerting she found this. She almost wished Keira was still there so that she could check if this lengthy sleep was normal.

She was as nervous as a mother with a brand-new baby. Twice she crept to the door of Jude's room and opened it a crack just to see if his chest was still rising and falling.

The rest of the time, she kept herself busy in the kitchen, making a beef casserole and a batch of muffins, as well as a proper homemade chicken soup with vegetables and barley. Clearly, Jude's illness brought out the homebody in her.

It was dark when he finally woke. He came into the kitchen, tousle-haired and barefoot, with a hand shading his eyes.

Quickly, Emily turned the overhead light off. 'Sorry.' Now there was just a soft light coming from the pantry. 'Is that better?'

'Thanks, that's fine.'

'How are you feeling?'

'Fabulous. I really needed that sleep. Could never get enough in the hospital.' He shot a frowning glance to the stove. 'You've been busy.'

'I thought you might like a bit more than tinned soup.'

His mouth tilted, not quite cracking a smile. He was wearing a long-sleeved grey T-shirt and jeans and the light from the pantry cast chiaroscuro shadows, highlighting the masculine planes and angles of his face. Despite the dark stubble on his jaw, he looked a little pale, but Emily was quite sure no one had ever looked more lovable.

She wanted to go to him, to slip her arms around him, to press her cheek against his chest, her ear against his heart.

Alternatively, she wouldn't have objected if he wanted to put his arms around her just as he had when she'd been standing at the sink on the day before the operation.

Neither of them moved, however.

'Are you hungry?' she asked.

Jude rubbed a hand over his stomach. 'Starving.'

'There's a beef casserole or there's chicken soup.'

'That's very kind of you, Emily.' His darkly lashed eyes glinted silver in the soft light and he sent her a sad smile. 'I'm really grateful for the food.'

'No problem,' she said uncertainly, sensing that he was about to say something more, something she didn't want to hear.

Jude looked uncomfortable. 'You weren't actually planning on staying here, were you?'

Fear tightened like an icy fist in her chest. 'Don't…' Oh, God, she couldn't believe she was asking this. 'Don't you want me to stay?'

At Jude's hesitation, her insides shrank.

With a pained grimace, he rubbed at his unshaven jaw. 'Look, I know this is your cousin's place.' His gaze flickered, not quite meeting hers. 'But could you give me a little space for a few more days?'

'How many days?'

'Till next week?'

Next week?

Dismayed, Emily grabbed hold of a bench top for support. Jude had told her he was feeling fine, and he'd sent Keira packing. Didn't that leave the door open for her to come back?

'I'm just not ready to be sociable,' he said.

'I wouldn't expect you to be sociable. But I wanted to help.'

'Thanks, but I don't need help.'

He said this with some reluctance, but that couldn't soften the blow.

He didn't want her.

She'd been so carried away, rushing here with her dreams of courage and winning. But her silly dream had been one-sided, based on a foolish hope that Jude and she might—

Oh, good grief, she was an idiot.

How had this happened again? How had she fooled herself into believing that this man was different, that this time she really was going to make a success of a very special relationship?

The kitchen blurred before Emily's eyes. Her throat ached horribly.

'I'm sorry, Jude,' she said in a voice that sounded way too tight and scared. 'I thought…I assumed…'

She couldn't finish. Not without breaking down and making a fool of herself. Not without losing the last tattered shreds of her dignity.

'I'll get my things,' she said instead.

Blinded by tears, she hurried from the kitchen. She hadn't unpacked her bag. It was still standing just inside the door to Alex's room, so it was a simple matter to grab it.

Jude was in the hallway, looking way too tall and gorgeous and grim. 'You do understand?' he said.

No, she didn't understand at all. But she sure as hell wasn't going to stand here and listen to his explanation of why her presence was suddenly a problem for him—

After everything they'd shared together.

She didn't want to hear his version of their relationship. She knew how it would go—that they'd had a brief pre-surgery fling with no promises.

'You don't mind staying at Sunshine Beach till next week?' he asked.

Emily didn't answer at first. She *did* mind and she wanted to tell him so. Loudly. If he wasn't still recovering, she might have.

'I may not need to come,' she said tightly. 'Not if you are coping just fine on your own. I'll have to see how I'm placed next week.' She opened the door. 'Oh, and I've left your car in the garage. Thanks for the loan.'

'Emily.'

Chin high, Emily refused to turn back. She couldn't bear to prolong the pain, knowing the result was inevitable. Marching through the doorway, she didn't copy Keira and let the door slam behind her, even though she now felt huge sympathy for the other woman. Clearly they were both Jude's victims.

To her immense relief, she was able to hail a taxi as soon as she reached the footpath. Clambering in, she sat hunched in the back, wrapped in a pain that was all too familiar.

She was such a fool. Jude had actually rescued her from this kind of hurting over Michael, and yet…once again… she'd fooled herself into thinking that she was safe to fall in love one more time.

It didn't help that she understood why Jude was doing

this—that he was so much the he-man he hated having anyone see him in a weakened state. That attitude didn't really make sense when she'd already been living with him and she'd seen him laid low by headaches.

At least she was certain about one thing—this was the last time she'd push her way into Jude's life. She'd gone to his mountain home at Alex's request, even though she'd known she wasn't really welcome. She'd gone to the hospital against Jude's wishes, and she'd come here this afternoon instead of waiting for him to invite her.

Three strikes and she was out.

Finally, she'd got the message.

Jude's reserve had all the hallmarks of a sinking relationship. She'd been on the receiving end of enough rejections and disappointments to recognise the warning signs.

Why hadn't she seen this coming?

Jude made no promises. I knew that, and yet I still fooled myself.

Somehow—some-*crazy*-how—she'd managed to trick herself into believing that this time with Jude had been different. This time she'd experienced a truer connection, a *two-way* connection. She and Jude had understood each other and together they'd helped each other through difficulties.

Jude had consoled her about Michael, and she'd tried to distract him during the lead-in to his surgery. There'd been a balance of give and take. They'd been a team.

A temporary team, apparently.

Oh, God. She'd promised herself this wouldn't happen again. She should have known. Unlike Michael, Jude had at least warned her. *No promises.* One thing she could say about Jude, he hadn't deceived her.

She'd done that entirely on her own.

* * *

I've left your car in the garage. Thanks for the loan.

Emily's last words had been delivered so coldly. Jude couldn't believe the pain they'd caused him, worse than any physical discomfort.

He'd totally stuffed up. He was a gold-plated fool. He'd convinced himself that he was asking her to leave for her own good. After all, a recovering patient wasn't very good company for a beautiful, vital young woman. But he hadn't meant to hurt her feelings, or to make her feel rejected.

In his weakened state, he couldn't run after her, damn it, but he was desperate to make amends. He grabbed his phone and pressed her number, but his call went straight to her message bank. No doubt she'd turned her phone off.

She was mad with him. No question.

Angry at his stupidity, Jude almost hurled the phone across the room. He couldn't believe he'd been so hung up about his damn eyesight that he hadn't taken any time to consider Emily's perspective.

Perhaps the surgeon had removed his entire brain?

It was just as well he'd slept all afternoon because sleep eluded him for most of the night.

In the morning, on the dot of seven-thirty, Jude tried Emily's phone again, with the same result—her voice asked him to please leave a message.

Emily, it's Jude. Please ring back.

He ate breakfast—baked beans, unheated, straight from the can—then he tried Emily's phone again. He tried twice more during the day, but pride prevented him from leaving a string of pleading messages. He wasn't going to explain or apologise to a machine. He wanted to speak to Emily.

By evening, he still couldn't get through.

OK, so he'd proved spectacularly that he was a thickhead—but even he could work out that Emily was deliberately *not* answering his calls.

He heated some of her chicken soup. It was delicious but each mouthful reminded him of his stupidity. In the living room he turned on the CD player. Not wanting to bother his eyes with a new selection, he let the machine replay the last disc inserted.

It filled the room with a slow, sultry beat.

His heart thudded.

From now until forever he would never hear this music without thinking of Emily.

From the first deep throb of the double bass he was remembering the little high kick she'd given as she came into this room wearing a scrap of copper silk and long black stockings.

In spite of everything, Jude smiled at the memory— smiled so hard that he was damn near fighting tears, all too aware of the Emily-sized hole in his life.

Having learned his lesson, Jude didn't call Emily again till the end of the week and, during that time, his body performed exactly as the surgeon had predicted. His headaches eased and then disappeared completely, and his vision gradually cleared. At his post-op check-up, he felt as well as he ever had, and the only hurdle ahead of him now was an MRI in five weeks' time.

This news was too good not to share, but when he tried Emily's phone again, she still didn't answer.

More distressed than he could have believed, he gave in and dialled Granny Silver's number.

'Oh, Jude,' she said brightly. 'How are you?'

'Very well, thanks.'

'That is good news. I'm so pleased.'

'I was hoping to speak to Emily.'

'I'm sorry, Jude. Emily's not here. She's gone home to Wandabilla. She left three days ago.'

'Three days?' He almost choked on his disappointment. 'What happened? Was there a problem at the office?'

'More or less,' Granny Silver said evasively.

Jude waited for her to expand on this unsatisfactory situation, but there was silence on the other end of the line. 'Granny, is there anything else you can tell me?'

'I don't think so, Jude. Emily decided that it made sense for her to go home now. She wanted time to get a few things for her new business sorted before she was due back at the bank.'

Her new business.

She'd been excited about it at the hospital, but he'd been so caught up in his own sorry mess that he hadn't given her a chance to explain her ideas.

Granny sighed. 'I'm sorry, Jude. I don't think I can tell you any more than that. I know that Emily really appreciated your company in Brisbane and she enjoyed getting to know you. We've been keeping you in our thoughts, and we're hoping for a full recovery.'

'Thanks,' he said grimly.

There was a sound, as if she was about to say something else, and Jude tensed. Right now, he would take anything, even a lecture from an octogenarian on the foolishness of his ways. Anything that would help him to heal the yawning gulf that separated him from Emily.

'I believe you're finishing a book,' Granny said. 'I hope that goes well.'

The book? He couldn't care less about the book. Not now. Not when his perfect girl had slipped away from him. Not when she'd flown out of his life with the same speed she'd escaped that Michael character. Clearly she'd placed him in the same league as the rat.

Jude was still grappling with shock and struggling to find words when Granny said, 'Have you heard that Alex is staying overseas for a few more weeks? I believe he's picked up several international clients. Isn't that wonderful? It means you'll be on your own for a few more weeks. I expect you'll enjoy the privacy.'

Emily had been coaching her grandmother. No doubt about that.

CHAPTER ELEVEN

WANDABILLA was a typical Queensland country town with
wide streets edged with old-fashioned shops and offices,
and a strip of well tended garden down the middle. Jude
parked his vehicle outside the bank where Emily was manager.

In the six weeks since she'd returned here, he'd walked
a tightrope. He'd desperately needed to see her, to explain
and to make amends, but his instincts had urged him to
hold back till he'd had the final all clear and everything
was in place. He'd gone with his instincts and now, at last,
he had all his ducks in a row.

Just the same, chances were this reunion would be
tough. But he was ready.

He tested the knot in the tie he'd teamed with a sports
jacket, cream moleskins and a blue chambray shirt. No
point in looking too citified.

Now, as he stepped onto the footpath, he tried to ignore the band of tension that tightened around his chest.
He pushed open the bank's old-fashioned swing doors.

'Good morning. I'd like to see the manager,' he told the
girl at the front desk. 'I'm sorry about the short notice. I'm
just passing through and it's urgent.'

The girl let her gaze linger, clearly checking him out,

before she turned to her computer screen and scrolled down a page. 'Your name, sir?'

Jude hesitated, and prayed that Emily wouldn't refuse to see him.

'Jude Marlowe,' he said.

The girl looked up with a beaming smile. 'If you'll take a seat, Mr Simpson will be with you shortly.'

'Mr Simpson?' Jude stared at her, stunned. 'But I want to see the manager, Emily Silver.'

Without even checking her computer, the girl shook her head. 'Sorry, sir. Emily Silver doesn't work here.'

This was crazy. Jude had researched on the Internet, and he was sure he had the right bank. He'd even double-checked with Alex. Emily hadn't returned his calls, so this was his only option. He *had* to see her.

'There has to be a mistake. I know she works here.' Jude reached for his tie, wishing he could loosen the knot. He was choking in the damn thing.

'I'm sorry,' the girl said again. 'I should have been clearer. Emily Silver doesn't work here any more.'

Jude felt as if he'd run smack into an invisible glass wall. 'Has she been transferred?'

'No, she resigned.' The girl looked up at him from beneath mascara-thickened lashes. 'It was a big shock to everyone. Emily left a fortnight ago. Left the bank and left town.'

'I see.' Jude spoke calmly despite his rising panic. 'I'm sure she left a forwarding address.'

Once again, the girl shook her head. 'I have no authority to hand out personal information.'

Of course. He knew that. He'd been desperate, clutching at straws.

'Thank you,' he said, even though he was anything but grateful.

Turning on his heel, he strode out of the building into sunshine and a blank wall of fear.

Saturday mornings in the city were very different from Saturdays in Wandabilla. Emily sat at a café table on a footpath crowded with small tables, drinking coffee and reading the weekend papers. All around her, people were doing the same thing—drinking coffee, eating breakfast, reading alone or chatting in groups.

No one paid Emily the slightest attention, and she couldn't recognise a single face. How wonderful was that? After years of living in a tiny country town where she knew everyone and everyone knew her, plus every single detail of her private life, this urban anonymity was bliss.

She'd been living in Brisbane for a month now, renting a flat in Red Hill. In that time she'd thrown herself into starting up her fledgling business—a sun-safe fashion line for mothers and children. Sports shirts with long sleeves, casual tops, hats made from cottons that breathe, but sturdy enough to run about and play in.

She'd been struck by the idea while staying at Sunshine Beach. As a redhead, she'd always had to cover up in the outdoors, and in her childhood especially she'd found it such a bore. These days, it wasn't just an issue for people with really fair skin. Everyone was more conscious of sun protection and, with so many 'yummy mummies' enjoying an active outdoor life, Emily was sure her idea was a winner.

There was a lot to do. She'd teamed with a talented young designer who was actually the granddaughter of one of Granny Silver's friends, and the garments were being made by a cooperative of farmer's wives from Wandabilla. They'd been looking for a project that allowed them to work from home, and they'd leapt at Emily's idea. She was offering them very fair rates, of course.

Now she was also busy with marketing—sourcing a logo, organising a registered trade name, setting up a website.

Fortunately, she had enough savings and investments to see her through this early establishment phase, and she was quietly confident that this business was going to fly.

It was all very satisfying.

A waitress arrived with her breakfast—mushrooms on ciabatta bread. *Yum.* She folded her newspaper, keeping only the real-estate pages open to peruse while she ate. She'd been toying with the idea of buying a house of her own.

With the flexibility of an Internet business, she could more or less live wherever she liked. The world was now her oyster, but she rather liked Brisbane and being close to both Alex and Granny.

Emily cut a piece of toast and topped it with dark, succulent, peppery mushrooms, munching happily as she scanned the rows of photos.

She wasn't quite sure what kind of place she would prefer—a slick modern apartment or a cute cottage with a leafy garden. It would be rather nice if something leapt out at her, a kind of real-estate love at first sight, but she was in no hurry to buy. She turned a page, helping herself to more mushrooms.

Then she saw it.

Halfway down the page.

A photo she instantly recognised that made her go cold all over and caused a piece of toast to stick in her throat.

A distinctively beautiful home made of timber and glass with a wonderful view of rainforest-clad hillsides. Emily checked the address—Mount Tamborine—and her heart crashed against her ribcage.

It had to be Jude's house. Of course it was his. It was highly unlikely that another home on Tamborine Mountain would be built to exactly that same design. Besides, she could see the brick-paved driveway where she'd parked the hire car and the flat rock stepping stones that led to Jude's front door.

There could be no doubt. Jude's gorgeous home was for sale. Emily clapped a hand over her mouth to stop herself from crying out loud.

How could Jude sell the place he loved so much? Why would he?

He'd told her once that he would be prepared to give up his mountain home and lifestyle if he found the right woman. Surely he hadn't found his perfect someone in the few weeks since his operation?

What else could this mean? Had he returned to one of his previous girlfriends?

It was unlikely, Emily decided, given all the messages on her phone that she'd ignored.

What else might have prompted this sale? Financial difficulties were a possibility, but somehow Emily didn't think that was Jude's problem.

Had his eyes deteriorated? Could he no longer risk living in such an isolated home?

Much as she hated this thought, it was surely the most likely explanation. Even though Granny Silver had reported that Jude had rung and said his vision was fine, something must have gone wrong since then. Some kind of relapse.

And if the worst had happened, he probably couldn't stand to live there surrounded by a view he couldn't see.

The thought was almost too sad to bear.

Emily had tried so hard to focus on enjoying her post-Jude life and put him out of her thoughts. But her avoidance of him had been based on the assumption that he was fine.

Now, any possibility of remaining aloof from Jude had been wiped out by one photo.

Abandoning her breakfast, she snatched up the page with the picture of his house, folded it swiftly and stuffed it into her shoulder bag.

'How was your meal?' the girl at the cash register enquired.

'It was delicious,' Emily assured her. 'I'm sorry I couldn't stay to finish it. There's been an emergency.'

The girl sent Emily a look of sympathy as she rushed away. She was halfway down the footpath before she came to a skidding halt, realising she had no idea where she was running to. She'd taken off in a blind panic.

Now, as she came to her senses, she pulled her phone from her bag and keyed in Alex's number.

'Jude's selling his house,' she told her cousin the instant he answered. 'Do you know why? Is something wrong? Is there a problem with his eyes?'

'Hey, calm down,' Alex soothed. 'One question at a time. What's this about Jude's house?'

'It's for sale. I've just seen the ad in this morning's paper.'

'Really? Are you sure it's Jude's house?'

'Positive. I can't believe it, Alex.'

'I haven't heard anything about it but, to be honest, I think Jude's avoiding me. He hasn't answered my phone calls or my emails. I'm assuming that's because he's way overdue with delivering his latest manuscript.'

'Is he?' This news only deepened Emily's fears. Jude

had been close to finishing the book weeks ago. 'I thought his eyesight was OK.'

'So did I. There was no mention of a problem last time we spoke, but that was quite a few weeks back. Now you've got me worried. I'll try calling him again.'

'Thanks. So will I.'

But Emily didn't ring Jude straight away. After she ended the call to Alex, she slid the phone into her pocket and started walking back up the steep hill to her flat. She hoped the long climb would help her to stop panicking. She needed a chance to think about this situation with a clear head.

The ad in the paper said that Jude's house was to be auctioned on Wednesday and the property was open for inspection over this weekend. This meant that potential buyers could be traipsing through that beautiful house right at this moment. They would be falling in love with its hilltop location, with its stunning views and its distinctive and elegant architecture.

Anyone who stepped through the doorway to Jude's house was bound to fall in love and want to buy it.

But Jude loved the house, too, just as he loved his mountains and hiking the skyline and watching the weather roll in over Sunset Ridge.

How could he bear to let all that go?

Emily wanted to ring him. Desperately.

But what did a girl say to a man after two months of silence, after she'd taken off with very little explanation and refused to return his calls?

I'm sorry. I was saving my sanity.

I was trying to be tough.

It was all about survival.

She'd retreated, afraid that she'd read too much into that

wondrous short time she'd lived with Jude, and knowing she was a relationship dunce.

But how did her hang-ups about her relationships stack up against Jude's serious problems—losing his eyesight and losing his beautiful home?

A major thing holding her back was the fact that she'd already been way too pushy with Jude in the past. Heavens, the only reason she'd met him in the first place was because she'd turned up on the poor man's doorstep, completely out of the blue.

That had just been the start. She'd gone to the mountains, she'd done that fateful striptease and, after his surgery, she'd come back to the apartment too soon. Now she cringed at the thought of yet again pushing her way uninvited into Jude's life. Hadn't she given up that right when she ran away?

Her phone sat on her kitchen table all weekend while she circled it, thinking about Jude, worrying about Jude and missing him so badly she felt sick.

Alex didn't ring back, so he probably hadn't got through to Jude, either, but on Monday Emily was very tempted to rush over to Alex's place and tell him the whole sorry story of her brief relationship with his client.

Like old times, they could open a bottle of wine and she'd pour out her troubles, and Alex would be sympathetic, and she'd feel better...

Except...

Except...she wouldn't feel better, would she?

Not this time. Not about Jude.

Besides, she didn't want to tell Alex about watching herons and sunsets with Jude. There were some memories that felt too precious to share. She certainly wouldn't tell her cousin about her attempted striptease...or the night that had followed.

Instead, Emily threw herself into a cleaning frenzy, vacuuming, mopping and polishing until her tiny flat shone. She spent the afternoon fiddling with her new website.

On Tuesday, a parcel arrived from Wandabilla—the first sample collection of sun-safe shirts and caps. They were just beautiful and Emily was thrilled, but she would have been more thrilled if she hadn't been so distracted.

In less than twenty-four hours Jude's house would go under the auctioneer's hammer. She still didn't know why, but she was sure the reason had to be desperate and she couldn't bear to think of Jude going through such an ordeal alone.

Shouldn't she be there, too?

The realisation dawned on her like a slow, warming sunrise.

Even if Jude had problems with his eyes, he would almost certainly be at the auction—and she could be there, in the background. She wouldn't be pushy. She wouldn't make her presence obvious. She would blend in with the crowd, keep an eye on Jude from a distance, be circumspect. If she sensed that he needed her help in any way, she would be ready. On call. To step in as a friend. She would make sure Jude understood that she wasn't barging back into his life.

Emily went to bed happy. She had a plan.

CHAPTER TWELVE

THE large number of cars parked along the edges of the winding mountain road didn't surprise Emily. She'd guessed that Jude's house would be popular. Just the same, she felt sick knowing that in an hour or two, someone else would own his beloved retreat.

It was cool in the mountains so she pulled a denim jacket over her T-shirt, making a quick check of her reflection in the rear-vision mirror. She'd dressed casually and kept her make-up subtle, aiming to blend into the crowd—but she was sadly aware that none of this was necessary if Jude couldn't see her.

She gave a little shake, needing to banish such thoughts. *No tears now.* Locking the car door, she set off, chin high, determined to be brave. And circumspect.

An assortment of people had gathered in the driveway—businessmen in suits, several couples of retirement age, a few people who looked like hiking types, lean and slightly weather-beaten.

Many of these people were probably hoping to buy their dream home today, and the auctioneer was on the move, smiling and chatting, no doubt trying to suss out the genuine bidders.

Emily's stomach fluttered nervously. She didn't care at all when heads turned to stare at her curiously. She just wished she knew where Jude was and how he was feeling right now.

The auction, they were told, was to be held on the back deck, and everyone filed up the external timber stairway. Emily held her breath as she followed the crowd. On the deck, she melted to the back of the group, shocked by how dreadfully anxious she felt—anxious for Jude.

Over the past weeks, she'd been trying to keep her thoughts Jude-free but, from the moment she'd seen the house in the paper, she'd been learning all over again how very deeply she cared for him, and now she was flooded by a host of feelings that she'd tried for two months to suppress.

She loved him.

There was no escaping it.

It didn't matter where Jude lived or whether or not he could see, she was still in love with him. Weeks of separation hadn't changed that. Nothing would change it. She would probably go to her grave knowing that he was The One.

But if Jude's circumstances were even worse than they'd been two months ago, he would almost certainly push her away again.

Still, she had to hope there was some way she could help.

The auctioneer opened the large timber-framed glass door that led into the house and spoke to someone inside. Emily's heart picked up pace. He was probably asking Jude to come out.

Despite the chatter of the people all around her, she was sure she could hear a firm tread on the floorboards inside the house. Then she saw a familiar figure in the doorway—tall, dark-haired, broad-shouldered—Jude, sexier than ever in a dark blue shirt and jeans.

Her heart thudded painfully. Seeing him again brought such a crush of memories…his smile, his conversation, his kisses, his touch… She'd missed him during every second of her self-imposed isolation.

And then she realised something else.

Jude didn't seem to have a problem with his sight. He wasn't wearing dark glasses and there was no hesitancy in his movements, nothing careful about the way he strolled onto the deck, hands sunk casually in the pockets of his jeans. He smiled and nodded to a couple of the men in suits, shook their hands, waved to someone else at the back of the crowd.

It was quite obvious that he could see, and Emily's first reaction was a rush of brilliant, over-the-moon euphoria.

But this was quickly followed by confusion. If he was OK, why was he selling his house? Had he found Miss Right, after all?

Then Jude froze.

Across the crowd, his gaze locked with Emily's, and shock registered as he stared at her.

She wanted to smile, but she hadn't a chance. She couldn't move a muscle. She'd turned to stone.

Without a word or a gesture to anyone, Jude crossed the deck towards her. People moved out of the way, making room for him as if they sensed a man on a mission.

In no time he was standing directly in front of Emily, his grey eyes burning. 'What are you doing here?'

'I…' Her mouth was so dry she had to run her tongue over her lips and try again. 'I was hoping to see you.'

He gave a helpless, stunned shake of his head, and then he gripped her arm. 'Come with me.'

He grasped her tightly and she was aware of the force of his tension as he steered her across the deck while curious eyes followed them.

As soon as they were inside the house, Jude released her. Then he stood back, running a shaking hand through his hair. 'I can't quite believe this.'

'It must be a…a surprise,' Emily admitted and she swallowed nervously. 'You look well, Jude.'

'I'm very well, thank you—apart from shellshock.'

Now she could see that he did look a bit dazed.

'What are you doing here?' he asked again.

'I saw the for sale ad in the paper and I had to come.'

For painful seconds he stared at her and his eyes reflected a breathtaking mix of emotions. 'Why, Emily? Why did you have to come?'

'So many reasons.' Now her heart was going crazy. She could scarcely breathe. 'Some you might not believe.'

'Try me.'

Oh, help. Emily hadn't expected to reach this moment so quickly. She'd rehearsed all kinds of explanations, but now, with Jude standing so stiffly before her, watching her so intently and fiercely, the answers flew out of her head.

She had no choice. She had to give him the only excuse she could think of—

'I was desperately worried about you.'

Jude looked unconvinced.

'I just had to see that you were OK, Jude. I couldn't think why you were selling this house, unless something had gone wrong with your eyes.'

'My eyes are fine.'

Now she couldn't bring herself to add the other reason, that she feared he might have found the perfect woman and that he was giving up this lifestyle to be with her.

The pain of that possibility was too much.

'Why have you come here after all this time?' Jude asked her again.

There was only one true reason. 'I'm…I'm in love with you.'

Oh, good grief. Had she really said it aloud?

'I'm sorry, Jude. I know that's the last thing you wanted to hear.'

His eyes were glistening now, and his throat worked as if he found it painful to swallow. He shot a quick glance out to the deck, where several people were peering in through the glass door.

'We need privacy,' he said, turning his back on the crowd and nodding to a door leading off the living room.

Emily frowned. 'What…about the auction?'

'This is more important.'

Her heart was trembling as she followed him into his study. She was aware of thick carpet beneath her feet, walls lined with crowded bookshelves, a computer and a scattering of pens and paper on a large silky oak desk. She was also nervously aware that she'd once again barged back into Jude's life—this time with the ultimate intrusion—a declaration of love.

Jude closed the door, then turned to her. There was no window in this room and they were completely alone, and she wondered if he was going to tell her off for interfering and then send her packing.

He stood tall in the middle of the carpeted floor, took a deep breath and folded his arms across his considerable chest. 'Did you know I've been to Wandabilla looking for you?'

Emily felt her knees shake with shock.

'When?' she asked, unable to wipe the disbelief from her voice.

'A couple of weeks back, after you'd already left town.' Jude eased back against his desk. 'I planned to come looking for you again, just as soon as I had this sorted.'

'Had what sorted? Selling the house?'

He nodded.

'But I don't understand. Why do you want to sell this place? It doesn't make sense. I thought you loved living here.'

'I have loved it,' he said simply.

She gave a helpless flap of her hands. 'Then why sell? Your eyes are fine, aren't they?'

'Absolutely. I've been very lucky. At the six week MRI, I scored a clean bill of health.'

'That's wonderful news.' It was such good news and she wanted to rush to him, to wrap him in a joyous bear hug. But she didn't dare, of course. Not after his grim reaction to her embarrassing, poorly timed confession of love.

'I'm even more confused now,' she said instead. 'Forgive me for speaking like a bank manager, but I do understand that finances are very tight for everyone at the moment.'

'I don't have a problem with my finances,' Jude said.

As if on cue, the auctioneer's raised voice reached them from outside. He was giving his introductory spiel.

'Don't you need to be out there?' Emily asked.

Jude shook his head. 'As I said, this conversation is more important. I'd like to explain to you why I'm selling the house.'

Something in his voice and in his eyes made her feel as if he was leading her to the very brink of a precipice.

A wave of dizziness overcame her, and for a terrible moment she thought she was going to faint. 'You've found her.'

'Excuse me?'

Oh, help. This was so painful. Why couldn't he just tell her instead of dragging this out? 'You told me you'd give up this house for the right woman. I'm guessing you must have found her.'

Outside, the auctioneer's voice grew louder and more excited. The bidding must have started, but Jude didn't seem the slightest bit interested.

His eyes were lit by a funny-sad smile. Directed at her. 'Yes, I've found her,' he said gently.

'That's—' Emily tried to form the word *wonderful*, but her lips were too wobbly.

'Emily, can't you guess?'

No, she was too scared to think. Her heartbeats were pounding too loudly, thundering in her ears. She shook her head. Tears threatened.

In one stride Jude was beside her and his arms were around her, supporting her, holding her against the strong, safe wall of his chest. He pressed his face into her hair and then he kissed her brow, her cheek, her chin. 'Emily.'

For a moment she was too stunned to think. Then she pulled back with a gasp.

Jude's smile was lighting his eyes and making the skin at their edges crinkle. 'You're more important to me than anything.'

'But you're not selling this house because of me, Jude?' Her heart stumbled, picked itself up and did a cartwheel. 'That's crazy.'

'No, selling my house isn't crazy. The crazy thing was letting you go.' With his thumb, Jude traced a soft line down the curve of her cheek. 'The crazy thing was being too afraid to admit that I loved you.'

His smile made her want to cry for all the right reasons. 'That's why I went to Wandabilla and it's why I was gearing up to cross oceans or slay dragons. I was going to find you, my dear, sweet girl, to tell you that I love you. I love you so much.'

He said this as if loving her changed everything.

As if nothing else in the entire universe mattered.

'Being with you is more important than where I live. I wouldn't want to live here without you. I was planning to start over somewhere else if I couldn't find you.'

He reached for her hands. 'I told you I could give up this house for the right girl. And I meant it. You're the right girl, Emily. The only girl.'

It wasn't easy to tell a man he was hopelessly crazy and kiss him at the same time, but Emily did her best, with her arms wrapped around his neck, with her body pressed close to his hunky muscles, and with tears streaming down her face.

She might have gone on kissing him for ever if there hadn't been a pressing question she needed to ask.

As she reluctantly pulled back, she could hear the auctioneer's voice outside growing increasingly more persuasive and agitated.

'Jude,' she said with sudden urgency, 'what if *I* don't want you to lose your house?'

She saw a flash in his eyes—and she had her answer. Now there wasn't a moment to lose.

She tugged at his hand. 'Come on. We've got to hurry.'

Thinking more clearly, she dropped his hand, and began to run ahead of him. 'Correction, *I've* got to hurry.'

Another sunset...

'This calls for bubbles,' Jude said as he carried a bottle of chilled champagne and two flutes onto the deck.

The auctioneer and potential buyers had left now, and the two of them were alone. Emily was leaning against the deck's railing, enjoying the view. She turned and grinned at him. Her hair gleamed like autumn leaves against the spring green of the rainforest, and he thought how perfectly relaxed and happy she looked in this setting, so different from the cool and collected professional who'd so competently joined in the bidding on his house.

Then again, he should have guessed that Emily's career as a country bank manager enabled her to morph into an auction genius.

He worked the champagne cork free and it gave a soft pop. The wine sparkled and fizzed as he filled their glasses and he handed one to Emily. 'Congratulations to the new home owner.'

'Thank you, sir.' She touched her glass to his. 'Here's to us.'

He stood for a moment, smiling a little dazedly into her eyes, sipping his drink as he came to terms with everything that had happened in the past hour.

His world had taken a three-sixty degree spin.

And here he was…celebrating.

He was a lucky man.

Un-flaming-believably lucky.

Emily waved her glass towards the house. 'I still can't believe you were prepared to sacrifice your lovely home for me.'

'Well, I can't believe you've sacrificed the money you'd set aside for your business just to buy this place.'

'Being crazy is fun, isn't it?' She laughed. 'But thank heavens we've worked as a team. You've heroically offered to finance my business, and I've graciously invited you to stay on living here.'

She reached for his hand. 'But don't forget, Jude, I can sell this place back to you in a blink. It's only a matter of paperwork.' She looked up at him, her blue eyes suddenly serious. 'Perhaps we should sort that out sooner rather than later. I certainly don't want you to risk your capital on my little business.'

'I wouldn't dream of reneging on that promise. You've seen enough small businesses come and go. You know the financial ropes better than I do. I'm sure my money's in safe hands.'

'That's very trusting of you.' Emily drank more bubbles and smiled at him over the rim of her glass. 'So I guess it's official. We're both as crazy as each other.'

'I guess we are.' Setting his glass aside, Jude placed his hands on the timber railing, on either side of her. Trapping her.

Her eyes widened and pretty colour rose in her cheeks. Her lips softened and parted.

'If we're both so crazy,' he said, 'we must be a perfect match.'

'I think we must be.'

They smiled into each other's eyes and it was a smile that reached all the way inside, a smile that made and kept promises.

They'd taken such a roundabout route to be together. They'd both held back, for all kinds of reasons. But now, as Jude kissed Emily, she linked her arms around his neck and their kiss was deep and lush and long, and buoyed by a happy confidence that sent Jude's last barriers tumbling.

He felt so good to be free. No fears. No regrets. No doubts, or what ifs.

Who would have thought total commitment could be so liberating?

'And now,' Emily said, breaking into his thoughts and giving him a cheeky grin, 'I think it's high time you showed me the rest of this house that I've paid an exorbitant amount of money for.'

'So you want a grand tour?'

'Well, there's at least one room I haven't seen.'

'What's that?'

'The master bedroom.'

Jude grinned. 'Which just happens to be the best room in the house.'

Emily totally agreed. The master bedroom was beyond amazing, with an enormous platform bed plus an en suite bathroom with a sunken spa looking out through a wall of glass into a totally private patch of forest. *And* there was even a sliding glass roof.

'For watching the stars at night,' Jude explained.

'Hmm…I think I've made a very sound investment.' She slanted him a questioning smile. 'I hope the master himself is part of this bedroom package?'

'That's a guarantee.' With a sexy growl he pulled her into his arms and set about proving he was as good as his word. Tenderly, but masterfully.

EPILOGUE

THE door to Alex's apartment opened and light spilled onto the steps.

'Jude! Emily!' Alex sent a startled grin to both of them in turn. 'What a surprise.'

'Sorry we didn't warn you we were coming,' said Jude.

'No problem. I'm glad to see you. Come on in.' In the hallway Alex turned back to look at them again. Clearly, he was puzzled. 'What's going on with you two? I know you're an item now, but you both look like you're about to burst.'

'We have good news,' said Emily. 'At least we think it's good news. I'm sure you will, too.'

'Don't tell me Jude's finally finished his book?'

'Actually, yes, I have.' Jude waved a large packet. 'I've even brought you a printout of the manuscript.'

'And I've read it and it's brilliant,' added Emily.

Alex's eyes widened. 'That definitely calls for a celebration. I wasn't sure he'd ever finish it with you as a distraction, Ems.'

'Well, he's not only finished it, he's started another. And I've also brought wine,' said Emily. 'And cheese and crackers.'

'There's no question then—it's party time.'

Alex hurried ahead of them into the kitchen, grabbing

glasses and a plate for the cheese and crackers, as well as olives and pâté from his fridge.

Emily thought how nice it was to be back inside these familiar walls. It was especially nice to have Jude here with her, looking hunky and gorgeous, and with none of that haunting uncertainty in his eyes.

Almost like coming home.

She remembered the meals she and Jude had prepared and shared in this kitchen. The conversations and the revelations. And the tears.

This was where it had all begun and where it had almost ended.

She and Jude had talked about it often. He'd told her how he'd fallen for her on that first night when she'd arrived on his doorstep. And they'd talked about everything that had followed—the morning of the cream nightgown, the kiss where she'd slapped him, the trips to see the heron and the sunset, the fateful striptease...

Jude had been amazingly understanding and patient. He totally *got* how hard it was for her to truly believe and trust that a man could love her as deeply and as permanently as she loved him.

Now, coming back here, Emily realised how wonderfully well Jude's reassurance had worked. She felt truly strong now. Safe and certain. And bone-deep happy.

'Well, well,' said Alex, handing her a glass. 'So what's the news? Apart from the fact that you two are an item.'

'Jude's asked me to marry him,' Emily announced, unable to hold back a moment longer.

Alex's jaw dropped. 'Amazing!'

Jude cuffed his friend on the shoulder. 'You're supposed to say congratulations.'

'I will. I am. I'm saying it now. Congratulations.' Alex's

face broke into an enormous grin. 'I didn't know you had it in you, Jude.'

'Granny's not surprised,' countered Emily.

'She's probably been hoping for weeks, the old romantic.'

Just the same, Alex held his arms wide and enveloped Emily in a bear hug. 'Truly, darling, I'm thrilled. You've made an excellent choice.' He shot a wink over his shoulder to Jude. 'So have you, mate.'

'Glad you approve,' Jude responded dryly. 'Just as well you do approve, actually. I was thinking of asking you to be my best man.'

'But then I came up with the brilliant idea that you could be our best person,' Emily broke in. 'Because you're so important to both of us.'

'Oh, goodness. Look at me. I've gone all jammy. If I'm a mess now, how am I going to be on the big day?'

'Perfect,' Emily and Jude said together.

They grinned at each other and Emily felt the happy shiver of desire and the solid kernel of warmth that she felt every time she looked into Jude's eyes. Finally, she'd found happiness—of the lasting kind—for now and for ever.

* * * * *

MILLS & BOON®
The Billionaires Collection!

This fabulous 6 book collection features stories from some of our talented writers. Feel the temperature rise with our ultra-sexy and powerful billionaires. Don't miss this great offer – buy the collection today to get two books free!

Order yours at
www.millsandboon.co.uk/billionaires

MILLS & BOON®

Mills & Boon have been at the heart of romance since 1908... and while the fashions may have changed, one thing remains the same: from pulse-pounding passion to the gentlest caress, we're always known how to bring romance alive.

Now, we're delighted to present you with these irresistible illustrations, inspired by the vintage glamour of our covers. So indulge your wildest dreams and unleash your imagination as we present the most iconic Mills & Boon moments of the last century.

Visit **www.millsandboon.co.uk/ArtofRomance** to order yours!

MILLS & BOON®

Why not subscribe?

Never miss a title and save money too!

Here is what's available to you if you join the exclusive **Mills & Boon® Book Club** today:

* *Titles up to a month ahead of the shops*
* *Amazing discounts*
* *Free P&P*
* *Earn Bonus Book points that can be redeemed against other titles and gifts*
* *Choose from monthly or pre-paid plans*

Still want more?

Well, if you join today we'll even give you
50% OFF your first parcel!

So visit **www.millsandboon.co.uk/subscriptions**
or call **Customer Relations on 0844 844 1351***
to be a part of this exclusive Book Club!

*This call will cost you 7 pence per minute plus your
phone company's price per minute access charge.